I0675568

BROTHERS OF A DIFFERENT CREED

Volume 3 of the Oscar Series

A Novel

HENDRIK WITMANS

Other books by the author

The Thought Killer
Volume 1 of the Oscar Series

The Mind Cleansers
Volume 2 of the Oscar Series

Problems with Portals
An anthology of short stories about teleportation

New next summer!
The Quantum Thinkers
Volume 4 of the Oscar Series

Please watch for this exciting sequel to
Brothers Of A Different Creed.
Coming to Amazon.com in 2016

This is a work of fiction. All characters, places and settings are a product of the author's imagination. Any resemblance to people, living or dead, and institutions or organizations is purely coincidental.

All rights reserved. No part of this publication may be reproduced, or transmitted by any means, electronic or mechanical, without written permission of the author.

Cover image by Fiverr
Copyright © Hendrik Witmans, 2015
ISBN 978-0-9699190-4-9

Dedication and Acknowledgements

For every bestseller, there are thousands of books that only make it to the bookstores' bargain tables. The Internet is a double-edged sword. It has made publishing easier, but getting one's book out to readers is getting more and more competitive. I dedicate this novel to all struggling authors, who keep going, despite the incredible odds against them.

A word of thanks to the people who helped me write this book, in one way or another. Thanks for the input and critique of the members of the Writers in Progress group in Qualicum Beach. Their discussions were invaluable. Special thanks also to my wife Brenda and our friend April Tomiye, for their patience and help in proofreading. A final word of appreciation for you, the reader, who showed interest in my work.

Previously in the Oscar Series

The origin of the commune called the Church of Oscar lay in a chance meeting between a human diver and a bottlenose dolphin along the California coast in the spring of 2031. Ted Taylor was a shy young man of nineteen, who enjoyed exploring the Pacific Ocean near Gaviota State Park. On one of his dives he met a dolphin that had been wounded in a chase with poachers. Luckily, the injury was only superficial and with Ted's help the dolphin was soon fine again, and began to join him on his dives. Ted named the dolphin Oscar and they became good friends.

One day, Oscar brought Ted a metal flask he had found. When Ted opened the flask, he was exposed to a strong hallucinatory drug that changed his consciousness forever. After returning from his dive, Ted shared the drug with his friend Joachim Rasnell, and Ted's mother Diana. In their altered state of consciousness, they saw it as their divine duty to save humanity from evil, greed and inequality, by going back to Nature and living according to Its laws. To do so, they created a religious commune called the Church of Oscar, and they named their secret recruiting drug Oscar's Breath, or the Breath for short.

After a few years, the church's drug supply ran low and, since there was no way to get more, the commune's efforts to change the world seemed short-lived and fruitless. It began to stagnate. In a strange twist of fate, the group was saved when Carol and Patrick Johnson joined. Carol's previous husband was the late Dr. Yabul Kozak, a brilliant, but megalomanic scientist, who had created the hallucinatory drug. It was lost off the coast, when the helicopter he had chartered, crashed, killing him and the pilot. On her arrival in the commune, Carol offered the church a DVD with the complete formula for the drug that her late husband had given her for safe keeping, in case something would happen to him. The church councilors were ecstatic, since they would soon be able make as much of the Breath as was needed.

The group's happiness didn't last long, however. A few months later, the entire commune was razed to the ground by a group of terrorists. The only survivors were the church councilors, who had been away to set up a research center they had bought to produce their recruiting drug. They now faced the monumental task to rebuild their commune from scratch.

REBIRTH

1

On October 7, 2052, a sleek business jet gracefully landed at Washington National Airport after a six-hour flight from Beijing, China. Stenciled on its side was the distinguished Panda logo for *Doyon Enterprises*, one of the largest Chinese state-owned companies. After the jet rolled to a halt, a door in its side opened and an inflatable set of stairs was released. Three passengers walked down onto the tarmac and were met by two officials of the State Department. Little was known about the delegation, or why they had come. There had only been a terse message from the Chinese Embassy that officials of the People's Republic of China requested a private interview with senior members of the U.S. Department of Transportation.

The officials soon left in a black limousine. Their destination was the office of the current Secretary of Transportation, Malcolm Mondroban, at 1200 New Jersey Avenue. Once inside the humongous building, the visitors met the Secretary and his second in command, Brendan Harshman. A young interpreter was standing by, but it soon became clear that his services were not required.

The leader of the Chinese delegation was in his thirties. His eyes and facial features seemed more Caucasian than Asian, and Malcolm wondered if the man had been born and educated in the West. Like the other government officials, the spokesman for the delegation was dressed in an immaculate dark business suit.

"I am Wung Hoo, President of the Doyon Group of companies," he said in flawless English. "One of our subsidiaries manufactures the Haydo electromagnetic Bullet trains. These state-of-the-art trains run entirely without wheels or moving parts; they float on compressed air and are pushed forward by a strong magnetic force. We have

1

operated this system for many years, and it is a fast, effective and clean method to move people and cargo. We are so excited about this technology that we want to share it with you. Our government has noticed your country's economic decline and, in the spirit of cooperation and goodwill, we are here today to announce that we would like to create such a transportation system in your country."

"You cannot be serious, Mr. Hoo." The Secretary of Transportation, known for his short fuse and no-nonsense attitude, couldn't keep the sarcasm out of his voice. "Sir, if you have studied us, you know that our economy is in the ditch because of your government's embargo of cheap goods. You want to sell us your Bullet trains? Not in a million years!"

Wung Hoo smiled. "You misunderstand, Mr. Secretary. We want to build the railway system for you. Furthermore, we will construct a plant to produce natural gas from the shale deposits in your country to generate the electricity to run the trains. It is part of our offer."

"Hold on now," Malcolm said. "Am I to believe that the People's Republic of China wants to do this out of empathy with the fate of the American people? What will *you* get out of this deal?"

"We shall take a percentage of the gas, liquefy it and ship it back to China."

Malcolm was silent, and it was Harshman who asked the next question. "Such a plan would be a tremendous economic stimulus for us, but what about labor? Would you bring your personnel or can we use our people?"

"Many parts of the trains and gas extraction plant can be manufactured in our factories in Ying San," Hoo said. "They can be shipped over and assembled here at our cost. We shall bring in the few senior officials whose experience you will need. The rest of the workers can be hired locally, and we shall pay them commensurate with present wages in other sectors of your economy."

Brendan Harshman was sitting next to Malcolm and he leaned over and urgently whispered in his boss's ear.

2

"Malcolm, take it! It's a fucking Marshall plan!"

Malcolm Mondroban sat in deep thought. He looked at the delegation, wondering just how far he could trust them. It was odd they had decided to help. Did they need the U.S. back as a trading partner? Why not lift that odious trade embargo instead? Still, whatever the reason, he knew Brendan was right; this was too good not to look into further. A thin smile lit up his rugged face.

"Thank you for your offer, Mr. Hoo. We shall need to discuss this further in private, and I must inform our President. You can leave your proposal with us. Our lawyers will study it, and you shall have our decision within a week. May I ask you to join us at an informal cocktail party we have arranged for you next door?"

Nine months later, the U.S. Senate passed a bill that gave Doyon Enterprises of Ying San, China, the right to build a Haydo Bullet train, connecting Los Angeles, California, to Washington, D.C. In the spring of 2055, a prototype of the train made a flawless inaugural trip, and a few months later the construction of a new U.S. train network began. A wave of optimism ran through the country as an economic reversal was finally happening. On June 12 that year, the euphoria was dampened, when a group of mercenaries attacked and destroyed a commune called the Church of Oscar, killing nearly five hundred innocent American citizens.

◊ ◊ ◊

The Secret Springs tower was not the tallest building in Chicago, but it was the most impressive one. Twelve hundred feet tall, it looked like the top half of a giant egg, made of thousands of hexagonal windows that sparkled in the sun, like a humongous diamond. The architects who designed the building had decided to use an open-plan structure. The office floors were large balconies encircling the entire dome wall, leaving a central open space called the Atrium. This was a park-like setting, with trees, flower beds, walkways and a pond. It also had facilities for the staff: tennis courts, exercise rooms, running tracks, and a swimming pool. Secret Springs looked after the welfare of its employees.

In 2020, a rich American software engineer by the name of Carl Heigin created the first virtual social network. He called it Secret Springs. It was a virtual extension of sites like Facebook, LinkedIn, and others. For years, orbiting satellites had taken high-definition, 3D laser pictures and videos of every spot on earth, mostly for military use. After extensive lobbying in Washington, Heigin managed to buy time on the satellites and downloaded some of the declassified videos and photographs into a database. A group of engineers edited the rather large file, adding visual and auditory information of buildings, sites and structures where it was needed. Then they compressed the file and rendered it into a hologram. It was the first prototype virtscape—a virtual landscape of Yellowstone National Park.

Using Secret Springs' proprietary software programs called avatars, people could enter the virtscape and explore the park and 'Old Faithful' without leaving their homes. All they needed was a powerful computer, a virtual reality suit and an account with Secret Springs. The results were overwhelming. The accounts department was flooded with new applications from people who wanted to experience virtual reality. Buoyed by the success, Secret Springs started to produce more virtscapes. It soon became the most successful company in history, as more and more holograms were added to the library.

Travel, entertainment, study, research, social gatherings, sex—there was no limit to what subscribers could experience in their virtual world. Heigin became a multi-billionaire, but he did not enjoy his fame for long. Five years after he created Secret Springs, he was killed by a religious fanatic who opposed the pornography and violence in some of the virtscapes.

On the fourteenth floor in a North-Easterly direction—14NE for short—was Secret Springs' quality control department. Here, in a theatre called the Matrix, six electronic experts checked every virtscape for picture- and sound quality, continuity, loading time and stability, to make sure the program met the company's rigorous standards. The leader of the quality control team was a young man called Philip Kozak.

Philip was born in Santa Barbara in 2031, at a rather inopportune moment. His father, Dr. Yabul Kozak, a renowned scientist, had died under mysterious circumstances seven months before Philip's birth, leaving his mother, Carol, in a state of disarray and fear. Added to that, Carol was embroiled in a controversial court case that could ruin her financially or even send her to jail.

Luckily all went well in the end. Carol married Patrick Johnson, a retired police lieutenant, and Philip was brought up on a hobby farm near Santa Barbara. Though technically his last name was Kozak, everyone referred to him as Philip Johnson.

At age sixteen, he decided he wasn't cut out to spend his days on a farm and applied for a job with Secret Springs, much to the disappointment of his mother and stepfather. On arriving in Chicago, he took a crash course in virtual reality, and after two weeks he started off as a customer representative.

For eight hours a day, Philip sat behind his computer in a huge room in the basement of the Secret Springs building with more than two hundred others like him, helping customers navigate the virtual world his company provided. It could be very frustrating.

No, Madam, you cannot get VD, or become pregnant, from cyber sex. Our avatars are very realistic, but not that realistic. Yes, you can enjoy all the pleasures without any consequences.

Sir, the reason you still feel hungry after eating in a virtscape is that your senses have fooled you. You may be convinced you have eaten a big meal, but all you have done is moved holographic energy from one place to another. Avatars do not have a digestive tract, and your stomach is still in your body at home.

After only two days he hated it, but he had little choice. His boss, a dour man of thirty-three, reminded him that he was on probation.

"Do well and you'll be fine," he said. "If you don't, I have hundreds of others waiting for the job."

At night, hoarse from talking, Philip began to study the five computer languages that made the virtscapes possible. He did not have a social life, no friends, male or female, nor did he have time for anything or anyone outside the complex. He called his mother two days after he arrived to let her know he was safe. But after a whole day dealing with people, talking, sometimes even shouting, he had no voice left to have long chats with anyone. He was driven by a force inside him that demanded that he make something of his life. Being a customer representative would only be a stepping stone.

As time went by, the ties with his past became weaker and weaker, and after a call to his mother on her sixtieth birthday, he didn't call home again. Nor did his parents call back, or if they did, the calls never reached him.

After three horrible years of customer support, Philip entered a competition for a software debugging position, among a crowd of forty other hopefuls. To his intense relief he got the job. Henceforth he would be working with computer software and not people. His sore throat found time to heal.

At age twenty-one, he legally changed his last name to Kozak. Not that he disliked the name Johnson, but he had never clicked with his stepfather. He knew instinctively that he was much more like his real father.

After two years as a software debugger, he was transferred to the inner sanctum of Secret Springs: the production and organization of virtscapes. Three years later he was promoted to quality control manager. By that time, he got himself a lovely girlfriend, Jennifer Higman. At twenty-four, she was two years younger than Philip. She worked in the Cleaning room, as it was called.

Virtscapes came in two kinds: public and private. In public virtscapes the material was censored and tailored for all ages. Real-life killings, and sexual perversions of any kind were not permitted. In the private, more restricted virtscapes there was less censorship. It was similar to the old movie rating system in the U.S. In the Cleaning room Jennifer and her three coworkers removed any unsuitable material from the public virtscapes. It was a boring job, gruesome at times, but it needed to be done. The last thing Secret Springs wanted was to offend its clientele.

Jennifer was a stunning young lady, tall and slim, with a sexy smile that made men look twice when they passed her. She had arrived at Secret Springs only a few weeks before, and Philip knew time was short. There were other available bachelors. When he asked her out, Jennifer immediately agreed, and after two more dates in one week both knew they were right for each other. Philip Kozak had every reason to be happy. He had achieved what he had set out to do when he left home sixteen years ago and found love as well.

To his frustration, a persistent little voice inside him told him he still needed to do better.

◊ ◊ ◊

The twelve church councilors had their hands full. After several days of grieving for the loss of their fellow members, they faced the task of changing the research center into a communal church. The Excalibur Center for Mind Research was founded by Philip Gallagan, a philanthropist who had made his fortune building quantum computers. Part of the Center was Gallagan's old mansion. During its time, Excalibur had used the mansion for office space, and an added annex for the laboratory and computer sections. Though the councilors were happy to have a roof over their heads, a lot of work was needed to make their new home workable. Joachim Rasnell was the Head Councilor for the Church of Oscar, and

7

also its co-founder. The first thing he did when the church took possession of Excalibur, was to lock up the laboratory. It became the home of Bert Kwiss, a colleague of the late Dr. Kozak at Excalibur before his conversion to the Church of Oscar. Bert would be in charge of the secret production of Oscar's Breath.

One immediate problem was accommodation. Though Philip Gallagan had been a billionaire, he had not been overly ostentatious. The Gallagan residence had only ten bedrooms. Some of the councilors would have to share a room. That in itself wasn't a big problem. But where to put up new church members? Luckily, the grounds around Excalibur were perfectly suited for a commune. The expansive lawns could be used for vegetable gardens, areas for livestock and living space for the commune's members.

Inside, the ballroom could be converted into a new church area, with a pulpit, an anteroom for food and drinks, and also the room to recruit new members. But where to get the tools and materials for the renovations? Dale Pinehurst, Chief of Security, Brian Rasnell, in charge of the daily upkeep of the church, and Father English, their religious leader, went exploring the Excalibur site and found a large garden storage shed. When Brian finally located the right keys to get inside, the councilors couldn't believe their eyes. There were tools of all description: saws, lawnmowers, hand tools, bench tools, even several chainsaws that could be used to cut down trees in the back of the property. Everything was dirty and covered in cobwebs. The one thing missing was a portable sawmill. It would be needed to cut the tree logs into boards, and Brian and Dale decided they needed to rent one in the future.

The councilors rolled up their collective sleeves and began the transformation of Excalibur into a commune. To Joachim Rasnell it seemed as if they had gone back in time, to when they had built their first church. Everyone was full of energy and in good spirit, the dark memory of the massacre fading by the day. Even Father English could be seen walking around with a tool pouch over his shirt and a crowbar in his hand.

On one of those busy days, Jo and Dale were sitting in the old Excalibur boardroom that Jo had set up as an operational center. They were studying the drafts and plans for the renovations.

"I wish we had an architect on board," Jo said. "I'm afraid this is the best I can do."

"It'll be fine," Dale said, smiling. "They're only renovations, not major construction. The mansion is still in good shape, and it's mostly interior work. The huts for the church members can be made very simple. We've got lots of wood and with a bit of luck—"

There were hurried footsteps on the stairs, and the door burst open. Erwin Johnson, the youngest councilor, stood in the doorway, his muddy boots marking the carpet.

"Jo, come quickly! There's a car coming down the driveway."

Dale and Jo followed Erwin, down the stairs, through the hallway, into the living room, where Daniel English and Carol Johnson stood looking out of the window. In the far distance, an official looking car had just turned from the main road into the Excalibur driveway.

"Who do you think they could be, Daniel?" Jo asked nervously.

Father English, dressed in khaki shirt and pants, a carpenter's apron around his ample stomach, did not look much like a servant of the Lord. He stood in front of the window and peeked outside, shielding his eyes against the low morning sun. His face was sallow and he was breathing with difficulty. "By the grace of Oscar," he said. "That's government, Jo. Only they still drive big gas-powered cars like that. It's trouble, I tell you!"

"Erwin, go call the others," Jo said. "I have a feeling this will be a matter for the entire Council."

While Erwin ran away to call the other councilors, Jo's good spirits crashed, as the memories of the massacre returned. Almost five hundred people of the Church of Oscar bloodily massacred, without a chance to defend themselves, and now an official visit by the very people who could well have been responsible. His heart was pounding and his mouth felt very dry all of a sudden. By the time the vehicle reached the circular end of the driveway and stopped in front of the main entrance, the councilors, still dressed in their working clothes, were ready and waiting. They watched, as four car doors opened and four men and one woman got out. One heavy-set man carried a brief case, and the young woman was pulling a small suitcase on wheels.

"Lawyers," Carol Johnson said. "You can spot them from miles away. No offence, Patricia."

Patricia Sheppard, in charge of the commune's legal affairs, just smiled. "I think you'll agree, Carol, that I have been very different from other lawyers since I joined the church."

Jo opened the door and motioned the others to remain inside for now. He walked over to the group of people, just as they reached the portico.

"Can I help you?" he said. "What is the purpose of your visit?"

One youngish looking man, around thirty to thirty-five, stepped forward and held out his hand. "I am Robert Stansing, of Internal Revenue. These are governments officials. Could you please inform the leader of this establishment that we would like to have a word?"

"I am Joachim Rasnell, Head Councilor of the Church of Oscar," Jo said. "I am in charge. What is your business here?"

"Could we perhaps discuss this inside?" Robert was smiling with his mouth, but not his eyes. "If you cooperate, this will only take a few minutes."

Grudgingly, Jo stepped aside to let the five officials in.

"This way, please." Dale Pinehurst stood in the hallway, pointing his arm to what once had been Philip and Lillian Gallagan's dining room. A polished, twelve feet long teak table with matching chairs offered seats for the visitors. The big

10

man carrying the briefcase opened it, and began to pile documents on the table. The woman unzipped her canvas case. There were twelve chairs, and the visitors sat down, but the twelve church councilors remained awkwardly standing.

"You must forgive us for the way we look," Jo said. "We are renovating our new home. As you may know, we have recently lost our entire church and all our people, and we are still in a state of shock."

"We are fully aware of that, Councilor Rasnell," Robert Stansing said. "In fact, it is one of the reasons we are here. I know it is rather belated, but we want to bring you the condolences of the U.S. government. This was an unbelievable act of unprovoked terrorism and cowardice towards innocent American citizens. The people who committed this terrible crime will be tried and held accountable, we promise you that." He shifted a pile of papers on the table in front of him, and looked up at Jo.

"Before we begin, let me introduce the others. On my very left is David Marshal from the FBI. Next to him, is Randolph Hardman; he is with the U.S. census bureau. Then Armand Dinges, of the Justice Department, and the lady is Wendy Boots, Armand's paralegal."

"Right," Jo said, "these are our councilors, from left to right: Diana Taylor, Carol Johnson and her son Erwin, Brian Rasnell, Daniel English, and Dale Pinehurst. Standing behind them are Sylvia Rasnell, Jeremy Burlon, Bert Kwiss, Penny Weatherby, and Patricia Sheppard. Each one of us brings his or her personal expertise to the daily running of our church."

"Thank you so much," Robert Stansing said. He brought a hand to his clean-shaved chin and reflected, as if he was trying to compose his thoughts. Then he turned to Jo. "Councilor Rasnell, could you all please sit down? It'll make things easier."

"We'll need more chairs," Dale Pinehurst said. He and Brian Rasnell left the room, while the other councilors took the vacant seats behind the table. After the chairs arrived and everyone was finally seated, Robert Stansing began.

11

"Councilor Rasnell, how many people perished when your commune was attacked?"

"Everyone except us," Jo replied. "Four hundred and eighty-nine."

Stansing sat back in his chair, arms folded across his stomach. "So far three hundred and ten bodies have been accounted for; many are too badly burned to be identified. It must be a gruesome task, and I am glad that is not my department. The FBI found something rather peculiar; a great number of the dead were listed, or had been listed as missing persons. Can you explain this, Councilor Rasnell?"

"I think I can," Jo said, nodding. "We are not a middle-class church, where people meet once a week to sing a few songs, have a nice chat with their friends, bow their heads and close their eyes, listen to a good story, and then head home again to forget everything until the next time. No, sir, the Church of Oscar asks for a lifetime commitment. It is not for everyone. We are looking for distraught people who can't cope with society anymore, for whatever reason. They need help, and our church is there for them.

"We take care of our people, Mr. Stansing. We do not ask questions. What they did before they join is of no interest to us. If people want a fresh start in life, the Church of Oscar welcomes them. If it weren't for us, they might end up homeless and addicted to drugs, or even dead. But there are other organizations that also try to solve this problem, and you can't blame us for sheltering all the missing persons in the country."

"That is true, of course," Robert said, slightly taken aback. "Nevertheless, this process cannot be allowed to continue."

"What? You've come to close us down?"

"No sir, you need not worry about that." Armand Dinges smiled at the councilors, then continued in his powerful baritone voice. "Every American citizen can choose a religion he or she wants; it is a constitutional right. We have absolutely no problem with people joining your commune. We just want to be informed when they do. Mr. Marshal here will concur with me, that it is very frustrating to spend a lot of manpower, federal and local, searching for missing persons, only to find that they are safely ensconced in your communal church. That time could be better used finding real criminals."

"But the church is sacrosanct!" Sylvia exclaimed. "If people want to disappear for whatever reason, I thought that a church was a safe—"

"I was just getting to that, young lady," Armand interrupted. "That may have been an unwritten law for centuries, but in this day and age we can't allow that anymore. See, it would be very convenient for a hardened criminal, or terrorist, to drop out of sight by joining a commune like yours, especially since you don't ask questions. We can't allow that to happen. Mr. Stansing here, would very much like to know if a potential church member's taxes are paid in full, before he or she joins you. And it would make Mr. Hardman's job with the census much easier if he knew how who has joined your church and who passed away, and when. Surely, you can all see our point, Councilors? In fact, you will be saving us time finding missing persons.

"Now, my good helper here, Wendy, has drawn up a series of simple documents. From now on anyone who wants to enter your commune will have to sign a form of consent. We also want to know when someone dies. Once a month, you must forward these forms to us. They will be kept strictly confidential, of course. If a potential church member is wanted by the authorities, for whatever reason, we shall have the final say as to whether or not that person can remain in your commune, or will face charges outside. If you follow that simple rule, my department will leave you and your church in peace."

"There are a few other points," Robert Stansing added. "Internal Revenue wants every member of the Church of Oscar to sign a Form of Perpetual Poverty, as it is called. Failure to do so will result in an audit, and federal tax may be charged. Money brought into your church by new members to

13

be used for upkeep or expansion will be allowed. However, if any donations to the church are invested outside the church, we will charge tax on the interest of those investments. It is all explained in the instructions we shall leave with you." Robert looked around at the other officials. "I guess that's about all, isn't it? Anyone else?"

"Yes, I have a question," David Marshal said. "Councilor Rasnell, why did your commune buy the Excalibur Mind Research Center?"

"Isn't that obvious?" Jo said. "Our old church building was demolished, and we needed a place to start all over again."

"I see." Marshal was a stocky man. His massive frame strained the dining room chair. He had dark, curly hair and a well-tanned rotund face. He shuffled some of the papers he had taken from his briefcase.

"I have a problem with that, Councilor," he said, after a few seemingly interminable seconds. "You see, your church was razed to the ground on June 12th this year, yet according to our records you acquired Excalibur on April 15th, almost two months earlier. Did you have a divine insight that bad things were going to happen, Councilor? Or did you buy it for other purposes? It seems rather an odd thing to do for a church, buying a Mind Research Center."

There was a short, intense silence, then Carol Johnson spoke.

"Mr. Marshal, I wonder if I may answer that question?"

Marshal nodded. "Sure. Fine with me."

"I am in charge of coordinating and maintaining the membership list of our church, since I have a background in working with people. About twenty-five years ago I worked for Excalibur. I was in charge of their volunteer program for brain scans. Perhaps you remember the program? Excalibur collected brain scans from millions of people all over the world, to compare and sort them to find a cure for certain diseases."

14

"Yes, I remember that. Excalibur did some real good work in those days. Too bad they went out of business. But why is the church interested in brain scans?"

"We're not. It is the database we wanted. Before the, uh . . . massacre, we had begun to make plans for expansion. I was very familiar with the Excalibur database, since I used it every day. Apart from medical records, it also had information about personalities, hobbies, and religion. It could be an invaluable tool for our church; a searchable list of potential recruits that we could use to advertise and promote the Church of Oscar. We could sort the records by religion for instance, and show people the difference between theirs and ours. It would save us a tremendous amount of work. And they had a Q-computer as well. When we learned that Excalibur was up for sale, we contacted them. The price was right and we bought it."

"Very commendable, Councilor Johnson, I must say." Dinges' deep baritone broke the ensuing silence again. "Are you sure this church is the right place for you? With a business acumen like that you could do wonders in the real world. Lots of small new places could sure use your expertise. Get at your competitors whichever way you can." He chuckled. "Not bad, not bad!"

"So are we done here, David?" Robert Stansing asked, looking at his watch.

The big FBI man nodded pensively, then began to collect his paperwork. "I guess so."

"All right." Stansing stood up, and one by one the others followed suit. "Mr. Rasnell, please go through the information and the forms we are leaving here with you. On completion, you can send the required documents back to us via mail or e-mail, whichever way you prefer. If all goes well, there will be no reason for us to visit you again." Like a trade delegation, they all walked back to the front door. Here Stansing awkwardly halted and stuck out his hand to Jo.

"Thank you for seeing us," he simply said, then shook hands with the other councilors. One by one the officials

15

disappeared through the massive front door, the last one Wendy Boots, who had not said a single word. She gave the councilors a quick, shy smile, then moved her little case on wheels and herself through the door.

"Bastards!" Daniel English snarled, while they watched the black sedan drive off. "Condolences my foot. Who says one of them didn't give the orders to attack us?"

"We don't know who was behind the destruction of our church, Father," Erwin Johnson said. "It was done by terrorists. And even if the government was somehow involved, it would be a very secret, covert operation. No regular law enforcement forces would kill five hundred of their own citizens."

"I thought we were finished, when the FBI guy asked that question about Excalibur," Jo said. "Imagine if they had found out we are using it to make Oscar's Breath! Carol, you seem to make a habit of saving our church. Thank you yet again."

"Don't be too sure about that, Jo," Carol said, shaking her head. "If they ever dig into it, they'll find out it was just a ruse. That database was valuable, yes, but not to us. All Excalibur's research was anonymous. There were no names on those records."

"So what do we do now?" Jo said, sitting down. "We don't have a church and from now on our members will be checked by the government. This is intolerable."

"Not necessarily all our members, Jo," Patricia said, picking up one of the papers the visitors had left. "See this form? Here's what it says: The before-mentioned government agencies must be informed, in writing, of the names of all new members of the commune, called the Church of Oscar."

"So?" Jo asked. "They already told us that. How can we run our church that way?"

"I think I see where Patricia is heading," Daniel English said, nodding. "Yes. Only the commune. We must make our church bigger than the commune. I have spoken of that before. We must recruit members who won't be living with

16

us, people we can send secretly out into the world to infiltrate society. A secret organization, like the Free Masons, or the Illuminati. I like it!"

"Have two kinds of members?" Jo was still not convinced.

"Why not?" Carol joined in. "We could call them our Ambassadors. They could change the world a bit at the time, put in a word here and there, steer a discussion in a direction that would help us, things like that. Nobody would ever connect them to our church."

"All right," Jo said. "Let's discuss it further at our next council meeting. Right now, all I want to do is sit down with a nice cup of tea."

It was Dale Pinehurst who put everything in perspective. "Daniel, do you remember that fiery speech you gave at the time of the massacre? About how it would put the Church of Oscar firmly on the map, and how people would notice us? Well, it appears they have."

2

"Stop it, Phil, you're hurting me! What's wrong with you?" Jennifer Higman pushed her lover away and sat upright, covering herself with her blanket. "Look what you've done!" She pointed at her right arm, where Philip had grabbed her hard during their lovemaking.

"That'll bruise, damn it. Why do you have to be so aggressive? If you want rough sex, you've got the wrong person, Phil!"

Philip lay on his back, next to her, staring at the ceiling of Jennifer's apartment. Already sorry for her outburst, Jennifer turned around and faced him. "Look, love, it's OK, really. Something is bothering you, I can tell. Does it have to do with work? Or are you on drugs or something?"

"Of course not! I'm really sorry I hurt you, Jen."

It was difficult not to like Philip. To Jennifer he was the most handsome man in Secret Springs. He was quite tall, just a fraction under six feet. She'd fallen for the soft gray-blue eyes, the quiet voice and the crooked smile. His usually relaxed demeanor made him look like an easy-going college professor or a introvert writer, yet he could also be tough and unrelenting if events at work warranted it. But he had never been rough like this before.

Philip stood up and began to put his clothes on. With a sigh, Jennifer draped her housecoat around her, and walked over to the kitchen to make coffee. It wasn't the first kink in their relationship.

At first, it had been heaven. It seemed that Philip had saved all his affections especially for her. Then one day, he'd arrived at her apartment rather drunk. She had invited him for dinner, but he had not touched it. He had blamed it on work and they had left it at that. In a few days it was all forgotten. About two weeks later, when she was supposed to meet him

18

in his penthouse, he wasn't there. Jennifer had waited for an hour and gone home, furious. She suspected he had found someone else, and had confronted Philip in his office next morning.

"All right, Phil, we need to talk. If you don't want me anymore, at least have the decency to tell me. Don't be such a coward. Is there someone else?"

"What are you talking about, woman? Of course not. Why do women always suspect men to be unfaithful?"

It incensed her. "The name is Jennifer, in case you've forgotten. Where were you last night?"

"If you must know, I was in a virtscape, climbing Mount Everest. I needed some time to think things over, and before you blow up again, it has nothing to do with us. I'm having some personal problems." They had made up that evening, but Jennifer knew something was not right.

She filled the kettle about three quarters full to make tea. It was Sunday and they had nothing planned, so it would be a good time to get things out in the open. When Philip came out of the shower, she had two steaming mugs of coffee and a plate of blueberry scones ready. "Come on, Phil. Tell me what's bugging you, no hard feelings, just an honest talk. What is wrong?"

He sat down in his white morning coat and gingerly picked up the large mug. He reached over and took one of the scones. Then he sighed.

"I don't know, Jen, and that's the truth. I've got this feeling that I haven't reached my potential yet. Ever since I left home, I've had this drive, this compulsion to exceed, to be different, to do something special . . ."

"You have," she cried out. "You're in charge of quality control of the biggest company in the world, and you're only twenty-six. You're having an incredible career. What more do you want? Be the CEO at your age?"

"No, even being a CEO wouldn't be good enough, Jennifer. There are thousands of them. I need to be unique, to be remembered in history. The feeling is getting stronger, and

I can't handle it. Every night I feel as if I've wasted another day. It's all in here," he pointed at the side of his head. "It's driving me crazy. And to drink, as well."

"Perhaps you should see somebody about it," she suggested, expecting a tirade. To her surprise he nodded. "Yeah, all right. Know any good shrinks?"

"Not offhand, but I'm sure we can find someone in Secret Springs' medical department."

◊ ◊ ◊

It was the year 2057, the Whitsun Massacre a fading memory, though every councilor knew he or she would never forget it. The church was doing well. With over a hundred new members, the renovations were soon done. Part of the gardens behind Excalibur were transformed into vegetable plots and animal pens, and two hundred huts were built for future members.

Due to the new government regulations, the councilors had to screen everyone who wanted to enter the church, and check people's backgrounds as much as possible. The Internet made this relatively easy.

In the beginning, Jo worried about the forms the new members had to sign. The perpetual poverty clause might confuse or deter people. Then Erwin suggested an elegant solution: new members would sign the forms *after* they received Oscar's Breath. Nobody in the government would ever know.

The church had not as yet started its Ambassador program though Jo daily looked for possible leads. One day he was surfing the Net for ideas, when he noticed a discussion panel on a news channel. Three people sat behind a round table, the moderator and two guests. One panelist was a plain-looking man of about fifty, the other a stunning woman who could be anywhere between twenty and forty-five. The program had just come back from a commercial break, and the moderator was introducing the panelists.

20

". . . with us today are Dr. Henry Waterford, an economist from San Diego, and Dr. Helin Sparling, a psychiatrist from New York. Before we begin, a quick word for those who have just joined us. This is the fourth part of our documentary about the continuing economic and moral decline in the United States. We see more and more people abandon their personal and social responsibilities to join radical new churches, communes, or other survival groups. Dr. Waterford, can we have your opinion on this, please?"

"Thank you, Jim. What you just mentioned is indeed a very disturbing trend that has been going on for many years. These are difficult times, and our government is doing all it can to improve things. There are new jobs available, and tax breaks for small businesses and individuals. The Bullet transportation system has given our economy a great boost. Yet despite all this we remain in a slump.

"I think the problem is a human one. People's values are changing. They don't want to work, and no longer care to have a job and a home to provide for their families. The old, established laws of economics no longer apply.

"This is a serious issue. Without consumer confidence, our economy will never recover. At best, we shall stay in the chaotic state we are in today. A worst case scenario will bring complete anarchy and the end of our western civilization."

"Dr. Sparling, your comment, please," the moderator said. "Do you agree with Dr. Waterford?"

"Up to a point, yes." Dr. Sparling was a beautiful woman. Her skin was without blemish, her delicate nose and mouth just the right size for her small, young-looking face. Her deep brown eyes were flashing with energy and intelligence.

"You are correct, Henry," she said. "People have changed, and it was all predicted by the Mayans."

"*The Mayans?*" Henry Waterford looked flabbergasted. "That's old hat of forty years ago. They were just plain wrong when they predicted the end of the world. We're still here, aren't we? Why bring them up here?"

21

"I am a bit puzzled also," the moderator said. "Are you suggesting that the Mayans are somehow responsible for the mess we are in, Dr. Sparling?"

"Of course not," Helin Sparling replied. "Let me put one misconception to rest here. The Mayans never predicted the end of the world. They pointed to a new era, very different from before. A time were materialism would fade away, and spirituality and human consciousness thrive. That is what we are seeing today. Why do people join communes, like that Church of Oscar, for example? That church wants nothing to do with material possessions. The answer lies in human consciousness. It is changing, and I can prove it."

Almost in trance, Jo stared at his screen. The psychiatrist had mentioned the Church of Oscar! Right there and then, Jo decided Helin Sparling was an ideal candidate to become their first Ambassador. He kept his eyes and ears glued to the debate.

"Jim, this will take a few minutes to explain. May I?" Helin asked, almost apologetically.

The moderator held up his hands. "Of course. In laymen's language, please."

"Thanks." She gave the others a brilliant smile and began. "It's all to do with the proverbial straw that breaks the camel's back, or the final drip that makes the bucket run over. We are talking critical mass here. Put some uranium together and for a while you're OK, until it reaches a critical state and can become a bomb. Human consciousness works the same way.

"From the moment our ancestors walked upright, their brains began to grow. Moderately at first, but faster as time progressed. Think of the stimuli a human being receives every day of his life. We experience and learn more in one day now, then we did in a whole year four centuries ago. Think of that as energy that gets into our brains.

"Look at electrons in a molecule. They're moving in pre-determined orbits. When they get too energized, they jump to a higher energy level. The same happens with our consciousness. It is evolving into a state of higher mental energy, just as the Mayans predicted. People want to break with the past. They see that our world is like a runaway train without a driver, heading for a crash at the end of the line.

"That's why people join communes, or churches, or any other group of people who think differently. To stop the madness of consumerism and create a better world. And there's nothing any government can do. It is the next stage of human evolution, and it will change the earth in ways we can't possibly predict. It can happen to anyone, at any time, anywhere. This is not the end of our civilization, Dr. Waterford, but the end of consumerism. We're heading for a time where intelligence and compassion will replace ignorance and greed."

Helin Sparling had finished and sat back in her chair.

"Just how do you think this will happen, Dr. Sparling?" Waterford asked, mockingly. "Are you suggesting that a person wakes up one morning and decides to walk away from his job, to join a commune, just because he sees the world in a different light? Do you believe something is short-circuiting in people's brains?

"I can tell you that sometimes, after a late party, everything feels very different to me the next morning. That doesn't mean I'm going to join a commune that day, change my religion, or sit on a mountain to meditate. Let's be realistic here. You have no proof for your outrageous theory."

"You mentioned the proof, yourself, Henry," Helin Sparling said. "People's values are changing. They no longer want to be part of a global capitalistic system. They are thinking local instead."

"We've run out of time, I'm afraid," the moderator said. "Thank you both for a most interesting talk. In our next segment, we'll have an agriculturist squaring off against a local farmer on the controversial topic of reduced government subsidies. Please stay with us."

Jo closed the program and sat behind his computer, his heart racing. He stood up and walked to a cupboard to the side of the bed. It contained a small bottle of excellent brandy. He'd had it for more than a year, and he rarely touched it. This time he poured himself two fingers. He walked back to his computer, and opened his browser to look for more information about Dr. Helin Sparling.

◊ ◊ ◊

The psychologist was a rotund little man. It seemed that when Nature had created him, She'd given him a loving pat on the head when She'd finished, but unfortunately had hit him a shade too hard. He was compressed to about two-thirds of average height and since his bulk had to go somewhere, he was much wider around the waist than most people. He wore a dark worsted suit with a pale-blue shirt and grey tie. A halo of white hair seemed to be glued onto his pate. His eyes sparkled behind dark-rimmed glasses, and he had a strong, mellifluous voice.

"Dr. Clarence Kilzinger," he said, sticking out a beefy hand. "How do you do?"

"Philip Kozak," Phil said, shaking hands. Then he waited awkwardly.

"Sit." Clarence pointed at the couch. "Or lie down. Whichever you prefer. Just make yourself comfortable." He picked up the form Philip had filled out when he had registered with the receptionist and began to read it. Philip hesitated, then sat down on the edge of the couch.

"Secret Springs? I get a lot of business through that company," Dr. Kilzinger said.

"Really? I didn't think our employees were that unhappy."

"Excuse me? Oh, I see. No, I don't mean it that way. I meant business in general, from ordinary people all across this land. You know how it goes: people meet others on your site, they fall in love, their marriages suffer and they call me. Bad for people, I guess, but good business for me. Now it says here you have this urgent drive, this feeling you have to do

24

better than you're doing. Why don't you tell me how that all started."

"I don't know how it started," Philip said. "I've always had it."

"Why Secret Springs?" Kilzinger asked. "Why did you come to Chicago?"

"They advertised on the Internet and I applied for a job."

"It says here on your resume that when you were young you were good at assembling and disassembling things. Toasters, blenders, that sort of thing. There has always been a good market for that kind of expertise. Car mechanics, repair shops, jobs like that. Myself, I can't even take a pencil sharpener apart. Why didn't you pursue a career in that field?"

Phil stared at the psychologist. "I honestly never thought of it," he said.

"And your stepfather's farm? Surely a person with your excellent dexterity could be a great asset there, fixing and repairing things. You didn't give that a thought either, apparently. Why not, do you think?"

"I don't know. I never considered it."

"Now your father, Yabul Kozak, he was famous, wasn't he? I remember what happened from the TV and the newspapers. Did you like your father when you were young?"

"If you look at that form, you'll see that I never knew my father. He died before I was born."

"Oh, I have read that, but that doesn't answer my question, Mr. Kozak. Even children who have never seen their father carry a picture of him in their minds; a picture of what they think their father would have been like. So my question, again, Mr. Kozak, did you like the picture of your father that you had in your mind when you were young?"

"Of course. They should never have hunted him down like a criminal. He was a genius!"

"Why did you change your name back to Kozak, Philip? Was it to honor your father? To show him you cared? To show him you loved him, even though you have never seen him?"

25

Philip felt ill at ease. He shifted around, not looking the psychologist in the eye.

"I suppose so," he finally said.

"Now your father had a very specialized job, didn't he, Mr. Kozak. Studying the mind is very difficult and requires an awful lot of research. But virtual reality is also about manipulating people's minds. Is that perhaps the real reason that you joined Secret Springs? To have a job as closely related to your father's line of work as possible?"

"No. I never thought about it that way," Philip said. "It just happened."

"Ah, yes. That is what people say. No, Mr. Kozak, it did not just happen. We create our own reality through our thoughts. You made a deliberate choice, but it was your subconscious mind that made it, and it is giving you problems. How much do you know about your father?"

"Very little. I have no aunts or uncles. My mother is the only person I could ask, but she couldn't help me. What the papers said is not true. My father was not a criminal."

"I'm not saying he was, Philip. Tell me what you know about him."

"He was a brilliant scientist. All his life he worked on something special that would make people remember him in history. He created something unique and then he died. It was unfair! He should have been famous . . ." Philip swallowed hard, and his eyes filled with tears. He bent his head between his knees and cried.

"That's right, Philip. You're almost there. Let it happen." Dr. Kilzinger handed Philip a box of tissues. For a while Philip cried quietly, then he wiped his eyes and sat straight up again.

"Sorry. I feel like an idiot, crying like that."

"And why is that? Do you think there is basically something bad or childish about crying? That's what society would make us believe, yes. But it is not. It is emotional relief, and you need it, just like laughter. Now, Philip, do you understand what is happening to you? All your life, two forces have created havoc in your mind.

26

"First of all there is envy, for never having known a father. The other factor is a profound animosity, a hatred, almost, for all the things and people that caused this situation to occur. We all want certain things out of life, but some of your urges are not realistic, Philip. They are not your own, but your father's. So how does your conscious mind compensate for these unknown feelings? It forces you to live the life that you think your father would have liked you to live.

"Now before we end this session, just one more thing. From what you've told me so far, I feel that you haven't had much contact with your mother and your stepfather over the years. That is a shame, really. You can't hold a grudge against them for not having the answers about your father. Your mother had her own problems with him, I'm sure. Don't be too hard on her."

"Well, that's all for today." Clarence Kilzinger jumped up off his seat, as if an internal alarm had sounded. He reached over to a bewildered Philip and pumped his hand.

"It was very nice meeting you, Mr. Kozak. I think we can do some good work here. Please make an appointment with my secretary for next week. Until then."

◊ ◊ ◊

"What? You want to take that Bullet train to New York?" Father English, eyebrows raised, stared at Jo and Erwin as if they had just told him they were leaving the Church of Oscar for good. "I don't think that's a good idea, Jo. Supporting the enemy isn't what the Church of Oscar preaches. I'm surprised you're even considering it."

"We have to go to New York, Daniel. Helin Sparling must be recruited. She is a freethinker like us, and she hasn't even had the Breath yet. She'll be invaluable to our church."

"That part I'm fine with," Daniel said, "but why the Bullet train? There are alternatives, you know."

"Oh, come now, Father!" Erwin snapped. "Flying is out of the question financially, and we can hardly take the church's armored van. Where would we get the gas? We have barely enough for local trips."

"Well, you can take the bus," Father English said. "What's the hurry?"

"To go all the way to New York on the bus will take days, Daniel," Jo said. "We'd have to stay at hotels, and it'll be too expensive, inconvenient and dangerous."

"Why are you so opposed to that new train, Daniel?" Diana Taylor asked. "It's a quick and clean way of transportation, much better than flying, or driving cars."

"It is the principle, Diana. That train was built with foreign capital and help to get our economy going again in a hurry. No wonder the government accepted it with open arms. It may be good for them, but it's not good for people. Don't you see what is happening here? Society must go through a long period of anarchy and purgatory before it can re-emerge as a new world order, just like the Phoenix arose from its ashes. We must have small, local economies that look after the needs of ordinary people.

"Soon this newfangled transportation system will cause small businesses to get bigger again and spread out across the country, and before you know it we'll have a global society again. That's how it started the first time, when the railways opened up the country in the nineteenth century. The Bullet trains will just give us a rehash of the way things were before, not a complete rebirth."

"But Daniel, that train will run, whether Jo and Erwin are on board or not. It makes no difference in the big picture," Diana said.

"Yes it does," Sylvia came to Father English's rescue. "When you buy your ticket, you support the people who built it, and they're not even Americans."

"I still think we should go," Erwin said. "It'll save us much time."

"Well, you suit yourself, young man," English exploded. "I've had my say." He pushed his chair back and headed for the doorway.

"Daniel, come back at once!" Jo barely raised his voice, but it made Father English slowly return to his seat.

"There may be anarchy in the world out there, Daniel, but not in the Church of Oscar. We'll vote on this in a civilized, democratic way. Those in favor of Erwin and myself taking the Bullet train, please raise your hand." It was a count of ten to two. Father English, and Sylvia were against, and the motion was accepted.

Three days later, on a Friday at 4:30 a.m., Jo and Erwin drove the church's van to Los Angeles and parked it at gate B of the railway station. After entering the large hall, they bought two boarding passes from a machine and headed for the departure gate. Here they stuck the passes in a scanner and entered the security checkpoint. Jo carried a satchel with their lunch and a thermos with tea. In the bottom of the thermos was a small secret compartment for one mask and a small amount of Oscar's Breath. The guard looked at them, casually inspected the satchel and let them through.

"So how fast does this thing go?" Erwin asked, while they headed for the train.

"Plenty fast," Jo replied. "Los Angeles to New York, that's twenty-five hundred miles, divided by eight hours, that's just over three hundred miles an hour. We'll be in New York around three o'clock this afternoon. But you'll never know it, because you don't feel a thing. They should have done this a hundred years ago, instead of building more planes."

"Wow! What a machine. It is beautiful!" Erwin stood back and looked at the sleek Haydo Bullet train that lined the platform like a ribbon of mercury. Then he frowned. "I'm not supposed to like it, am I, Jo? Daniel English would object, I'm sure."

Jo gave him a quick smile. "Probably. The church's rules and dogmas can be murky. Ted and I had long talks about it in the early days. Just how much of the world's time and money saving devices and services can we allow in the Church of Oscar? It's hard to make decisions like that, Erwin. What if we turned our backs on technology and went back to the horse-

and-buggy days? How could we ever recruit Helin Sparling? We wouldn't even know about her without the Internet. The trick is to use technology as a tool, but not become slaves to it."

"How does Daniel know so much about things, Jo? Does he secretly use the Internet?"

Jo smiled. "Only in emergencies, like that time when he hurt his hand in the old church. No, Daniel has his own ways, Erwin. He may be dogmatic and sometimes short-tempered, but he's a good person. He had a superb education when he was younger, and he has his books. Apart from saving our planet, the only thing that matters to Daniel is teaching people the ways of our Church. Have you noticed how he welcomes every recruit? He can talk to people for hours. That's why he wants to be addressed as *Father*; it puts new members at ease, and they confide in him, the way they do in confessions. He has that effect on people. He's a clever man, our Daniel."

The boarding passes showed their cabin numbers and they walked through the crowd to find the right compartment. Since they were traveling the cheapest way, they had a small private compartment with two chairs that could be tilted back. They'd have to walk down the corridor for washrooms and food. The seats were comfortable, and they sat down, waiting for the train to leave.

"So why are we both going?" Erwin asked. "Couldn't you have talked to Helin Sparling on your own?"

"No, the Council has decided we need two people for a recruitment. Our appointment is for four o'clock and hopefully that will give us enough time to see Dr. Sparling and catch the overnight Bullet back home. If not, we must arrange for a hotel."

"How are we going to recruit her? There's bound to be security."

"Don't worry about that for now. We'll have to improvise. Come on, I could do with some breakfast."

3

Philip Kozak slowed his Honda Cobalt XRS to turn off Highway 101. He stopped behind the cars in front of him, and when it was his turn, he headed left to follow the secondary road that would lead to his old home. It was time. He needed to see his parents again. His mind was torn between conflicting emotions; excitement he was going to see them again, battled with fear they might reject him for ignoring them so long. He was also worried he had not been able to contact them. Something had happened. The phone had apparently long been disconnected and the e-mail he had sent came back as undeliverable. When he finally reached his home, he saw that his fears were justified.

The last thing he had seen when he left, ten years ago, was their magnificent mansion, surrounded by lush, green gardens. A long, well-kept driveway had led to two natural stone walls on either side of the property entrance. In between the walls, attached to two wooden pillars, a heavy-duty metal gate had closed behind him. He saw something very different this time, and he knew his parents didn't live there anymore.

Pieces of the metal gate, bent, rusted, and corroded, lay on the ground in front of the walls. The main part of the gate had either been stolen or was used for other purposes by the new occupants. The beautiful wooden pillars had been chopped off, leaving only stumps in the ground. Great pockmarks defaced the walls, as if someone had tried to knock them down with a sledgehammer and given up halfway. Chunks of stone lay everywhere. The remnants of the walls showed ugly graffiti and blobs of spray paint. On one side, someone had sprayed an ominous warning on a rusty, metal board. *Private Property, Keep Out!* The once pristine driveway showed its wear and tear: deep ruts, cracks and

31

potholes everywhere, and weeds blossoming from the cracks. There was an awful smell in the air. It permeated the car even with the windows closed.

Philip stopped at the entrance to the driveway, unsure what to do. His eyes followed the damaged driveway until he saw his old home, his family's pride. The roof had lost many shingles, and three of the windows were broken. Whoever lived there now hadn't bothered to board or fix them. The siding needed painting. At one place the flashing around the chimney had come loose, inviting rain to run in. There was no garden anymore, just an overblown jungle with three large trucks, haphazardly parked. To the left of the property stood an enormous building with rows of small windows under the roof. When Philip opened the car window, the nauseating smell of pig excrement wafted in, and he could hear the raucous voices of pigs waiting to be slaughtered. He closed the window again.

At this stage Philip knew he should turn around and head back the way he had come. But he couldn't. He had to know what happened to his parents and the caretakers Alyn and Michelle. He debated whether to drive in or walk. If he drove it would be faster, but if he had to get out in a hurry he could not turn around in that jungle. He decided to back in.

He was a third down the driveway when he heard exciting voices behind him. in his rear mirror he saw two men standing ten feet behind his car. They had been hiding behind a truck. One of them aimed a handgun at him. While Philip put the car in forward gear, there was a loud bang, and the back window shattered in a shower of pieces of glass. Several of the pieces hit him in the back of the head. The bullet had landed in the front window frame about a foot from his head. Philip feared the next shot might kill him.

He stopped and slumped over the wheel, realizing that for the last ten years he had not just lived in an air-conditioned, super-panoramic office, but also in an ivory tower. This was the real world of the 2050s—a place of guns, mayhem, fear and death. And he had walked right into it. On

32

his own, without help. He locked his car doors and windows and took his phone out of his pocket to call for help. To his dismay, he couldn't get a signal.

The two men walked to the side of the car. One of them, grinning maliciously, made short rolling movements with his hands, showing that the wanted Philip to open the window. Philip opened it a few inches. The man was about twenty-five. He had a full black beard that blended with the long hair hanging around his face. Dark sunglasses shielded his eyes, and an Australian bush hat perched on his head, as if his unruly hair was trying to push it off. He wore a dirty khaki shirt without buttons that didn't quite close in the center, revealing yet another crop of dark hair. Faded blue jeans and heavy construction boots completed his outfit. Strapped around his shoulder hung an hunting rifle, and around his waist looped enough ammunition to start a small war.

"You've got yourself two choices, Mister," the hippy said. "You can come out peacefully, so we can have a chat. Or, if you decide to be difficult, we'll both empty a round in the door lock. What will it be?"

In a daze, his heart beating like a drum roll, Philip unlocked the door and stepped out of the car. The two men roughly pushed him towards the house. Inside, Philip hardly recognized the place, but he had no time to worry about it. The men pushed him down in a chair in the middle of what once had been the dining room. One of them tied Phil's hands together around the back of his chair.

"Right." The man who had spoken to Philip took off his glasses and hat and put them on a chair. "I'm Mark and I bloody well want to know what you're doing here. Can't you read? Says *Private* in big red letters. Why have you come here?"

"This is my home. I used to live here. Where are my parents?" As a reply, Mark's fist hit Philip on the nose, and he cried out in pain. "We're asking the fucking questions here, OK?" Mark shouted. One of the hippies held Philip, while

Mark quickly patted him down and grabbed the wallet out of his pocket. By now, two others had joined in the excitement.

"Yuppee doo," Mark exclaimed, punching the air with his fist. "It's our lucky day, chums. We found ourselves a Vee Ai Pee. He'll be good for a few million bucks!"

"What's going on here?" A woman had joined the crowd. Phil guessed her to be in her mid-thirties, and he thought that at one time she might have been beautiful, but life had done its best to eradicate it. Her skin was pale and a large scar disfigured her left cheek. Her tousled hair hung around her head as if she'd been out in a windstorm. Next to her stood a warrior-like hippy, complete in warfare outfit, including a red bandana around his forehead.

"We've won the lottery, Jose! This guy's an executive for that shit company, Secret Springs," Mark shouted.

"What do you want with us?" the woman asked Philip. She had a pleasant, cultured voice. "What is your name?"

"I'm Philip, and this is my home. What have you done to my parents?"

Mark raised his arm to hit Philip again, but Jose held him back.

"When did you live here?"

"My parents built the house when I was two years old. I lived here until I was sixteen."

"What did your father do for a living?"

Phil was about to say scientist when he realized she was talking about his stepfather.

"He was a retired policeman. Homicide."

Shouts of annoyance and anger filled the room.

"I smell bacon! I'd say take him . . ."

"Fuck! Let's bleed that company. Make them pay to get him back."

"OK, guys, back off!" Jose's partner with the bandana moved between Philip and the others. "Mark, give him back his wallet."

The other hippies stood in shock. "What?" Mark exclaimed, "You don't want his money? Have you gone mad,

Vernie? Come on, let's call that company. He's our ticket to the good life. What's bloody wrong with you?"

"Give him back his wallet, Mark, and untie him. I won't ask you again." A red-faced Mark removed the cord around Philip's wrists and threw the wallet in his lap. "You'll be sorry you did this Vernie, and you too, Jose! You may be in charge, but that can change."

"Here's the story," Vernie said. "Thirteen years ago, Jose and I were shacking up in the house next door." He pointed to his left. "Times were different. In those days squatting still landed you in jail. Two cops came to the door and found us. One of them said he lived here. He wondered what had happened to his neighbors. Point is, they could have arrested us, but they gave us a break and let us go. That cop was this guy's father, so we're paying off a debt here. If you want to harm him, you'll have to harm us first. Anyone has an issue with that?"

Jose grabbed Philip by the elbow and dragged him off the chair.

"Come," she whispered, pulling him away, while Vernie argued with the others. When they got to the door, she roughly pushed him out.

"Run! They will not be very happy with us."

"My parents! What happened to my parents?"

"Don't ask stupid questions! Get the hell out of here!"

◊ ◊ ◊

Helin Sparling leaned back in her chair, raised both hands above her head and stretched. Ah, that felt good. Just one more appointment and then she could lock her office and head to their cottage in Albany to spend the weekend with her husband Claude.

Why do I still practice here, she thought for the umpteenth time. She could work from home, give lectures via the Net, or spend her time on research, rather than sit in her office all day—spacious and comfortable as it was.

35

After graduating from medical school, she had specialized in psychiatry. Dealing with life-threatening situations wasn't her forte, and she could not see herself as a surgeon or trauma physician. Obstetrics wasn't her line either. Her interests lay in the human mind and its many secrets. After five more years of specialized study and two stints as an intern in New York's Bethesda hospital, she set up practice in New York City.

For a while, she enjoyed helping her patients cast out their demons. Lately, she had gotten tired of it, as mainstream psychiatry had turned to drugs to treat mental issues. It was far easier—and more profitable—to prescribe a pill, rather than take time to address the complex, emotional forces that had taken many years to build, and might take just as long to resolve. At age forty-seven, Helin wondered if she shouldn't give up her practice altogether and concentrate on the research for the book on expanded consciousness she was planning.

The buzzing of her intercom startled her from her reverie.

"Mr. Porter and his son are here, Helin," her secretary announced.

"Thank you, Marsha. Show them in, please."

Mr. Porter was around forty, Helin guessed; heavy-set, but not overly so. What caught her immediate attention were his deep, penetrating brown eyes. They seemed to pierce right through her, yet she felt no threat. Sometimes it felt as if a patient was mentally undressing her during a consultation, but not so with Mr. Porter. His stare was melancholic, almost hypnotic.

The file that Marsha had brought in earlier had not stated Mr. Porter's profession and Helin wondered what his line of work was. He looked ill at ease in his suit, as if he usually wore a sweater and jeans. The son cast his eyes down and wasn't very happy. The two men didn't look similar; perhaps the son was adopted. She stood up behind her desk and shook hands with the older man.

36

"I am Dr. Sparling," she said, smiling. "Please take a seat. How can I help you?"

Instantly, time stopped for Helin Sparling. With no warning, the younger man moved behind her, folded his arms around her in a bear hug and pulled her back against her seat. She was paralyzed with shock, unable to speak or call out. At the same time, the older man held a mask against her face, and an acrid substance entered her nose. She could feel it expand through her nostrils, like a burning gas, and she gagged. It all happened in a split second, and she tried to scream and push the mask away, but couldn't.

"It is best if you do not struggle, Dr. Sparling," Mr. Porter said. "It will make things easier for you. We won't harm you. It lasts only a few minutes, and you should feel better soon."

It was true. The stinging had gone, but Mr. Porter still held that horrid mask against her face. Helin frantically shook her head to force it off, but he was very strong. She felt light-headed. They had drugged her. But why? The thought echoed in her head, as if her mind had turned into a huge, cavernous chamber. *What was happening to her?*

Her muscles relaxed, instead of preparing to fight. It had to be a psychosomatic drug, like Rohypnol or Ketamine. Far away, she heard her own voice inside her head. *Helin, for Christ's sake, do something! Call Marsha! Don't just sit there!* Then the voice faded away, and she slid into a relaxed, contented state. Had she died and gone to heaven? No, Mr. Porter was still standing there, looking at her. There was no malice in his eyes, only concern.

"I shall remove the mask now," the father said. "Our apologies for what we did, Dr. Sparling. There was no other way. I have studied your work and I admire you greatly. You will be a great asset to us." He took the mask away, and at the same time the son released his grip. Helin wanted to shout for help, but something stopped her.

She saw Mr. Porter's head sharply defined against the fluorescent light above her, with an energy field fluctuating around him, like a colorful aura. The vision filled her entire mind, and there was no room to think of other things.

Helin Sparling could have sat there for the longest time, studying Mr. Porter. She saw the creases in his skin, the wrinkles around his eyes, the bushy, uneven eyebrows, the blood vessels in his hands, the pores in his skin and the veins in his neck.

"Who are you? Why have you drugged me?" she asked, when she finally found her voice again.

"We are councilors for the Church of Oscar, Dr. Sparling. I know you have heard of us because I watched you on TV the other day. Your theory about expanding consciousness is not just a theory but a fact."

"Why didn't you tell me that before, instead of coming on to me like that?" she said. "I would have listened to you. I admire your commune. It does much good. There was no need for this." Helin shook her head, put her elbows on the desk and cupped her hands under her chin.

"Yes, there was," Mr. Porter said. "Even though you are more open-minded than others, you were still programmed to stick to the status quo. We have cleansed your mind, so you can see the world as it really is."

"It was very much a religious experience," Helin said. "Like being born again. I feel wonderful, but you had no right to assault me. I don't understand why I haven't called security and have you both arrested. What is stopping me?"

"You yourself are, Dr. Sparling. You would already have done so if you wanted to. Revenge and retribution are negative emotions that have no place in the Church of Oscar. We need your help."

"Do you want me to move into your commune?"

"No. We want you to continue your life as before. You will be our first Ambassador. If you meet others who share your view of the world, please mention the Church of Oscar as an alternative way of living. Do not let them know you are a member, just refer them to us. That's all we're asking. Some time in the future we would like you to visit us, so we can show you our church. You know where we are, in Santa Barbara, California."

"I am exhausted," Helin said, standing up. "Please leave now. I need some time alone, to come to terms with this new way of thinking."

In the taxi on their way back to the Bullet Station, Erwin voiced his concern.

"We have taken an awful risk, Jo. Is it going to work?"

"Don't worry, everything will be fine, Erwin. If Dr. Sparling wanted to stop us, we would never have gotten out of that building. I have complete faith in Oscar's Breath."

At the station, luck was with them, as they had less than a half-hour wait for their return trip. Erwin looked around for trouble. He saw lots of armed patrolmen, but nobody paid them any attention, and soon they were on their way back to L.A. Jo rested back in his seat and closed his eyes, but Erwin let his mind wander.

They had been lucky. If Helin Sparling had been stronger and managed to pull free, or if someone had entered her office at the critical moment, things could have ended quite differently. Oscar's Breath was an amazing substance, but the delivery method was cumbersome and dangerous. There had to be a better way. While he sat there, his head leaning against the glass windows, with the countryside whizzing past in one continuous blur, Erwin felt an idea germinate in his mind.

◊ ◊ ◊

The Santa Barbara Police Station looked like an ordinary brownstone house, except that the garden in front had been leveled to make room for parking spaces. Philip didn't know much about architecture, but to him it looked like an old colonial kind of place, with a balcony around the front and a little porch to shield visitors in case of rain. This was a police station?

When he walked up the steps leading to the front porch, he noticed a small sign above the door: *Santa Barbara*

Oceanic Department. There was more parking to the side where two police cars were parked. One of them had just arrived and he could see the officer sitting inside. Phil found it a very strange place for a law enforcement agency. When he stepped up onto the porch to go inside, he noticed billboards and pictures of missing people stuck on the siding of the house, and one particular notice caught his attention. Curiously, he stepped closer to take a look. It was a dog-eared, yellowed sheet of paper, containing the list of names of people killed in the Whitsun Massacre two years ago. Philip had heard about it on the news. None of the names meant anything to him.

He stepped inside and saw an information counter and a set of stairs with beautifully carved banisters. It reminded him of a hotel, not a police station. Behind the counter stood a young sergeant who gave him a pleasant smile.

"Yes, sir. What can I do for you?" he asked. His name tag said *Watersma*, and he looked in his early twenties.

"Excuse me, please," Philip said, his curiosity getting the better of him. "This is the strangest police station I have ever seen. It's an old house."

Sergeant Watersma laughed. "It is. We're here only temporarily. We had a big fire in the main station; arson is suspected, and it is still closed for investigation. This was the best place they could come up with on short notice."

"I see. As you can tell I'm not from the area," Philip said. "I am looking for my parents, Carol and Patrick Johnson. They used to live on a farm in Carpinteria. Stowaway it was called. When I went there, our old home was occupied by a group of hippy squatters. Do you know what happened there?"

The sergeant frowned. "I'm sorry, I don't." He turned to the officer who had just entered the station. "Excuse me, sir. Do you know a place called Stowaway, in Carpinteria?"

Philip guessed the newcomer was the senior officer in charge. He was about fifty and looked very friendly.

"Sure do," the officer said, staring at Philip. "My old boss used to live there. It's off the 101, about twenty minutes. Why?"

"I am Philip Kozak," Phil said. "I wonder if—"

"Well, I'll be!" the detective said, taking off his cap and holding it in his left hand. He stuck out his right one towards Philip and gave him a firm handshake.

"I'm Lieutenant Tom Cramer, Philip. We've met before, but you were only a few years old then. Karl, this is Patrick Johnson's son. I can't believe it, after all those years. Why do you call yourself Kozak, though, Philip? Come on in." The lieutenant took Philip by the arm and led him down the hallway into an small office. It looked as if it might have been a dining room at one time. There was just enough room for a round table and four chairs, and they sat down. The lieutenant looked serious.

"I know why you're here," he said. "Did you look at the list on the bulletin board?"

Flabbergasted, Phil nodded.

Cramer scratched the back of his head. "Dreadful business that, but I'm still hoping. They're not on the official casualty list, so that's probably a good sign. Still, many of them could not be identified. Some of those church members have gone into hiding in the old Excalibur Center. Perhaps you can try there. I can't help you, though. We're not allowed to go anywhere near the place. They don't like police, or any other authority for that matter."

"Excuse me, Lieutenant Cramer. I have lived in Chicago for the last ten years and I know about the Whitsun Massacre, but what has that got to do with my parents?"

Cramer gaped at him. "You don't know? They didn't tell you? Your parents joined the Church of Oscar, son, a few months before that massacre. The caretaker, Alyn, told me. I was in the neighborhood on a case a while ago, and dropped in to see how things were with my old boss. They had already left. Patrick was quite ill, and Carol was very upset about that

41

pig farm next door, so they decided to make the move. Erwin also. How come you don't know that?"

Philip was mortified. Had his parents been killed? Nauseating waves of despair and guilt flowed through him.

"We never really talked that much," he said. "They may have written or e-mailed me, but I never got a message. I work for Secret Springs and all my mail is screened."

"Now, Philip, Patrick and Carol are two of my best friends and I know they both loved you very much. Why did you change your name back to Kozak? Did you not tell them? No wonder their messages didn't reach you. Why, Philip? Why did you shut yourself off from your parents?"

Philip just lowered his head, and for a while all he could hear was the ringing of the phone in the hallway. The lieutenant had no right to grill me like that, he thought angrily. It was personal.

"OK," Cramer finally said, as if he'd read Philip's thoughts. "Sorry, son. It's really none of my business how you run your life, and I apologize for what I said. It's the job, you know," he added with a faint smile. "Whenever I talk to people I automatically go in interrogation mode. My wife hates it at times! Anyway, I'm glad you finally have come to look for them. Did you go to your old home?"

"Yes. Almost didn't make it out. A bunch of crazy hippies has completely wrecked the place. They were going to keep me for ransom, but I managed to get away. How can villains just take over and throw people out of their homes? Isn't that what police are for? To preserve law and order? They've probably killed Alyn and Michelle. How could you let this happen?"

Lieutenant Cramer sighed. "There wouldn't be enough police in the country to go after every break and entry and squatting incident, Philip. We have our hands full with homicides. It's a survival of the fittest out there and it's getting worse every day. Unless you bring me definite proof that those bastards deliberately killed the caretakers, there's nothing we can do. I don't like it a bit, but that's how it is these days.

"There's something else you should know. You took an enormous risk, driving around in the country by yourself. You can't do that these days, not someone important like yourself. You were lucky to escape without being harmed. I think you should go to Excalibur, to see if by any chance your parents are there, but you're not going alone. I'm sending Watersma with you. I want to make sure you're safe; I owe that much to your parents. Just don't let the church people see him; they don't like us. Can't blame them after what happened to them. Perhaps they'll listen to you, since you're family. If you find Pat and Carol, say hello from me, will you."

Cramer stood up and shook Phil's hand again. "All the best, Phil. I hope that your parents are still alive, and that you find them. For their sake as well as yours."

◊ ◊ ◊

"I received a rather odd e-mail this morning," Jo said, buttering a slice of toast. "From a member of Congress."

It was Monday morning and the church councilors were having a working breakfast to plan their activities for the week ahead. Daniel English looked up. The hand bringing the coffee cup to his mouth froze in mid air. He frowned, and stared at Jo.

"A congressman? Who?"

"Richard Duval. He's a Democrat from Illinois in the House of Representatives."

"That is bad news," English said, putting his cup back on the table again. "Very bad. What does he want?"

"He wants to set up a date for a visit. He didn't say why, but I think he wants to find out what we're doing in our church."

"That's rubbish," Patricia Sheppard exclaimed. "He can't just come over to inspect us. Only if he has a suspicion that we're doing something wrong, and even then he needs a warrant or a court order."

"Maybe he wants to join us," Erwin said.

Carol Johnson laughed. "Fat chance, Erwin. Politicians love their cushy jobs. He'd be the last person to join a commune like ours."

"This reminds me too much of Jonestown," Daniel said, shaking his head. He pushed his plate with eggs and fried potatoes away, as if he had suddenly lost his appetite. The hand pushing the plate was only a claw with three fingers missing. His face was pale, and many sharply defined crease lines showed his age. His long hair badly needed cutting, as it reached below the collar of his khaki shirt.

"Jonestown?" Jo frowned. "I'm not with you, Daniel. Jonestown where? What's the relevance?"

"You should study your history, Jo," Daniel said tiredly. "In the mid 1970's, a certain Reverend Jones ran a religious compound in Guyana, very similar to our own. Individuals who for one reason or another couldn't conform to society anymore. There was a cloud of suspicions about that compound, rumors that people were being brainwashed and held against their will. A congressman by the name of Ryan went over to investigate. In the end it all got very nasty, and everyone in the compound, including Jones, died. Most were suicides. We can't allow this Duval to snoop around and talk to our members, Jo. One slip of the tongue and our church will be finished."

"That e-mail doesn't make sense," Patricia said. "What exactly did it say, Jo?"

"I have the printout here," Jo said. He produced a sheet of paper from his gown pocket, and began to read. "This is to advise you that United States House of Representatives Member Richard Duval would like to pay your establishment a short personal visit to discuss a matter of mutual interest. Please reply at the above address to set a suitable date and time. Duval, Richard, United States member of Congress for the State of Illinois."

"That's absolutely ridiculous," Patricia burst out. "Matters of mutual interest? We have no mutual interests. A suitable date and time? As if a congressman would ask permission to visit someone. This is a practical joke, Jo. A hoax!"

"I was up early this morning," Jo said, pouring himself a cup of coffee. "After I read my e-mails I did some research on this Duval. He's thirty-two and a real go-getter. Not the type to be satisfied with just a seat in the House, and there are rumors he has taken aim for the Presidency. But he is still relatively unknown, so he needs leverage to get where he wants to go."

"Like exposing our church," Daniel growled. "Wouldn't that be a feather in his cap. I do not believe this is a hoax, Patricia. This is a very clever ploy to get a look inside our church. Perhaps people have talked to him; disgruntled family members, unhappy that someone close to them joined our commune. I've always worried about that possibility. He wants something, that's for sure."

"Well, what are we going to tell him?" Jo asked impatiently. "We have to reply."

"We could just say no," Father English suggested. "Say that our church does not want to be involved in matters of state. We have a constitutional right to our privacy."

"There's something fishy about this," Jeremy Burlon joined in. "Remember what happened to my sister? According to the official explanation for the massacre, Angela got involved with that Army Sergeant, Matt Friesen, who's been charged. Friesen followed the proper channels and went to the authorities first and tried to get Angela back. Remember that policeman who came to our door, asking questions? When that didn't work, Friesen lost it and decided to wipe out the whole church.

"If this Duval suspects we are doing something wrong, why hasn't he arrived at the gate with a bunch of federal marshals, the FBI, or members of whatever other government agency he needs? Instead, he meekly asks permission for a personal visit? No, I think our Congressman is up to something shady and secretive, and he doesn't want anyone else to know about it. That's why he wants to come himself, instead of sending his underlings."

"But why?" Jo exclaimed. "What does he want from us? Why the e-mail? If it is something do to with the massacre, why has he waited so long? From what I've read about him, he is out for personal gain. I just can't figure out what this Duval hopes to gain from visiting our church."

"I am still convinced this it a ruse," Daniel English said tiredly. "Once he has seen what he wants to see and heard what he wants to hear, he'll head back to Washington to confer with other Members of the House and then plot our coup de grace. You'll see. The government is very touchy about getting involved with us, because of the massacre. It gave the Ramsing administration a big black eye, even though they somehow wriggled themselves out of it. If they suspect something this time, they'll want to be absolutely certain they've got it right. They don't want another scandal. Someone needs to check us out first, and that someone is Congressman Duval."

"So what do we do?" Diana said. "If we ignore the e-mail it'll make him suspicious and he might come back with the cavalry. If we refuse, he may think we're hiding something. Yet if we invite him in and he somehow hears or sees something he doesn't like, the results could be just as bad. We need another option."

"There is one," Erwin said, and eleven pairs of eyes focused on him.

"And what would that be, Councilor Johnson," Daniel asked, peering over his half frame glasses.

"We could give him Oscar's Breath. That way he won't harm us."

"Oh, that's rich, Erwin," Patricia Sheppard said, standing up. "Sure, we just kidnap a member of the U.S. government, and nobody's going to miss him, right? He may act secretively, but I can guarantee you if he doesn't get back home, our church will be swarming with security agents within twenty-four hours, like wasps circling a jam jar."

"No, no," Erwin said. "That's not what I meant. We don't want to keep him here. We send him back to Washington, as an Ambassador." In the ensuing silence, Patricia slowly sat down again, staring at Erwin. Then Carol spoke.

"I think that's a brilliant idea. Look, we've already recruited Helin Sparling, so why not? Imagine if we could have a say in the House of Representatives, and with a bit of luck later on in the White House. I think we should go for it. We may never get an opportunity like this again."

"Perhaps," Jo replied. "It is not as easy as it seems, Carol. As a commune, we're all together with the Council in tight control. Are we really ready to expand our Ambassador program? Helin Sparling was thinking very much like us even before she was recruited. But this is different.

"We don't know much about this Duval at all. He may look exactly the same after he is converted, but his actions may change. In a position of power like that, people will notice. Especially people close to him, his wife, his secretary, and co-workers. This could be traced back to the church. I think our plan for future Ambassadors for the church should involve a period of teaching and coaching, to make sure they come to terms with their new outlook on life *before* we send them out into the world."

"Well, perhaps it is time to jump into the deep end without testing the water," Carol said. "It's the best of our options and having a member of our church in government would be invaluable."

"There's still the issue of security," Patricia said "We need at least ten minutes, minimum, for Oscar's Breath to do its work. We'll never get a chance to have Duval alone for that period of time. He will have security with him, that you can count on. No congressman in his right mind will travel the road alone these days, not even on private business. Unless we can recruit his security at the same time, the whole thing will be impossible."

"Perhaps he'll only have a bodyguard," Diana suggested. "What possible harm could he expect in our church? If he is on a secret mission, a large entourage would raise suspicion."

"Agreed," Dale said. "Our new recruiting room is almost finished, Jo. It's not as big as the one in the old church, but it will have to do. With some extra help I could have it operational in a week or so. We'll be able to recruit the congressman and his security at the same time."

"Right," Jo said, raising a finger in the air, "just a quick show of hands, people. In principle, who wants to invite Duval and recruit him for our church? Hands up, please." Eleven pairs of hands shot up and, lacking his gavel, Jo used his knife to bang on the table top. "Carried unanimously. I shall ask the Congressman to visit us ten days from now, to give Dale some extra time."

4

Philip stood in front of the old Excalibur Mind Research Center. Behind him lay the long driveway to Gallagan Drive, winding through the beautifully landscaped gardens and fields, like a huge black serpent in rigor mortis. They had come to a locked gate at the beginning of the driveway, but Sergeant Watersma had proven to be a resourceful young policeman and, after some encouragement, picked the lock.

The mansion was fronted with brownstone, and two marble columns supported a portico. A magnificent wooden door was centered between two windows. Philip let a brass knocker hit the door twice. When there was no response, he knocked again, wondering what on earth had made his mother and stepfather join the commune.

Finally the door opened and a middle-aged man stepped onto the porch. He was dressed like a gardener, or workman. Heavy-duty khaki work shirt, jeans and boots. He was not in a good mood.

"You are trespassing!" he shouted. "That gate is there for a purpose. How did you get through? The church is closed today. The next service is on Sunday. If you want to learn about us, try our website: www.ChurchofOscar.rel. Now leave us." He turned back to go inside again.

"Wait!" Philip yelled. "I have come more than two thousand miles for this and I've been through an awful lot. You can't just dismiss me like that. All I want is some information. What is your name?"

The man slowly turned around and faced Philip again. He had bloodshot eyes and an unhealthy pallor. "I am Father English, religious leader and a councilor of the Church of Oscar. Who are you, and what is your business here?"

"I am Philip Johnson, and I am trying to find my parents, Patrick and Carol. They joined your church a few years ago,

49

and I want to talk to them." When Philip mentioned the name Johnson, he saw a look of recognition cross the other's face, and he felt a surge of relief. Perhaps his parents were still alive. Father English took a while to answer, then made up his mind, shaking his head. "I'm afraid I can't help you." He turned around again and began to shuffle back towards the door.

"Can you at least tell me if my parents died in that massacre? You must have a list of names of the people who were killed."

The priest turned around and peered at Philip. "And just which part of the word "no" are you having trouble with, young man? We do not want to be reminded of that horrid day in our history. If you want to look at a list, go to the police station. They have one. Leave us alone." He began to walk back to the church again.

"I won't go away, you know," Philip shouted. "Can't you just answer a simple question?"

"Why does everyone always stick their noses into our business?" English snapped. "All right. Your mother is still alive, but your father died some time ago from lung cancer. Now please, will you go?"

"I want to see her."

"That is out of the question. The church does not keep visiting hours."

"Now here's the thing, Father. I can make life very difficult for you. I work for Secret Springs. Most people have used our site during their lifetime and now that I know your name, it'll be very simple for me to check up on you. If you ever did anything of a secretive or shady nature in Secret Springs before you joined this church, I shall leak that information to the other church members."

"Go right ahead, young man. You will not find my name on that devilish website." Daniel English turned around and headed back.

"I'm going to stay here, until you let me see my mother. That's all I want, just five minutes of her time. Why are you so spiteful?" There was no reply, as Father English had gone back inside.

Deflated, Philip paced up and down in front of the building. It had been a long shot. Not everyone did something in virtual reality they might not want others to know about. But he had run out of ideas. He tried to look inside, but dark blinds in the windows made it impossible. In the quiet, Philip could hear farm machinery somewhere, so there were other people around. A bored-looking Sergeant Watersma waited silently in the car.

Utterly frustrated, Philip kept his eye on the door. He realized how eager he was to see his mother after all these years. He had come all this way, he damned well was going to see her, if he had to camp out here for a week. There was something very odd about this church. Why the secrecy to the point of hostility? Why were all the blinds drawn during daytime? Why had that priest not invited him in and called his mother, so that they could have a nice chat over a cup of tea? It all made very little sense.

To Philip's relief, the church door suddenly opened again and three people stood there but didn't come out. Two men and a middle-aged woman. Was that his mother? Philip knew Carol would be sixty-six, and the woman looked about that age, but he realized she was a different person from the one he had left at age sixteen. Waves of guilt crashed through him, like an emotional tsunami. How could he have ignored her all this time? Why hadn't he called more?

"Mother!" he shouted, "Mom, it's me, Philip!" He raced towards the door, and was about to step inside and embrace her, when he halted. He looked at the two men, standing next to Carol. It was Father English and another man, slightly younger and in better shape. Both men were standing very close to his mother, as if to protect her. Their body language was threatening. The priest had his right hand in the pocket of his jeans. Was he hiding a gun?

"Well, come in," Father English said impatiently. "Don't keep your mother waiting."

Philip didn't move. "No. I want her to come out. Alone. We can sit in the car." He could see they hadn't expected that. Father English and the other man exchanged glances. They had been up to something! Philip stepped away from the door, keeping his eyes on the others. Then his spirits lifted, as his mother stepped on the porch by herself.

He ran over to her and passionately hugged her, but her response was not what he expected. There was no emotional spark, no feeling of belonging. She felt limp in his arms, as if he was holding a stranger. He felt a sudden blockage in his throat.

"Are you all right, Mom?" he asked. "What happened to you? Aren't you glad to see me?"

"Hello, Philip. Of course I am, son. I'm just so surprised, after all this time."

"I am sorry. There was just never the right moment for a call or visit."

She gave him a thin smile. "Oh, I know, Philip, I went through it all before, with your father."

"Father English told me about Patrick," Phil said. "How awful for you."

"Yes. The Church has helped me through it. Come." She pulled him towards the car. "I can only stay for a few minutes." Philip told Sergeant Watersma to go for a walk, and they both sat down in the car.

"Why did you and Pat join that church, Mom? Is Erwin here also?"

"Yes, but he is on a trip. We did it for security in our old age, Philip. We just couldn't stay at the farm anymore. Everything had changed for the worse, and it was just getting too dangerous. It was the best thing we ever did. The Church of Oscar made me see things differently and it gave me a new purpose in life. Patrick died in peace here."

"But he didn't like that church at all. Remember, how we talked about it when I was young? He loved his home. Oh, Mom, it's so awful! Our house has been taken over by a bunch of hippies, and they were going to hold me for ransom; they might even have killed me if I hadn't escaped. The whole place is in ruins. No sign of Alyn or Michelle. I think they killed them. Alyn would never have given up without a fight."

"It was to be expected," Carol said calmly. "The world is full of violence and killing, and that's why we came here. What about you? How is your job at Secret Springs?"

"I'm in charge of quality control of the virtscapes, Mom. I could be the CEO one day."

"I know you wouldn't settle for anything less. A girlfriend?"

He nodded. "Yes, Jennifer."

"And you're both happy?"

"We are doing fine. And you?"

"Of course. I am at peace here and this is where I want to spend the rest of my days. You heard about that dreadful massacre?"

"Yes. It was lucky you were away at the time."

She looked him straight into the eyes. "So what made you suddenly decide to come and see me?"

"I wanted to find out how you were, and apologize for not calling you before. And I also want to learn more about my father. You were married to him, surely there must be something you can tell me. What was he working on?"

"Yabul was a genius, Philip. He created something very controversial, to do with the mind. That's all I know. He had his life and I had mine."

"I can't believe that, Mother," Philip said. "You can't live with a person for eight years and not know more about him. Why do people say he was a traitor? I want to know."

"Of course your Dad wasn't a traitor. He was a very clever, misunderstood and lonely man, but what he did lies behind us now. There are more important things to consider. The church is all that matters."

Carol's body was tense, and she stared at her son with such intensity that Philip thought she was trying to reach his soul. He felt uneasy and backed off a bit.

53

"Why was that priest so rude to me, Mom? All I wanted was to talk to you."

"Father English is not a priest, Erwin. He just likes to be called *Father*. We have nothing in common with other religions. After that dreadful massacre we must be very careful whom we talk to. He was just trying to protect us."

"I don't trust him. First he wants nothing to do with me, and then he suddenly invites me in. What's going on, Mother?"

She relaxed, like a puppet that had its strings cut, and lay a hand on his chest. For a second Philip thought she was going to cry, but she didn't. "Oh, Phil, all those questions! After ten years you suddenly show up and give me the third degree. I love you son, and I wanted to see you, but there are things I can't tell you. I will not betray my people." She pushed herself upright, gave Phil a quick kiss on the cheek, scrambled out of the car and rushed to the porch without looking back.

"Wait! Mom!" he called after her, but she had already disappeared inside.

◊ ◊ ◊

"It looks as if you were right, Diana," Daniel English said, looking down the driveway. "The congressman is traveling light, and he is very punctual." It was exactly twelve o'clock and in the distance a small car had just turned off the main road. All twelve councilors were assembled in the Excalibur living room that looked out over the front of the property. They were nervously awaiting their guests.

"Everyone is clear on what to do?" Jo asked. "Be polite and open, answer questions if you have to, but don't volunteer information. I shall do the introductions and the questioning. Dale, at my sign, get the recruitment room ready, please, but not before. OK?"

"Right," the head of Security nodded.

While their visitors drove up to the front of Excalibur, Jo stepped outside on the porch. Two men got out of the car and stood for a few seconds, looking around at the Excalibur buildings. Jo walked towards the smallest of the two and reached out to shake his hand.

"Thank you for coming, Congressman," he said. "I am Joachim Rasnell, Head Councilor of the Church of Oscar. Please come in."

Congressman Duval was short and stocky, his slightly overweight frame a sharp contrast to the wiry, muscular body of his tall assistant. Duval was wearing a dark-blue business suit with the white shirt and dark tie that his profession required. He looked a bit stiff, probably from the cramped seating in the small subcompact they had traveled in.

"Richard Duval," he said, shaking Jo's hand. It was a firm handshake, the hand cool and dry. When Jo looked at Duval, he noticed a pair of steel-blue eyes that were very focused. The man had the look of someone who didn't miss much of what was going on around him. Yet the wide smile was disarming, and Jo's first impression was favorable.

"This is Clive Wadding, my assistant," Duval said. The bodyguard looked like a wrestler, boxer, and street fighter, all in one. The man was all muscle and looked in top shape. Wadding was wearing dark training pants, a grey sweater and white sneakers as if he had just come from the gym. If things got out of hand he could be a formidable opponent, Jo thought. Incongruous with his healthy appearance, the young bodyguard wore heavy-rimmed glasses, and Jo had an immediate feeling there was something peculiar about them, but he had no time to think about it.

"Please, come in and meet the other councilors," Jo said, pointing at the front door. One after another they walked into the living room and after Jo did the introductions, everyone sat down.

"I thought you might be thirsty after your trip, so I have arranged refreshments and a light lunch later on," Jo said, while Diana, Carol and Patricia began to busy themselves getting tea, fruit juices, and slices of blueberry cake.

"I must say, I am impressed with your hospitality and the ambience here. This doesn't look like any church I've ever seen."

Duval looked at the old bookcase filled with Philip Gallagan's books, still regularly dusted by the house staff, and the beautiful landscapes that graced the walls, painted by the computer tycoon's wife, Lillian, many years ago.

"You have preserved the Gallagan residence as some sort of museum?"

"No, only this room and the library," Jo replied. "This was the original living room, later used as an office. We had to make extensive renovations, but we were happy to make Excalibur our new home after our church was destroyed."

"Yes, that is what I wanted to talk about," Duval said, sipping from his glass of orange juice. "It was really a most horrific act of wanton destruction and, late as it may be, I want to offer my full condolences for the tragic loss of life it entailed. Now from what I have learned, one of you was actually a witness to this horror?"

"That was me," Daniel English said, nodding. "I barely made it out alive."

"Well, I would certainly like to talk to you, Councilor English," Duval said. "There are things that bother me about this whole dreadful business."

"There really isn't much to say, Congressman," Daniel said reluctantly. "I told the local police all I knew at the time. We are trying to forget the whole thing; it is still quite painful."

"Of course, I realize that. Nevertheless, if you could spare me a few minutes, I would be thankful. After all, it was you who pointed at a possible government connection."

"I shall help you as best as I can," Daniel said.

"Right, Councilor, cast your mind back to that fateful scene and try to remember. Did any of the men who destroyed your church wear uniforms? Army, Special Forces, Police, anything?"

56

"Not that I recognized," Daniel said, shaking his head. "I only saw green khaki shirts and pants; could be camouflage, I don't really know. It was dark, and I'm not familiar with uniforms in the first place. I've always been a clergyman, never a soldier. They did seem to be well organized, but I have no idea who or what they were. The only thing that pointed to the nearby army base was a small decal on one of those big earthmovers."

While Daniel and the congressman were conversing, Jo kept his eye on the bodyguard. There was something very odd about him, the way he followed the conversation by turning his head from speaker to speaker, almost as if . . . The truth hit Jo like a sledgehammer. The glasses the bodyguard was wearing weren't spectacles at all, they were video cameras. He was filming everything! Jo felt ripples of fear running along the hairs on his back. What was going on? Why record the meeting? Did Duval want to show it to his colleagues in the government later on? Or was it perhaps being broadcast live, so that others could see it? They would have to be very careful what they said.

"I feel a strong reservation, a hostile feeling almost, that I am stirring up these horrendous memories and wounds you must all still have," Duval said, helping himself to a piece of blueberry cake. "I can understand that. However, we must go over those facts again—painful as they are. I do not believe the conclusion the Beaching Commission reached is the correct one. Sergeant Matt Friesen was most likely not responsible for the attack on your church, or if he was, he was not acting on his own."

Jo studied Duval attentively, trying to understand where he was going. Like the other councilors, Jo himself had great misgivings about the official explanation of the massacre. It was too easy, too straightforward.

"What do you mean by that, Congressman?" he asked politely.

"I can't really go into detail here," Duval said evasively. "Friesen was a member of a White Arian Supremacist Movement; that has been established. However, he did not frequent their meetings. Most of the members had never heard of him. Secondly, the WASM as the name suggests, is firmly opposed to immigrants, homosexuals, Jews and certain other groups of our society, but they do not specifically oppose churches. In fact, some of them are fundamentally religious. I do not think it was the WASM that attacked your church, Councilor English."

"I know for sure that Friesen was the wrong guy," Jeremy Burlon said. "Angela Burlon was my sister, and she would never have gone for someone like him."

"Then who did it?" Daniel asked.

"That is what I wanted to find out," Duval replied. "I had hoped you would have information that was missed before. Had anything happened before the massacre? Did you perhaps have a warning the attack would take place? The reason I am asking this is that all the councilors were miraculously saved because they were not in the church at the time."

Jo felt bile coming up to his throat as his heart went in overdrive. The gloves were off! Duval suspected something. This was all going horribly wrong. He saw the others were in shock also.

"I resent that statement, Congressman," he said firmly. "The councilors were not in the church that horrid night because they had been staying in Excalibur for a few days. For some time our old church had been overcrowded and we were cleaning and planning the Excalibur site for future expansion. To suggest that we knew about the imminent attack and fled the scene, callously leaving almost five hundred of our people to be massacred is a very low blow and if that is what you believe, this meeting is over."

Jo could see he had hit home. Congressman Duval's face went scarlet and his lips formed a tight line of anger. He was obviously not used to being rebuked like that. With a sickening feeling in his stomach, Jo realized his outburst had been recorded through Clive Wadding's camera. There was no way back now; they had to recruit Duval and his guard. He glanced at Dale Pinehurst and nodded slightly, hoping that the other would get the message. *Go and prepare the recruitment room.*

Duval composed himself and when he spoke there was no anger or threat in his voice. "I am sorry, Councilor Rasnell. I do not want to lay any blame for this horrible incident on the church itself, of course not. I only wondered if you had perhaps an idea why it happened. What did you think when police cadet Watersma came to visit you, a few days before the massacre, inquiring about a female member of your church?"

"We have always worried about that," Jo said. "You see, Congressman, when people join our commune, their friends, relatives, or lovers may miss them and be upset or angry. As it may have been in the case of Angela Burlon. But every person is responsible for his or her own life and beliefs, and for Army Sergeant Matt Friesen to blame our church for losing his girlfriend is ridiculous. To take this anger and resentment out on the entire church proves that he was psychotic."

"If he did it at all," Daniel joined in. "Congressman, you yourself said that you didn't think it was Friesen. Whom do you suspect?"

"I'm afraid I can't tell you that, Councilor," Duval said. "You must understand my position."

"Well, perhaps we should leave this subject for now," Jo said. "We have an informative video we would like you to watch. You can see for yourself what the old church was like. Afterwards, we can show you our gardens and orchards, and you can talk to our people, if you like. Then we shall have some lunch."

"That sounds like a wonderful idea, Councilor Rasnell," Duval said, smiling. He seemed relieved the awkward moment had passed. "We shall be delighted."

"Splendid," Jo said. "If you'll follow me please."

◊ ◊ ◊

Dale Pinehurst had done a splendid job. Originally used for storage, the new recruitment room had been renovated and cleaned up. Racks that had held boxes with winemaking gear and bottles had been removed. The four walls were freshly painted a light pastel green. Recessed fluorescent lights and soft secondary lights had been installed along two walls. The air conditioning system had been altered to allow Oscar's Breath to be diffused. There were no windows and on one wall a large TV screen was mounted about four feet above ground level. The other walls showed photographs of the early days of the Church of Oscar, as well as the surrounding areas of Santa Barbara.

To accommodate Sunday visitors, the room held rows of wooden chairs, but for this special occasion Dale and Brian had removed them and brought four lounge chairs from the library. Standing in the doorway, Jo was about to usher his guests inside, when he took a deep breath and addressed Duval.

"When we show our visitors the history of our church we ask them, as a courtesy, to leave all photographic or electronic equipment outside," he said, as casually as he could, his heart pounding, in case he was wrong. "We have no objections about people learning the facts about our church for themselves, but we do not want to advertise things publicly, or watch it on tomorrows newscast. Would you please ask Mr. Wadding to remove his photographic recording device, Congressman?"

To his relief, Jo saw he had been correct. A surprised Clive Wadding glanced at his boss, and the Congressman nodded almost imperceptibly. Clive removed the glasses and handed them over to Jo, who put them on a side table in the hallway.

"Thank you. Please step inside and take a seat." Duval, Wadding, Daniel and Jo entered the room, and each took one of the four lounge chairs. When they were all comfortable, the lights dimmed and the TV screen came to life.

"Before the video, we have a few still photographs of the very early days on our church," Jo said, as the photograph of a young man appeared on the screen. It was taken in a state park along the coastline, with frothy waves and black rocks in the background. The young man was wearing diving gear, and was about to step into the ocean.

"That is Ted Taylor," Jo explained. "He was my best friend and together we started the Church of Oscar." The next photo showed old Bernard Tows' barn, after it was made into their first meeting place. A much younger Diana, Jo and Sylvia sat at the table with Bernard. The next slide showed the vegetable gardens and fruit trees in the garden. Jo was getting restless. *Come on Dale!*

It had been almost twenty years since Jo had breathed in Oscar's Breath, yet he could still remember what it felt like. A short stinging sensation, then the expanding consciousness. Bert Kwiss and the late Dr. Williams had added a special muscle relaxant to Oscar's Breath, and they also had brought down the stinging effect. But they had no idea how it would affect Duval, and more especially his bodyguard. If Wadding became violent it could be hard for them to stop him. Jo had therefore asked Dale to stand by with four security guards. There was also another unknown element: no one had ever been subjected to Oscar's Breath more than once. What would it do to Daniel and himself? All would be revealed in the next ten minutes.

The photos on the screen had stopped and the video began. The screen showed a fabulous view of the old church at sunset. They had chosen Jo's sister Sylvia for the narration. She had just the right type of voice: deep, melodious, hypnotic almost. One just couldn't help listening to her. Jo and Daniel had carefully selected the words and recorded it on a disk. It was played every Sunday during the recruiting service.

The first signs of the Breath were the same as one might have after a stiff drink. Jo began to feel relaxed, worry-free and a feeling of drowsiness began to envelop him. He looked around and noticed it was affecting Duval and Wadding as well. Their eyes glued to the television, they slouched in their chairs and relaxed. All of a sudden, Sylvia's voice filled the room.

"We are the Church of Oscar, a church unlike other churches this earth has seen. We do not prepare our members for imaginary bliss in the hereafter. Our aim is to save the world, by forcing mankind to step down from its self-created pedestal of superiority . . ."

Jo listened to his sister's voice as she narrated Oscar's Doctrine. Though Jo's muscles had relaxed, his thinking was not affected at all, nor did his consciousness expand the way it had done twenty years earlier. He still vividly remembered how scared he had been that time when Ted had given him the original cylinder with Oscar's Breath. Scared to become an addict again, scared to fry his brain once more. Yet the drug was not addictive at all. One exposure was all that was needed. He idly wondered how Yabul Kozak could have ever created it. It was truly one of the greatest miracles of all times.

" . . . we are all connected to all living creatures through a great Universal Consciousness, but our dependence on material things has broken this connection. Our minds must be cleansed and repaired . . ."

From the corner of his eye Jo looked at the others. Daniel lay back in his chair, asleep by the looks of it, and Jo himself felt a bit sleepy also. Duval and Wadding seemed to be in a deep trance, slouched back in their easy chairs. The video on the screen was showing scenes of the original church, and Jo took a deep breath. He had liked that church. It had been perfect. The perfect size, the perfect spot. He wondered who had really destroyed it. Did Duval know?

". . .we welcome you into our church, and may the Lord's blessing be upon you all."

Sylvia's voice faded and slowly the lights brightened in the room. This time Oscar's Breath had had no measurable effect on Jo, but he could see that Duval and his guard were confused. They sat up, staring at themselves, each other and the room around them. Then Duval spoke.

"You have drugged us," he said, sitting up straight and looking Jo in the eye. "I know I should take immediate action and hold you accountable for physical assault and bodily harm, yet I cannot. I have never felt so good in my life. Is this some strange, esoteric rite of passage to make us members of your church, Councilor Rasnell? I feel very strange indeed and I need to step outside to get some fresh air."

"Of course, by all means," Jo lead the two men to the back door and out into the gardens. Jo and Daniel stayed behind. Dale and two guards approached, but Jo waved them back.

In the garden, the two visitors strolled around like the best of friends, engaged in happy conversation. They stood and studied the multicolored flowerbeds and the productive vegetable patches. Next was the commune's livestock area with grazing sheep and cows. Crossing the small bridge across the pond, Duval pointed at fish and plants below, and both men laughed when they spotted two ducks chasing each other.

"What do you think, Daniel," Jo asked. "Has it worked?"

"It is too early to tell," Daniel replied, pensively. "This reminds me of my childhood in Nebraska. We had four horses and we always kept them inside in the harsh winters. It was quite a sight in the first weeks of spring, when we allowed them out again. They were just raring to go, chomping at the bits. I think Duval and Wadding have a similar urge to explore the exciting new world their freshly cleansed minds have suddenly opened up for them."

◊ ◊ ◊

It was a late lunch. Diana and Carol had laid out a good spread, sufficient, but not ostentatious. Trays of cold cuts: ham, sliced pork, a variety of cheeses, filleted trout, deviled eggs, several kinds of bread and two choices of soup. Jo prided himself that everything they ate was grown or bred in the commune, including the fish, caught in the lake behind Excalibur. The two visitors were enjoying the food, but none of the councilors seemed very hungry.

Jo listlessly stirred his potato-and-leek soup, thinking about what they had set into motion. After their tour of the garden, Duval had wanted to see the rest of the commune and it had been a well-spent afternoon. Jo had shown their new members the church itself, with Daniel's new pulpit and the small statue of Oscar high up in the nave. Then he had explained to Duval why the church worshipped a dolphin.

After that, they had visited the people's quarters, the workshops, the carpentry, and the newly-built community hall in the back of Excalibur. Duval had talked with some of the commune members and the time had just flown by. Yet important things had to be discussed still, and Duval and Wadding probably had a plane to catch. What would happen now, Jo wondered, while he spooned up some of his soup. Would the church still be around a week from now? Or would an army of investigators, police, FBI and goodness knew who else, swarm their commune? He wasn't afraid of another massacre, but exposure would be almost as bad. After desert was served, Jo decided it was time for some serious talk, and he turned towards the congressman.

"Congressman Duval," he began, "You are one of us now, and we, as members of the Church of Oscar, have no secrets from each other. Perhaps you can now tell us why you came to visit us?"

Richard Duval looked up and stared at Jo. For a moment he didn't speak. Most people couldn't meet Jo's penetrating stare for long, but Duval did. He continued to look at Jo as if they were engaged in some kind of mental tug of war to decide which one of them was in control. The other councilors shifted nervously in their seats, waiting. Finally, both men broke their mental deadlock and looked away. Then Duval spoke.

"I was curious to find out what really happened to your church," he said. "You must understand something, Councilor. May I call you Jo? The massacre of your people was one of the darkest pages in our history, right up there with Pearl Harbor and 9/11. The government desperately wants everyone to believe the Beaching report and forget the killings. The last thing our president needs is another investigation. However, like yourself, I do not believe that a love-torn sergeant was responsible for the massacre and I wanted to find out what really happened."

"There are many other people who do not believe the Beaching report," Jo said. "None of them have asked to visit us. Yet you did. Why? Was it perhaps to use us for your own political gain?"

"Yes," Duval admitted frankly. "I could smell a good story; something that would help me in my bid for the presidency three years from now. But then I got frustrated. Apart from the official explanation, I could not find a single solid lead, not even in the classified material. I was about to give up the whole idea, when I had a interesting conversation with General Petterson."

"Who is he?" Erwin asked.

"He was in charge of the army base where the heavy equipment for the massacre came from. Poor man, he took early retirement. It must have been awful for him, the massacre happening on his watch, so to speak. Anyway, at first, Petterson didn't want to talk about anything. Then, after a few drinks and some prodding, he finally told me that he thought Alex Ferndalo was somehow involved. Ferndalo was a member of GLATO, and —"

"GLATO? What's that?" Sylvia interrupted.

"It is the global anti-terrorist organization, part of the United Nations. Their headquarters are in Geneva, Switzerland. The United States joined in 2030, and Ferndalo was their North American representative in Washington. Anyway, Petterson said that Ferndalo believed the Church of Oscar was using some kind of secret initiation rite, involving drugs, to recruit its new members. He wouldn't say why he thought so. Nobody in the U.S. government knew anything about this, and the general himself didn't believe a word of it either. He thought Ferndalo had become paranoid and lost his mind. But Petterson was in a pickle about the massacre, since he had supplied the equipment that was used.

"Then Ferndalo killed himself and Petterson immediately washed his hands of the whole affair. He found a scapegoat by the name of Sergeant Matt Friesen and used him to get himself off the hook. Yet the conversation left me wondering. A church, using an inauguration ritual, like a secret society? It seemed an outrageous idea, and if true, it might create a scandal even bigger than the massacre itself.

"I saw an opportunity, but I couldn't tell anyone, not even the President, because then I would have no control over the story, and if I was wrong, I would lose all political credibility. So I decided to pay your church a private visit and find out for myself. It seems Ferndalo was right after all, wasn't he? You are using some kind of drug to recruit new members. I would never have dreamt that you would have the temerity to expose Clive and myself to it, even if it is the best thing that ever happened to us."

"So what our your plans now, Congressman?" Jo asked.

"Call me Richard, Jo. Well, it is very simple. We shall return to Washington and resign our positions. Then we shall make arrangements to move and join your commune as soon as possible. We shall be very happy here."

Jo firmly shook his head. "With all due respect, uh . . . Richard, that is not an option. You are too important a person, and if you resign just like that, questions will be asked, and they will certainly point to our church. We will be investigated and closed down. You must stay in Washington in your position as a member of Congress, and become our Ambassador."

"What? You can't be serious, Jo! You have no idea what it is like out there, on the Hill. Your life is not your own in politics. It took a Herculean effort to even keep this little visit a secret. From the moment I arrive at work, someone's near me, and hovers over me, and my whole day is laid out for me. My aides tell me who I have to kowtow to next. Working breakfasts, luncheons and dinners. Meetings with lobbyists, committees, business representatives. My life is measured in minutes, not days. Split decisions have to be made, and some of those decisions I may not always like making.

"The only way I have been able to do this for the last ten years, is because I believed in what I did. I seriously thought I was serving my country and the American people. Now your church has washed that feeling right out of my head and I am a new person. How can I possible continue as if nothing has happened?"

"You must," Father English said sternly. "There is no alternative. Your mind may have been cleansed, but you are still a rational person, in control of your actions and ideas. It may be difficult at first, but you will get used to it. You could casually steer conversations in the direction that would benefit our cause, or plant the seed of the Word of Oscar in some of your friends and acquaintances. Soon you will also be able to recruit other Ambassadors for us. Your position will be invaluable for our church, Congressman, especially if you were to become President."

Clive Wadding looked at his watch. "Sir, we must go."

Duval stood up. "Councilors, I do not know what to say. This is the most important day of my life. I am a re-born person, but I have no idea what tomorrow will bring. We shall go home and digest not only your wonderful food, but also what we have learned here today."

"Congressman Duval," Jo exclaimed. "We have laid our church bare for you, and I pray that the Lord will guide your decisions."

"Thank you, Jo," Duval said. His face was serious. "I shall consider my options. Thank you also for your splendid luncheon and your hospitality."

Jo led the way out into the hallway. When they walked past the recruiting room, he halted and picked up Wadding's photographic glasses from the side table. "Don't forget these," he said, handing them to Duval.

"Oh, we don't need those any more, Jo," Duval said, smiling, while he touched his head with his right hand. "I've got everything up here now; lots of room there all of a sudden. Keep them as a souvenir of our visit."

The councilors saw Duval and Wadding to their car. Then it was time for handshakes and goodbyes.

"We shall talk again, Councilors," Duval said. "No matter what happens." He stepped into the small car and Wadding got behind the wheel. Then they were off and the others stared after them as the car headed down the driveway.

"What have we done, Daniel?" Jo whispered, his hands trembling. "I am very scared."

"So should we all be," Carol said sternly. "One tiny slip up by the Congressman, one word said in anger, or taken out of context, and we shall all spend the rest of our lives behind bars."

"Perhaps not, Carol," Daniel English said softly. "We must have faith in Oscar's Breath. It has guided us all these years, and I am certain It will also guide Duval when he makes his decisions." No one said anything else while they watched the little car until it reached the end of the driveway and turned right on Gallagan Drive. Then it accelerated and was gone.

5

"I think it is a bad idea," Daniel English said sternly. "Taking Oscar's Breath out of the church in large amounts? Over my dead body. It is an open invitation for things to go wrong. It could be lost or stolen. A clever chemist could do an analysis and find out what it does. Then where would we be? No, I think the best way to recruit new members is the way it is done, under strict control, in the church."

"But we've already taken the Breath out," Carol objected. "Jo and Erwin carried it with them all the way to New York. There will always be some risk."

"Ah, yes, but that's different, Carol. A very small quantity, carried by church members, is acceptable. What Erwin is suggesting is something different altogether. The logistics would be impossible. Flooding entire compartments of a Bullet train with Oscar's Breath? Or airplanes in flight? Or using the climate control system in sealed offices? We might not even be able to produce that much. How can we possibly move such a large amount of the Breath without getting caught?"

"Can someone please explain to me what we are talking about?" Diana asked. "What exactly is Erwin's proposal?"

"I got the idea on my trip in the Bullet train to New York the other day," Erwin said. "For security reasons, as well as climate control, the windows in the compartments don't open. While I was sitting there, dozing, I suddenly felt cool air streaming in from a vent, as the air conditioner started working. Then I wondered if it would be possible to use that system to vent Oscar's Breath into the train. Exactly the same way as we do in our recruiting room, but on a much larger scale. Those trains are packed, and we would have a thousand or more new members in one go."

"And then what?" Sylvia asked, horrified. "You would have a train full of liberated, free thinking people like us, from all across the country, without any ties to the Church of Oscar. We would not know anything about them, what kind of people they were, or where they lived. Nothing. They would start their own little groups, and change the world their way. We would be worse off than before, because they might compete with us for new members. What's wrong with our present system? We advertise our church, and people come in to hear our sermons. If they like what they see and hear, they watch a video and we recruit them. If they don't, they go home again. We have complete control. Everything is working well, and I don't see a need to change anything."

"Sylvia is right," Jo said. "Erwin's idea for a large scale recruitment program is ingenious, maybe, but not logistically feasible."

"Even so, we can't keep Oscar's Breath locked up in Excalibur forever," Jeremy Burlon said. "How can Duval, Wadding, and Helin Sparling spread Oscar's Word if they can't recruit new church members?"

"A good point," Jo replied. "Somehow we'll have to supply them with the Breath."

"But how?" Sylvia queried.

"A courier," Carol suggested. "One of us could deliver a small amount of the Breath to our Ambassadors. Just a quick trip and back."

"I want to volunteer," Erwin said enthusiastically. "I rather like those trains."

Jo sat back, considering. "Operating like a drug cartel? Very dangerous. You know how paranoid our government is about drugs. They have spies and agents everywhere. It might work for a little while, but sooner or later someone would become suspicious. We have to be extremely careful. What do you think, Daniel?"

Daniel English sat quietly, deep in thought. He looked very tired, Jo thought. Finally the vicar nodded. "We need to support our Ambassadors, Jo. There is no question about it;

they cannot operate in a vacuum. One small cylinder and a box of masks should be plenty for a while. The risk would be minimal. We can start with Duval. Let Erwin do it."

"Just one more thing, please, Jo, before we close?" Brian held up his hand. "I want to say something about Erwin's proposal. With a few exceptions, we are giving people a choice to join our church, through advertising, the Internet and our Sunday sermons. In the long run that won't be satisfactory. We must make people *want* to come to us."

"And just how do you propose to do that, Brian?" Jo asked, intrigued, despite his reservations.

Brian shrugged. "I don't have all the answers. I think Erwin's suggestion could be a starting point to a new way of recruiting people and we shouldn't just discard it."

"Perhaps we don't need to spread Oscar's Breath itself," Bert Kwiss suggested. "We could use a drug with some kind of posthypnotic suggestion to lure people. Scopolamine would do it. Once they get to the church, we can recruit them the same way as before. I make a motion that we take a serious look at Erwin's idea some time in the future."

"Seconded!" Erwin shouted. "Take a vote, Jo."

Jo nodded. "All those in favor?" He looked around questioningly and, after some hesitation, eleven hands were raised. He raised his own hand to make it anonymous.

"Motion carried." Jo watched Erwin, as the latter sat there, elated, smiling to himself. That young man would go far in the church, Jo thought.

"All right," he said, "If there's nothing else, I'll call this—"

There was a sudden commotion in the hallway. Sounds of running, more footsteps further down the hall. Then a voice. "Stop! Or we'll shoot!" The door to the boardroom burst open and an agitated man ran in, wielding a gun around him for cover, the way a SWAT team member would enter a danger zone. He turned to the flabbergasted councilors, pointing his weapon to one councilor after the other. "Porter!" he yelled. "Which one of you clowns is Porter?"

Daniel English was the first to react. He jumped up so fast that his chair toppled onto the floor with a loud bang. "How dare you come into the house of our Lord, brandishing a deadly weapon!" he shouted. "There is nobody here by that name. Who are you?"

"It's all right, Daniel, I'll handle this," Jo said, putting a hand on the vicar's trembling shoulder. He turned to the intruder. "Now you, sir, before anyone gets hurt, lower that weapon, so we can deal with this in a civilized manner." At that moment, two red-faced security guards entered the room, their weapons drawn, but Jo held out his hand to stop them. Though outwardly Jo hoped he would radiate confidence, inside his heart was thumping as if he'd just ran a marathon.

"I used the name Porter," he said. "Some time ago, Erwin and I went to see Helin Sparling, a psychiatrist in New York City. I didn't want anyone else to know about it, so I used a false name. Who are you?"

"I am Claude Sparling, her husband. Helin is a changed person. What have you done to her?"

"*Done to her?* We haven't done anything! She gave us a consultation, wrote a prescription and we headed back home. What is this all about?"

Jo could see a moment of doubt and uncertainty in Claude Sparling's eyes. The man nervously touched his cheek with his free hand, and stared at Jo, then defiance crept up again.

"She's not the same person anymore," he snapped. "That day, when you visited her, she was supposed to come to the cottage right after work, but she didn't get there until much later that night. I was sick with worry. When I asked her what happened, she said she stopped on her way at a beach to watch the sunset. She wasn't even sorry for not letting me know."

Dale and Erwin had stood up and slowly joined Jo and Daniel standing in front of the table. To Jo, they seemed like characters in a stage play—a murder story. Only this was very much for real.

"I am sorry to hear about your marital problems," he said sharply. "What have they got to do with us? Why have you come here, scaring us all like that?"

"She mentioned your commune, that's why. And it's not just that one thing," Claude continued, still aiming his gun at Jo. "We haven't slept together since that night. She daydreams a lot, and she's no longer interested in anything I say, or do. I can't please her no matter how hard I try. She lives in another world. I know the signs. You're having an affair with her!"

"Don't be stupid!" Jo shouted. "Are you suggesting I seduced your wife? That she became romantically involved with me after a one-hour professional conversation more than two months ago? Everyone here can confirm that I haven't left our commune since then. That is the most ridiculous accusation I have ever heard. I suggest you head back to New York, or we will press charges." Jo gave a sign to the two security guards and they stepped towards Claude to apprehend him. In a flash the intruder backed off, aiming the gun at Jo's head.

"Come one step closer, and I'll blow his brains out!" he shouted at the guards. "I mean it." Uncertain of what to do, the guards halted.

"You won't get rid of me that easily, you know," Claude snarled. "I've checked out this place, and there's something very fishy going on here, people just deciding to drop everything and live in poverty. I won't let Helin have anything to do with you or your damned commune. If you ever come near her again, I'll kill you."

It was Dale Pinehurst who saved the situation. Gradually creeping closer to Claude, he suddenly leaped at him, grabbed the arm with the gun and pushed it up into the air. There was a terrific explosion and the smell of burning. Then Dale had the gun, and the two guards had Claude under control.

73

"Dale, man, thanks," Jo said. He brought the sleeve of his gown up to his head to wipe off the sweat. "That was a close one. *What the . . . Daniel?*" Father English had suddenly slid down on the floor and fell face-down on the carpet. Jo quickly turned him around and grabbed his wrist to find his pulse, while he shouted at the others. "Call Doctor Fleming, quickly."

"What happened?" Sylvia shouted. "A heart attack?"

"I don't know. I can't find a pulse."

The two security guards were taking Claude into custody and the council members all gathered around Father English. He lay absolutely still, eyes staring vacantly without blinking. Sylvia sat down next to him and hastily began to give mouth to mouth resuscitation, while the others stood by, helplessly. Then Jo bent down and looked closer at the side of Daniel's head.

"Oh, for the love of our Lord, no!" He pointed a shaking finger at the vicar's right ear. Just in front of it was a neat round bullet hole.

"It can't be!" Dale exclaimed. "The shot went straight up into the air."

Everyone except Sylvia looked up at the ceiling. It was made of square cork tiles, hung between plastic support rails. There should have been one tile with a hole in it, but there wasn't. A heavy-duty metal conduit pipe for an electric light connection ran along the ceiling and at one point the pipe had a dent in it. While the councilors stood there, gaping, they realized what had happened. The bullet from Claude's gun had ricocheted off the steel conduit and hit Daniel just above his right temple. Because the pipe had taken most of the impact, the bullet had only caused a small, bloodless wound. Jo took Sylvia's arm and gently pulled her away from Daniel's body. She stood up, shaking her head.

"I don't understand it," she said. "The Lord saved him once before when he was shot. Why didn't He deflect that bullet just a few inches more this time? It doesn't make sense." There were hasty footsteps in the hall and Doctor Mark Fleming rushed in. He was a energetic young man of

74

about thirty. He usually had a charming smile, but this time he looked serious. He looked at the small head wound and felt for Daniel's pulse again. Then he shook his head.

"He's dead, and even if he weren't, there is nothing I could have done without a fully equipped operating room. He would have died, no matter what. I'm sorry." Absolute silence followed the doctor's statement, as if it was the final confirmation that Daniel English, religious leader of the Church of Oscar was no more.

"So what will you do, Doctor?" Jo asked. "Before you joined this church, it was your duty to report a violent death like this to the authorities. In our commune you are no longer bound by that rule. I do not want a police investigation, so can you please write out a death certificate to the effect that Daniel died of natural causes?"

"Very well." Dr. Fleming nodded. "I shall make out the certificate for a pulmonary embolism."

"What about Claude Sparling?" Diana asked. "We can't let him go. We must bring him into the church."

"Of course," Jo said tiredly, "but I'm not in the right frame of mind for that at the moment. We shall deal with him later. Right now, we must mourn for our good friend and mentor Daniel. I shall lead a service to send his spirit on the way to the hereafter. In due time, Dr. Fleming will look after the cremation, so that Daniel's ashes will be the first to be stored in the new Vault of the Ancient."

◊ ◊ ◊

The restaurant didn't do its name honor. Erwin stared at the neon light that showed the diner's name: *The Happy Lunchbox*. The lights under the 'L' and the 'b' had burned out. *The Happy unch ox.* Somehow it seemed a bad omen. The building had obviously seen better times and it fitted well in a neighborhood effused with poverty and neglect. The paint on the siding and around the doorframe was chipped. A downspout on the side of the building hung loose. The

75

windows were covered in grime and dirt and looked as if they hadn't been cleaned in years.

It was two weeks after Daniel English's death. After a short period of mourning, the councilors had decided that life had to go on, despite the loss of their spiritual leader. Congressman Duval and his partner Clive Wadding in Washington needed the Breath, and Erwin was here to deliver it. He would meet Clive in the restaurant the next morning, but had decided to check the place out first.

The appearance of the restaurant was probably the reason Clive Wadding had chosen the place. Erwin could not enter Washington for two reasons. One was that Clive had made it very clear that he and Erwin could not be seen together anywhere in the City, as it had eyes and ears everywhere. Gossip was a commodity almost as essential as food and water in the nation's Capital. The second reason was the tight security.

For about six months now, a RFID implant program had been in operation. People could get an implant, allowing them free access into the city, just by running their arm in front of a scanner. The alternative was to line up and be searched at the security stations. Erwin would certainly never dream of having an implant, and he couldn't go through the tight security either, because they might find the flask of Oscar's Breath and the masks. So Clive had suggested they meet outside the city, in this rather sordid looking restaurant, away from prying eyes. The squalor of the restaurant wasn't the only thing that put a damper on Erwin's spirit. Although he had looked forward to his trip, things had not started off well.

Jo and he had left Excalibur at 6:00 a.m. They had driven to the Santa Barbara seafront, where a bus would take Erwin to Los Angeles. There were only six people on the bus, and it took its time, as if the driver was on a leisure trip. The Bullet station was not near the bus terminal, and when Erwin finally arrived in L.A., there were no taxis or buses. He had to walk, and the train would leave in an hour.

On arrival at the Bullet station, after a strenuous, forty-minute walk, he had to line up to go through security, and he feared he might miss the train. In his knapsack he carried his lunch and the flask with Oscar's Breath and the masks, hidden in a secret compartment. A busy security guard took a quick look at Erwin and his knapsack and waved him through. He had barely sat down when the train began to move.

Like the bus, it was slow going. On several places the Bullet went only about eighty miles per hour, due to constructions on the track. None of the passengers spoke to him, and Erwin soon dozed off. They were more than an hour late, and didn't arrive at Longport, the last stop before Washington-City, until four-thirty.

After Erwin exited the station and walked to the hotel that Jo had booked for him online, there was another problem. His booking didn't exist. Apparently there was a big conference in Washington and the hotel was fully booked. There were no budget rooms available. Though Erwin had some money with him, the price of the few rooms left was so exorbitant that he decided to look for another place, nearer to the restaurant where he would meet Clive.

Jo had given him directions to the Happy Lunchbox and it had taken Erwin thirty minutes to get there. It wasn't a pleasant neighborhood, and Erwin felt vulnerable and insecure. Perhaps he had been a little too eager to volunteer for the courier job. He was on his own and a long way away from home. Feeling a sudden pang of hunger, he decided he needed food and company and entered the restaurant.

It was bigger inside than he expected. There were about twenty comfortable looking booths, ten on either side of the large room. He slid in one halfway down the middle and put his backpack next to him and waited. It wasn't very busy.

A waitress approached him. She was about his age, slim and tall, dressed in a white blouse and dark skirt. A nametag on her blouse read *Tammy*. The skirt was short, the top button of her blouse undone. Her chestnut hair was tousled, as if she been walking in the wind. She had sparkling, blue-grey eyes, a great smile, a rather large mouth and scores of tiny freckles, as if someone had thrown the contents of a peppershaker in her face.

"Here you are, hon," she said, in a lovely sing-song voice, handing him a menu. "Special today is baked seafood lasagna. Divine. Anything to drink?"

"Just water," he said, giving her back the menu. "I'll have the special, please."

"Good choice." She lingered for a few more seconds, bending down a bit, so that he could see her cleavage. "Where are you from? I can tell you're not from this part of town."

"A place near Santa Barbara," he said awkwardly, and her face lit up.

"Oh, California! What I wouldn't give to be there right now and lie in the sun on those lovely beaches." She gave him a great smile and sauntered off to put his order in. There were only six other customers, four middle-aged men and two old ladies. Most of them had already been served and the aroma of the lasagna floated his way, making him even hungrier. While he was waiting, he wondered where he was going to sleep that night. He hadn't seen any hotels or inns on his walk to the restaurant. The waitress seemed quite pleasant, perhaps she would know a place.

He thought about the next day. He wouldn't see anything of the city and he didn't care. Up early to meet Clive, hand over the Breath and the masks, and then catch the 12:30 Bullet back home. All of a sudden he felt homesick for the quiet security of the church. He knew this was only the first of many courier jobs to deliver Oscar's Breath. Well, he wasn't going to volunteer anymore; someone else could do it. Jeremy perhaps. He could suddenly smell garlic.

"There you are, love." Tammy placed a huge plate of lasagna in front of him, with two pieces of garlic toast on the side. "You looked hungry, so I asked cook to give you a bit extra." She gave him a wink and a smile and was off again. He immediately dug in and after two forks full, he agreed with

78

the waitress. The lasagna was the best he'd ever tasted. There were fresh shrimps, and bits of whitefish, or crab. When he took a bite of the garlic bread, the smell assailed his nostrils, and for some peculiar reason he thought of Oscar's Breath. He ate slowly to enjoy every bite of his meal, and when he finally pushed his empty plate back he felt happily satiated, his gloom gone. As if on cue, Tammy was back to take his plate.

"Well, didn't I tell you? Wasn't that the best lasagna you've ever eaten?"

"Absolutely." He smiled back at her. "Wonderful. Thanks very much."

She hovered for a moment. "So what brings a nice-looking young man like you to a ghastly place like this?"

"I'm supposed to meet someone here tomorrow," he said. "I'm surprised this place is so quiet, with good food like this."

"Oh, it won't be quiet for very long," she said. "You picked the right time. Another hour or so and it will be packed. We're basically a commuter's place here, for people working in the city. Would you like some dessert? We've got great cheesecake. Coffee?"

"No thanks, just the bill, please." She smiled again and walked away.

The door opened and a party of four walked in, two men and two woman, dressed in casual working clothes. Perhaps the beginning of the rush. He watched as Tammy led the new group to a booth in the end of the restaurant. Then she disappeared behind a curtain, probably to ring up his bill on the computer. After a few minutes she was back and placed a tray with the bill on his table.

"Thank you very much. Will we see you for breakfast tomorrow?"

"I don't know. Do you know a decent hotel around here? Not too expensive?"

She frowned. "No, nothing in this area. Closest place is the German Guesthaus, but they'll probably be full with that neurologists conference in the city." She looked up as six more people entered the restaurant. "Tell you what, love. I finish work in half an hour, so why don't you meet me then, and I'll see what I can do. If you can wait that long."

"Oh, sure, thanks very much," he said. The bill was for $14.50. He gave her a twenty dollar bill, and told her to keep the change. She gratefully accepted and winked at him. "See you in a while. Come to the back, there's a lane on the side."

Just as Erwin walked out, two more people walked in. The rush was definitely on. As he'd been sitting most of the day, he decided to go for a short walk to stretch his legs. It was almost dark, and with every step he took, he felt his backpack with the flask with Oscar's Breath hitting him on the shoulder. He wondered if he'd done the right thing. He didn't know Tammy at all. Could he trust her? He suddenly smelled smoke.

Loud voices filled the air. An old two-storey house was dark and boarded up. In the front garden, overgrown with weeds, a makeshift barbeque of half a metal drum was set up. What seemed like a small pig was being turned over the flames. About ten hippies were sitting around, drinking beer, laughing, kissing. The smoke filled the entire street. One of the men noticed Erwin, and called out to him. "Hey, bud! Want some fun? Fuck one of our girls, and if you survive, you can eat for free!"

Loud laughter followed Erwin, while he hurried along, fearing for his safety. Most of the houses he passed were derelict, or partially demolished. Some were occupied, and behind blinds he saw the flicker of television screens. There was hardly any traffic and it was getting darker by the minute. An old man, taking his dog for a walk, hurried past silently, his head down. This was definitely not a place for a friendly chat. After fifteen minutes Erwin turned around. He had seen a few side streets, but he didn't dare leave the main road, in case there was no connection back. He crossed the road and walked back on the other side, to be at least further from the squatters and their stinking barbeque. He was getting quite worried about where he would sleep.

When he reached the restaurant, he glanced through the window and noticed hardly any empty seats. There was no sign of Tammy. Two other waitresses were running about, keeping everyone happy. He quickly turned the corner into the lane and found the back entrance to the restaurant. There was a big dumpster, full of empty boxes and garbage. The door was still closed and he hid in the shade of the dumpster and waited, cursing the hotel that had lost his reservation. He wished he was three thousand miles away, in his cozy room in the church.

About ten minutes later, there was a sharp click and the door opened. Tammy appeared, pushing a small electric scooter ahead of her. She waved at him, and Erwin rushed over.

"Bad new, I'm afraid," she said. "Just as I thought. The German Guesthaus is packed, not even a closet left. I phoned." There was a small light bulb above the door, and in the yellow light Tammy had a ghostlike appearance. To Erwin it all seemed like a bad dream. No place to stay . . .

"Thanks for your help," he said meekly.

"Don't give up yet," she said. "There may be room in one of the bigger hotels in town. I'll give you a ride."

"No, thanks. I can't go there."

She eyed him sharply. "Why not? Are you in some kind of trouble?"

"I am sorry, I can't tell you."

He could see she hesitated, deciding what to do. Finally, she shook her head. "I hate to leave you here. This is a bad neighborhood. Oh, what the hell. Hop on, you can sleep on my couch."

Erwin carefully swung his leg across the back of the scooter. He sat up awkwardly, trying to hold onto the baggage holder behind him.

"No, no, you'll fall off," Tammy said. "Put your arms around me."

He pushed himself forward and pulled his arms around her, holding her tight. In his entire life he'd never held a woman like that. It felt strangely comforting, yet also scary.

◊ ◊ ◊

Hands in the pockets of his tracksuit, Philip Kozak ambled down the beach. In the distance he saw the Santa Barbara Pier, and to his left the Pacific Ocean came crashing down in decent size waves. In reality, he was in the VR room behind his office in Chicago. He'd chosen this particular virtscape because the West Coast had been his home turf for sixteen years. Philip had been glad he'd finally seen his mother again. In his mind's eye he could still see that fanatic glare in her eyes that had chilled him at the time. Was there really something going on in that church, as he has suspected long ago? Were the church members truly brainwashed? Or was it all a product of his vivid imagination? The main thing was that his mother was safe and happy in that church. A burden was lifted off his shoulders.

Some people, intrigued by a story, could never let it go, like a ferret chasing a rabbit, not to be satisfied until it had made the kill. Not so Philip. He considered himself a pragmatist, and he was not about to spend his precious time trying to understand why a group of people lived the way they did. He had other things to do in his life. Yet there was one aspect of the Church of Oscar that did concern him. There was every reason to believe that commune would continue to grow. People wanted the security of a group, just like his mother had done. Others wanted to go back to Nature, eat good food, and live a healthy life. Whatever the reason people joined, it was a good bet that followers of the Church of Oscar would not be spending time online with Secret Springs. Membership was already dropping, and Philip feared for the company's future.

There was another thing that had greatly affected Philip during the visit to his old home. It had opened his eyes to the world outside Secret Springs. Not everyone was addicted to mind candy. A lot of people were fighting for their lives with real guns, without avatars and safeguards. And their number was growing steadily.

Secret Springs was caught between two opposing forces that were shaping society, and in his heart Phil knew that the company had already reached it zenith. From now on, its support base would begin to decline. The warning signs were there. Four weeks ago he'd been promoted to CEO, and he felt personally responsible for the company.

His avatar was purple-flagged, the maximum level of privacy. He wanted to think, and the last thing he wanted was someone else popping up next to him, looking for conversation or sex. Besides the problems that faced Secret Springs, he also had his own dilemma of finding a new challenge in life. Being a CEO wasn't enough; he had to do more. But what?

He suddenly decided he'd walked enough and punched a button on his left glove. A menu screen appeared in the sky. It had hundreds of little icons, and after some consideration he pointed his right index finger at one of them. A sub menu appeared with questions regarding time of day, weather conditions, position. When he had entered the necessary information, he pointed at a key in the right hand corner. Instantly the beach at Santa Barbara vanished, and he hung precariously from a cliff on Mount Everest.

The program had placed him about fifty feet below the top, and he suddenly had cleats on his shoes and a pickaxe in his hand, while he began the climb that no sane climber would ever attempt in real life. Below him there was nothing but empty space and sharp protruding rocks, crevasses and lots of snow. Had it been for real, it would have been suicidal, but even if his hands or feet missed, he'd only lose his balance and fall down onto the floor in the VR room. Still, his eyes and heart were telling him there was danger.

When he finally reached a little plateau at the very top, he sat down and looked around. Here he was on top of the world. There was nowhere further to go; it was the end of the line, just like his job at Secret Springs. He felt a little melancholic when he realized how symbolic it was. He looked up. It was a sunny day, with a few clouds high above them. He idly wondered what it would be like to fly, not just in a virtual world, but in real life. Like an eagle, or a seagull. He began to feel very strange indeed, as if the rarefied air was real and affecting him. What was he going to do with the rest of his life?

He thought about his father and felt a blockage in his throat. Why had he never met him? Why did Yabul have to die before Philip was born? Why could no one tell him anything about him? His dad hadn't lived in a vacuum; they had no right to keep what he had done secret. If only he could meet him, somehow. The beauty of the scenery, the vast expanse of peaks and the white blankets of virgin snow, finally released his pent-up emotions, and he cried.

He noticed he began to rise up in the air, very slowly. When he looked down at his feet, they were still firmly planted in the snow. Yet he was moving up towards the clouds. In another place and time it would have been frightening and he would have struggled. Thoughts of ancient Hindi levitations ran through his mind. But this was no levitation; his avatar was staying behind. Some part of his mind told him he was having an out-of-body experience and he should not worry. He was steadily rising towards the clouds, enthralled and overwhelmed by the experience. It was strange to be floating in the air without any substance, yet feel his entire body, arms, fingers and toes. The avatar below was just a black spot on the white cushion of snow. Higher and higher he rose.

There were scores of small, individual clouds. One near to him looked like a fluffy ball of cotton, and Philip's mind could see right inside. Alyn, the caretaker stood there, just like he had been on the farm, dressed in his denim work clothes, his dark face partially hidden under a sun hat. Alyn smiled at him, and Philip realized the caretaker had probably died in a fight with the marauders who had taken Stowaway. Then Alyn was gone, and Philip's mind moved on to the next cloud. When he looked inside, he saw his stepfather. Patrick just nodded his head in recognition. He didn't speak, or smile. Philip felt sorry for him. Why had he never loved him? Patrick had treated him like his own son, yet to Philip there had never been a spark, or a feeling of intimacy. Patrick's cloud began to fade away, and Philip approached another, bigger cloud. Even before he entered, a voice greeted him inside his head.

"Hello, Philip. Finally we get to meet each other. It is good to see you."

His real father was standing there, looking just like the few pictures Philip had seen in his youth. The dark-blond hair framing a youngish face, with blue-grey eyes that sparkled, and a smile that touched Philip in the pit of his stomach. He tried to speak but couldn't.

"I know, son," Yabul's voice sounded in Philip's head. "I love you also. No need for words here. We're all part of the same consciousness here. Don't fight it, just open your mind and the thoughts will flow."

"Am I dead?" Philip asked.

"No, your time has not yet come," Yabul replied. "There is something you must do first."

Philip was filled was such ecstasy and bliss that it seemed as if the cloud was his entire universe. He wanted to stay there forever, with his father. Nothing else mattered. His consciousness mixed freely with Yabul's, and there were no longer any secrets, as Philip understood what his father had gone through in his life. For the longest time they were quiet in their joint universe. Then, like weeds marring a perfect lawn, thoughts about the real word appeared in Philip's happy mind.

"I need your help, Dad," he said. "Why can't I be happy in my job? Why do I always want to be better than I am?"

"You are trying too hard, son. Worry and fear are your biggest enemies. Do not despair; everything will fall into place when the conditions are right. You are meant for bigger things, and they will happen, but now it is time to face the world again, Philip."

"No, please, I want to stay with you!" Philip cried, but a sudden thought shot through his mind, like a pin, bursting his balloon. *This isn't real, it's all a trick of your imagination!* In a flash he was back in his avatar again, the clouds just ordinary puffs of white above him. He feverishly punched the exit button on his glove and stood back in the VR room behind his office. Quickly he stripped off his suit, then without bothering to put his clothes on, he sat down on a bench and cupped his head in his hands. He was sweating, as if he'd climbed the entire mountain. What had happened there?

He shivered in the cold air, and after a few minutes he stood up and dressed, still in a state of shock. While he hung his VR suit in the cupboard, he suddenly thought of something. His left glove contained a chronometer. Every time he entered a new virtscape he reset it to zero, so he knew how long a particular trip had lasted. When he looked at the time record of his latest trip, he was astonished. He was sure he'd talked to his father for hours, yet the chronometer registered only three minutes for the entire trip.

◊ ◊ ◊

Tammy had said she lived about fifteen minutes from the restaurant. Holding on for dear life, Erwin had absolutely no idea where he was being taken. They were cruising at a fair speed, and when Tammy finally slowed down and drove into a small alley, Erwin took a deep breath, thanking his lucky stars he'd made it. He got off and stretched his legs. Tammy used a key to open a small garage. Then she pushed the scooter inside and closed the garage door.

"That's handy transportation," Erwin said.

"I don't like it. It's a dinosaur. OK on good days, but miserable in the winter. Half the time it won't go in the cold. I want a car. If I ever get my hands on seventy thousand dollars, I'll buy one of those new peppy Tatshu cars. They are lovely. Have you seen them?"

"No, I don't know much about cars," Erwin replied.

"They're made in China, and they do everything. They drive and park themselves." Tammy opened the door to her apartment and stepped inside. "Come on in."

Erwin had never been in a young woman's home and he had no idea what to expect. It was quite spacious, the entire basement floor of an older house. Through a short hallway, into a fair-sized living room with an easy chair, a small side table, and a large couch—most likely his bed for the night. Two matching standing lamps, an old fashioned TV, and three house plants. On the wall, shelves with little knickknacks, small furry creatures, little dolls and rows of books. A kitchen nook with a table and three chairs. Two more doors off the hallway, presumably leading to Tammy's bedroom and a bathroom. Three small carpeted steps leading towards the front door. The furniture was cheap, probably second-hand.

"Well, sit down," Tammy gestured. "I think I'll have a beer. Would you like one?"

"No thanks, I don't drink."

"Coffee or tea? I got some nice peppermint tea."

"OK, that's great, thank you."

He lowered himself into the comfortable couch, while Tammy busied herself with the teapot and a kettle. After a few minutes, she sat down in the easy armchair opposite him.

"So, are you going to answer my question now?"

"What question was that?"

"What's a good-looking young guy like yourself doing in this crappy neighborhood? You seemed lost and needed help. This is not a place to be out alone at night."

"You are very trusting," Erwin said.

"Oh, I don't know. First things first. You know my name, but I don't know yours."

"It's Erwin."

"Well, Erwin, it's like this. Working in the restaurant gives you a good chance to meet people and find out what they're like. I know most of our regulars, and I tell you there are quite a few I would not bring within ten miles of my place.

You get a pretty good idea in judging people, whether they're phony, dangerous or even psychopaths. Believe me, I've seen all kinds. But I've never seen anyone like you."

"How so?"

"Well, there's something unusual about you. First, I pegged you as some kind of salesman. But you weren't really dressed like one, and no salesman would ever ask me if I knew a hotel around here. This is your bottom-of-the line, grade ten neighborhood, with drug addicts, sexual perverts, and other bottom feeders of our society. Of course, there are a few good people here also, who can't afford to live anywhere else."

"Like yourself."

"Well, thanks. I need a place close to the restaurant, don't I? Anyway, if not a salesman, what were you? This place isn't featured in any tourist brochures, you can bet on it. We get lots of drug dealers, but you didn't seem the type. I just couldn't understand why someone nice like you would come to this dump."

Erwin felt hot and apprehensive. He didn't like where the conversation was going. Did Tammy suspect something? He crossed his legs, then uncrossed them again. "I told you, I'm supposed to meet someone here tomorrow. That's all. After that I'm heading right back. Why do you want to know all these things about me? I can't say any more."

At that moment there was a loud whistling noise from the kitchen. Without a word Tammy got up to make the tea. Nervously, Erwin sat back in the couch, feeling bad about what he'd said.

"I am sorry, Tammy, that was rude of me," he apologized, when she returned. "You've gone out of your way to help me, and I am very grateful. The hotel I booked lost my reservation, and I should have looked for somewhere else instead of coming to the restaurant and bother you. I'm not used to this kind of thing. We live in a commune and don't travel much."

"Hey, no bother at all," she said. "Your tea will be ready in a minute, and I'm just going to change. Make yourself at home." She went into the bedroom.

Erwin looked at his watch. 8:30. What was he going to do for the rest of the evening? Watch TV? Sit and talk? About what? He took a magazine from a wooden stand to the side of the couch. It was an old copy of *Nature.* He flipped the pages, then put it back, when Tammy came out of the bedroom, wearing dark pants and a mauve, low-cut sweater. She went into the kitchen area, and he could hear her pour the tea. Then she came back, carrying a tray with a glass of beer, a cup of tea, and a plate with biscuits.

In the light of one of the standing lamps he noticed she had done something to her face. The freckles didn't quite stand out so much, and her chestnut hair was neatly combed. She put the tray down on a side table, sat down in a chair next to the couch, and reached for her beer.

"Help yourself," she said, pointing to the plate of biscuits. "Do you want to watch TV?"

"Not for me, but you go ahead, it is your house."

"All I watch is a good movie sometimes," she said, taking a swig of her beer. "It's all garbage what they show you on TV, anyway. Why should I watch the news about people getting killed all over the world? That's all you see, murder and mayhem, economic depression and ads for new cars and other expensive things. Really, who can afford a new car? Or a boat? Makes you sick."

"That's why we don't watch TV either. We're down to basics. Good food, grown on our own farm, great company, and healthy minds."

"Really? What kind of commune . . . Wait a minute! Santa Barbara, you said. Not that big commune there, the Church of Oscar? I've heard about that. Are you a member of that church?"

He nodded, furious his cover was broken.

"Well, would you believe that! I would never have guessed. You know, I almost joined a commune myself, when

89

my boyfriend Ronny and I split up. We just couldn't talk about anything. We'd start off on a topic and always ended up having a screaming argument. What made you join?"

He shrugged and drank some of his tea. "My parents owned a farm and everything was going wrong in the end; we got bad neighbors, and they lost most of their money, so one day they'd had enough and decided on a communal life. I went with them. Our church is growing real fast these days, you know. There are a lot of people out there who can't hack life anymore. I mean, it's all wrong, isn't it? Nice people like yourself having a hard time making ends meet, and up the road, in the city, the rich don't know what to do with their money."

She smiled at him. "Dead on! At this point Ronny and I would have our first argument. He thought everything evolved naturally and that was it. It you became rich, you'd worked hard for it, and it was your right to be rich. To hell with everyone else. Oh, the fights we had."

"That's the problem with the world, Tammy. People make the wrong decisions, because they don't think right."

She sat back and took a large swig of her beer. "You know, I can't get over this. I am sitting here, in my living room, with someone I hardly know, having an intelligent conversation. Tell me, Erwin, why do you think everything is in such a terrible mess? People blame it on greed, the job market, anger, envy, or other reasons, but what do you think is the real cause?"

Erwin looked at Tammy, as she sat there, looking at him, almost in adulation. What did she want? He felt very uncomfortable.

"It started in the past, I think," he answered after a few seconds. "Someone long ago, made the decision that people were the most important life form in the universe, and everything else came second. It's part of Christianity and other religions. That kind of thinking seems to be the root of all our problems. People only think about themselves."

Tammy drank some more of her beer, and without asking if he minded, she sat down on the couch next to him.

"You know, I've thought about this for a long time, and you don't know how good it feels to hear someone say this," she said in an emotional voice, as if she was on the verge of crying. She lay a hand on his arm, and he could feel the moist heat through his shirt. "You can't talk about this with other people. They think you're crazy. Everyone always blames others: the government, or big corporations. Nobody has the guts to blame people. If that is what that your church preaches, I want to hear more." She suddenly brought her head forward to his and kissed him full on the lips.

Erwin knew things had totally gone out of control and quick action was necessary. In a flash, the solution was there, like a supernova in a pitch black universe. He gently pushed Tammy away and reached for his backpack that lay against the side of the couch.

"I've got to go to the bathroom," he said, and rushed into the room next to Tammy's bedroom. He stood in front of the sink, taking deep breaths, trying to stop his panic. When he finally had calmed down a bit, he opened the zipper of his backpack and removed his lunchbox. He looked around for something thin and sharp, and noticed a nail file on the side of the sink. With shaky hands he pressed the point of the file into two small holes in the bottom of the lunchbox, and lifted the top of a hidden compartment. It contained twelve masks. He quickly took one out and closed the false bottom again. He took a few more deep breaths, thinking about what he was about to do. It was the only way. Keeping the hand with the mask behind him, he returned to the couch, where Tammy looked at him with inquiring eyes.

"What's wrong? Are you ill? I'm sorry if I scared you. I just . . ."

"I'm fine," he said, sitting down next to her. Before she had a chance to speak again, he suddenly turned towards her, and put an arm around her, as if he was going to kiss her. He felt her go limp in his arms. Then he brought his hand from behind his back and pressed the mask on her face, making sure it covered her mouth and nose.

It took her half a second to realize what was happening, and he used it to press her tight against the couch. She began to struggle, and made gagging noises, trying to scream. She tried to hit him with her long arms, but he was stronger and held both her wrists together. She couldn't move.

"I am sorry, Tammy," he said softly, "You leave me no choice. Don't fight it. You'll be fine. Just relax."

At last she couldn't hold her breath any longer, and he saw her take gulps of Oscar's Breath. After that it was easier. Tammy ceased to fight, and he relaxed his grip a bit. She was breathing slowly and steadily. Her eyes, wide with fright just minutes ago, slowly returned to normal and searched for his. He held her for a little while longer, while he recanted the welcome message for new recruits.

"Welcome to your new life, Tammy," he said solemnly. "You have been chosen to become a member of the Church of Oscar, with all its privileges and rewards, but also its duties. You will be fully instructed when we welcome you into our commune."

He cautiously let go of her, ready to restrain her, if necessary. She sat up, stretched her legs, and wriggled her shoulders a bit. Then she stared at him.

"I am very tired," she said. "What was that stuff you gave me, Erwin? I have a right to know."

"Later, later," Erwin hushed her up. "Don't worry about it now. You are fine. Get some sleep. I'll explain everything tomorrow."

She suddenly lost her balance and held on to him, her head against his chest. "So you're a drug runner after all," she said. "I bet I'll have a hangover like never before." Then she closed her eyes.

Erwin was quite pleased that everything had gone so well. He's saved himself from a precarious situation and recruited a new member for the church. On top of that, he'd saved a considerable sum of money by not having to pay for a hotel. He watched as Tammy peacefully slept against his chest. It was best if she could come with him tomorrow. Otherwise the church would have to arrange for her transportation. Maybe Clive could help.

After a few minutes, he carefully picked Tammy up and carried her into the bedroom. She wasn't heavy. With one hand he pulled the cover off her bed and stared at a red teddy bear lying on her cushion. Smiling, he lowered Tammy into the bed and covered her, putting the bear next to her.

He walked into the bathroom, removed his toothbrush from his backpack, brushed his teeth and washed his face. He quickly relieved himself, took his backpack and walked back to the couch. He removed the cushions and lay down, covering himself with the blanket Tammy had supplied. He almost dozed off, then thought of something. He sat up and reached for his backpack, hid it under his pillow and lay back again. It was a bit uncomfortable, but he was too tired to worry about it. Within minutes he was sound asleep.

6

"Oh, don't stop! Philip, oh, God, keep going, come on!" Like two randy teenagers, Philip and Jennifer were having it off in her bed. When it was finally over, she rolled on her side, and stared at him. "Jeepers, Phil, that was fantastic! And you were so gentle this time. Twice in a row, and in the middle of the day? What brought that on? Did you feel guilty for neglecting me, or something?"

"No, I just feel great. I wanted to talk to you about something that happened to me this morning, but I got sidetracked." He gave her a sly smile.

"I'd say you did. I'm not complaining, mind. You can talk to me after I have a shower." Jennifer jumped out of bed and ran to the en suite bathroom. Philip lay back, totally spent, wondering why his experience on the mountain had caused such a sexual arousal in him. Was it because he had finally met his father? Had some old blocked emotion finally been released, just as Dr. Kilzinger had said it would be? Or was it just the relief that he had found a new direction in his life? Whatever the reason, he felt like a new person. Once more he ran that morning's events through his mind, the experience of his consciousness just floating out there, the talk with his Dad, and then the full realization of what had really happened.

It was Sunday, and they would have plenty of time to discuss it. He was at Jennifer's place. Philip had a penthouse in Secret Springs, Jennifer just a small apartment. They'd been talking about moving in together, but so far it hadn't happened. Philip especially, needed his privacy now and then. Jennifer returned into the bedroom, wearing blue jeans and a white top. "Have your shower, and I'll make us something to eat," she said, winking at him. "You must be hungry after spending all that energy."

When Philip walked into the kitchen after his shower, lunch was ready. Jennifer had laid out a meal of ham, cheese, and salmon, with bread, cucumber slices, and radishes on the side. On the counter top stood two cups of steaming coffee. Before he sat down, he walked over and kissed her. "Thank you for this."

They ate in silence for a while, then she said: "So what did you want to talk about?"

"I had a very exciting experience this morning," he said, buttering a slice of bread. "A very vivid OBE."

"An out-of-body experience? Really? Wow, I've never had one. What was it like?"

He told her how he had met his father, high above Mount Everest.

"Was he like the pictures your saw of him?" she asked.

"Yes, but even without them I would have recognized him. My consciousness knew it was him, even before my eyes saw him. I can't describe it any better. It was just the most wonderful experience of my entire life, and it showed me the path I have to follow. I thought about it all morning, and I also realized something else that made it even more astounding. It wasn't an ordinary OBE."

"Is there such a thing as an ordinary OBE?" Jennifer asked, sipping her coffee. "I thought it would always be a most extraordinary event."

"Oh, it was. What I meant was that it was different from any other OBEs I've read about. During surgery, a person may feel his consciousness float out of his body, and when he looks down he sees himself on the table while the surgeons are operating on him. My experience was different, but at first I didn't realize it."

"How so?"

He licked his lips. "Oh, Jennifer, this is so weird. I don't know if I can even explain it. While my spirit was rising towards the clouds I could still feel my body, my arms, my toes, everything. Then when I looked down, I saw my avatar standing there on top of the mountain, getting smaller and smaller. I didn't think anything of it at the time, but later on I realized that it was all wrong."

"What do you mean?"

"I shouldn't have seen the avatar. I should have seen my own body in my VR room."

"Now you have lost me completely."

"Think about it. In an OBE, a person's consciousness leaves his body and returns to it afterwards, right?"

"Not always. Sometimes it doesn't, and the patient dies on the operating table. Anyway, yes, that part I understand."

"Well, my consciousness didn't float back into my body, it went into my avatar. I had a virtual OBE."

"That's impossible, Philip! An avatar is just a piece of 3D software. It is not alive."

"Exactly. There's only one possible explanation. After I talked to me father, I somehow transferred my consciousness into my avatar."

"Oh, Philip, this is getting too spooky for me. Are you telling me you were actually inside Secret Springs, the real you, as part of a virtscape?"

"That's right," Phil said, finishing the last of his breakfast. "I didn't return to my body until I exited the program."

"That's the weirdest thing I've ever heard. If the essential *you* was in that avatar, how could your body still function? Your heart, or your lungs? It doesn't make sense, Phil. Some part of you must have stayed in your body, otherwise you would have been dead, like that patient on the operating table."

"Oh, I know, Jen. I'm only just beginning to scratch the surface of this. I think we may have it all wrong. We assume that a virtscape is something outside of us, like an old 3D movie that you can objectively watch and enjoy. I don't think that's true. I think that every time you enter a virtscape you're having some kind of an OBE, and you become part of the virtscape. Your consciousness, or at least a major part of it, leaves your body temporarily and moves into your avatar, only you don't realize it. I want to pursue this further, Jen, and

I have an idea that I want to present to the next board meeting."

"I wish you wouldn't, Phil. We're dealing with something totally unknown here. It could be very dangerous."

"That's exactly what I want to do. Face the unknown. That is my new challenge in life."

◊ ◊ ◊

Wide awake Tammy Tilburn lay in bed, staring at the ceiling. Sleep was out of the question. Without a doubt, this had been the craziest day in her entire life. And it had all started when that guy had walked into the Happy Lunchbox. Right away, she had noticed there was something odd about him. In her twenty-two years, Tammy had learned how to judge people's character. She knew she wasn't particularly beautiful—those damned freckles, for a start. She could also use some more curves here and there, for sure. But she still had lots to offer, and she'd met plenty of men who showed admiration, attraction, desire or even lust for her. Of course there were also the gays, but she could spot them a mile away, and she had no problems with them at all. Some of her friends were gay.

But this guy had been different. She didn't get any readings from him at all. He looked fine from the outside, but his body language was missing. He'd been sitting in that booth like a mannequin—a human shell without any substance. When he'd asked her for a place to stay she had seen a possibility. He was so harmless; a case for easy picking. She had planned to get him drunk, give him a good fuck, and then let him sleep it off, while she searched his backpack and wallet. It had misfired when all he wanted was tea. Tea, for Christ's sake! And then that esoteric, highbrow conversation.

Tammy agreed that the world was in a mess, and it was getting worse every day. She knew some people were trying to fix things, but it was all talk. The world was the way it was, and it would probably stay that way. Then, when she took the initiative and kissed him—she had to go to work the next day, for Pete's sake—he had bolted like a scared horse. He'd been absolutely scared shitless. She'd never had that effect on any man. And then he had drugged her!

That part she truly didn't understand. He'd proven stronger than she expected, managing to hold her down, while he pushed that stupid mask onto her face. She'd been petrified, expecting a high and the sudden rush of adrenaline. But nothing had happened. He'd gone all soppy. *Don't fight it, Tammy. It won't harm you, just relax.* Fight what? What was he talking about? Was she immune to what he had used?

Then he had welcomed her to that Church of Oscar. Was that how they got their new members, by subjecting them to some kind of secret drug? It was diabolical. That commune was an impressive cult that was growing stronger by the day. Stronger and richer! They wouldn't want their dirty secret revealed to the world.

An idea formed in her head. She would go to the authorities tomorrow and tell them. Perhaps she would get some kind of reward. On second thought, nah, they'd just close that damned church down and give her a pat on the back for being such a good citizen. A juicy case of blackmail would suit her much better. She turned around and looked at the clock on the little table to the side of her bed. Shit, only 2:30!

She wanted to be out of there before he woke up, but she didn't really want to go outside by herself in this part of town in the middle of the night. She fidgeted and tossed and turned for a while longer, her mind whirling, deciding what to do. She had to phone in sick tomorrow morning, that was for sure. No way did she want to be in the restaurant when he would come in for his meeting. Then she had an idea.

She sat up and swung her legs over the side of the bed. She had a little flashlight by her bedside and in the sudden bright light she walked over to the chair where she had put her bag. She took out her cell phone and climbed back in bed, pulling the covers snugly around her. She turned the phone on and punched in her ex-boyfriend Ronny's speed-dial number.

He would go ballistic, but what the hell. After four rings, she was connected and before she heard his voice there was a loud bang and she cringed. She knew exactly what had happened. Ronald Harbor lived in a small attic and his bed was placed under sloping roof beams. She had spent many happy hours there, but it was very cramped. He had looked at his phone, seen who it was, and been so surprised he'd sat up and banged his head against the ceiling.

"Shit, that hurts. Damn it all, Tammy, is that you? What the hell! I don't hear from you for months and then you call me in the middle of the night. You've got a nerve." His voice was very loud, and she turned the volume down, hoping that it hadn't awakened Erwin. She also heard something else: a concerned female voice, fussing about Ronny's head.

"Hello to you too, love," she said in a soft voice. "Sorry to ruin your night, but I've got to talk to you. It's very important."

"Oh yeah? Well, you can hear I'm not alone, and if you have the hots for me again, forget it. Go away. Why are you whispering?"

"Because I'm hiding under the blankets and there's a strange guy sleeping on my couch."

Silence.

"Ron? Are you there?"

"Of course I'm here, where'd you think I'd be? Are you in danger? Why don't you call the cops?"

She smiled, while she cupped the phone between her two hands and brought her mouth close to it.

"Very funny," she whispered. "Now listen, and don't interrupt me. Do you remember that time when we were snowed in and we hardly got out of bed for three days? We vowed that one day we would go somewhere warm together, just the two of us. The Bahamas, Mexico, Australia. Remember?"

His voice softened. "Of course. So?"

"Well, I've found us a way, love. I can't tell you now, but you won't believe what happened to me. You've got to come and pick me up."

"OK. What time tomorrow?"

"Not tomorrow. Now. Soon as you can. I've got to get out of this place."

"Are you insane? Why can't it wait till tomorrow?"

"Stop asking questions, dickhead! I've got to be out of here before he wakes up. Are you coming or not? I can always find someone else to share my time in the sun."

"Give me an hour."

"I'll give you thirty minutes. That gives you ample time to get rid of her. Wait for me out front." She quickly broke the connection and shut the phone off, just in case he'd call back.

For awhile she lay back, her mind whirling with excitement. She wondered if she knew Ronny's partner. What would have happened if things had been reversed? Would she drop everything and help him out? Probably not. She relaxed for a while, thinking about what she was going to do. She didn't want to wake her visitor, so a shower was out. Just a change of clothes would have to do. She got up, went to her closet and took out a bra, a light-blue blouse, a black-and-white-striped sweater, denim pants, and her comfortable runners. Careful not to make any noise, she quickly dressed.

In the bottom drawer of the dresser she rummaged for her ID card and money. She turned the flashlight off and carefully opened the door a crack and listened. Erwin was sound asleep; she could hear his soft breathing. She waited till her eyes had adjusted to the dark, then crept into the living room. In the little light coming in through the window she could see him sprawled out on the couch. She walked towards the chair where he'd put his jacket, and felt through the pockets. Nothing. There were no other garments; he must have fallen asleep with his clothes on. No sign of his backpack. She walked a bit closer and saw he'd put it under his pillow. Smart move.

Oh, well, so much for that; it didn't matter. With a bit of luck she'd have plenty of money soon. She took a last look around, then carefully walked up the three steps that led to the front door. It was a bit tight against one of the jambs, but she managed to open it without a noise and stepped outside. She carefully closed the door behind her and was suddenly worried. What the hell was she doing, leaving a stranger alone in her house? He could rob her.

She almost laughed out loud. What was there to steal? Soon she'd be able to buy all kinds of new clothes and furniture. She shivered in the early morning cold, pressing herself close against the door, hoping that nobody would see her. After about ten minutes a small car approached and stopped in front of the house. She quickly walked over, opened the door and got into the passenger seat.

"This had better be good, Tammy," Ronald Harbor exploded. "You have no idea what you interrupted. If it hadn't been for all the good times we've had together, I'd have hung up on you. What the devil is going on?"

"Later, later," she gestured, pointing through the windscreen. "Your place, please, and I hope you've got rid of her. I need to go to the bathroom big time, have a shower and something to eat. Then I'll tell you all about it."

◊ ◊ ◊

With heavy heart, Philip Kozak entered the elevator that would take him up to the boardroom on the eighteenth floor of the Secret Springs complex. He had taken the short ride hundreds of times during his time with the firm, always eager to discuss with his team the next move in the eternal struggle to keep everything in top shape. The Secret Springs' Board of Directors was very different from the boards of other large corporations.

Whereas the executives of many large firms could wear multiple hats, and work for other companies, in Secret Springs this was not the case. Its Board of Directors was accountable only to the company's shareholders, many of whom were also employees. The company could best be described as a multi-national co-op, and each board member was also a manager. As CEO, Philip was in charge of the giant servers for the virtualization software and the millions of virtscapes, organized in thousands of libraries, annotated and indexed, so that subscribers could easily choose any virtual trip they wanted.

Usually, Philip looked forward to the weekly meetings to discuss the running of the company, but this time he was not in a hurry to meet his fellow executives. He was apprehensive, worrying how his latest ideas would be received. Perhaps it was best to start them off on a jocular note, he thought. After he exited the elevator, he walked down the luxuriously carpeted hallway and opened the door to the boardroom. Everyone was there, his the only vacant chair. He nodded a greeting and sat down.

"Sorry I'm late. Had to do my laundry." That brought out the smiles on four of the faces. Only Armonde Takir and Sandor Donavon kept a neutral expression.

"Today is April 14, 2059," Philip continued. "The President of the United States is Stuart Ramsing. Water boils at 100 degrees Celsius, and the ratio of a circle's circumference to its diameter is called Pi." He halted, wondering if he'd overdone it. Six pairs of eyes stared at him, not understanding. Then Charles Reprino, one of the program analysts, laughed out loud.

"Good old Philip, always such a great sense of humor. I take it that you want to convey to us that you are fully cognizant and in control of your thoughts and actions? Well, well! Don't you think we should know that after all this time? What gives? You may have some strange ideas at times, but on the whole you're one of the sanest persons I've ever met."

"You may want to reconsider that statement before this meeting is over," Phil said.

"Another one of your controversial ideas?" Armonde Takir said, smiling thinly. "I thought you would have run out of those by now." Armonde was in charge of the photographic units that went out to shoot 3D videos and the still pictures that were integrated into the company's virtscapes. He was a young man, originally from Turkey. He looked very healthy, with a deep tan, and delicate features that made him look like a male fashion model. Trim, in top shape, with no excess fat anywhere. Phil wondered how Armonde found time to work; with a body like that he would have to spend several hours in the gym each day. Phil didn't particularly like the man, but he had no complaints about his work.

"Yes, Armonde. I am afraid you're all going to be very surprised at what I have to say. Please bear with me, and let me finish the whole story before you bring out the daggers." He halted and nervously wetted his lips with his tongue. Never in his entire life had he felt so uncomfortable.

"As you know I made a short trip a while ago," he began. "This was for personal reasons. However, what I saw and learned on that trip, made me realize there's a different world out there, a world that we at Secret Springs have conveniently pushed aside. To put it bluntly, I believe our future is not quite as rosy as we think. There are two great storm clouds gathering ahead, and we would be wise not to ignore them." He halted, to give the others time to comment. And they did.

"Are you sure we're talking about the same company here?" Donna Charming said. She was dressed in smart, dark blue pants, a white blouse and grey jacket. A mother of four, she still somehow found the time to be the Chief Financial Officer of the company. She probably wouldn't want to open the company's purse for his ideas, Philip thought. "According to our last quarter earnings, we're doing very well, Phil," Donna continued. "I don't think the future will be that much different."

"There are signs," Philip persisted. "People just don't want to see them. I'm telling you, we've reached the top of the bell curve, and from now on we'll be sliding downhill, perhaps as fast as we climbed up."

"What are those two storm clouds you mentioned?" It was Sarah Marrion, a woman of about sixty, who looked like a librarian with old-style half-moon reading glasses perched on her nose. Her brown hair was done up in a bun behind her head. She was small, and bent forward, as if she'd shrunk in accordance with her age. Her voice was like the chirping of a bird. Her department was in charge of continuity in the virtscapes.

"Let me explain," Phil said, coordinating his thoughts. "On one side we have a coming anarchy. Nobody can deny that. The efforts of our government to create new small businesses is collapsing, because we can't make goods at the price people want to pay. We've been spoiled for too long. Many people are roaming the country side, looking for food and shelter, and they have little money for the fantasies Secret Springs provide. The second cloud is the possibility of a dogmatic tyranny by the Church of Oscar."

"What? That bunch of losers?" Donna said, laughing. "What threat do they pose? A group of peasants, growing natural foods, hiding away from everyone? Come on now, Phil, this is too much."

"What do we really know about them?" Phil retorted. "They don't talk to anyone, they don't mix with other people, and don't leave their compounds. I believe they are determined to take over the world, like some modern, twenty-first century crusaders. I know, because my mother is one of their members. Haven't you noticed how that commune has grown lately? They started out small in Santa Barbara, and now they have many churches around the country. Everyone thinks they are harmless, but what if they are not?"

"Look, even if I'm wrong about them, and they're not set out to conquer the world, you can bet your paycheck that none of their followers will ever use the services of our company. With anarchy on one hand and that church on the other, I think we're heading for very difficult times. Secret Springs could well be finished in five to ten years."

"That's rather a sweeping statement you are making, Philip," a cultivated voice with a slight Indian accent broke the ensuing silence. "Without any kind of proof. This country still has people with money and they are the backbone of our business." Marvin Tuppal was smartly dressed in a dark grey suit with white shirt and tie. He was of average build, clean shaven, and he wore a small Ghandi cap. Marvin was a very likeable, even tempered man, and a very good electrical engineer. He was responsible for the distribution and control of the raw power that fed Secret Springs. Philip desperately needed him on his side.

"Of course," Phil replied, "they're still rich because of their connections to the big corporations outside the U.S. I am well aware that China and the Middle east are still basking in wealth. But this thing is global, and their time will come also."

"So why exactly are you telling us all this, Mr. Kozak," Armonde asked formally. "Are you suggesting we should all go home and wait for the inevitable? Do you have a solution, or are you just a prophet of doom? Perhaps you have read too many conspiracy theories."

"Let's not get personal here," Sarah said. "Just listen to what Philip has to say."

OK, here goes, Philip thought. *The point of no return.*

"Marvin, at the present stage of technology, what is the best known yield for solar energy collectors?"

"Excuse me?" Marvin Tuppal was taken aback by the sudden change in subject. "You mean solar cells? Well, I believe the best we can expect at this moment is about 100 Watts per square foot, give and take a few Watts. The company that makes them is located in China."

"Well, here's a brain teaser for you. Assuming we created a huge bubble over Secret Springs and covered it with solar cells, could we create enough power to operate?"

"Oh, don't be stupid, Philip," Charles Reprino burst out. "Secret Springs uses the same amount of electricity as an average city. We get about three billion hits a day on our site, each using tons of bandwidth. You want to draw all that energy from solar power? If you covered the entire State of

Illinois with solar cells, maybe, just maybe, you would get enough. But one little bubble? No way."

"I must concur with Charles," Marvin said. "It is not possible. Why do you ask such a question when you very well know the answer yourself, Philip?"

"I didn't phrase my question very well," Philip said, feeling his face get flushed. "Imagine there are no calls coming in. Would we have enough power for a no-load scenario?"

"I don't know," Marvin said. "I would have to do some proper calculations, but on a rough estimate, I'd say, if the bubble was big enough, yes, perhaps it could be done. But why? Where are you going with this?"

"Just bear with me," Philip said. "Suppose we allowed some callers in, just a limited number, say a thousand. How many virtscapes could we run then, using solar power? A hundred? A thousand?"

The electrical engineer was getting nervous. "I couldn't possibly tell at this stage, Phil. I need computer simulations. My guess would be a hundred, max, but I could be way off. This has never been proposed. Why do you want to go solar?"

"Because solar power will be forever, or at least for millions of years. I want to create a new Secret Springs that will last that long."

"Rubbish!" Charles Reprino said. "This is insane. You want to turn a profitable, established company into a mere shadow of itself, to serve just a few elite people. Why for goodness' sake? What are you getting at here?"

"Excuse me," Sandor Donavon said in the sudden silence. He had originally come from the Czech republic, and was a young physicist, specializing in the quantum physics that lay at the core of the Secret Springs operation. He was not very outspoken and usually kept to himself. But Philip had learned long ago that if Sandor spoke, is was best to listen carefully. "These few people you're talking about? Who would they be? How would you choose them? Where would they call from?"

"Actually, they would all be living inside the dome," Phil said nervously.

Confusion reigned in the boardroom. Even the usually unflappable Marvin shook his head. "You've lost me completely, Philip. Why go through such an elaborate process? Why a solar powered dome for a thousand people? The electric grid is here to stay for a long time, I'm sure. The Secret Spring complex already houses almost six hundred people. If you want to add more, I'm sure we can expand the normal way. I don't get it."

"Philip, all this makes little sense, and I am very disappointed in you," Armonde said, pushing his chair back, and standing up. "You have made us waste valuable time that we could have put to better use."

"Agreed," Charles added, also getting up. "If it weren't for your little spiel at the beginning, I'd say you'd really lost your marbles, Phil. I think this meeting is over."

"No, wait," Sarah called out. "Let him finish."

"Only if he talks sense," Charles muttered, while he sat down again. After a slight hesitation, Armonde sat down also.

"OK, I must talk about something else first," Philip said. He quickly described his OBE experience. When he finished, Charles Reprino just shrugged.

"So? You left your body for a while, Philip. It must be a very intense emotional experience, I am sure, but what has that got to do with anything we're discussing here?"

"Perhaps everything," Philip said. "I believe it is possible to move one's consciousness outside one's body permanently."

Armonde cocked his head to Philip. "How do you figure that? Without a consciousness you would be dead. I don't follow you at all."

"I think Secret Springs should start a research project to look into the possibility of virtual people, Armonde. Don't you understand? People move part of their consciousness into an avatar every time they enter a virtscape, sometimes hours at a time. There is no law in physics that says it isn't impossible to move it permanently. It would be the next step in human evolution. We're more than just our bodies. We could create virtual people who live forever. All they would need is a little energy to keep their avatars charged. It would be the greatest discovery of all times, Armonde. Think of what it could do for Secret Springs."

"I'll tell you what it would do," Charles shouted. "it would cause Secret Springs to go belly-up, Philip. I think this time you have really lost it. You want us to engage in some sort of harebrained scheme and commit economic suicide? What could we possible gain from such an insane experiment? Get serious, man."

"Agreed," a tightlipped Armonde said. "Even if what you suggest could be true—and I know it can't be—how could we possibly justify it ethically and morally? Without a body, people would officially be dead, and Secret Springs could be charged with murder. This is beyond outrageous, and I've had enough." He pushed his chair back and headed for the door.

"Wait, I'm coming also." Charles Reprino quickly got up and joined Armonde on his way out, leaving the remaining board members in a state of uncomfortable quiet. Then Donna Charming spoke.

"Virtual people? How cute! That's the kind of stuff my six year old kid reads about in his comic magazines. You want to try that for real? You're out of your mind, Philip." Shaking her head, she followed the others outside.

"Philip, this is just too far-fetched," Marvin said. "You've only got your own ideas to go by. Even though it might be interesting to pursue your theory, Secret Springs is not the venue for this. What do you think, Sandor? Sarah?"

The last two board members shook their heads, and Marvin looked at Philip.

"We've done this democratically, Phil. Six out of seven against. I'm sorry. I don't think the world is quite ready for your idea."

◊ ◊ ◊

He stood motionless in the center of the track where the Bullet trains ran at almost four hundred miles per hour. It was a stupid place to be, but no matter how he tried to move, his feet seemed glued to the ground. Panic stricken, he heard the train's horn nearby. At that speed there was no way the Bullet could ever stop in time, and he would be squashed, like a bug on the windscreen. Why did it take the train so long to get there? Suddenly he knew there would be no train; it was only a bad dream, and the horn was a telephone ringing.

It took Erwin several seconds to realize where he was. Then it fell in place. Tammy! Why didn't she answer the phone? What time was it? He took the backpack from under his pillow and looked at his watch. 8.00 o'clock! Only an hour before his meeting with Clive and he had no idea where he was. Then he heard Tammy's voice.

"Hi, I can't talk to you. Leave a message." There was a short beep, followed by an agitated man's voice.

"Tammy, where the hell are you? Get your ass over here quickly, this place is rocking!" Another beep and there was silence again. Erwin ran to the bedroom and knocked on the door.

"Wake up, Tammy," he called out. "Your boss just called. He's not very happy. Tammy?" When there was no answer, he turned the door handle and opened the door. Her bed was empty. He checked the bathroom and the rest of the house. She was gone! When he looked in the garage, he saw she hadn't taken her scooter.

He ran back into the bathroom, poured some water in the basin and quickly washed his face, wondering why she had left. Back in the living room, he picked up his backpack, realizing he needed some kind of map to find his way back to the restaurant. He checked the book case, the magazine holder, the mantel piece. No maps.

It had taken them twenty minutes last night. By foot, it would take more than an hour, especially since he didn't know the way. Impossible; he needed transportation. He stepped into the garage, opened the outside door and pushed the scooter outside. Tammy would understand; he was only borrowing it and he'd leave it at the restaurant. He closed the garage door again, and looked at the scooter. There was a starter button, and when he pushed it two times the engine came to life. After a few minutes of trial and error, he figured out how to work the controls. He stuck his backpack into the luggage basket and carefully drove off.

He was very short of time, but he felt he should try to find Tammy. If she was walking she might not be far. He decided to make a big square and look in the side streets. Even though it was early morning, it wasn't very busy and none of the other drivers and pedestrians paid him any attention.

After he finished the square, he stopped in front of the house again, frustrated. He was wasting time. Tammy could have left hours ago. He just had to let her be, and hope she was all right. She wouldn't be too happy he'd taken her scooter, but he'd apologize later.

It had been dark last night, and he had absolutely no idea which way they had come. He rode on for a while, hoping the little motor wouldn't quit. At a small convenience store, he parked the scooter and walked in, but stayed near the window.

"Yes?" An older man in a dirty leather jacket eyed him from the till in the center of the store.

"Do you know where the Happy Lunchbox is?" Erwin called out.

"Yes."

"Well, can you tell me how to get there?"

"Are you buying?"

"Got a map of this area?"

"No maps. Anything else?"

"I'll take a chocolate bar."

"Help yourself, over there." The man pointed at a rack with various sweets and candies in front of him.

"Can you bring it here? I want to keep an eye on my scooter."

"What are you, some kind of nutcase?" The man stepped from behind his counter, grabbed a bar and shuffled towards Erwin. "Hope you got five bucks," he said, puffing. "I don't want to walk back with change again." Luckily, Erwin had the right bill. "So about the Happy Lunchbox?" he demanded, looking at his watch. 8.30!

"It's easy," the man muttered, pocketing the money. "Keep on Jerkins for about ten minutes, then turn left at the church. Can't miss it. It's Casslings. Follow Casslings, and it becomes Universal Avenue. Head north, turn left at the second light, and you'll see the Cage. Just follow that."

"Cage? What cage? What are you talking about?"

"Huh? What planet are you from, son? They build metal mash cages wherever the Bullet trains run through built-up areas, to stop accidents."

"Right. I get the picture, thanks."

The store keeper's instructions proved to be accurate up to a point. Erwin found Casslings, but there was no sign of Universal Avenue. Traffic got much denser, and he probably had missed it, trying to concentrate, riding around cars. After another five minutes, he angrily gave up. The place was like a maze.

He was about to ask a young woman, who was walking briskly along the pavement, when he saw the Cage in a valley on his left. He rode on, trying to follow the track as best as he could. Twice he had to backtrack a bit, but finally, in the distance he saw the restaurant. He'd made it!

He was about to park the scooter in front of the building, then decided to leave it in the back, behind the dumpster. Anyone opening the back door would see it and know it was Tammy's. He rushed back to the entrance and entered the restaurant. It was very busy, and he recognized Clive Wadding in a booth at the far end.

"You're late," the former bodyguard greeted him dourly. He'd just finished his breakfast and pushed the empty plate away from him.

111

"Couldn't help it, I had rather a bad experience," Erwin defended himself, but the other didn't seem interested.

"Have you got the Breath?"

"Of course." Erwin unzipped his backpack and handed over the flask and his lunchbox.

"Push something sharp into the two holes in the bottom, and it will come off," Erwin said. "It's a hidden compartment for the masks".

"Thanks." Clive put everything in his briefcase, and stood up. "Come, I'll drive you to the station."

"Just a moment. I need to tell you something."

Clive looked at his watch. "Is it important? I've got to get back into the City."

"Yes it is." Reluctantly, Wadding sat down again, and Erwin told him what had happened.

"I don't believe this. How could you get involved with a two-bit hooker, Erwin?"

"Tammy is not a prostitute! She's a nice young woman who gave me a bed for the night. You don't even know her."

"Keep your voice down," Clive hissed. "I've been here before, and I've seen Tammy. You took an awful risk going home with her, you know. She could have stolen Oscar's Breath, for goodness' sake. And your money."

Wadding sat quietly for a few seconds, tapping his fingers on the tabletop. "OK, here's what we'll do. It's best if we're not seen leaving together. I'll head for my car. It's the Xanic parked in the lane. You wait a couple of minutes, and then join me. I'll drive you to the station, and you head home pronto. I'll look after the rest."

"Can I have breakfast first?"

"No. I can't wait. Eat at the station."

"What about Tammy?

"Were you listening? I said I'll look after her. You just go home."

Erwin nodded, and the other stood up. Erwin watched him amble to the till in front and pay his bill, then leave the restaurant. Feeling sick and angry at what Clive had said,

Erwin got up and headed for the washroom. He looked in the mirror at his unshaven face. In his backpack was a razor, but there just wasn't time.

After relieving himself at the urinal, he washed his hands and slapped some water on his face. He slung his empty backpack on, left the bathroom and headed for the exit, stepping aside to allow a young waiter to pass him. The sight and smell of the breakfasts he carried made Erwin even more hungry. When he got outside he walked to a small blue car parked in the lane and got inside.

"Sorry I was a bit short with you, Erwin," Clive said. "I should have realized you've never been out on your own. Things are a bit different here than in sunny California. But you've got me the Breath and that's the main thing."

It took them only ten minutes to reach the station, and Clive stopped the car in a no-parking zone. He stuck out his hand. "Safe journey home, Erwin. I'll be in touch."

Erwin got out and watched the blue car disappear towards the city. He wondered how Duval's ex-bodyguard would bypass city security. He looked at his watch: 9.15, an hour before the train would leave, and he already had his ticket. He was very hungry, and resolutely headed for the food court in the terminal.

At Harold's Pancake House, he ordered a full stack of blueberry pancakes with bacon and sausages on the side. Their hot water dispenser was out of order, so he couldn't have tea. He settled for vitaminized mineral water instead. While he wolfed his meal down he thought of Tammy. What would become of her? Would she continue to work at the Happy Lunchbox? He suddenly felt bad he hadn't told the restaurant about the scooter, but how could he? There would have been questions. He somehow had to find a way to write or e-mail her. If only she had told him she was going out. He could have gone with her, helped her get used to her new life. There was nothing he could do now.

Half an hour before departure time, he entered the Bullet and found his seat. Several people were already seated,

113

and it looked as if it was going to be a busy trip. Erwin made himself comfortable and leaned against the window. He felt exhausted, and by the time the train began to move he had dozed off.

The trip was worse than the one going. Somewhere in the middle of Kansas the train slowed down and came to a smooth halt. He woke up, wondering what had happened. The train was packed, every seat taken. Next to him an old lady in a blue chiffon dress and matching hat smiled at him. For about ten minutes they just sat there, and all he could see was fields and a few country roads. An official looking man in uniform appeared in the corridor that connected the compartments.

"About half an hour's delay," he announced. "Vandals clamped a metal bar on the magneto rail, and we need to shut the power off." He walked on, repeating the same message down the corridors. Great, Erwin thought. Now he'd probably miss his bus and have to phone Jo to come and pick him up.

Finally they were on the move again, and he tried to look out of the window. It was painful to the eyes. He could see houses and cattle far away, but everything nearby was a constant blur since the train was probably going faster than normal to make up time.

"I would have flown, you know, but I can't afford it," the lady next to him said. "Do you live in L.A?"

"Santa Barbara," he said.

"Oh, that's nice." She nodded. "I've been there. I'm going to my great-nephew's wedding in Oxnar. Do you have a family, young man?"

"No. I live in a . . ." He stopped just in time. No use tempting fate again. "I live alone." He turned away from her, and looked outside, hoping she would get the message. The old lady did, and started a conversation with the passenger on her other side.

For the longest time Erwin looked out, mesmerized by the constant movement just outside his window, and he dozed off again. When he woke up, it was early afternoon.

114

The train had slowed down and after a few minutes there was an announcement. "Los Angeles Terminal, five minutes." Despite the best efforts of the engineer, they were twenty minutes late. Because of the time difference, it was only a quarter past three, but he still had to get to Santa Barbara.

After a fifteen minute cab drive, half an hour wait for the bus, and a two hour journey, he finally reached the Santa Barbara bus terminal at ten minutes past six. As he stepped outside, he heard his name being called, and there was Jo waiting for him. Erwin's spirits lifted, then immediately took a nosedive again. Jo's face was drawn without a smile to greet him. He knew.

"I'm glad you're back safely," Jo said, "Why are you so late?"

"Some idiot sabotaged the Bullet line. It has been quite a day, believe me."

Jo nodded. "I know. Clive phoned." Nothing more was said until they reached the car.

After they got in, Jo didn't immediately start the engine.

"Not quite your finest moment, Erwin, was it?"

"I don't understand it, Jo. Why would Tammy run away?"

Jo's features softened. "Perhaps she was scared. I should never had let you go out all by yourself on such an important mission."

"I'm twenty-four, you know," Erwin retorted. "I did my best, considering the hotel screwed up the reservation. Has Clive found Tammy yet?"

"No. She's probably very confused after getting Oscar's Breath, and all we can do is hope that she is OK." Jo started the engine. Before he drove off, he looked Erwin straight in the eye. "I think it is best if this stays between you, Clive and myself. No need for the others know, not even your mother."

Erwin nodded, and they joined the traffic to head home.

7

When Lieutenant Cramer was summoned to his boss's temporary office, he feared the worst. The inspection had gone relatively well, as far as he could tell. But Pittard had been evasive, avoided eye contact and had hardly talked to anyone. Cramer didn't like the Chief in the first place and there was no love lost on Jim Pittard's side either, he was sure. Was something else brewing? Had the Chief come here for other reasons than an inspection after the fire at the station?

Since there was very little room in the old house, the Chief had set up in the garage, among supplies, tools and other paraphernalia. They'd found him an old table as a desk. Pittard had brought his own assistant, a pretty young cadet, who told Cramer that the Chief would see him soon. Would he like a coffee? Cramer declined, as he didn't think he would be in there very long.

Soon turned out to be fifteen minutes later. The door to the garage finally opened and Pittard invited him in. He was a fit-looking man for his fifties, and the crisp, spotless uniform fitted him like a second skin. He was clean shaven, with a short, almost military hair cut. His teeth were too white and uniform to be natural, and Cramer didn't like his smile. It was forced. Pittard invited Tom in as if he hadn't seen him for weeks, instead of just two days.

"Ah, Tom. Sit down." The Chief didn't quite seem to know where to start and Cramer instantly knew the news would be bad. His boss scratched the back of his head and shifted around in his uncomfortable looking chair. Then he looked Cramer straight in the eye.

"You're a good man, Cramer, and you've run a tight ship here, I can tell. But times are bad, Tom. Money is worth less every day, and the government coffers, both state and

116

federal, are practically empty. Truth is, Tom, we're not going to rebuild the station, and we'll be closing this one down next month. We're going to police the area from L.A." Pittard raised a hand to stop Cramer from interrupting him.

"I know, I know. There may be problems, but there is no other way."

"With all respect, sir, you can't do that. We've been expanding for the last fifty years: Buellton, Goleta, Montecito, they are all under our jurisdiction these days. It's a huge area with over five million people. You can't possible run everything from L.A."

"We'll have to. That's the way it is these days, Tom, unfortunately. There simply is no money available. The California State Patrol will help out in emergencies."

"The CSP? You can't be serious! They were never meant to police a huge area like this. If you close this station the troubles we face today will be like a picnic in the park compared to what's coming. We need a police force here."

"Oh, there will be. We'll be deploying an army of drones and fast helicopters from L.A. Any problems in the area, and we'll be right there, believe me. Anyway, enough of that. I didn't call you in to discuss police matters, Tom. This has to do with you. I've got some good news. Since you're senior here, you'll be transferred to L.A., the Beverly Hills precinct. A cushy job if there ever was one, just right for you—a nice shoe-in to your retirement. Very little crime there. L.A. is like one giant gated community these days. I don't have the exact figures, but I think there might even be more pay, and we'll help you find a place to stay. I think the force owes you that much. You'll be able to relax, play golf, and hobnob with the elite, Tom. You'll start next month."

Tom Cramer didn't answer immediately. Part of him wanted to grab the opportunity. Only four more years and a full pension. Yet another, much stronger part of him knew he would be selling his soul for a few more dollars. He'd never be happy there, looking after the rich. *To thyself be true.* He could see the other was waiting for his response.

"I don't think so, sir. I must decline, thank you."

Pittard's eyebrows shot up in genuine surprise.

"You don't want it? What's wrong with you? I'm doing you a big favor. You can make new contacts for later on, you know. Lots of these places have got their own security. You're in good health still and you can keep working after you retire. Lots of opportunities for a security job there."

"I don't want to work in L.A., sir. Protecting the rich is a baby-sitting job and it's not for me. I don't need to hobnob and I don't play golf. Sir."

He could see the veins on Jim Pittard's head darkening. He obviously wasn't used to being talked to like that. But years of frustration had steeled Cramer. He wasn't going to spend his last few working years looking after the elite, who still thought that money could buy anything at the expense of the rest of the population. And that was that.

"You don't have a choice, Tom. This place is going to be closed, and you'll be out of work. Come on, even if you don't like it, what is four years? After that you can do what you want. I had to pull quite a few strings to fit you in there, Lieutenant. Don't make me regret it."

Cramer didn't answer. He took his badge and put it on the table in front of his boss.

"I'm sorry sir. I can't do this."

"You're way out of line here, Lieutenant Cramer," the Chief exclaimed. "This comes from the highest level and you're not making the decisions here."

For a while the two sat there, Pittard, red-faced and angry, Cramer breathing hard, hands tightened into fists, fighting the urge to reach over and punch his boss on the nose. Then Jim Pittard calmed down and softened a bit. "Look, Tom, let's be adults about this. You've been a good cop, and the force would hate to lose you. There's an opportunity waiting for you. I hear what you're saying, and I don't like closing this place either. But that's life, Tom. Policing costs money, and if there's none, well, that's it.

Centralizing is the way of the future. Sometimes we must do what we don't like. Four years will fly by before you know it."

He put his hand on Cramer's badge, ready to push it back to him. He even managed one of his sickening smiles. "Come on, Tom. Won't you reconsider? A full pension, versus seventy-five percent? Heather will thank you for it."

Cramer almost laughed at the absurdity of it all.

"In all due respect sir, I don't think I am the one who should reconsider."

Jim Pittard's lips tightened in a thin smile. He sat straight up and roughly pushed the badge back towards Tom. "You'll be needing this for another two weeks," he said. "I hope one of the other guys will show more sense, when it comes to relocation."

◊ ◊ ◊

Jo had a terrible night. A lot of things were running through his mind and sleep eluded him. After the drive home with Erwin he'd taken a stiff brandy and thought things over. He wasn't at all happy about what had happened in Washington, not even after Clive had assured him that finding Tammy would only be a matter of time. It was a bad idea to have a new church member wandering around on her own. Why was she hiding? Was she scared? There was no reason to be. Nobody recruited for the church was ever scared afterwards. Confused for a little while, maybe, but not scared. There was something about Erwin's story that bothered Jo. Something didn't feel right.

He could feel it in the back of his neck: a stiffness, a feeling that he was missing something. Around six o'clock he got up and took his shower. He felt tired, ill at ease. A long walk would do him good. He dressed in his casual walking gear: woolen socks and hiking boots, brown corduroy pants, a brown-checkered sport shirt and his khaki walking jacket. He took his toque out of the closet and was about to leave, when he decided to check the mail first.

119

The church received many e-mails every day. A lot of them were junk and spam. People begging for money, or promising it. This time was no exception, and he quickly deleted them. It left three messages. The first one was a report from Helin Sparling and the commune in New York. Everything was fine, and she had some good news: John and Marg Butterman, owners of Butterman's Books were very interested in the church. As soon as they could get some of the Breath to her, Helin would try to recruit them. There might be a lot of money involved for the church.

Jo took a deep breath, his heart pounding with the news. Thank you Helin! The next e-mail was from Clive. Sorry, he hadn't found Tammy yet, but he was still trying. The stiffness in Jo's neck started up again. He hated loose ends. Then, when he read the third message, Jo's world collapsed and he felt a pain in his stomach that almost made him sick. This wasn't possible. It couldn't be. With shaking hands he re-read the e-mail, and things began to fall into place, as he realized what had been bugging him all night.

We have discovered your church's secret. We know you are using some kind of drug to recruit new members. Unless you immediately transfer one million dollars into account 1.989.7743 of the Washington Secure Saving Bank, we shall make your shameful practice known to the media. This is not a joke, or hoax: $ 1,000.000 dollars, or the Church of Oscar will be disgraced and shut down forever. You have twenty-four hours.

Jo's chest was hurting and he had difficulty breathing. He slumped in his chair as everything around him seemed to swerve and move around. He closed his eyes, his mind filled with only one name: Tammy! She hadn't been converted at all, and he knew why. He had to act at once. He punched in Dale's number, impatiently waited for the connection. *Come on, come on, Dale, you should be up by now . . .*
"Dale."

"Jo. We have an emergency. The church has been compromised. Get the others in the boardroom at once, no excuses. Make sure everyone's there in five minutes." Jo put the phone down and left his room. Sylvia had a room a few doors down the hallway and he banged on her door.

"Sylvia! Open up! Quickly." After a few seconds he heard movement behind the door, then it opened ajar and there was Sylvia's perplexed face.

"Jo? It's barely six, what's going on? Are we under attack?"

"Worse than that. Boardroom, as quick as you can." He left her standing behind the door and rushed off.

About ten minutes later, the normally staid boardroom was in absolute mayhem. Most councilors had just thrown on the first clothes they could lay their hands on. Everyone was talking, as no one had any idea why they were there. When a disheveled Dale appeared with Erwin in tow, Jo stood up and demanded attention.

"OK, everyone! We are on the brink of a disaster that could finish our church forever. Sit down and listen." When the noise died out, Jo carefully selected his words.

"Oscar's Breath has been compromised," he began. "Someone knows about it. I have received a blackmail message. Unless we pay one million dollars by tomorrow morning, the media will be informed about our recruitment procedure."

For a fraction of a second there was absolute silence, then pandemonium broke out.

"It can't be . . . "

"What happened?"

"It's a hoax!"

Jo held up his hands. "Quiet, everyone, quiet! I know exactly what happened. Erwin, sit down over there." Jo pointed at the chair at the head of the table. Erwin looked at the chair as if it was one of those mediaeval Judas torture chairs. He'd lost all color and seemed fixed to the floor.

"Sit down!" Jo shouted. Shaking like a leaf, Erwin finally took his seat.

"Tell the Council what happened on your Washington trip," Jo demanded.

Erwin shot him a hurt, angry look. "You promised . . ."

"*Tell them!*"

In a shaky, hesitating voice, Erwin told them about Tammy. When he had finished, Jo took over.

"Clive Wadding in Washington is looking for her, but so far no success and I know why. She's gone into hiding."

"But why, Jo?" Carol asked. "What has this got to do with that e-mail you received? Tammy wouldn't possibly do this if she's one of us. She couldn't. Why would she go into hiding? It's got to be someone else."

"Wrong," Jo retorted. "Tammy was never recruited."

"She was so!" Erwin shouted. "I gave her the Breath. I should know."

"I'm confused," Diana said, shaking her head. "What's going on here, Jo?"

"Erwin, tell us exactly what you did, after Tammy kissed you," Jo demanded.

"She wanted to make love to me and I panicked. I grabbed my backpack and ran to the bathroom. I thought she was going to throw me out into the night, and it was a horrible, dangerous neighborhood. The only way to stop her was to make her one of us, so I just grabbed a mask and recruited her."

"Did you prime the mask?"

"What do you mean? I told you, I panicked, and didn't have time to think. Those masks were ready to go, weren't they?"

"No, Erwin, they were not. In the church they are, yes. Father English always made sure they were primed and ready, but the mask you used was brand-new. You gave Tammy nothing but ordinary air."

"No! She got all weak and groggy, and when I told her about the church she understood and fell fast asleep."

"That's because she's a good actress, Erwin. She out-smarted you. She struggled at first, fearing she was being drugged, but then she saw an opportunity and decided to go along with it to see if she could use the information you gave her. Thank the Lord you hid your backpack under your pillow, otherwise things would have been even more catastrophic."

"Right," Dale said in the ensuing silence. "Now we know what happened and we can't change it. We've got to find her, but what are we going to do about the demand? We only have one day. We must make sure the money is in that account tomorrow morning. Otherwise we're finished. We know from Erwin that she's not very rich, so my guess is she'll be hiding in the area and check the account first thing in the morning. We're going to need some high level help here, so I suggest we call Clive again and explain the situation to him. I also think we need to go out there. When she takes the money out, the bank should detain her and we can pick her up then. It could take a few days, but we must be ready."

"All right, you head down there, Dale. Brian, can you go also?"

Brian nodded, and Jo continued. "I'll look after the money transfer today. Any other suggestions?"

"I want to go also," Erwin said meekly. "I know I fouled up badly and I want a chance to get even with Tammy. I can recognize her, and—"

"I don't think so, Erwin," Brian interrupted. "You have done enough damage."

"No, hear me out," Erwin said. "I know Tammy better than any of you. She's not stupid. No way is she going to try and cash a million dollars at once. She'll take out a small amount first, to see what happens. If the bank detains her, all she has to do is make one phone call to the media and the church is finished. I think we should let her take out a certain amount before we go after her."

"Actually, that's a good idea," Carol said. "Lure her into a false feeling of security. She must know we'll keep an eye on that account. How much shall we let her get away with before we grab her?"

"I think she'll withdraw about seventy thousand dollars," Erwin said.

"Why that amount, Erwin?" Jo demanded suspiciously. "Is there something you're not telling us? May I remind you that the future of our church is at stake?"

"You just have to trust me, Jo," Erwin said. "I got the church into this mess and I think I know a way to get us out."

◊ ◊ ◊

"Sorry, Jen, I can't do it." Philip pushed the covers off the bed and swung his legs over the side. He walked over to the nearby chair, grabbed his housecoat and walked into the bathroom. He stood in front of the mirror, frowning at himself, taking deep breaths. He sighed, wondering what was wrong. It was the second time in two weeks that he had failed to satisfy Jennifer and himself, and he felt very worried. He took a quick drink of water, then returned to the bedroom. Jennifer was still under the blankets, with only her head showing. She eyed him sympathetically.

"There's nothing wrong with you, Phil," she said. "It's all in your mind. Something is bothering you again, and it's not just the sex. What is it?"

"It's partly the job, I guess. We're not doing too well, haven't you noticed? We're losing customers, and I'm really worried about the future."

"Come off it, Phil! You're not personally responsible for Secret Springs, even though you think you are. It's just part of our economical system that's falling apart. Nothing you can do about it. What else is bothering you?"

He hesitated for a few seconds, debating whether to drop it, then he suddenly let it all out. "It's that board meeting of the other day. I mean, I hardly expected them to go gaga over my new idea for virtual people, but to laugh it off as hocus pocus, that really hurt. They didn't even want to consider the possibility. Sure, it sounds impossible at this time, but what about ten, twenty years from now? They could have been a bit more open-minded about it.

"Hell, if someone from last century visited Secret Springs today, he wouldn't believe his eyes. Things are changing exponentially, and in the future virtual life could well be possible. Then there's that Church of Oscar. Something odd is going on there. I can't forget that look on my mother's face, Jen. It was almost fanatical, but at the same time she seemed very happy. I can't figure out what has happened to her."

"That's ridiculous, Phil. Why should anything have happened? You're looking for a bear behind every tree. It's a communal church, highly respected everywhere. Your mother is getting old, and it could the onset of dementia, or Alzheimer's. You can't blame that church for her condition."

For the longest time neither of them spoke. Then, finally, Jennifer shook her head. "You were doing so well, Phil," she said. "I think you should go back to Dr. Kilzinger. Perhaps he can give you some medication."

He smiled at her, but it was more of a snarl. "Sure, I'm going crazy, right? Just take a pill and everything will be fine. No way. Dr. Kilzinger helped me a lot, but there's nothing more he can do. I'm not going mad or anything, Jen, I'm just more perceptive than most people. Anyway, I'll take my shower now." He abruptly disappeared into the bathroom and closed the door.

Philip was under a lot of pressure, that Jennifer knew. It was no secret that the social network was not doing well. In it's zenith, ten years ago, the sky had seemed the limit for Secret Springs. New virtscapes were added almost daily and they had subscribers in almost every part of the world. Then, gradually, despite Philip's best efforts, the decline had begun. Some called it an awakening from the mass hypnosis of television and its cousins, the virtual social networks. Disturbing as it might be to Secret Springs, Jennifer knew it wasn't the only problem Philip faced. He was also fighting some kind of personal battle.

She heard the water rushing while he took his shower and she decided to get up and start making breakfast. It was Saturday morning, so there was no rush. She put on her housecoat, walked to the kitchen and started laying the table. She thought about Secret Springs. Perhaps it did need a new direction, a fresh approach. But Philip's idea of virtual people? Human spirits without bodies, permanently living in avatars? No wonder the board members had scoffed at the idea. It seemed ridiculous to her as well.

She took the kettle from the countertop and held it under the tap, thinking about what Philip had said about his mother. She was almost seventy and perhaps couldn't help it if she was going a bit gaga. Jennifer had known Phil for more than ten years, and he had hardly ever spoken of his mother. How would that poor lady have felt all those years, when Philip had never contacted her? Jennifer didn't get to see her parents in Wisconsin as often as she wanted, but she tried to visit them at least once a year and she phoned them regularly. She couldn't imagine not talking to them for years.

The bathroom door opened and Phil walked out, hair dripping, towel wrapped around his lean body. He came over to her and gave her a happy smile.

"Feeling better?"

"Yeah. Sorry, about that." He embraced and kissed her. "How about I make breakfast while you shower? Buttermilk pancakes OK?"

Half an hour later they were enjoying wafer-thin pancakes with maple syrup, strips of bacon, ham and fresh coffee. Then he surprised her. "You're right," he said. "I think too much and I get depressed too easily. Why don't we go for a walk? A real walk, through real trees. How about Beaverdale Park, we haven't been there for ages." It was the nearest park to the Secret Springs headquarters. Not a nature woodland by any stretch of the imagination but it would do.

"We should go barefoot," Jennifer said. "Did you know it is important to ground yourself now and then? All the positive

126

ions flow right out of your body, back into Mother Earth, and you feel energized. It's a great remedy for depression."

"Not true," he smirked at her. "It's the other way around. The electrons flow from the ground into your body to neutralize your positive ions."

She stood up and hugged him. "All right, smartass, let's go collect some electrons."

◊ ◊ ◊

With a squeak of her front brake, Tammy came to a halt in front of the car dealership just outside the Washington city limits. Entering the luxurious site with scores of new cars lined up in rows, she felt out of place on her scooter. It was fine in Longport, the dump where she lived, but not in a citadel of power and money like Blenkin Motors. Still, it didn't matter anymore. She'd made her last ride on the damned thing. No more cold, rainy mornings, no more sliding in the snow. She decided to leave it at the dealership; perhaps they knew someone who might have a use for it.

She had asked Ronald to drive her, but he had given her various excuses and finally reluctantly admitted he'd rather not. He hoped she would understand. Tammy understood, all right. Lasha, Ronny's new girlfriend, had probably read him the riot act, and although he knew about Tammy's sudden windfall, Ronny had given in to Lasha. He was smart enough not to burn all his bridges, just because Tammy might have struck it rich.

But he had agreed to keep her secret and help her in case something went wrong. Tammy had written a captivating account of her experience with Erwin, saved it on a USB stick, and given it to Ronny for safekeeping. One call from her and he would take it to the media.

She left her scooter against the fence that surrounded the property and stood for a second, admiring the new clothes she had bought the day before. Blue pants and jacket, white blouse, and new shoes. It wouldn't do to get into a brand-new car, wearing old, grubby clothes. She took her compact and lipstick from her new handbag and made herself as presentable as she could. Then the headed for the ornate glass door and entered the showroom. Her eyes were immediately drawn to the neon-blue Tatshu, the latest model for the American market. She wondered how many people could afford it.

"Ah, Miss Tilburn," a salesman suddenly stood beside her and pointed at the car.

"It's all ready for you, fully charged. If you could just wait in my office, we can finalize the paperwork. I'll be right with you." He guided her towards one of the offices and she stepped inside, taking a seat behind the desk. For the first time, Tammy really understood how her life had changed.

After spending the rest of the night with Ronald, she had sent the e-mail to the church. At first, she'd been petrified. Was it going to work? No way was that church just going to part with a million dollars. They'd find out from the bank where she lived and someone would come for her. The church couldn't go to the authorities, because that would incriminate them. But they could hire someone to kill her. She hadn't dared to go back home or to work, and had booked a room at the German Guesthause.

Even though only Ronald knew where she was, she'd stayed in all day, waiting for the knock on her door, or a call on the phone. After another sleepless night, she'd gone to her bank, her phone handy, in case there was trouble. She'd inserted her bankcard, expecting bells to ring and lights to flash, but nothing happened. When she checked her balance it was just over one million dollars.

Her first idea was to go inside, take out all the money and disappear. Then she'd silently cursed herself for being so stupid. If the police or security apprehended her, how could she explain a check for a million dollars in her purse?

She'd take out a small amount, to see if everything was all right. If she was caught, she could always say the bank had made a mistake and the money wasn't hers. Keying in her PIN number, she made a withdrawal for two hundred dollars, and watched as the machine spat out the stack of notes without any trouble.

She had gone out to buy herself a new outfit and the snazzy handbag she'd wanted for a long time. The next day she'd been more daring and taken out a cashier's check for seventy-three thousand dollars. Again, there had been no problem. She'd gone to Blenkin Motors, shown them the check and chosen the car she liked best. And as of today it would be hers!

She heard footsteps in the hallway and eagerly awaited the return of the salesman. But instead of one person, three men entered the office. She didn't recognize two of them, but when Tammy saw the third person, the dream of her new life collapsed. "You!" she yelled, "How did you know where to find me? How could you possibly know I would be here?"

"Hello, Tammy," Erwin said, locking the door behind him. "You should be careful what you say to strangers next time. '*If I ever get my hands on seventy thousand dollars, I'll buy one of those peppy new Tatshu cars*'. Remember you said that? There is only one Tatshu dealership in the area, so we just kept an eye on it." Tammy's hand quickly moved to her bag, but one of the men wrested it from her. Despite Tammy's heated protests, he rummaged through the bag until he found her phone.

"Not quite clever enough, Tammy," Erwin said, smiling. "I think you and I have some unfinished business." Tammy's eyes widened when she saw the mask in Erwin's hand.

"No! Don't! *Help!* Someone help me!"

"You can shout all you like, Tammy. We persuaded Mr. Langford to go for a fifteen minute coffee break. Hold her, Dale, Brian." Erwin held the little mask up in the air, then walked over to Tammy. She was fighting and thrashing her head, but the two had her under control. Without any hesitation Erwin pushed the mask hard against Tammy's face.

"You can be assured of one thing, love," he said. "This time I'm not shooting blanks."

8

"This has to be it." Charlie Ng lowered the binoculars from his eyes and handed them to his mate, Ken Chu. "It's built like a bloody fortress. We'll never get inside. That moat is at least hundred yards wide."

"Going to be tough," Ken agreed. "I can see trip wires. We have to cross that open field first, no protection at all. Look at the floodlights. There could be mines, for all we know. Friendly lot, aren't they?" He handed the binoculars to Monty Chang next to him.

"What do you think they're doing in there?" Monty asked. "It doesn't look like a research center." He passed the binoculars to the last member of their group, Harry Ihsu.

"Brain research, according to Jo," Charlie said. "That's what the old Excalibur place was built for, and this is supposed to be a subsidiary, called Excalibur-Asia."

"It's not called that now," Harry said. At nineteen, he was the youngest of them. "It says *Doyon Enterprises* on the front. Are you sure this is the right place?"

"Got to be," Charlie said. "The GPS coordinates are spot on, and there's nothing else around. Who would want to work or live here?"

"Your grandparents, maybe?" Monty quipped. "Not that long ago all our people lived here."

"No, way," Charlie replied. "My family is from Shanghai. I wonder why they built this place in the middle of now—"

His speech was cut off as Ken placed his hand across Charlie's mouth. The four of them lay motionless, until Ken carefully raised his head and pointed at a small outcrop of rocks and bushes a little further. "I thought I saw something there," he said.

The team had set out two months ago, from a little village called Ionsing, near the ocean, more than four hundred miles back. It was there that a small submarine had dropped them off. They didn't know how Jo had managed to procure a submarine for the Church of Oscar, and they hadn't asked. The four of them had been specially selected because they were young, in good physical shape, and second generation Chinese who spoke Mandarin fluently. For months, they had been trained like spies, to go behind enemy lines and survive. There mission was critically important, yet surprisingly vague. They were to locate a large industrial complex, if it existed. They needed to find a woman, Alison Hu, if she was alive. If she was, they had to recruit her for the Church of Oscar, and then help her set up a commune.

It had been tough going. Though they were dressed like peasants, they had decided to move only at night and hide during the day. They had no identification or communication devices, just a knapsack each with the tools for the job: binoculars, a flashlight and a knife. One of Ken's shoes had a small GPS device built into the heel. In a specially sewn secret pocket in Charlie's knapsack were two masks with Oscar's Breath, ready to be deployed. As far as food and drinks were concerned, they had to forage for themselves. At one stage of their trek they had not eaten for four days. But they had survived, and now they were ready for their most difficult task.

"Must have been an animal," Charlie said, and they sat up again. He looked at the fortress. "Do you think we could kill those floodlights?" he ventured.

"With what?" Ken asked. " Bare hands? And then what? Crawl through a booby trapped field? Why couldn't they have armed us a bit better, for Pete's sake!"

"In case we got caught, I guess," Charlie replied. "Without weapons we could pass for farmers, but if they found arms on us it would be curtains. We do have our knives."

"Sure, big deal," Ken said. "I suggest we try the road."

"Agreed. It's our best bet," Charlie said. "There'll be a gate or something, but at least they wouldn't booby-trap the only way in or out. And we don't have to cross that moat. But we're not going in yet. We'll just lie low for a while and get a good look at—"

The gunshot was loud and offensive in the morning quiet, and they dove for cover. How could they have missed us, Charlie thought. We were perfect targets.

Four men on horseback approached them from the bushes where Ken had heard the noise.

"Don't move!" one of them shouted. "We won't miss twice." Three of the men stayed on their horses, while one, the obvious leader, dismounted. He had a slightly rounded face that betrayed Mongolian heritage. He was dressed in a dark-brown uniform with the words *Doyon Security* on his breast pocket, as well as his name: *Ho Chjin*. Strapped around his body he carried a modern high-powered rifle.

"So what have we here?" Chjin asked, walking over to the four. "What is it this time? Environment? Animal Welfare? Religious fanatics? Always some people who can't leave us alone. Or perhaps you're spies from other companies after our secrets? Well?" It was a northern dialect that Charlie knew, and it was he who answered.

"We are no spies. We have an urgent message for Alison Hu."

Chjin whirled around as if he had been bitten by one of those giant spiders the four men had seen in the area.

"The Head of Doyon Enterprises? *Tamade!*" He spit on the ground in anger. "Why would she speak to peasants like you? What message could you have for her?"

None of them answered, and Chjin nodded. "Ah, yes, of course. No reply. We shall soon fix that." He gestured to one of the guards who had a length of rope looped around his shoulders. The guard dismounted and began to unwind the rope. While the captives watched, Chjin and two of the guards made four noose-like loops in the rope. The third guard stood awkwardly next to his horse, as if he didn't want any part of the process.

132

Chjin roughly pushed the guard to the side and walked over to Charlie. He placed the first noose over his head, then secured it so that Charlie couldn't wriggle free. Next was Harry, then Ken, and finally Monty. The other end of the rope was tied to the leading horse.

"They're gonna kill us, aren't they?" Harry whispered. "Why didn't we fight, damn it!"

"Unarmed against four rifles? Not a chance," Charlie said. "They're not going to kill us, at least not yet. Keep your eye on that lone guard, there is something odd about him."

They could say no more as the guards had mounted again and spurred their horses. Soon they were running for their life behind the galloping horses. If one of them fell, or couldn't keep up, the rope would be pulled taut, the nooses would tighten around their necks and strangle them. Charlie put his hands around the noose, trying to pull it a bit less tight. He was the oldest of them, and he was well trained. But how long could he run at full speed? The complex didn't seem to get any closer. He ran as he'd never ran before, and he heard the others laboring behind them.

Then, as if to give them some respite, the horses slowed down to a mere canter and it was easier to keep up. Obviously, Chjin wanted them alive. They continued at the slower pace until they came to a large drawbridge. While they waited for it to open, the four captives gasped for air after their ordeal. At the other end of the bridge there was a sudden commotion, as the reticent guard took off towards the main building. Chjin and the two other guards continued towards a series of huts. When they came to the last hut in the row, the guards stopped and dismounted. One of them lifted his rifle and aimed it at the prisoners. Chjin roughly removed the nooses and pushed his prisoners into the hut.

It was a storage hut for horse gear. Along the wall hung saddles, stirrups, jodhpurs, and other riding equipment. In the middle of the room stood a wooden horse-like structure, on which saddles could be cleaned or repaired. Chjin picked up a large saddle from the wall and tied it to the structure. Then the three guards walked over to Charlie. One of them grabbed his backpack and threw it in a corner. He tore off Charlie's shirt and trousers, while the other undid his boots. Then they heaved Charlie on the wooden horse and tied him down with his torso on one side, and his legs on the other. Chjin took a thick wooden stick from a workbench. It was about two inches in diameter, the size of a baseball bat, perhaps used to pound leather. He walked over to Charlie, smiling.

"Your last chance. Who are you? Why have you come here?"

"I have a message for Alison Hu," Charlie said again, preparing himself, though not enough. Like a sledgehammer, the baton hit him in the back and he screamed in agony. From the side of the room, Harry, Ken, and Monty watched helplessly, knowing they would be next. Blow after blow rained down on Charlie: on his back, his sides, arms, feet and legs.

"When I get tired, my two friends here will take over," Chjin said merrily. "Just tell us what we want to know." Then a strong female voice filled the room.

"Chjin, have you gone mad? Stop that at once, or you won't wear that uniform again. Don't you think I should be informed if someone has a message for me?"

In the doorway stood a young woman, dressed in a white coat. She was Chinese, but there was also a touch of the West in her. Raven-black hair hung down her shoulders. Behind her stood the fourth guard.

"Oh, Miss Hu. These are obviously industrial spies, trying to steal our secrets. I wanted to find out what they were up to before I called you."

"Untie that poor man at once, you silly fool."

In the ensuing silence, Charlie's agonizing sobs sounded loud and intrusive, while the guards delicately lifted him off the wooden horse. After looking at Charlie for a few seconds, the woman walked over to the three other captives.

"I am Alison Hu, president of Doyon Enterprises. I am sorry for what Chjin has done to your friend. He will be

134

disciplined." She studied the three of them intently for a while, then stood in front of Harry.

"Open your mouth, please." Harry's eyes opened wide in surprise, but he obeyed, and Alison peeked inside his mouth. She repeated the process with Monty and Ken. Then she walked over to Chjin.

"I have only been in here thirty seconds, and I already know more about these people than you do, despite your primitive, medieval methods. These are not industrial spies from our competitors. They are Americans of Chinese origin. I can tell from their build; they have trained very well, but there is still too much fat around their bellies. Their dental work is also very different from ours. We do not use gold crowns, but they still do in North America." Alison walked over to Charlie, who sat in a heap in the corner, still in utter agony.

"This man needs a doctor," she said to the guard beside her. "See to it, Izzo." Alison turned to the three captives. "Izzo is my personal guard," she said. "He told me what happened."

"Keson," she called, and one of the other guards came running. "Show these men to our visitor's quarters. Let them clean themselves up, and give them something to eat. Afterwards tell Izzo to bring them to my office, so we can find out why they have come here."

◊ ◊ ◊

It was the feeling of power. The knowledge that you had all this incredible energy at your fingertips. Just by pressing the mouse button, the engineer made five hundred thousand pounds of aluminum, titanium and steel woosh along the magnetic track that snaked ahead of him, like a black ribbon into eternity. There was absolutely no sensation of movement as the Silver Arrow shot through the Californian landscape on its final push to L.A. Most of the thousand passengers were sound asleep in their beds, bunks, or their folding seats. The Bullet train had all the comforts of home: television and WiFi in every seat, a restaurant, a movie theater, even an exercise and workout facility. All this to alleviate the boredom of the nine-hour journey.

The engineer's name was Alberto Robini. He sat in a spacious, quiet cabin at the head of the train, about eight feet above the ground. It looked like the cockpit of a large airliner. In front of him was a wide panoramic window, with a whole array of dials and gauges below it, like the dashboard of its counterpart in the sky. It had a lot of the same controls: gauges for outside and inside temperatures, air pressure, humidity. There was radar, a large GPS screen, advanced HUD display, and scores of other gauges and readouts, displaying the conditions of the engine and the track ahead. The only control missing was an altimeter.

Technically, an engineer was not required, as the Arrow could run entirely on automatic pilot. Yet the company had given in to public demand for safety, and made sure a human being was always there, to override the computer, if necessary. Absolutely nothing was left to chance. If somewhere along the monorail track even the slightest thing went wrong, be it an obstruction, an animal, or icing in inclement weather, the train would automatically slow down and stop without even the slightest discomfort to its passengers.

Alberto was doing the overnight Washington to L.A. run. He'd left the Capital at nine o'clock sharp, and was due to arrive at the Albert Cowlings Terminal in East L.A. at 5:40 a.m. While the train spat past the outskirts of Riverside, he began to make his preparations to go home. He did as much as he could on the train to save time. First, the log of the trip. Nothing out of the ordinary had happened, so that was easy. Next he checked the instrument readings and marked them down in the log also.

At exactly 5:36, he slowly took his baby into the bay, and when he parked the train exactly one inch in front of the bumpers at the end of the bay, it was 5:40. Behind him the passengers began their usual free-for-all to get out of the train, on their way to whatever the reason was they had come to L.A. It was none of Alberto's concern, and after making sure everything was off, he picked up the logbook, grabbed his totebag and locked the cabin behind him.

He walked down to the company office, checked himself out and headed for the service elevator that would take him down to the crew parking lot. It was very quiet, the day shift had already checked in, and the elevator wouldn't take long. When it arrived, Alberto noticed to his surprise that he wasn't alone. A young man stood in the small cabin. He smiled and nodded.

"Morning."

"Morning."

Alberto pressed the button for the lower parking level and the elevator began its noisy ride down. Halfway between the third and second parking deck, it came to a sudden halt and all the lights went out. Alberto immediately realized something was very wrong, because the emergency lights went out also. He stood in total darkness.

"What the hell?" he said, but there was no response from the other. Alberto felt the first shivers of alarm.

"What do you think happened?" he inquired, hoping the other fellow would at least say something. There was only silence, and Alberto began to feel spooked. "Say, are you all right?" he asked, a bit more forceful. When the other still didn't answer, Alberto took his cell phone from his pocket to call 911. Just his luck to be stuck in an elevator with a weirdo. Before he could make the call, the phone was wrested from his hands.

"Hey! Give it back! Are you crazy?"

Then Alberto saw a tiny cone of red laser light moving around, and his first thought was that he was going to be shot. He tried to stay out of the range of the light, then noticed there were two lights, about three inches apart, and he realized what was happening. Whoever was in the elevator with him was wearing infrared night goggles. This was way past crazy!

137

"OK, hold on. Slow down. Let's talk. What do you want?" The lights were shifting around and Alberto had no idea where the other was. It was like playing a game of cat and mouse, but the cat could see and the mouse couldn't. Sudden anger filled Alberto, and he thrashed out at the lights, missing completely. Then he felt two hard bumps against the back of his knees and he fell down on the elevator floor, his tote bag flying noisily through the elevator cabin. Before he could get up, his assailant was straddling him, and he was pinned against the floor, both hands secured under the other's knees. Then the man finally spoke.

"Don't be afraid, Alberto. You will not be harmed, and it will only take a few minutes. You will feel much better afterwards. Trust me." From the corner of his eyes Alberto stared at the two red lights above him. They looked like two hot coals from hell, and seemed to burn right into his skull. Then it was suddenly darker than ever, and something was pushed against Alberto's mouth and nose. He could not breathe.

Alberto was not a big man, but he thought he was in good shape. He tried to struggle and push the other off, but his attacker felt like a deadweight on his chest and arms. He tried to turn his head sideways to force the mask off, but his assailant pushed it to the floor. Then the man spoke again.

"It would be better if you didn't fight it, Alberto."

"How . . . how do you know my name?" Alberto mumbled through the mask, trying to push the knees off his arms, so that he could at least try to defend himself. But all he felt was the dead weight of the other's body and he couldn't move a muscle.

"Why are you doing this?" he croaked, trying not to breath the stuff that the mask forced into his nostrils. It felt slightly acrid, but didn't hurt. He was getting very tired. What was happening to him? He desperately moved his head to the left and right, trying to kick up his knees at the same time, but it was all in vain.

He was getting weaker and weaker, and finally gave up and took a few deep breaths. He began to feel light-headed, as if he was hyper-ventilating. All energy left him, and he lay back, no longer struggling. After a few more minutes, the man lifted the mask from Alberto's face, and he could breathe again.

"There. It's all over, Alberto. You are one of us now. This is the luckiest day of your life."

"No, it isn't," Alberto retorted, trying to get up in the dark. "What have you done to me? You're a lunatic, and I'll get you for this."

Then the lights went on again and he had a good look at his assailant. The man was about twenty-five, handsome, dressed in slacks and a sports jacket. He didn't look at all like a robber, or someone on drugs. He actually smiled at him, and even stuck out his hand.

"Hi, I'm Erwin. I apologize for what I did, but it was necessary. How are you feeling?"

Alberto reflected. What was going on? His thinking was all screwed up. He knew he should be livid, hit the other, kick the shit out of him for what he had done, but he couldn't. He looked at the younger man, who really seemed a nice-looking kind of chap, not a punk or anything. He shook his head as if to clear his confused mind, and finally shook the other's hand.

"Alberto Robini. But you already know that. What have you done to me and why? What do you mean, one of us? Who is us?"

"All your questions will be answered soon, Alberto." Erwin pushed the L-2 button on the elevator panel and they started moving again.

"Who is us?" Alberto repeated.

"We are the Church of Oscar. You have been selected."

"What? That can't be. The people in that commune were killed long ago."

"Not everyone, Alberto. A few were saved, and we are rebuilding. We need people like you."

There was a sudden shock, as the elevator halted at the L-2 level and the doors opened. Erwin stepped out, but Alberto hesitated.

"They'll lock you up for this, you know. Grievous bodily assault and intimidation."

"So why aren't you running for the cops, Alberto?"

While he stepped out of the elevator, Alberto asked himself the same question and he couldn't find an answer. Something inside him wanted Erwin to pay for what he had done, but the feeling of revenge was draining away by the second, as if his mind had sprung an emotional leak.

"So what's going to happen now?" he asked. "I could sure do with a coffee or something."

Erwin took Alberto's cell phone from his pocket and handed it back to him. "All right. Here's what we'll do, Alberto. You call Amanda, that lovely wife of yours, and tell her you are doing a double shift today, to get some overtime. You've done that plenty of times before and it's not just for the money, is it? I know your girlfriend's name in D.C., but if you cooperate Amanda will never hear about her."

Alberto stared at Erwin, flushed. "How do know so much about me?"

Erwin shrugged. "Oh, just research. Come on, call her, and then we'll go for breakfast. It's on me, and I'll tell you all about our organization." Alberto quickly phoned his wife, and after he ended the call, he suddenly smiled at Erwin. "You know, breakfast sounds great, I'm starving. It's crazy, but everything feels so different all of a sudden. I'm not even worried about my affair anymore. Whatever you did to me, I feel great, man!"

"Didn't I tell you?" Erwin said. "Let's go. Where's your car?"

◊ ◊ ◊

On the fourth floor of the opulent Doyon building, Alison Hu sat in her chair facing the window that overlooked the barren, tundra-like landscape as far as the eye could see. It wasn't a very exciting view in the first place, but this time Alison wasn't looking outside at all. She was staring at a photograph on her desk and thought about the three American men who would soon be shown into her office. Why now? Almost forty years later? And why where they dressed like farmers? It didn't make any sense.

The photograph showed a middle-aged woman with a striking resemblance to Alison. Though older, the face showed the same jaw line, the same delicate shape of the nose and the same dark-brown eyes and pitch-black hair. It looked like an older version of Alison, which, in effect, it was. Alison Hu, twenty-five, President of Doyon Enterprises was a clone, created from a single cell of the late Alison Hu, who had started Excalibur-Asia. While looking at the photograph, Alison allowed her mind to flash back to the stories her mother had told her, about a time before she herself was created.

Thirty-four years ago, the first Alison Hu had arrived in Ying San from the United States with a large amount of money and great plans to build a mind research facility on the site that now housed Doyon Enterprises. Part of her cash was immediately diverted into the various pockets and palms of people of the central and local governments, long before the first shovel of earth was moved. Permits had to be issued, contractors hired, plans approved. Everything went smoother with money.

Alison Hu took charge of the planning and preparation of Excalibur-Asia, and shortly afterwards construction began. It would be a modern, six-storey high building, with laboratories, freezers, a state-of-the-art computer center, and facilities for the staff.

When the research center was near completion, Alison became apprehensive. All those years, she had heard nothing from Dr. Kozak. He had given her carte blanche, as far as

141

money and time went, and told her to communicate only with him. Why wasn't he responding to her messages? It didn't make sense. The center was soon to be staffed and opened, and she needed Dr. Kozak to come over and look after it. She sent him another urgent message, asking him to come to Ying San. To her dismay and annoyance there was again no reply.

Alison had disliked her boss from the moment he took control of Excalibur. She found him overbearing, sarcastic and secretive. She was in charge of Supplies and Equipment at Excalibur at the time. It wasn't the best job in town, but she was willing to learn and climb the corporate ladder, just like anyone else. She did her best and hoped for a chance to improve herself. And she soon found out that there was something about Dr. Kozak that wasn't quite kosher. She didn't know what, but she didn't trust him.

Then, to her surprise, she was suddenly given the opportunity to go to China and set up a research center there. She suspected that for some reason her boss had wanted her out of the way, and she had almost refused, but after some soul searching she had accepted. After all, it was a challenge and a fantastic promotion. Yet after the building was constructed, somewhere in the back of her mind Alison knew that something was very wrong. Why was Dr. Kozak not responding?

Around this time she was visited by an official delegation of dignitaries from Beijing who made her a surprising offer. Since Excalibur-Asia had stood idle for a while, the government was wondering if the building was up for sale. Doyon Enterprises, one of the largest conglomerates in China, manufacturing houses, trains, weapons, and more, wanted to set up a new subsidiary, specializing in genetic engineering and human cloning. It was in desperate need for a new facility. Could they perhaps buy the new research center?

It was a dilemma for Alison. She could certainly use the money. Most of her original funding had been used up, and no new money was coming in. But selling Excalibur-Asia was not her decision. While she decided what to do, mulling over

142

the pros and cons, she received a phone call from Beijing that changed everything. Two American marshals had arrived with a subpoena for her to testify at a court hearing in America. Dr. Kozak had died, and was accused of fraud and treason.

Fearing the worst, Alison told the marshals that she had absolutely no inclination to come to the United States, and since she had become a Chinese citizen long ago, there was nothing they could do about it. She immediately explained the situation to Doyon's Board of Directors, and a week later the Chinese government nationalized Excalibur-Asia and Doyon Enterprises moved in. There was one particular clause in the takeover agreement: Alison was to be on the company's Board of Directors.

After the building was updated and modified to suit Doyon's needs, the company was ready to begin human cloning. Alison found it a fascinating science. Comparing the latest methods of human cloning to the reproductive cloning of the first cloned sheep, Dolly, was like comparing the latest quantum computer to the first monster size computers of the mid 20th century. Great progress had been made, and the somatic cell nuclear transfers were a thing of the past.

Alison's husband, Jonathan Hu, tired of waiting for a family, had long left her for the more socially acceptable environment of the big city, Beijing. Alison knew she'd left it a bit late to have children the normal way, as she was forty-five and without any suitable candidates for marriage. Here was a chance to have a child without pain and troubles and a very special child at that. She was accepted as a donor and the cloning process worked flawlessly. After the required eight months gestation time in the artificial incubator, a new Alison Hu entered the world.

From the start, the two Alison's were inseparable, and as she grew up little Alison learned everything from her mother. She didn't need any schooling, or private tutors or nannies; her mother supplied her with all the knowledge she would ever need. There was an emotional bond between them unlike any other bond between two humans.

Apart from general knowledge, Alison also confided her personal and most private thoughts to her daughter. Is was like pouring out one's soul to oneself. She told her about Excalibur, about America, and Yabul Kozak, and his betrayal. She also told little Alison about her worst fear—that one day people from America would come to take back everything she had worked for.

Luckily it had not happened during the older Alison's lifetime. At age sixty-five, she had a stroke and two weeks later she was gone, despite the best medical treatment Doyon could provide. After a small period of intense grief, the new young Alison followed in her mother's footsteps and progressed rapidly through the company, until she ended up as the President at age twenty-five. For years everything had gone well, and Alison had almost forgotten her mother's warning. Now the Americans were here, and she was very ill at ease. She had felt sorry for the one who was hurt. Had she allowed her emotions to cloud her judgment by treating them like guests, instead of first finding out why they had come?

A series of short knocks on the door shook her out of her reverie. That would be Izzo with the visitors. "Come in," she called out, glad the matter would soon be settled.

When the three Americans walked in, there was no sign of Izzo, and Alison knew she had made a terrible mistake. One of the men carried Izzo's gun and aimed it at her. She was furious at her own stupidity. How could she have been so careless?

"I allowed you to freshen up and fed you, and this is how you thank me?" she asked, as fear, coupled with anger, spread through her. "Have you killed Izzo, and am I next in line? You won't get away with this, and Chjin will make sure your deaths will be long and painful."

One of the men approached her. He was carrying some kind of mask in his hand, and smiled at her. "There is no reason for concern, Miss Hu. You are not in any danger, and your guard is unharmed. We are members of the Church of Oscar and we have come to save you."

144

9

"You quit? With only four more years to go?" Heather Cramer stood at the kitchen sink, rinsing spinach in a colander. The olive-color skin of her slightly oval face had hardly any wrinkles, despite her fifty-seven years. The dark-brown eyes that had so enchanted Tom from the day they had met, showed surprise and just a touch of annoyance.

When they had married, Tom and Heather made a pact that they would never get angry at each other. It had held through twenty-three years of marriage, but this time Cramer knew he had pushed his luck. Though Heather didn't seem outwardly angry, he noticed the small signs. The frown, cutting through her otherwise perfect forehead. The hands that suddenly stopped tossing the salad and put the colander down just a little too hard. Still, it was probably the combination of worrying about his job and her mother's condition. Rose Paring wasn't very well; she was eighty-three and a diabetic with circulatory problems. On top of that she had Alzheimer's. She lived in Minneapolis, Minnesota.

"I'm sorry, Heather, I had to make a decision that I couldn't live with."

"What does that mean, exactly?" Heather asked, sitting down at the table with him. "Do you want a drink?"

"Do I ever."

She stood up and walked over to one of the kitchen cabinets and opened it. A half-full bottle of Barlett's Five Star brandy stood on the shelf. She took two glasses from the cupboard above the sink and poured just a touch into one glass and a liberal amount into the other. She gave Tom the latter, and he accepted gratefully.

"I've got to take it easy," she said, pointing at her own glass. "It's my bridge afternoon and I don't want to get sloshed before I even start. So what could you not live with?"

"A transfer. Pittard is closing the station down and wanted me to move to Beverly Hills. A nice, cushy job he called it. A shoe-in for an easy retirement."

"Why didn't you take it? Couldn't you have managed it for four years?"

"Have you ever tried to do something you hate for four long years, Heather? It would be like a prison sentence. That part of L.A. county is almost crime free these days. It is a large gated community for the very rich. I called it babysitting and Pittard didn't like that. But that's what it is. It would go against everything I've always lived for. And something else. There's talk about the government introducing RFID implants for everyone living in the big cities. They've already started in Washington. I don't like that idea at all, so I declined."

"No chance to fight the closure? What if everyone gets together? Couldn't you stop it?"

"I don't think so. People are scared, and tired. They have lost any confidence in the system and don't want to rock the boat. I'll get seventy-five percent of my pension. Some of the other guys will get nothing."

"So I'll have you around the house all day long?"

She said it with a twinkle in her eye, and Tom knew the worst was over. His wife stood behind him, and he loved her for it. She had been a detective with the force, but when Penny was born Heather had given up her job to look after their daughter.

"Don't worry," he said, "I'll find a way to stay out of your hair. I think I'll do some private investigating so I can set my own rules, instead of having to kowtow to someone else." Cramer took a swig of his brandy.

"You know, the whole world is upside down these days," he said after a while. "We used to go after the villains and protect ordinary people. Now it's reversed. The police protect the rich because they're paying their wages, and to hell with the poor people. There's no middle class anymore. Either you're with the rich, or you're in the ditch. Simple as that. Imagine, an area the site of Greater Santa Barbara with no

146

local police protection. It's insanity. They'll have to reverse it, and keep at least a small place open. But that's Pittard's problem. I have a long list at work of people who disappeared without a trace. Every time someone reported a missing person, I dutifully added it to that list. That was the end of it. No action was ever taken, and the whole thing is a complete waste of time. Nobody speaks for the people anymore. Well, maybe I should." He took another sip of brandy. "What do you think? Am I right? Or just an out-of-touch dinosaur?"

"Of course you're right," Heather said. "But I don't know how you're going to do it all on your own without the resources of the force behind you. Are you planning to get a PI license?"

"Perhaps later. I'll start off as a concerned citizen and see how it goes. I'll be doing a lot of computing and Internet stuff, so we've got to get a new computer. The old one is way too slow. I'll go to some of those social sites: Friends For Ever and Secret Springs. These missing people all have relatives, friends, lovers, acquaintances. Someone must now something."

"A lot of people join that Church of Oscar," Heather said. "Did you know that's the fastest growing church ever? They say it'll eventually be bigger than the Roman Catholic church. Can you believe it?

"It's a secretive place," Cramer said. "Once you're in, you don't come out. At least that how it seems. That place on the old Excalibur site is a fortress. And they don't talk to the outside. Can't really blame them after what happened to their old commune."

"Well, whatever you do, be careful," Heather said. "I've got to get ready. Dinner is done, so when I come home all we have to do is heat it up." She reached over and kissed him, then disappeared into the bedroom.

◊ ◊ ◊

Alberto Robini walked through the giant station hall on his way to the Silver Arrow that was waiting for him to be driven to Washington, D.C. He was early, because he had an extra chore to do this time. He hummed along to the music that a rock band gave out in a large number of decibels. The Bullet terminal was much more than just a station: it had shops of all kinds, recreational and exercise facilities, and also a large entertainment area, run by the Secret Springs Social Network. Here, the public could enjoy 3D movies, concerts, or any kind of entertainment.

This time, a rock band from the Ukraine, the *Volhyns*, gave a virtual performance. Many of the waiting people sat in easy chairs, watching the show. Alberto didn't know any of the songs, and he didn't care for either the Ukraine or its rock band, but he tried to hum with the music anyway. The concert looked extremely realistic, as if the singers and musicians were performing live on the stage. Since they were only holograms, Alberto could have driven his train right through the band without hurting anyone.

He entered the restricted door that led to the company's office. It was a large room with four partitions, like an old-fashioned newspaper office. He walked to the desk and smiled at the young girl behind it, while he signed the log. He grabbed his tote bag, headed out of the backdoor towards the tracks and walked along the busy platform to his cabin in front of the train.

Alberto was in a good mood, knowing that joining the Church of Oscar had been the best thing that had ever happened to him, despite the strange way in which it was done. He was a new person, focused, alert, without any worries. As part of the recruitment deal, he would visit the church in Santa Barbara once a week, to learn and understand what was required of him.

On his first visit, he mentioned to Councilor Johnson that his feelings for his wife, and his mistress for that matter, had changed. Erwin had sympathized and said it was the result of his new outlook on life. The most elegant thing to do was recruit his wife and mistress also. Alberto had followed the church's advice and it had worked out fine. He, his wife Amanda, and Nataly in D.C., shared an important new goal in life: spreading the Word of Oscar and saving the planet. On his next trip to the church a week later, he had received his first mission which he was about to execute.

After Alberto settled in his engine cab, he began his start-up routine. He checked all the gauges, to make sure everything was working: the cabin lights, air conditioning, thermostats and the backup batteries. He opened his log, and marked down the time and number of his trip, the 10:45 to D.C. When he had checked everything, he reached for his bag and placed it on the floor next to the panel for the electrical controls.

Security was fairly strict on the Bullet train, but Alberto had worked for the company for more than twelve years and the security agents all knew him and didn't bother to check him most of the time. Had they done so today, they might have wondered why Alberto carried a length of thick vinyl tubing in his bag, as well as two thermos flasks instead of one.

Alberto reached over and locked his cabin door, just in case. Then he removed the cover of the electrical control panel. It showed a series of gauges and dials, where he could set the temperature, humidity and pressure of the cabin air. There was also a regulator that adjusted the ratio of fresh and recycled air. It was connected to a powerful compressor that blew the air through the train cabins. Everything was programmed automatically but, as the train's engineer, Alberto could override it.

He began by turning the regulator to the setting for recycled air only. Next, he had to replace the line that connected the regulator output to the compressor. He had to loosen several clamps that held the tubing in place but he had the tools, so it was easy.

He carefully removed the existing line and lay it to the side. He measured a length of new one-inch tubing, cut it in half and inserted the Y-joint he had brought with him. Next he connected one side of the new line to the regulator valve, and the other end to the compressor intake, making sure he tightened both clamps securely. Finally, he cut off a another length of tubing and connected the last Y connection to a small black thermos. Luckily, there was a space to the left of the regulator, and he carefully placed the thermos inside the control compartment. It was perfect.

There was one more unusual item in his tote bag: a small digital player. He would hook it up to the train's intercom system and play its message as soon as the drug from the thermos bottle had mixed with the air supply. Alberto had no idea what the message was and he wasn't curious. It was none of his business.

After he connected the player to the sound system, he carefully replaced the panel cover and looked at his watch. Still time left for a quick coffee. He unscrewed his regular thermos and poured himself a cup. He decided to activate the drug around one third into the trip, in the mid-Western plains were the train would reach its top speed on the longest stretch between two stations.

At exactly 10:45, Alberto pushed his chair in front of the control console. He checked the video screens that showed him the platform and the entire train. When he was sure all the doors were closed properly, he clicked his mouse on the first of a series of numbers, and the train began to move. They were on their way.

◊ ◊ ◊

It was a glorious Sunday afternoon. Sitting in easy lawn chairs on the back patio of Excalibur, the church councilors were enjoying tea with butter tarts and scones. It was a party in honor of Jo's fiftieth birthday. The morning had started rather auspiciously, when forty-eight people had joined the church—a record for one day. It had perhaps partly been due to the outstanding sermon by Father Dubois, their new religious leader.

150

Gilbert Dubois was a big, robust man of forty-three. He was from Montreal, Canada. Helin Sparling had recruited him while he was visiting New York, and since her commune already had a spiritual guidance councilor, Helin had suggested that Dubois would be a good candidate to replace the late Father English. Jo had agreed, and soon after Gilbert had arrived in Santa Barbara. Though he came from a very different religious background than Father English, Dubois soon proved himself to be just as staunch a believer in the Church of Oscar's mission as his predecessor had been.

The afternoon was quiet and peaceful. It was a welcome change from the noise and dust of the last few weeks, as earthmovers, small bulldozers, and tractors had been busy clearing and leveling an area at the back of the property, to reclaim more fertile land from the wilderness.

Excalibur was bursting at the seams. The commune had more than five hundred members, and the original research center had never been designed to house that many people. Extensions and improvements had helped, but the councilors knew that the facility had reached its limit. Helin Sparling's commune was flourishing near New York City, and new communes were being set up in Denver and Chicago. For Jo it was a time of reflection.

"I think we should all be tremendously grateful for what we have accomplished," he said, holding his teacup and saucer on his lap. "And to know that it all started here, right on this patio."

"How do you mean, Jo?" Sylvia queried. "We started off in Bernard Tows' barn, didn't we?"

"Ah, yes," Jo agreed. "But I have studied Excalibur's history, Sylvia. On this patio, about thirty years ago, Thomas Gallagan, heir to the Gallagan billions, was stung by a wasp. A relatively minor incident for a healthy person, it was fatal to Thomas, because he suffered from epilepsy. So think about it, Sylvia. Without that wasp sting, Thomas might have lived for many more years, and Philip Gallagan probably would not have built the Excalibur Mind Research Center. Yabul Kozak

151

would not have created his mind-altering drug, and the Church of Oscar might never have been founded. Makes you wonder how everything is connected, doesn't it?"

"Oh, I don't know, Jo," Erwin said. "You can explain everything that way. Who can tell for sure what causes what? Yabul was a genius and he would most likely have found another way to bring his ideas to the world. I mean, where does it all end? You could even argue that the Lord ordered the wasp to sting Thomas, in order to create our church."

"This is turning into a crass, blasphemous case of second-guessing our Lord," Father Gilbert Dubois said. "You should know better, Councilors. Can we change the subject, please."

"I only wanted to—" Erwin said, but Jo cut him short.

"My fault totally, Gilbert, I am sorry, I got carried away. Let's not ruin a perfectly fantastic day. By the way, where is Bert Kwiss?"

"In the lab most likely," Carol said. "He practically lives there these days."

"Why? Is there a problem with the production of Oscar's Breath?"

"I don't know, he hasn't mentioned it. He knows we're celebrating your birthday, so he'll probably show up sooner or later. You know what he is like. Once he gets into something he forgets all about time."

"Talking about Oscar's Breath, Jo," Father Dubois said. "We really ought to think about how we're going to distribute it. Both Duval and Helin Sparling have only one little flask of it, and now we have communes in Denver and Chicago, and more planned. Every time we send a courier with the Breath there is a chance that something will go wrong."

"Yes, Daniel was worried about that also," Jo replied. "It does pose a problem."

"I think I have arrived at the right time," a high-pitched voice joined the conversation. Bert Kwiss stood there, looking disheveled, his hair all tousled, his lab coat creased and dirty.

But his tired looking face showed a wide smile. "Happy Birthday, Jo. Sorry I'm late, but I have exciting news."

"Bert! Sit yourself down, and thanks for coming," Jo beamed. "What's this about?"

Bert Kwiss was sixty-five, and many years of looking through a microscope had given him a slightly stooped appearance. He was not very tall, and his head hung down slightly as if he was continually looking at his shoes. He didn't sit down, but produced a small bag of white powder from his lab coat pocket and held it up for everyone to see.

"This little bag, my friends, is the equivalent of five hundred bottles of the Breath," he said. "One pouch, the size of a brick, will supply our church for years."

There was absolute silence, while everyone considered the implications. Erwin was the first to react. "You crystallized it?"

"Yes. It's similar to what happened in the old days, when people transported milk in huge containers," Bert said. "Someone cleverly realized it was much more cost-effective to transport milk powder and add the water later. Oscar's Breath is a little more complicated, of course. This powder does not dissolve in water and it needs a special activator. Something like this." He took a small vial with a clear liquid from his coat pocket and held the two items in front of him.

"Powder and a catalyst. Mix them together and you create Oscar's Breath, ready to be used."

"Brilliant, absolutely brilliant, Bert," Jo exclaimed. "That'll take care of our shipping problems."

"Just a minute now," Father Dubois said, frowning. "Isn't shipping white powder dangerous? You know how paranoid the government is about drugs, and don't forget the drug cartels. If we start transporting that white stuff we'll be in mega trouble on two fronts."

"Uh, uh." Bert Kwiss shook his head. "No, Father, not at all. There is a major difference between Oscar's Breath and other drugs. What makes the drug trade so lucrative? The fact that drugs are addictive. It's repeat business. You need more and more of the stuff. Not so with Oscar's Breath. One small bag per church? You can hardly call that a drug trade."

"Well, Bert this is fantastic news," Jo said.

"There is more, Jo," Bert continued. "I have basically turned Oscar Breath into a binary drug. The white powder is harmless and inert; you could eat it if you wanted to. Similarly, the propellant. With the proper tools, the powder could perhaps be analyzed, but you would still need the catalyst to activate it. If we ship the two items separately, Oscar's Breath will be completely safe."

"Diane, please, bring two bottles of blackberry wine," Jo called out. "This is an important milestone in the church's history and we need to celebrate."

◊ ◊ ◊

"Has anyone seen the boss?" Joanna Radcliff stuck her head around the cafeteria door. About six staff members looked up, but most shook their heads and went back to their lunch.

"Try his VR room," a short, buxom young woman suggested. "That's where I would go if I didn't want to be found." Her nervous giggle followed Joanna into the hallway, as she marched back to her office, muttering. Being a secretary to Philip Kozak was like being a zookeeper in charge of a tiger. She never knew where he was, and whether he was going to purr or growl when she finally found him.

She sat down behind her desk. It was clean and uncluttered. Her laptop, a notebook, a tray with pens, paper-clips and staples, her phone, and a picture of her husband John and their two kids, Irvin and Pandora. Filing cabinets and bookshelves lined one side of the room. On the other side, between a rubber plant and a small tank with tropical fish, a large window overlooked the Atrium. To her right was the door to Philip's office. It was closed.

It was 2:30, half an hour left before Philip's meeting with the representatives of Q-computers, who were going to show their latest computer models. Philip needed reminding of everything, especially lately. He'd been in a real bad temper the last few days, definitely a growl period.

Joanna didn't mind her boss's occasional mood swings. She loved her job. Being Philip's secretary put her ahead of all the other secretaries and it had its perks. A good salary. An office with a view. Deferential nods from the security people at the entrance.

2:45.This was getting serious. Could he have met someone and forgotten the time? Philip sometimes had lunch at a cute little café in the Atrium. She could actually see it from her window. She reached over to pick up her phone and punched in the number.

"This is Philip Kozak's secretary. Is he there? Could I speak to him for a moment?"

She listened attentively. "Hasn't been in today? OK, that's fine. Thanks." She hung up. Where had he gone? She stood up and cautiously entered her boss's office, as if she expected him to leap at her from behind the door. The office was empty and seeing the vacant chair and clean desk, Joanna's annoyance turned to apprehension. Had Philip gone away without telling her? Surely he would remember an important meeting with Q-computers. There was only one other place she could look, but even thinking about it gave her goose bumps.

Philip let her run the office the way she wanted, and she was grateful for that. But there was one thing he had been adamant about, when he had chosen her from six other applicants. Under no circumstances was she ever to enter his VR room without his permission. It was his holiest-of-holy places. She had never broken that rule. What if she went inside and just at that moment Philip would walk in the door? She'd be out of a job. The sudden ringing of the phone made her jump. Philip? It was the security guard at the entrance downstairs. The delegation of Q-computers had arrived to see her boss. Could he come down and meet them, please?

"No, please, wait. Mr. Kozak isn't in yet, but don't tell them that. Just make them comfortable for a few minutes."

Standing up straight, Joanna Radcliff straightened her white blouse and tucked it into her dark pants. She suddenly needed to go to the bathroom. No time! This was an emergency. She drew a deep breath and walked towards Philip's VR room. It was locked. What was going on? He never locked it when he was inside. She walked back to her desk and took the spare key from her desk drawer. She unlocked the door and stepped inside. It was pitch dark.

She fumbled for the light switch and light flooded from the ceiling. Then, standing there, staring at the VR platform, Joanna knew her life would never be the same. Her boss lay on the platform and he wasn't moving.

A rational thought pierced her mind, like a lighthouse beam on a stormy, dark night. Her boss had just been tired and fallen asleep. If anything had happened, the Failsafe alarm would have sounded. She cautiously nudged him.

"Mr. Kozak, wake up, please! You've got an important meeting."

There was no movement, and Joanna walked to the computer control panel. What she saw scared her even more. The Failsafe control had been turned off! She ran back to Philip and turned him over. Two unseeing eyes stared at her and when she felt for his pulse there was none and his skin was cold. She felt bile coming up her throat and ran to the bathroom in the office and retched. She splashed cold water on her face, ran to the phone and called security.

"Joanna Radcliff here. Come quickly! There has been a terrible accident."

10

It was hard to believe that Jo had never been inside Los Angeles International Airport. In his younger days, before the Church of Oscar, there had never been a reason for him to go there. Flying was outrageously expensive, even then, and it had steadily worsened. His family never went anywhere, except locally by car. Jo wasn't quite sure what to expect, but he wasn't prepared for what he saw when the church's armored van reached the airport site.

"What's all this?" he asked, pointing at a large settlement of tents and lean-to's made with cardboard, wooden boards, and sheet metal.

One of the guards who had recently joined the church, moved closer to Jo, so that he could hear him above the noise of the engine.

"This used to be the parking lot for the airport years ago," he said. "Huge lots for personal cars, rentals and freight. When flying took a nosedive, this became an empty waste land. Soon the homeless moved in, and now it's just one large ghetto. The authorities don't like it and tried to move them, but the people just kept coming back. Finally the city put up huge fences all around, allowing two lanes for airport traffic."

"What do these people do all day?" Jo asked, floored by what he saw. "Do they work?"

"Some do," the young guard replied. "The lucky ones, who have identity cards. Most of the others are oblivious on drugs. At night they come alive and roam the country side, looking for money and blood."

They reached the central airport location and parked in a small parking lot. Inside the building, the small Arrivals hall looked like a dead zone. Jo looked at a TV monitor and saw there were only two flights that day. The weekly Air United flight from London, England, scheduled to arrive several hours later, and a private flight from Ying San in China that was due to land in about twenty minutes. Jo walked over to a nearby bench and sat down. A few minutes later Erwin joined him. "I don't understand it, Jo. Why is Alison Hu coming here? Isn't she supposed to form a commune in China?"

Jo nodded. "Something must have gone wrong. It was a long shot, anyway. All we had to go on was what Carol knew about Alison Hu, and that was a long time ago."

Through the observation windows they could see a tiny speck in the azure blue sky, growing rapidly. They stood up and walked to the window. Out on the tarmac, two men rolled a stairway out of a hangar. They watched while the speck turned into a small sleek executive jet. It had the company name in Chinese lettering, and also in English. *Doyon Enterprises.*

Once it had landed, the plane taxied to the terminal and the ground crew moved the stairway into position. The door hinged open and one man stepped out, walked down the steps, and waited at the bottom. Then a young woman, dressed in a long white coat that contrasted with her raven-black hair, stepped graciously down the stairway, like a queen on a state visit. Next, three young men walked down.

"Our Ambassadors!" Erwin shouted. "Look, there's Ken, Harry and Monty, but I don't see Charlie. Isn't that woman a bit young, Jo?"

"Yes, she is. She must be the wrong person."

All five passengers, accompanied by a waiting U.S. Immigration official disappeared into the building. Nervously Jo and Erwin returned to their seats. It might take a while. Jo had no idea how he was going to handle the unforeseen problem of a mixed-up identity. To their surprise, it took less than five minutes. The door to the restricted area hissed open, and there were the three ambassadors, all seemingly in good shape.

"Be careful what you say," Jo whispered. "We don't know what happened over there."

They quickly hurried over to the others, and it was a happy reunion. Then Jo turned to the lady in the white coat.

"I'm Joachim Rasnell, leader of the Church of Oscar. Welcome to our country." He stuck out his hand.

"Alison Hu," the woman said, shaking his hand. "Pleased to meet you. This is my assistant, Izzo. You have arranged for transportation to your commune?"

"I have indeed," Jo said. "A quick word privately, if I may, please, Mrs. Hu?"

"Certainly. It is Miss, Councilor." They walked back to the waiting area and sat down, away from the others. Jo clasped his hands together, trying to find the right words.

"I'm sorry, Miss Hu," he said. "I think there has been a mistake. I do not believe you are the right Alison Hu."

Alison's eyebrows shot up above her beautifully made up eyes. "I am sorry, I don't . . ." Then her face broke into a wide smile. "Of course. I'm supposed to be much older, right? About seventy? That was my mother, Councilor Rasnell. She died a while ago."

"I am sorry," Jo said, much relieved. "How stupid of me. But may I ask why you have come here? The plan was for you to set up a branch of the Church of Oscar in China."

"That will take a bit of explaining, Councilor. Can it perhaps wait till we get to the commune?"

"Of course. Just one more thing. What happened to our fourth Ambassador?"

"Unfortunately he was badly beaten by one of my security men. He is alive in hospital, but healing will take some time, I'm afraid. Don't worry, he receives excellent care, and will be returned when he has recovered."

"Thank you for that. Shall we go?"

It was a bit crowded in the armored vehicle, but soon everyone was seated and they started their return trip. And it wasn't long before Erwin asked the question that had burned on his tongue.

"Harry, how on earth did you get past immigration? You had no papers."

"No papers? What do you call these?" Harry proudly showed off a small booklet. "Official Chinese government issued passport. I work for Doyon Enterprises now, thanks to Miss Hu. By the way, Jo, you can relax, Izzo is one of us."

In Excalibur, Jo managed to corner Alison by herself once more, while Izzo and two guards took the suitcases to her room.

"Miss Hu . ."

"Please call me Alison, Councilor."

"Very well, Alison. We have arranged drinks and a banquet in your honor, followed by a closed council meeting. I know you have many questions about our church, but could you please hold your curiosity until the council meeting afterwards? It would make things easier for both of us."

She gave him a coy smile. "Skeletons in the church's closet, Councilor?"

"Not at all," Jo replied. "A business and a church may be two different kettles of fish, but they have at least one thing in common. Wouldn't you want to make your company decisions in the boardroom, rather than in the staff cafeteria?"

She gave a throaty laugh. "Touché, Councilor. I shall honor your wish."

◊ ◊ ◊

Run, run. Don't stop, don't think. Get it out of your system. Why did he do it? Why did he switch off the Failsafe? Why? Breathing hard with the effort, Jennifer Higman sprinted past the virtual version of her old high school in Madison, Wisconsin. It was an ugly old building, well over a hundred years old by now. It had dark brown shiplap siding and two rows of windows in the front. The building was dark and there was nobody inside.

To her right lay the recreational field were she had played hockey in her younger days. Disappearing under her fast moving sneakers was the composite gravel surface of the virtual running track. She'd been around three times already and her body was screaming for a break, but she kept going. If she stopped she would have to face it again—Philip's body on the gurney in the morgue. The image was etched in her mind, like a number burned into a cow's flesh. *Run, run . . .* Against her will, her mind flashed back to the scene.

"Quite common, you know," the pathologist had said. "It's like trapeze artists doing their high-wire acts. Some of them don't want safety nets. It gives them the extra thrill."

"No, Philip wasn't like that," she had said, staring at her lover's lifeless body. "Please don't cut him open."

"Hey, look here, lady, don't interfere, OK? He died a suspicious death, and I have to do an autopsy. Are you family?"

"No, I'm his . . . I'm a good friend. I'm Jennifer Higman and I worked with him."

"Well, Jennifer, I'm very sorry, but you shouldn't be here. Please go home and let me do my job. Otherwise, I'm afraid I'll have to call security."

"I'll go, but tell me what happened. I have to know. How did he die?"

"Literally scared himself to death. We call it the DAS syndrome, death from acute stress. I looked at the latest virtscape he was using. Climbing the Matterhorn, he lost his footing and fell. It wasn't a real fall of course, but it was so realistic that his mind believed it was real. He thought he was going to die and he did. I'm sure I won't find anything wrong with his body, but I've got to check it anyway."

"How awful!" She'd started crying and had ran out of the medical clinic.

Run, run, run . . . Don't cry, don't think, don't do anything. Just run. She'd attached a purple flag to her avatar. She didn't want to be disturbed by any one, for any reason. The track all around her was empty. *Got a stitch! Never mind . . . Keep going.* Someone else had shut off the Failsafe, had to be. Charles perhaps, or that creep Armonde. She'd kill him!

She was on her fifth round, and as her body told her in no uncertain terms, also her last, when the air in front of her

161

suddenly shimmered and another avatar popped up. Damn! She filled her lungs ready for a shouting match, with whomever it was who had ignored her warning. Someone was going to have his Secret Springs privileges revoked!

Then her legs suddenly gave out and she stumbled, while her knees buckled. She barely managed to avoid the other runner who quickly grabbed her to stop her from falling. When she finally came to a halt, she put her hands on her knees and held her head down, breathing as if she was having an asthmatic attack.

"It's not possible," she finally managed. "This can't be true."

"Breath slowly now, Jennifer," Philip Kozak said. "Slow long, breaths. That's right. You're hyperventilating; you'll be fine in a minute." He stood there, just like she'd always known him, wearing his blue jogging pants and sweatshirt. Jennifer pushed him away and closed her eyes, hoping that the apparition would go, but when she looked again, Philip was still standing there. A mix of powerful emotions bubbled up inside her: relief, happiness, wonder, shock, and fear.

"You are an hallucination," she said, still breathing heavily. "It can't be you, Philip. I saw your body go into the furnace. This is some kind of virtual screw-up." She had to stop for lack of breath.

"No, Jennifer, it's me, really. My essence saved in an avatar. I had to do it, Jen. I had to prove it could be done."

Suddenly Jennifer was flooded with a tsunami of anger, as if the mental cauldron that held her emotions had overheated and boiled over. She stood up straight and pushed Philip away.

"You arrogant, crazy bastard! You turned off the Failsafe and jumped just to prove your theory? You were killed in a freak accident, Phil. That's what the coroner's report says. I cried for you for two days. You are history, gone at the age of thirty. Is that what you wanted? What about me? Did you even think of what your death would mean to me? You selfish prick!"

162

To the side of the school building was a row of benches to accommodate spectators during game days. Philip gently pushed Jennifer by the elbow and they walked over, then sat down. Jennifer's anger was slowly dissipating.

"You shouldn't have come back, Philip! It will only make things worse. I would have gotten over losing you after a while. Oh, what am I saying? You're not real. Go away, leave me in peace!" She tried to walk away, but Philip held her back.

"No, Jennifer, hear me out. I was getting very depressed, suicidal even, because nobody would listen to my ideas about virtual people, not even you. The only way to prove my theory was to try for myself. I turned off the Failsafe system, entered a Matterhorn virtscape and jumped off the mountain.

"While I fell down, I concentrated on my avatar. I desperately tried to become one with it, to make it part of me. When I reached the ground, I didn't hurt at all and nothing had changed. It felt just like being in other virtscapes. I thought I had failed, and it had all been for nothing. Then, when I pushed my exit control, I got an error message: *No corporeal connection*.

"Virtual life is possible, Jen. I am the proof. I may no longer be alive, but I'm not dead either. I have moved into another dimension, somewhere between life and death. I know it sounds crazy, but everything I could do in the real world, I can do here, Jennifer. I can meet other people, or run along a beach. But I will never get sick or old, and I don't need air, food or water. All I require is a small amount of electricity to keep my avatar circuits going. I also need you, Jennifer, to tell me what's going on in the real world."

Jennifer looked at the image of the person she still loved and she was torn between two forces. It would be best to break her virtual connection and head home to start a new life. Forget about Phil. How could she love an avatar? Yet seeing him again made her heart remember all the good times they'd had together: the virtual trips, the laughs, the sex. She finally gave him a weak smile.

163

"Oh, Philip, I knew you wanted to learn more about consciousness and OBEs, and things like that, but I had no idea you were going to try your crazy theories out on yourself. My mind is overloaded right now, and I must get out of here before I go totally insane." She gave him a quick kiss on the cheek and pressed the exit control on her left glove.

◊ ◊ ◊

It was a council meeting like no other. Twelve church executives, dressed in their white ceremonial gowns, and their guest, Alison Hu, wearing a long blue evening gown, worthy of an emperor's ball. Everyone had enjoyed the special feast that had been laid out in honor of the Chinese visitors, and now it was time for questions and answers. Jo had called the meeting to order and formally handed control over to the chairperson of Doyon Enterprises. After taking a few moments to compose her thoughts, Alison began her address.

"Councilors, may I first compliment you on the fantastic reception you have given us," she said. "It is hard to believe that all that lovely food, the vegetables, fruit, even the lamb, were locally grown and raised. It was truly a feast, and Izzo and myself thank you.

"There are two reasons for my visit. Three days ago, four strangers came to my company's headquarters in Ying San, claiming they had a message for me. When I wanted to discuss this with them, the men caught me by surprise and exposed myself and my guard Izzo to some kind of mind-altering substance. Though it has given me great peace of mind, you can understand that I have many questions about this. What is the drug you gave me? Who is Oscar? How did a respectable scientific research center turn into a drug dispensing communal church?"

"Excuse me, Miss Hu, for not immediately answering that question," Jo said. "You mentioned you had two reasons for coming here. May we know the second one?"

"I am a very different person from all of you, Councilors," Alison said. My full name is Alison Hu II. I am a

164

human clone, created from a cell taken from my mother, the original Alison Hu, who died ten years ago."

"That technology is not available here," Father Dubois broke the ensuing silence. "Where did this cloning take place?"

"In our research center at Doyon Enterprises," Alison said. "We have been working on this procedure for over thirty years."

"Do you have the same personality as your mother? Is that even the right word?" Sylvia asked, confused.

"I usually call her my donor, but to make things easier I shall refer to her as my mother," Alison said. "I received my full genetic blueprint from her. I do have my own life and personality, but I also have many character traits that are identical to hers. My mother once worked for Excalibur and that is the second reason I came here, to see and experience the place where she worked and lived."

"I'm afraid the research center closed down about eight years ago," Jo said. "Our original church building had been destroyed and we bought Excalibur to start up again. We have left the buildings and surroundings in as much of their original state as we could. You are welcome to wander around, if you like."

"Thank you, Councilor. This afternoon, on first entering Excalibur, waves of deja vu went through me, though I myself have never been here. My mother worked here for three years before Dr. Kozak, her boss, sent her to China to set up a new research center. Excalibur-Asia was built, but Yabul never followed up on his idea and the facility lay idle for a while, until it was taken over by Doyon Enterprises. Councilor Rasnell, now that I have done my part, perhaps you can answer my questions?"

"Very well. The substance we used is called Oscar's Breath. It clears the human mind of negative, destructive, selfish thoughts. It also expands human consciousness, as you yourself have noticed. This drug was invented and created in Excalibur by Dr. Kozak, the same man your mother worked with. He was killed and his invention was considered lost at sea. But the Lord intervened and ordered a dolphin to bring it to Ted Taylor, my best friend. He named the dolphin Oscar, and started our church."

Alison sat quietly for a few moments, digesting what she had heard. Then she spoke again.

"What is going to happen now, Councilor Rasnell? Do you want me to go home and resign my position at Doyon Enterprises?"

"Just one moment, please," a sudden voice exclaimed. "Before you burn all our bridges, Miss Hu, I have a question for you." Jeremy Burlon, the zoologist, seemed ill at ease. He was the quietest of the councilors and usually did not say much at council meetings.

"Of course, Councilor. What is on your mind?" Alison asked.

"I am in charge of Oscar's welfare," Jeremy began. "Unfortunately, I am fighting a losing battle. I have experience with dolphins and I know their average lifespan is about thirty to forty years in the wild. In captivity their lifespan is much shorter.

"Even with the latest medical innovations we cannot keep Oscar alive much longer. His heart and liver are failing. Even if I could perform transplants, it would not be the answer. One cannot keep replacing parts of a living being. I wonder if you could comment on this, Miss Hu, considering the nature of your work?"

"You are absolutely correct," Alison said. "One cannot replace all the trillions of cells that make up a living being. Cells are programmed to die, and even if you replaced all major organs, other collaborating cells would die, causing the organism to fail sooner or later. That is why we decided on cloning as an alternative."

"Can you clone Oscar for us?"

Alison took her time. Finally she nodded. "Yes, I think so. Dolphins are mammals, like us. They are in fact more like us than most people realize. Yes, I think that with a few necessary modifications it should be possible."

"What about the dangers? We cannot allow our Lord to be harmed."

"There are no dangers to the donor," Alison said. "All we do is take a biopsy; one living cell is enough. The problem lies in the gestation process. Obviously a different kind of incubator would have to be designed and that will take some time."

"We cannot allow our Lord to travel outside his home. It might kill him. Can you take a biopsy here and use it to clone Oscar in your facilities?"

"I would have to clear it with my company, but I can't see why not. In our testing stages we cloned small animals with good results. But there will be a problem in the future. A clone is not absolutely an identical copy, and you cannot keep cloning an individual forever. There are random errors at the quantum level. Each copy is less perfect than the previous one. First and second generations are probably fine. However, at some time in the future, Oscar could not be cloned again."

"How many generations are we talking about, before that happens?" Jo asked.

"I don't know," Alison said. "So far we have managed twelve generations of rats. Dolphins or people will be different, and I cannot give you an exact answer. Perhaps at a future time our scientists can perfect the technique further."

"I suggest we go ahead with this, Jo," Jeremy said urgently. "If we don't, Oscar will die within the year, I guarantee it. And then where will we be? A church without an idol to be worshipped? Perhaps we should vote on this now."

"All right." Jo nodded. "Those in favor of cloning Oscar, please raise your hands."

To Jo's surprise only ten hands were raised. Father Dubois and Sylvia were against.

"Gilbert, Sylvia," Jo said, taken aback a bit. "I'd really would like to make this unanimous. It is of critical concern for our church, and we should not be divided over this. Why are you against the idea?"

"It is not the normal way of procreation and not in Nature's best interest," Father Dubois said sternly. "If we use cloning once, it could be used again. What will be next? Cloning the church councilors? I do not want this in the Church of Oscar."

"Sylvia?"

"I agree with Father Dubois," Sylvia said. "Cloning is not a natural thing."

Jo reflected for a while, wondering how they had suddenly got into this quagmire. Then he resumed.

"Daniel English had a favorite saying: If the church is in need of something, the Lord will provide. Three times in our church's history he has been proved right. When we were in dire money troubles, the Lord used Oscar to create a financial windfall for us. When our church was too small, He found us a temporary place in a hotel. And most importantly, when we ran out of Oscar's Breath, the Lord brought Patrick and Carol Johnson into our church, so we could make our own supply. Can both of you, in this special case, not find it in your hearts to accept cloning as a gift from our Lord, to be used only to keep His Representative on earth alive?"

It was Sylvia who raised her hand first, and after some hesitation, Father Dubois also raised his.

"Carried unanimously," Jo said happily, bringing down his gavel.

◊ ◊ ◊

As soon as Tom Cramer walked in, he knew something bad had happened. Heather, always there to greet him with a smile and a kiss, was sitting at the kitchen table, cutting carrots into small pieces. Her eyes were red, and he could see she had cried.

"Hon?" He rushed over and she stood up to hug him, her eyes wet with tears again. "What is it? What happened?"

"It's Mother, Tom. She's gone into a coma. They don't think she'll last very much longer. We'll have to go."

He let her cry against his chest for a while, thinking about the implications. Heather was originally from Minneapolis, where her parents had run a small hardware store. It was one of those quirks in life, that although Tom loved his wife, he had never liked her parents. There was just no nice way to say it. Neil Paring had been a redneck; opinionated and stupid. He had been one of those people who could not let go of the past; who couldn't accept the fact that the great American Dream had turned into an ugly nightmare. *We'll show those damned terrorists. We're still the greatest nation on earth. We'll teach them a lesson or two . . .* It had dragged on and on, until he finally drank himself into an early grave about six years ago.

Rose Paring, his wife, was less belligerent; in fact, she was almost the total opposite of Neil: mousey, rarely speaking her mind, always agreeing with him. Soon after her husband died, Rose was diagnosed with Alzheimer's, and it had gone downhill from there. Tom found it totally inexplicable that two people like that could have produced such a loving, intelligent, happy daughter.

"Will you come with us, Tom?" Heather asked, looking up at him. He loved her dearly, but he knew he'd have to disappoint her.

"I can't, Heather," he said, giving her a hug. He walked over to the counter and took a bottle of Scotch from the liquor cabinet underneath. "I've only got till next Wednesday to sort things out before we close the station. It'll be quite hectic. We've got to take it easy on our money from now on, also. Rose wouldn't recognize me anyway. You and Penny go."

"OK." She wiped away her tears. "You're right, it would be a waste of time for you. And it's better to have someone in the house, anyway. We don't want to come back home and find squatters." She said it with a thin smile, but he knew she was serious. Leaving a home for any length of time was inviting trouble. He'd seen them himself, young men in old

169

cars, cruising the neighborhood, looking for signs that people were away. Heather sat down again, while Tom poured himself a drink, glad she'd accepted his refusal to come with her. He couldn't think of anything worse than sitting beside the bed of a dying person he hardly knew.

"So how was your day?" Heather asked.

"Oh, chaotic. Last minute paperwork to be sorted out, you know, making sure the guys get good references. Not that it makes a lot of difference for most, but I want to make sure that Watersma gets a good job. He's such a nice guy."

Cramer sat back, enjoying his drink, letting his mind wander, thinking about his career that was about to end. He had no misgivings or regrets. He'd never killed, or caused harm to anyone and he hadn't been hurt himself. He thought about the early days, working as a sergeant for Patrick Johnson. Those had been the best times. He wondered how he and Carol were; whether they had survived that massacre. Perhaps he should have checked up on them before . . .

"Can you book the train, please?" Heather asked. "Soon as possible, tomorrow even, if there's space."

"Sorry, hon. I was miles away. Of course, I'll do it right now. When do you think you'll be back?"

"I don't know. One week? Two? See if you can get us an open ticket. Oh, and we'll have to let Jenny's school know. Will you be OK on your own for a while?"

"Of course. I can start thinking about what I'm going to do after next Wednesday."

11

Anna Kulik was nineteen, a pretty teenager, unfortunately wearing braces for her teeth. They were a bummer, she thought. She had other features that made up for them—a fact not lost on the many boys at John Handy High School in Redding, California. She was tall and slim, with the right curves in the right places; she had beautiful legs, a great natural tan and long blond curls that framed her unblemished oval face. She was an only child. Her parents, Walter and Jean Kulik, thought the world of her, as parents with one child usually do.

Walter suggested that Anna would do well as a model. After all, her braces would not be needed forever, and she had exactly the right figure for it. Even though economic times were tough and jobs rare, there were still rich people who spent money lavishly on clothes and other apparel, like shoes, wedding gowns, or holiday outfits.

Anna did not have an exact idea of what she wanted to do with her life, but she dismissed her father's suggestion. She did not want to become a living puppet to show off other people's ideas. She wanted to do something she could excel in for herself: an actress perhaps, or a professional tennis player. Something unique, not just an ordinary run-of-the-mill job.

She loved tennis, but becoming a pro was out of the question. Her father was an administrator for the municipality of Redding, earning a decent living, and her mother was a nurse in a local hospital. Even their combined income would not be enough to pay for such an extravagant career. Gone were the times of corporate university scholarships for sports or the arts.

Apart from money, time was of the essence. To become big in any kind of sport, you had to start early in life. Nineteen was already pushing it. Though Anna played as much as she could, she knew she needed coaching. One day she saw an ad in the local paper for a chance to win an all-inclusive weekend training workshop with some of the national and international tennis players, if she bought a racket made by a new company called Swifthead. Not one to let a chance like that pass, Anna collected all her savings, went to the sports store and bought the racket. She filled out her application and mailed it out with proof of purchase, not really expecting ever to hear from the company again.

Eight weeks later, to her utter delight, she received a parcel from the Swifthead headquarters in Redondo Beach, California. Her name had been picked, and she would be playing with the professionals! The workshop was to be held near Prescott, Arizona. Included in the parcel were a first-class airline ticket to Phoenix, a voucher for limousine travel to the resort, her resort reservation, games itinerary, and five hundred dollars spending money.

On October 13, 2061, at 11:05, Anna Kulik waved goodbye to her parents, went through the security checkpoint at Redding Municipal Airport and boarded Arizona Air flight 86. It would be a two hour flight to Prescott, and Anna happily sat down in her first class seat. About halfway into the flight, the captain's voice came in through the intercom.

"Ladies and gentlemen, we are making some adjustments to the cabin air circulation. You may feel a bit lightheaded since we are adjusting the air to oxygen ratio. Please keep breathing normally. Everything should be back to normal soon. Thank you for your cooperation."

Anna looked around her. First class was almost empty. A businessman sat in the row to her left across the aisle, busy with his laptop. Behind her she could see that economy was about half full. She quickly took a sip of water, while something in the air caused her to sniff a few times. She was getting tired all of a sudden, and her eyelids became quite heavy.

A voice filled the air. It wasn't the captain, or one of the stewardesses, but a lovely, melodious female voice, seductive

172

almost, like the audio on a television car commercial. The woman was enunciating every word slowly and precisely, as if she had all the time in the world and wanted to make sure everyone understood her.

"Your body is beginning to feel heavy, your muscles are relaxing, your eyelids are closing. Your cares and worries are slowly floating away and you want to go to sleep. Let it happen. Relax . . . Relax."

Anna felt very strange. Her body slouched in her seat, as if she was pushed back by the forces of several Gs, although the flight was smooth without any turbulence. She couldn't raise her arms, or legs, or even open her eyelids. All she could do was breathe slowly, her head resting against the back of her seat. Far away she heard the noise of the engine, a waterfall of white noise, filling her mind. Then the Voice was back.

"Your conscious mind is fully asleep now, but your subconscious is alert and will listen to my message. We are a secret society on a mission to save the human race from looming extinction. You have been selected to join us in this vital quest. I shall give you complete instructions on how to achieve this. After I have finished, you will hear a chiming sound and wake up. Your conscious mind will have forgotten everything I said, but your subconscious will remember my instructions and carry them out when the time comes. Here is what I want each of you to do . . ."

Anna awoke with a start. What was that? A noise, like a doorbell, had awakened her from a snooze. When she looked up, she noticed the captain had just turned on the seatbelt sign. It was the accompanying chime that had roused her. She stretched her back, reached for the seatbelt and strapped herself in. She didn't usually daydream, but with all the excitement ahead she hadn't slept much last night. The little catnap had actually done her good, and she felt refreshed.

A stewardess appeared to her side with a tray of snacks, and Anna gratefully took two small sandwich squares. "We'll be landing in about thirty-five minutes," the stewardess said, smiling at her. "Would you like anything else?"

Happily, Anna shook her head. "No thanks, this will be fine." Munching on her sandwiches, Anna picked up one of the in-flight magazines, wondering what it would be like to stay in a five star resort. Playing tennis with the pros would be heaven, even for just one game, let alone a whole weekend. For a while she just flipped the pages, thinking how incredible lucky she had been. After a while the captain's voice came through with preparation for landing instructions and Anna moved her seat back and tightened her seatbelt.

Half an hour later, she walked down the airport concourse, pulling her little suitcase on wheels, watching for people holding up little boards with names on them. When she saw a young man who held a board with her name on it, she waved at him. Ten minutes later she was whisked away to the Alpin Rio resort, looking forward to a fantastic weekend.

◊ ◊ ◊

Philip Kozak stood in front of the Arc de Triomphe, and looked at the constant flow of traffic heading down the Avenue des Champs-Élysées. He wasn't sure why he had selected Paris in April from the available virtscapes. Perhaps it had to do with love, and the freshness of a new spring. He was waiting for Jennifer.

While he looked at the cars, he wondered how much longer they would be around. Using a box made of metal and plastic to move people? It was so archaic. He could see the necessity for trucks or vans to move goods. Yet most of the cars he saw were driven for personal use. He wondered why. In Secret Springs, people could meet each other anywhere, without ever leaving their homes. They could work in virtual offices, and there was no need for commuting. Philip had thought that virtual reality would have lowered the number of cars, but it obviously hadn't.

A sudden shimmering of air next to him broke his reverie. Had to be Jenny. He had set his privacy flag to purple so that no one else would bother him. When she materialized, Jennifer seemed to be unsteady on her feet, and he rushed over to hold her.

"Hi, Phil," she began, then looked at him. "You are Philip, aren't you? What's with the strange avatar? I prefer you as yourself."

"Hey, a lot of people knew me when I was alive. If I go walking around in public virtscapes looking like Philip Kozak, someone is bound to recognize me and ask questions. I save my own avatar for when there's just the two of us. Are you all right? You were swaying when you materialized. Too much to drink?"

She smiled and kissed him. "It's that new helmet I'm wearing. It's the first time I've tried it out, and it takes some getting used to. Heck, I'm sitting in my easy chair at home, yet here I am, walking around as if this is real. How did they create these helmets, Phil? They are incredible."

"Let's go for a walk," he said, grabbing her by the hand. For a few seconds they waited at the traffic light, then joined the crowds of tourists and locals who were ambling down the Champs-Élysées, home of the fancy shops, expensive restaurants and car showrooms.

"VR technology changes by the day and I'll tell you what I know, but remember that I've been out of the loop for a while. Most bodily functions start in the brain, Jen. A chemical-electrical signal is sent to your feet or your arms to move them. What our scientists have somehow managed to do is temporarily reroute these signals to your avatar. Your brain thinks you're walking, but it is really the avatar that's moving. They did it to give handicapped people a chance to join Secret Springs. You know, old people who can't walk easily, or paraplegics who can't move at all. But enough of that. What is happening in the real world?"

175

"Nothing much really. Business as usual, I guess. The board has made Armonde Takir your successor, Phil, as expected, and they just hired a new guy to fill his position. Nobody has mentioned you at all, so I guess to Secret Springs you are really history. So how are you doing in that virtual body of yours? I don't like that disguise, by the way."

He grabbed her by the hand. "In there." He pulled Jennifer into an alleyway between a dealership for Ford cars, and an expensive shop for maternity wear. A few feet further down the alley stood a dumpster truck, and Philip quickly hid behind it. Curiously, Jennifer followed.

"Hey, what's gotten into you? What—"

She stared at Philip as he suddenly metamorphosed into his old self, like a human shape-shifter. He laughed and held her tight. "I can be anything I want to be, Jen." He could see a shadow cross Jennifer's face.

"What? Aren't you happy to see the real me?"

"Oh, Phil, of course I am. I just can't get over what's happening to us. You are so realistic, it reminds me of when me first met, and how happy we were. But it will never be like that again, will it?" She sniffed.

"Come on, let's go back." Philip snapped back into his disguise and without speaking they left the alleyway again and joined the crowds on the sidewalks. Something had changed between them. Philip saw that it had upset Jennifer.

"Perhaps we should only meet in private next time, so I can be myself," he suggested.

"How can we, Phil? I want to do things with you that normal people do. Go out and meet others, go dancing, have a nice meal. I don't want to hide in a virtual place all the time. When I was sixteen, my father and I had an interesting chat. I guess he wanted to tell me the facts of life, bless his soul. He told me never to get emotionally involved with anyone who lived more than a hundred miles away. It would not work, he said. I wonder what he would think of a virtual boyfriend."

He pulled her close. "Come on, Jen. It's not that bad now, is it? We can see each other any time you want, we can kiss, and make love, just like in real life. Look, I know I did something outrageous and I'm not sorry for it. I just had to do it and it'll open a whole new area of research. But I need your help, Jen, and here is your first assignment."

"Forget it. You may be my boyfriend, but not my boss." She winked at him when she said it, and he smiled. "All right. I'm begging you, then. I want you to arrange a virtual meeting with Marvin, Sandor and Sarah. If they see me, they will realize the importance of what I've done and help me with my project. Will you do that for me?"

She gave him a difficult smile. "I'll try."

◊ ◊ ◊

The neighborhood might at one time have been classy, with detached homes on large lots and lovely gardens, but not any more. Most of the homes were boarded up, the driveways cracked and full of weeds. Overgrown gardens, not mowed for many years, wrecked cars along the side of the road, left there when people couldn't afford to drive them anymore. It was obvious that this particular neighborhood had long been removed from the routes of city garbage removal trucks. Yet people still lived here, and there was power, notable by the light that shone above the porch at number 19 Hazelwood Drive.

Cramer carefully walked up the overgrown driveway, expecting a wild dog to appear from the side of the house at any moment. Seeing no sign of a bell, he banged his fist on a paint-flaked front door and waited. He was about to walk away, when the door opened a fraction, and an elderly woman peeked through the gap. A thick chain looped in front of her face. She just stood there, staring at him without a word, obviously leaving the introduction to Cramer.

"Mrs. Penstone?"

"Yes." He waited patiently, but she said nothing else.

"My name is Tom Cramer. I would like to talk to you about your husband. May I come in?"

"Are you with the police?"

"I was a lieutenant with the Santa Barbara Police, but I'm retired now."

"You should be ashamed of yourself!"

"Excuse me?"

"For waiting so long. My husband has been gone for more than nine months. I reported him missing, but nobody did anything. Why have you come now?"

"Mrs. Penstone, I'd rather not discuss things out here. Could you let me in? I can't show you a badge, but I am here to help you. Please?" She finally removed the chain and opened the door wider. When Cramer entered the home, he was shocked. The old lady had a gun in her hand, and it was aimed at him.

"In the living room, please," she said, showing him the direction with her other hand.

"There is no need for this, Mrs. Penstone. Could you please put that gun away?"

"I decide what happens in my own house," she said. "Sit down." Cramer sank into a comfortable couch, while Mrs. Penstone took a wooden chair at the other end of the room, still pointing the gun at him. It seemed like a surreal dream. What was he doing here? The old lady was just sitting there looking at him. Finally, she spoke.

"If you're not with the police any more, why are you doing this? How do I know you're not some kind of con artist, trying to get information or money from me?"

"I'll tell you why, if you put that gun away, Mrs. Penstone. Guns make me nervous. If you don't want me here, I'll leave. I just want to help."

She carefully lowered the weapon and put it on the coffee table, well within her reach.

"Why?"

"For years I have wondered why so many people are disappearing, Mrs. Penstone. Since I'm retired now, I need to do something with my time. I want to help people find others who are missing. Think of me as a private investigator who works pro bono."

"What does that mean?"

"Without getting paid. I picked your name from a list I had at the police force. Could you just answer a few questions, please?"

"OK."

"What did your husband do for a living?"

"Cyril used to work for a building supply company. Retired four years ago."

"Have you any idea why he left you? Did he say anything about where he was going?"

She shook her head. "One morning I woke up and he had gone."

"Had you had a fight, or disagreement before?"

"No."

"Can you remember anything around that time, anything that was different from normal? Was he angry? Ill, perhaps?"

"He was antsy."

"How do you mean?"

"He walked around like a chicken that couldn't lay an egg. It started about a month before he took off. Something was bothering him, but he wouldn't say what. Couldn't sit still, not even to watch TV. He just walked around the house, muttering to himself. He hardly slept. It drove me nuts."

"Did you and your husband belong to a church?"

She nodded. "But I don't any more. I can't drive and there's nobody to take me. We were Presbyterians."

"Have you heard of the Church of Oscar?"

"Don't like them; I am fine in my own church."

"Why don't you like them?"

"Too strict. We had some good friends, the Bilstons. They joined that church. We told them to stay in touch, but they never did. They were nice, Noah and Irene. They said they would call us, but they never did."

"That's because it is a communal church. People live together in a group."

"I didn't know that." She stood up and headed for the kitchen. "I'm going to make some tea. Would you like a cup?"

"I would love one, thank you."

While Mrs. Penstone busied herself in the kitchen, Cramer looked around. It wasn't a very big house, more of a bungalow. He noticed two heavy locks on the front door, as well as a big vertical bar that could be swung down horizontally and secured, to make sure no one could break down the door. The two windows in the living room had steel bars in front of them, and he could see the same protection in the kitchen. An old grandfather clock stood along a wall, alongside an antique cabinet that held glasses and old bottles. Empty ones.

Though the décor was hardly posh, the place was clean and tidy. There was no other furniture, but the wall held several pictures, probably of Mr. and Mrs. Penstone and their children. He couldn't really tell from where he was sitting, but he didn't dare get up, in case he'd scare the old lady. She came back carrying a tray with cups and a teapot and a plate of chocolate biscuits.

"I apologize for my unfriendly behavior," Mrs. Penstone said. "But you just don't know these days. Help yourself to a biscuit." She poured the tea into two delicate china cups.

"I completely understand, Mrs. Penstone," Tom said, while he took a biscuit of the plate.

"Call me Irene."

"All right. I know it is a while ago, Irene, but please try to remember if anything out of the ordinary happened around the time you first noticed your husband's strange behavior. Go back a bit further, if you want. Anything special he did."

She frowned. "We didn't do much," she said. "It's far too dangerous to go out, especially at night. Cyril did go to his school class reunion. He was brought up in Tacoma, Washington, and he kept contact with some of his old class-mates. About two years ago, they had this reunion and Cyril really wanted to go. He couldn't drive that far, so we saved for an airline ticket. I didn't go. He had a fabulous time over there. Afterwards, he was fine. He was thrilled to bits he had gone. It wasn't really until about two months before he disappeared that I began to notice that things weren't right. He seemed uptight, confused, not quite himself."

"Can you recall anything specific? The first thing you noticed was wrong?"

"I guess it was when I found that book he was reading. Cyril was never much of a reader, so I was surprised one day when I saw him reading a book about the occult."

"The occult? What exactly was he reading, Irene?"

"Oh, I don't know. The book I saw was about poltergeists. Later I found others about alien abductions and secret societies. When I asked him about it he said it was none of my business what he read."

"And he had never been interested in that before?"

"No. He always thought it was stuff for people who believed in conspiracy theories, or stories about UFOs."

"Was there anything else? Did he use the Internet?"

"No. We're not really computer savvy. He just withdrew into himself, and one morning he was gone. Took a bag with some clothes and half of our savings."

"Do you know why he took the money?"

"I have no idea. I guess he figured he would need it for whatever he was planning to do. I didn't know until a few days later, when I went to the bank. He'd cashed in exactly half our savings account. Some more tea?"

"No, thank you Irene. You've been very helpful, but I must be on my way."

"What good will all this do, if you're no longer with the police?"

"I don't know. It probably will not bring your Cyril back but I just feel that someone ought to do something, Irene." He stood up. "Thank you for the tea. If I find out anything more, I'll let you know."

"I'm sorry I was so paranoid before," Irene said. "You are a good man, Tom Cramer. God Bless."

◊ ◊ ◊

181

It was a happy reunion, albeit an unusual one. When Marvin Tuppal saw Philip's avatar, standing behind the virtual boardroom table, smiling at him, the usually staid engineer almost lost his footing and had to hold onto a chair.

"Heck, Philip, is that really you? You almost caused my heart to give out. How can it be? What the . . . Come here, man." He rushed over and gave Philip a bear hug. "I'm only dreaming, I know that. You feel real to me, but when I disconnect you'll be gone. It's great to see you, my friend, even if you are an illusion." He let go off Philip and sat down. Sandor Donavon and Sarah Marrion showed similar sentiments. Jennifer stood to the side, almost like a bystander.

"How can you exist in an avatar, without a body to go back to, Philip?" Sarah queried, wiping away a few tears, after she had hugged him also. "It would seem impossible."

"I agree with Marvin," Sandor said. "It's great to see you again, Phil, but we're in some kind of virtual quantum dream here. Weird. Spooky."

"No, my friends, you're not," Phil said. "Sit down and I'll explain. You yourselves have moved part of your consciousness into your avatar, just by being here with me. I say part of it, because some—most likely your autonomic nervous system—is left behind to make sure your body is still functioning.

"In my case, I moved my entire consciousness, and that's why my body died. I'm proof it can be done. Now I know it's not something everyone can or wants to do. Most people are afraid of dying, and fear destroys everything. But I think virtual life is the next evolutionary step for mankind."

"How did you do it, Philip?" Sarah asked, shaking her head. "Were you on drugs?"

"Not at all. You just have to be absolutely, one-hundred-percent convinced that you want to leave your body and it will work. I wanted to succeed more than anything else in the world, and it just happened."

182

"Excuse me, Philip," Sandor said. "There's something that isn't right here. You are officially dead, and Secret Springs has closed your account. How can you still be online?"

"Ah, Sandor, good question. When you go online, the avatar you choose is tied to your identity until you log off again. Then it is reset and returned to the library. The time you have spent in the avatar is charged to your account. That's how the company works and makes its money.

"The crucial thing is that Secret Springs does not track individual avatars. First off, there are millions of accounts and millions of avatars to choose from and it would be too time consuming and expensive to follow each avatar. Secondly, Secret Springs takes their customer's privacy very seriously.

"On the other hand, Secret Springs has to know where the avatars are, for emergencies, or when people want to meet each other in the virtscapes. For that reason, the software designers equipped avatars with identification transponders, much like airplanes have. When you want to meet someone in a virtscape, the log-on search engine looks for the transponder signal of the avatar the person used and connects you to it."

"Why didn't Accounts reset your avatar when your body died?" Sandor asked.

"They couldn't find me. Before I went on line, I turned my transponder off."

"That's impossible," Marvin called out. "Subscribers can't do that."

"I'm not your average subscriber, Marv. I used to run the company and knew how to do it."

"Wait," Sarah said. "I don't get this. You turned off your avatar's transponder, yet we found you. How can that be?"

"There was a big problem when I died," Philip said. "I could not go off line, because I had no body to go back to. Nobody in Secret Springs' history had ever switched off the Failsafe and died while in a virtscape. It was an unforeseen situation that caused the computer exit program to malfunction. When Accounts couldn't find my avatar, the management probably decided that it was destroyed in the same malfunction.

"The company's first task was to debug the logoff subroutine to stop a situation like this happening again. When that was done, they had a choice. They could either spend an awful lot of time and effort to find a way to locate one silent avatar among billions of others, or simply delete my account and forget about the whole thing. I waited for one week, then switched the avatar transponder on again. Nothing happened, so I guess they've forgotten about me."

"But Phil, you're taking an awful risk here," Jennifer said, shaking her head. "When we search for your avatar, the Secret Springs computer will find you, remember you are a rogue avatar and reset you. I'm surprised that hasn't happened already."

Philip smiled at her. "A computer program does exactly what it is asked to do, Jennifer. Nothing more. The log-on search program will find a specific avatar in a specific virtscape and connect you to it. That's its job. No more. It doesn't ask questions about what kind of avatar it is.

"The only way I can get into trouble is if Accounts starts to look for me again, but I'm confident they won't. It's an extremely busy place, and they simply won't have the time. Besides, it'll only be for a short while. As soon as Marvin has spoken to the rest of the board—"

"What do you mean?" Marvin interrupted. "Why should I talk to the other board members?"

"To explain what happened, of course," Phil said. "I want you to tell them that virtual life is possible. I am the proof. It is the greatest discovery of all times, and they would be fools not to help me develop it. I'm sure they'll listen to me this time."

The atmosphere in the room suddenly changed. It seemed as if a cold draught had wafted in from somewhere. Sarah and Sandor looked puzzled, and Jennifer just stared at Philip, worrying. Marvin had lost his exuberance at seeing Philip again, and sighed while he looked at his friend.

"Oh, Philip," he said wistfully. "You're so brilliant and yet so naïve. Do you really think what you have done will make the slightest difference to Armonde or Charles? Or Donna? Will it change their opinion of your ideas? Of course not. If I tell them you are still in the system they'll go ballistic.

"You're a virtual squatter, Philip, who uses company resources without paying a cent. Secret Springs will find you and neutralize your avatar, transponder or no transponder, I guarantee it. They'll order a complete shutdown if needed. With that new guy, Clifford Sting, it'll be four against us three when it comes to a vote. There will be nothing we can do to stop them. Sorry, Phil. Be realistic here. Talking to the other board members would be your death warrant. Secret Springs will never help you."

There was a long silence, and it was Philip who finally broke it.

"So you're all giving up on me?" he asked. "Leave me high and dry where I am, unable to pursue this any further?"

"Of course not, Phil. I'll help you," Jennifer said at once.

"Me, too." Sarah said, nodding. "You've done something so extraordinary that we can't ignore it. I'm on your side and I think I can persuade my husband Pedro also. He's a philosopher and loves this kind of thing."

Philip cocked his head towards the quantum physicist. "And you, Sandor?"

The scientist nodded. "I thought I understood physics, Phil, but this blows my mind. I definitely want to learn more about it."

"Marvin? Where do we go from here?"

The engineer sighed. "Oh, Phil, If you can find another way to follow your dream, I'll give you my full support, of course. But you cannot involve Secret Springs in your plans."

"Fair enough," Philip said. "That's all I can ask, my friends. An open mind. I'll do some serious thinking about this. I've got lots of time for that these days."

◊ ◊ ◊

185

"What is the matter with Anna?" Walter Kulik looked at his wife in despair. "She is not herself these days."

"Of course not, silly. It's called growing up," Jean said.

"She's changed, I tell you, ever since that damned tennis workshop."

"Oh, Walter, don't be so suspicious. I can tell you exactly what happened. She met Pym Tang, Donald Freemann and other top professionals. Anna knows she can never be like them, because she can't afford the training. I'd be moody and uptight too!"

"That's hardly our fault, is it?" Walter exclaimed. "Heck, we gave her a brand-new tennis outfit for her birthday: top, shorts, shoes, you name it. She has only used it once. If she's serious about tennis, I'll be the last one to stand in her way. But you need to practice, otherwise you'll never be any good."

"Since when are you an authority on tennis?" Jean said, eyeing her husband's girth. "It wouldn't harm you if you took it up yourself."

"Don't change the subject," he retorted. "It's Anna we have to worry about. Shall we take her to a doctor?"

"What? A shrink? Are you kidding? There's nothing wrong with Anna. She just graduated, for Pete's sake. Give her some slack, Walter. She has to decide on a future, and boys, and whatever else a young girl faces."

"Look, if she wants to take up tennis, why doesn't she just say so? We could scrape some money together and help her out. But she's hardly talking these days. I hope she's not on drugs. I don't particularly like that Timothy character."

"What's an awful thing to say, Walter. Anna has never taken drugs. Why can't you accept the fact that she's no longer your little girl of ten years ago. She's got a life of her own now."

"Yeah, yeah, you women always stick together."

There was the sound of a door opening and footsteps in the hallway. Jean pointed an admonishing finger at her husband. "Be nice now."

When Anna walked in, she didn't come over to kiss them, the way she used to. "Hi," she said, giving them a thin smile.

"What'yer been doing, girl?" Walter asked.

"Oh, this and that. Timothy took me to the beach on his motorcycle and we went for a burger at Ida's. I've just got back from the bus station."

"The bus station? Why did you go there?"

She didn't answer for a few seconds, as if she was gathering courage.

"Mom, Dad, I've got to go away for a couple of days."

"Where to?" Jean asked sharply.

"The L.A. area. There's another tennis meet going on, University Open Championship. I want to see if I can quality. I was wondering if you could lend me some money."

"What? Just like that? When did you hear about this?" Walter asked suspiciously. "You've hardly played any tennis lately."

She give him a nervous smile. "I know, it's rather all-of-a-sudden."

"Where are you going to stay?" Jean asked.

"Don't know yet. I'll find a place somewhere."

"I don't know if I like this, young lady, you going down there, all by yourself," Walter said, frowning.

"Oh, Dad, I'm nineteen! I've been away on my own before, haven't I?"

"Yeah, but that was all arranged and paid for."

"Walter, could you leave us alone for a minute, please?" Jean said.

Muttering to himself, Walter stood up, and without looking at Anna he left the room.

"Anna, what's going on?" Jean asked. "You've been so uptight lately. And now you just drop this into our lap. You can't blame your Dad and me for worrying about you. That is quite a long trip, especially by bus. Are you sure you want to do this?"

"Yes, Mom, honestly. The bus leaves early tomorrow morning and it takes only eight hours. I'll be there in the afternoon. Lots of time to look for a place to stay. I'll be fine."

"Tomorrow? That's cutting it rather fine, isn't it? Now tell me truthfully, Anna, are you in some kind of trouble? Drugs, or money? Boy problems? I will understand; please tell me. I don't know if I quite believe that tennis story."

"It's true!" Anna suddenly screamed, stamping her foot on the kitchen floor. "Why do you people always make such a fuss? If you don't want to give me money, I'll hitch a ride!"

"When do these games start?"

"Tomorrow, I told you! I've got to be there tomorrow! Now are you going to help me out or not?"

Jean Kulik had never seen her daughter hysterical. Anna's face was distorted with—what was it? Fear? Rage? Frustration? For a second Jean thought of having Anna followed to find out where she was going. Then she chastised herself for even thinking like that. Spying on her own daughter, heaven forbid. With heavy heart, Jean walked to one of the kitchen cupboards and took a can from the shelf that held soups, beans and other tinned foods.

"Don't you ever mention this to your father," she said, taking a wad of money out of the can. "No daughter of mine's going to hitchhike all the way to L.A. How much do you need?"

The next morning, at 4:30 a.m., a Yellow Cab stopped in front of 21 Orchard Road. Standing at the door, Jean hugged and kissed her daughter and watched as Anna quickly walked down the driveway to the waiting cab, carrying the holdall with her tennis gear. A quick wave, then she stepped inside. Jean watched as the cab drove off and disappeared around the corner. She closed the door quietly and walked back to the bedroom, where Walter was still snoring his head off. Carefully pulling back the cover, Jean got back into bed, worrying where Anna was going and why her daughter had deliberately lied to her.

188

12

"Where's your Mom?" Tom Cramer asked, when he walked in. "We're supposed to have an early dinner tonight. Hope she hasn't forgotten we're playing bridge at the Taggards." Then he noticed Penny was wiping her eyes. "She's gone," his daughter said, sobbing. "Couldn't you see it coming?"

"Gone? Gone where? What are you talking about, child?" Tom had never spoken like that to Penny, and he rushed over to hold her. "I'm sorry, hon. I didn't mean that, you're not a child. But you're not making much sense. What did you mean, about seeing it coming?"

"She has left us. Just after you went out this morning, she packed a bag and took off without a word. She's gone, Dad!"

"That is rubbish!" Cramer said. "Heather would never do that to us. We're a happy family."

"Are we?"

"What's that supposed to mean? Of course we are. Your mother and I have never said one bad word to each other. She would never run out on us like that, and even if she did, she would leave a note."

Penny pointed to the mantelpiece. There, leaning against his parents' antique clock was an envelope. Cramer stood still, unable to walk over to pick it up. This was not happening. This was absolutely, totally impossible. Heather had not left him; he would bet all his money, the house, even his life on that. Something else was happening here. Perhaps to do with her parents' estate? No, that was settled long ago. Another man? He felt a cold mess forming in his stomach, but he ignored it. No. He would have known. Finally gathering enough courage, he walked over to the hearth and took the envelope. With shaking fingers he pulled out a single folded sheet of paper. He opened it and prepared himself for the worst. For the benefit of Penny, he read it out loud.

"Tom, my love, I do not know how to say this. For a long time now, I have known this day would come. I have tried to hide it from you, I have tried to fight it with all my might. I even went to see Christopher, but he couldn't find anything wrong with me, and all he did was give me a sedative. For reasons I do not know, I must leave you, Tom. I couldn't talk about it, because you would not believe me, and only get angry and try to stop me. Something has happened to me. I must go somewhere and I can't tell you about it. You must understand, Tom, I beg of you, that it has nothing to do with you, or what I feel for you. I love you as always, and there is no one else. I am very much afraid I am losing my mind, Tom. Please do not take this out on Penny, she needs your support now, while I am gone. I do not know if, or when, I will be back. Look after Penny, and love to both of you, forever. Heather."

With his stomach a sudden pit of ice, and his heart beating like a pile driver, Tom stared at the note, wanting to put it back on the mantelpiece again, wanting to go back outside and return to the sight of a smiling Heather and the smell of dinner. But he didn't move, as reality slowly sank in. Heather had become a missing person, like Cyril Penstone and hundreds of others on the list. With shaking hands he put the note back on the mantelpiece, sighed deeply, and sat down at the table next to Penny. She was still crying. He ran his hand through her hair and pulled her close.

"Penny, I'm so sorry. I never expected this to happen. I had no clue, your Mom hid it very well. It's going to be awful for us, but we've got to stick together, you and I, until we get her back. I was a damned good cop, I still am, and I'm going to find her, Pen, I promise you. Even if I have to do it all by myself."

"But how, Dad?" she said, sniffing. "Where are you going to look? Do you . . . do you think she has found another man?"

"No. Absolute not," he said, with as much confidence as he could muster. "Not Heather; she wouldn't lie to me about that. It is something else."

"We need help, Dad. You've got to call the FBI."

"I know. I'll enter it into their missing persons website for a start. Don't except too much from that direction, though."

"Why not? They'll look for her, won't they?"

Tom sighed. "No, Penny. They used to, fifty years ago, but not any more. They no longer have the money or the manpower to go after missing persons. Not unless those persons are very important, high up on the social ladder. It's up to ordinary citizens to help each other. Besides, your Mom's not really missing. She deliberate went somewhere and I think she's hiding from something. Why couldn't she just tell us what was wrong!"

"Perhaps she is ill, Dad. Something serious, and she's gone to hospital to see a specialist. Maybe she didn't want to worry us."

"No, she said she went to see Dr. Taggard and he found nothing wrong. I'm going in my study for a while, hon, doing some research. I'll make us something to eat later, or we can order takeout."

She shook her head. "I'm not hungry."

"Neither am I."

He walked into his study and closed the door. Then he started his computer, and while he sat there, waiting for it to boot up, he suddenly put his head in his hands and cried like a child. For the longest time he stared at the computer screen, only seeing Heather in his mind. Then he grabbed a tissue from his desk, wiped his eyes dry and clicked on the browser icon. He typed in the url for the FBI missing person site and the screen displayed a database sheet that he had to fill out.

191

Details of the missing person: name, address, sex, age, weight, height, marital state, date last seen, close relatives and next of kin . . . Emotional condition of missing person, history of illnesses, including mental illness . . . Had this person gone missing before? Did he or she have a criminal record . . . Had there been a ransom demand?. . . Name, address, and e-mail address of person(s) filing the report.

Tom had done all this before many times for others, but never for himself. Mechanically, he filled in all the fields on his screen and when he had finished he clicked on *Submit*. The screen went blank and then there was a short message:

Heather Cramer, of 1250 Bermuda Drive, Santa Barbara, California, has been added to our Missing Persons database. You will be contacted when we have further information regarding her whereabouts. Thank you for using the FBI Hotline.

Well, Tom thought, he'd done what needed to be done, but no way was he just going to sit there and wait for others to find out where Heather had gone. The Hotline track record was abysmal, less then 10% of the cases were solved. For a while he pondered about what to do next. Where could Heather have gone? Perhaps she had joined some kind of commune, like lots of people did these days. It would be a start. He Googled for the word 'commune' and waited while his screen filled up with links and websites.

When he saw all the hits that came up, he was appalled. There were hundreds of religious communes, right-wing groups and other kinds of organizations where people could turn to if they lost faith in the way the world was run by the elite: The 2012 Warriors, The 2043 Freedom Fighters, The Aces of the New Millennium, The White Supreme Brotherhood, the Church of Satan, the Church of Oscar, The Church of the Last Days, the Rocky Mountains Freethinkers . . . At the bottom of the page was a counter: there were 12 more pages to be displayed.

Next came the conspiracy websites that ran from the highly unlikely to the outrageously inane. One of the sites warned about high-tech lasers that could evaporate a person in seconds without leaving a trace. Others mentioned secret additives to food and water supplies that would drive people mad and make them jump off cliffs like lemmings. One blog claimed that the HAARP transmitters could get into people's minds and force them to go to secret camps where they would be sterilized as a way to control the world's population.

Tom sat back and closed his browser. He rubbed his tired eyes. The world was mad, definitely. But that had absolutely nothing to do with what had happened to Heather. He was suddenly angry with himself. Why was he wasting his time on such rubbish. He never used to, in the force. He was a detective, for Christ's sake, and a detective went by facts, not idiotic ideas from lunatic minds.

Heather had carried a large canvas bag. That was a fact. It probably meant she wouldn't be coming back soon. Another fact was that she had left him a note, but it was not a suicide note. It somehow eased his worries a bit. Whatever Heather was up to she wasn't going to take her own life. She had written that it wasn't his fault, and there was no other man. From this he deduced that something else, something outside their own environment had caused her to leave.

She had not taken the car. That was important. Heather could hardly go very far, carrying a heavy bag. So somehow she had needed transport. The neighbors? Not likely. Mrs. Oldman, on the left, had no car; she was eighty-six and still lived by herself. The Tannings, on the right? No, they hardly knew them. Chuck left at the crack of dawn for a job in a nearby foundry, his wife Betty was a waitress at a downtown bar and she never surfaced before twelve noon. So the most likely explanation was a cab, and cabs could be traced. He felt suddenly invigorated. He was finally doing something. He Googled for taxi firms in Santa Barbara and got thirty-two results. He would check them out, one by one. Just when he started phoning, Penny came in, carrying a cup of tea.

"That's mighty nice of you, Pen," he said. "Thank you. I'll do some dinner shortly." She gave him a difficult smile and left again. She was really a wonderful girl, Tom thought. Quiet, considerate and loving, nothing like some of the precocious loud-mouthed brats in her class. He picked up the phone again and punched in the number of the first cab company on his list.

"Hello, can you tell me if you sent a cab to 1250 Bermuda Drive, Santa Barbara, this morning around 8 o'clock? Thank you." It was boring, repetitive work. Finally, after about twenty calls and thirty-five minutes later, a tired-sounding cabby told him he had come to their house and picked up Heather.

"Where did you take her?" Tom asked.

"Triagle."

"What? The Triagle Shopping Center?"

"Yes. What's so strange about that? Isn't that where women go shopping?"

"And from there?"

"How do I know? I took her there, she got out, paid me, and went inside. I left. That's what a taxi does; it drives people somewhere and drops them off. What else do you expect?"

"No reason to get snarky. I just wondered if you noticed where she went."

"No. Like I told you, she went inside. That's all I know. Hey, I got another call, I've got to go." The line went dead.

Interesting. For whatever reason, Heather had gone to a place where she could hide in a crowd. There were over a hundred shops and markets in the Triagle Center, and the place was always busy. A good place to lose oneself. The center would be closed now, but first thing tomorrow he would head down there. Someone might remember seeing Heather. Too tired to look at the screen any more, Tom switched his computer off and stood up. Just as he walked to the door, the phone rang and it felt as if his heart jumped into his throat.

"Heather?"

"No, it's Linda. Where are you? You guys haven't forgotten, have you?" It was Dr. Taggard's wife.

Oh, hell. Their bridge game. He should have called earlier.

"I'm sorry, Linda. Something dreadful has happened and I've been too upset to call. Heather has disappeared and I have no idea where she is. You'll have to do without us tonight."

"What do you mean, disappeared? What happened?" It was Christopher, listening in on another extension.

Quickly Tom explained. He wasn't in the mood to chat.

"That's just unbelievable," the physician said. "Is there anything we can do to help?"

"Not now, Christopher. I don't want to sound rude, but can I call you back tomorrow? I'm still in shock about this."

"Of course. You and Penny take care, Tom."

The call had upset Tom again, and he hurried into the kitchen to make some kind of late supper for Penny and himself. He had to do something, anything to take his mind off Heather.

◊ ◊ ◊

When China closed its borders for the export of cheap goods in the fall of 2047, the American economy was hit hard. It was the unexpected end of an era of overabundance. Hundreds of retail businesses folded, and luxurious shopping centers turned into decaying ghost buildings where crime and drugs moved in. Gone were the urban box stores and beautiful shopping arcades, where people once strolled among artfully designed shops that sold thousands of items imported from the Far East.

The super-rich in the big cities, like L.A, New York, Atlanta and others, where not affected, since they had no need for shopping centers. They ordered all their goods online, and everything was delivered to the city depots, and distributed along safe, protected transportation routes.

Triagle was an example of a new kind of shopping area for the poor and the ever-declining middle class. It was a large plot of country side, surrounded by high metal fences. Inside this compound, scores of small businesses, organizations, or just enterprising families sold their wares.

Some sellers operated from pre-fabricated wood structures on wheels that were moved there permanently, others used motor homes or campers. Still other businesses operated from tent-like structures, with tarpaulins stretched between poles to keep rain or sun out. To the far right, in an open field stood a battery of generators to supply electricity for lights and freezers for places that needed them.

Tom impatiently waited in line for the early morning opening. It was the first full day without Heather, and both he and Penny had been depressed and sad when they woke up. There was suddenly a big gap in their lives and they had a hard time coping. Penny wanted to help, but Tom decided that he'd rather work on his own this time. He had taken his daughter to school and told her to wait till he would pick her up.

After that, he had set off to the place where Heather had been seen last. It didn't look hopeful. There were hundreds of people waiting to get in and it would undoubtedly have been the same the day before. The chance of anyone having noticed Heather was small. The center opened at 10 a.m. and Tom had been there for at least half an hour, part of an ever-growing crowd.

Finally it was opening time. Two burly security guards rolled a large gate to the side, and the people immediately surged through. Tom let himself be moved by the throng, and once inside the center, he stood to the side to let the crowds pass. Where to start? He took a photo of a smiling Heather out of his pocket and stared at it, while his mood took a nosedive. He waited till the majority of the shoppers had passed through the gates, then approached the two security guards.

"Excuse me. Did either one of you by any chance notice this lady here yesterday, around this time?" He showed them Heather's picture. After taking turns to look at the picture, both men shook their heads.

"Can't help you, mate," the biggest one said. He was wearing a uniform that said *Belmont Security* on the breast pocket. He had a slightly pockmarked face and shifty eyes that moved from Tom to the few stragglers who walked in. "We're just here to keep law and order. You saw what a melee it was just now. Every day a few hundred people try to get in here at the same time. We can't look for individual faces. Sorry."

"Thanks anyway." Tom walked to the first of the shopping stalls and peeked at the merchandise. It was a butcher. Pheasants, chicken, rabbits and carcasses of deer hung from a bar suspended along the ceiling. A small refrigerated showcase showed the various cuts of meats. Tom was almost certain Heather wouldn't have stopped here and he began to walk past the stall, then he stopped. He was assuming things, one of the biggest mistakes in detective work. Heather might not have come here to buy meat, but she could have had another reason. He approached the stall keeper.

"I'm with the Santa Barbara Police Department," he said boldly. "Have you seen the woman in this photo?"

The butcher took a long look at the photo. He was about six feet tall, wearing a heavy-duty, bloody apron. Everything about him was big: his body, neck, chest, biceps, his hands and fingers. But apparently not his mind. He frowned and stared some more. Finally, he looked up at Tom with rather vacant eyes.

"Am I supposed to know this lady? I'm sorry, I can't recall. My memory's not what it used to be."

"No, no. All I am asking is if you saw her yesterday," Tom said, getting hot under the collar. "She's my wife and she's gone missing."

"Ah. Yesterday. I may have, I think. Or no, perhaps not. I can't recall . . ."

197

Tom gently pulled the photo from the man's huge hands and thanked him. Then he went on to the next booth. It was a furniture maker. There were two chairs and a table on display, and a sign that read: B.J. Barber and Son, Makers of Fine Furniture. Neither Mr. Barber or his son, if it was his son, had seen Heather, and Tom was beginning to feel stupid. This was crazy. It would take days to check out all the stores.

He moved to the next stall which held an artisan dealing in crystals and rocks. It was a thin young woman dressed like a gypsy. She had a crooked nose, and a small, pinched face with deep-set dark eyes that focused themselves like lasers on Tom when he entered her stall.

"You are a very troubled man," she said before Tom managed to say anything. "I can help with whatever ails you. My vibrational energy will cure anything. Quartz, blende, each crystal has its own specific frequency. Just tell me what's wrong and I'll select the right crystals for you to help your body find its natural balance."

"No thanks. Just tell me if you saw this lady yesterday."

"That was Monday. I'm closed on Mondays. Sorry."

His visit to the next stall was more successful. It was a bank, the First Triagle Cooperative. It wasn't a branch of one of the big city banks, but a place where the various merchants could deposited their money for safekeeping. Not only did the co-op deal with money, they also had barter cards that could be used by the various merchants in the center.

It said on a sign that the Cooperative cashed personal cheques, up to two hundred dollars, but didn't accept regular credit cards. They kept ten percent. Tom and Heather had never used the First Triagle Cooperative, since Tom's pension came into their local branch of First National. The little building was actually a prefab wooden structure on wheels that could be towed. Inside were two rooms. One housed the cashier in her little cubby hole behind a glass partition, the other one was hidden behind a door. Probably for private consultations, or maybe it was the vault. There were three chairs in the cashier's room and luckily they were all vacant. A pretty young woman with dark glasses, and curly black hair hanging down her shoulders, smiled at Tom when he entered.

"Can I help you?"

Tom handed her Heather's photo. "Have you seen this person here yesterday morning?" The replay was immediate and his heart jumped in his chest.

"Yes. She came in here to cash a check." Her face suddenly clouded over. "You're not with the police are you? Don't tell me it bounced. We're very careful, you know, but there is always a risk. That's why we keep our ten percent. She did look honest."

"Did she tell you why she cashed it?"

"No. It's none of our business. Probably none of yours, either. Why do you want to know?"

"I'm her husband. She has disappeared and I'm trying to find her."

"Oh. Sorry. No, she just said she needed money and since our limit is two hundred, that's what she took. I guessed she wanted to buy something in the market."

"Do you know where she went afterwards?"

The woman shook her black curls. "Sorry. She just took the money and left. It must be terrible for you. I hope you find her soon."

"Thanks." Tom nodded and headed outside.

He stood still in a little quiet spot between two stalls, letting the people file past him. Two hundred dollars. Not a good omen. If you lived carefully, two hundred dollars could last you quite a while. He looked at his watch and decided to take a look at some more stalls, and then go for a cup of coffee somewhere. He walked past a shoe and boot maker, where a middle-aged man with a leather apron was putting plaster on a woman's feet to make casts for a new pair of boots. In the back of the stall a young man was busily cutting leather. A strong smell of tannin filled the air. Cramer halted awkwardly, not wanting to disturb the workmen.

"I'll be a few minutes and then I can help you while this dries," the older man said, pointing to a chair. "Sit down

199

please." Tom sat down and watched while the man expertly sculpted the plaster around the lady's feet. Then the shoemaker stood up, and walked over to a sink to wash his hands.

"What can I do for you, sir. It is boots you want? Or just a pair of easy loafers?"

"Sorry, neither. I was just wondering if you had seen this lady yesterday?" He showed the shoemaker the photo.

"No." The shoemaker shook his head. "Nobody like that came in my stall yesterday. Are you with the police?"

"No, this is a photo of my wife. She's gone missing."

"Sorry to hear that. Can't help you I'm afraid." Without another word the shoemaker turned around and began to inspect the casts again. Taking the hint, Tom quietly got up and left.

The Organic Food Emporium was by far the biggest enterprise in the market. It consisted of several long tents, meeting in a center section, covered by a canvas roof. On the outside, above the entrance were the letters OFE. It was a busy place. People were streaming in to buy fresh vegetables, fruit, eggs, poultry and meats. Everything was laid out in cardboard boxes on long trestle tables, and it all looked fresh and clean, even the cuts of meat. Near the exit, an older Chinese man was weighing and pricing the items. It was a madhouse. Apart from him, there seemed to be very few staff. When Tom finally spotted a young man pushing a cart with fresh produce, he walked over and stopped him.

"Can you help me, please," he said, producing Heather's photo, well-worn by now. "Have you seen—"

"No time. You see supervisor. In office. Over there." The man pointed a long finger down the back of the tent, then pushed on with his cart. Carefully threading himself through the throng, Tom walked in the direction the man had pointed. He passed an archway, and noticed a midsize camper, with its door open. As he walked towards it, a man stepped out.

"Hey, you! Can't you read? It says 'PRIVATE' in big letters above that archway. Get back!"

"I am sorry, I just wondered if—"

"Not here." Giving Tom no choice but to follow him, the man strode through the archway, until they stood among the fruit and vegetables again.

"I haven't got much time. What is it you want?"

"My name is Tom Cramer. I just wondered if you have seen this lady yesterday." He handed the man Heather's photo. The store manager was about fifty or so. Overweight, with a beer belly, pallid, and hundreds of liver spots on both hands and arms. His dark hair was thinning badly and what was left of it was plastered against his pate. He was wearing faded blue jeans, a cream-colored T-shirt and worn sneakers. On the left hand side of his T-shirt was a peculiar mark: a small blue circle with three wavy grey lines inside. The manager frowned and shook his head.

"Haven't seen her. Why are you asking?"

"She's gone missing, and—"

"Sorry, can't help you." The store manage abruptly handed the photo back, and headed for the arcade again, leaving Tom nonplused. He decided it was time for a coffee and something to eat.

Phil's Coffee Hut was crowded, and it took a while to get served. However, the coffee was excellent and the oat bran muffin fresh. For a while Tom sat there, thinking about the store manager. Why had he been so rude? It had been a simple question. He had almost seemed on the defensive, as if he was hiding something. Had he perhaps seen Heather? Or had he just been annoyed that someone had invaded his privacy?

Tom sipped his coffee and thought he was probably imagining things. He sighed. Heather had come to Triagle and taken money out. She could have made contact with any of a few hundred people and gone goodness knows where. She could have just walked around for a while, called a cab and headed somewhere else. The shopping center was a dead end.

He finished his coffee and muffin and wondered whether Heather was still alive. Taking a deep sigh, he pushed that thought back to the most remote part of his mind. Heather was fine, she had to be; the alternative was unbearable. He looked at his watch, and decided to buy a few groceries for that evening and then head out to pick up Penny. Back into the Food Emporium, he selected a few carrots, a yam and a cabbage, and headed to the meat department to buy two fancy lamb chops. While he walked back to his car, he remembered something that had happened a while ago.

Heather was very health conscious. She exercised and looked after herself and provided her family with the best food she could find. She enjoyed cooking and preparing food. For years, she'd gone to the weekly market in at the Church of Oscar site. She had delighted in the fresh produce and meat they offered. There was a box for donations to the church, but everything was free for those who could not afford to pay.

After the terrible massacre there had been a lull, while the church had moved to the Excalibur site. Soon the market had reopened, albeit at on a smaller scale. Then one day, Heather had come home, frustrated and furious. She had driven all the way to Excalibur for nothing, because the church had closed its market. No reason was given. For a while Heather and Tom himself had scoured the country side, looking for farms that sold produce. It had not been easy. And then, just a few weeks later, like a sunny break in a cloudy sky, the Organic Food Emporium had opened.

Tom wondered if there was a connection. Had the Church of Oscar decided to sell their products through the OFE? Fresh food wouldn't keep that long, and it would all have to be trucked in, probably early in the morning, before the market opened. And if those trucks did indeed come from the Church of Oscar, they would return there. It could be a lead. Feeling much better than when he arrived, Tom got into his car and took off in the direction of Penny's school.

◊ ◊ ◊

He was cold and miserable. Sitting in his car with the windows steaming up, so he could hardly see outside, Tom wondered what the hell he was doing out there, in the middle of nowhere, at 4:00 a.m. in the pitch dark. He seemed to be the only living thing on the planet. He had parked under a lonely tree along the road that led to the Triagle shopping center, far enough away for the guards to spot him. Through his binoculars, he'd seen light in the guardhouse, and he suspected Triagle was guarded twenty-four-seven.

In front of the passenger seat stood a bag with his breakfast: two buns with ham and cheese, and a large thermos with coffee. On the passenger seat lay the handgun he had purchased for Heather several years ago, a Nano 9mm Beretta. He would have preferred his service pistol, but he'd had to hand that in when he retired. Luckily, it seemed that the criminal elements of society had taken the night off. He had not seen anyone on his way out here. His plan was to wait for the delivery truck to arrive and be unloaded at Triagle, then follow it on its route back from where it had come. He just wanted to find a clue, something he could work on.

When the eastern horizon was getting slightly lighter, Tom suddenly heard the unmistakable sound of a truck engine, slowing down as it left the highway and entered the service road that led to Triagle. The truck would pass close by; if the driver saw the car he might wonder why it was parked there, in the middle of nowhere. He might even stop to investigate, or alert the authorities. Tom would tackle that problem if and when it happened. He made himself as small as possible, crouching on the seat. When the truck finally reached him, the driver either didn't care or didn't notice him, and kept going without slowing down.

Relieved, Tom grabbed his binoculars and watched the vehicle as it drove the last mile or so to the gate. A searchlight went on in the Triagle compound and the gate slid open. The truck drove through and around the stalls, to a loading area at the back of the stores. Tom reached for his thermos and the last of the buns, wondering how long it would take to unload.

It was getting considerably lighter now, and he wasn't very happy where he was. The truck driver could easily see him on his way back. He might get suspicious and take down his license plate number. Perhaps he should head to the main road and wait there. He started the Volt and turned around.

On the highway, he made a left turn and drove for about a hundred yards, then turned around and parked on the side of the road. About twenty minutes later the truck appeared again, noisily stopped at the intersection, and turned right. Tom smiled to himself. Yes, the direction for the old Excalibur plant and the Church of Oscar. He waited a few minutes to let the truck get ahead, then slowly began to follow. There was hardly any traffic, and for a while he drove on, the truck a good distance ahead.

After about twenty minutes, he saw the vehicle's brake lights glow up, as the truck left the highway. Cramer also turned and followed at a safe distance, until the vehicle reached the driveway to Excalibur and stopped at the gate. Tom had kept well back, and pulled over on the shoulder. Looking through his binoculars, he watched as the cast iron gate swung open and the truck drove through.

The gate was lit up by lights on two stone pillars. Cramer could just make out an ornamental decoration on the left pillar, a miniature statue of a warrior on horseback with a large sword—the sword of Excalibur, most likely. On the right pillar, black gothic letters in a half circle showed the commune's name: *The Church of Oscar*. Tom watched for a few moments more, as the gate closed again, and the truck headed down the meandering driveway.

It was time to go home and warm up. Cramer now had proof there was a link between the Organic Food Emporium and the Church of Oscar. So what? It did not help him at all. Heather might have gone into the food market, or she might not. There were an endless number of possibilities. Perhaps he should concentrate more on why his wife had left him, rather than where she could be.

Heather's disappearance made no sense at all. If she was so unhappy she wanted to leave Penny and him, they would have discussed it together. They kept no secrets, or grudges. His wife loved him and Penny. No way would Heather just sneak out like that, yet she had. Something bigger was going on and Tom had no idea what it was. With a sickening feeling in his stomach he realized that as far as his missing wife was concerned, he still had his feet firmly planted in square one.

◊ ◊ ◊

When Carol and Patrick Johnson joined the Church of Oscar, they brought two DVDs with vital information for the commune. Father English had suggested that the contents of the disks should be transcribed onto paper. According to him, every church had its history and records written on stone tablets or old scrolls of parchment. Who had ever heard of a church based on a DVD? An intense, emotional experience, like the cleansing of one's mind with Oscar's Breath, just didn't jive with a product of modern technology.

Or so Daniel thought. If he had his way, both DVDs should be copied and then destroyed. Jo had thought that went a little too far, and they had kept the disks in the church's vault. One of the disks had a rather personal message from Yabul to his wife Carol, and after watching part of it, both Jo and Daniel had decided it wasn't necessary to transcribe that disk for the church. Sure, it was interesting to note that Yabul's ideas and those of the Church of Oscar were very similar, but that was hardly relevant to the daily running of the commune.

It was the second DVD that was worth gold. The first file on it, 'VTM.doc', held the complete blueprint and specs for Oscar's Breath. It was this file Daniel had transcribed first, so that Bert Kwiss could begin the manufacturing of their recruiting drug. Daniel had not been able to do any more work on the disks, since his life had been cut off so suddenly. It had been up to Jo to continue the process.

One early morning, around six o'clock, Jo was sitting behind his desk studying the DVD on his computer screen. He had finally decided to spend some time copying it. It was not just a matter of sending the files to the printer; the text should be read and edited first, to see what needed transcribing. It was a boring job, done a bit at a time, since Jo wasn't a scientist.

For about twenty minutes, he had peered at a file called 'Test.doc'. It was all about statistics, groups and sub-groups, testing criteria, abstracts, means and deviations. Jo understood very little of it, and he wondered if the file even needed to be copied. After all, they had all received the Breath and it worked flawlessly. Why worry about testing after the fact?

The next file on the DVD was called 'Myvisions.doc'. It was a recording of Yabul's philosophy about the world and how he thought humans were destroying it. Jo quickly browsed through the file and marveled at Yabul's genius. It seemed that somehow the scientist had imprinted his own ideas on his VTM creation. It was a remarkable feat. Jo was sorry he had never met Yabul; the scientist would have made a great Head Councilor. What a loss to the world that he had died so young.

The last file on the DVD was called 'Addendum.doc'. It was small and Jo assumed that Yabul had added it later, after he finished his other work. He clicked on the icon and a double page appeared on the screen. On the left side was a picture of a small plant. On the right side was a message.

Carol my love, I'm putting this in as an afterthought, since I have only just found out about this the other day . . .

Jo stopped reading and took a sip of his coffee. Should he be looking at this at all? It seemed personal. Yet Carol and Patrick had given the DVD to the church, to do with as they pleased. After a few seconds he continued to read.

I have done everything in my power to make VTM exactly the way I wanted it, but it must be tested first. Once found to be safe, it can be marketed for the good of mankind. However, one cannot possibly think of all contingencies and there is always the possibility that something will go wrong. I want you to know that I have found a way to counter the effects of my VTM, should it be necessary. The picture you see on the left of this note is a photo of a specific mushroom, called Psilocybe Cubensis. It is native to North America and wanted by some people for its hallucinatory properties. Quite by accident, I have found out that an extract from this type of mushroom can be used to reduce, or even counter, the effects of VTM on the human brain. I have no more information about this, since I did not have more time to pursue this any further. I only include this information to let you know there may be a way to protect yourself, should my invention fall into the wrong hands.

In horror, Jo stared at the picture of the little mushroom, as if it might come alive, jump off the page, fly into his face and crawl into his brain. An antidote to Oscar's Breath? He took a deep breath, while the importance of what he had just read sank in. Was this the Lord's way to solve the reproduction problem that the church faced? Jo still remembered one of the first church meetings, when the councilors had discussed their lack of sexual feelings. Father English had always stoically maintained that the Lord would supply the solution to their procreation needs in due time, when the earth's population had been brought down to a sustainable level. Everyone had accepted that and nothing more had ever been said about it.

Could this be the answer, right here, hundreds, perhaps thousands of years ahead in time? A tiny mushroom? If so, what should the church do about it? The knowledge was of tremendous importance for the future, but it also posed a great threat in the present. What if the authorities ever found out about this? They could use the mushrooms to change the members of the commune back to how they were before, negating everything the church had done. It would be as if it the Church of Oscar had never existed.

Jo suddenly couldn't think any more; his mind was overloaded. He decided the DVD could never leave the vault. Absolutely no one, except the Head Councilor, must ever know about it. He turned his computer off and carefully placed his papers and the DVD back into the vault. It was time for his morning walk. He took a light jacket from his closet, put on a pair of brown walking boots and headed out. After he walked down the steps into the lush gardens, he set out at a vigorous pace to clear his mind and get the circulation in his legs going.

His walk took him through the commune, past the Common Area and then via the vegetable gardens into the wilderness behind Excalibur. While he strode on, he thought about the church's early days in Bernard's barn, then in the Magnolia Inn, and later in their lovely new home near Mission Canyon and its horrible ending.

He thought of the councilors who had passed away over time. There were only himself, Brian and Sylvia left of the original founding fathers. Or should that be fathers and mothers? His old friend Ted and his mother Diana, Bernard Tows, Penny and Ian Weatherby, his mother Elvira, Daniel English, Dale Pinehurst—all gone.

Jo missed all the late councilors, especially Daniel, but it was the recent death of Dale Pinehurst that was a reminder of what the world outside was like these days. The Chief of Security had died in an altercation late at night, when two poachers had tried to steal the sheep that roamed freely in Excalibur's front garden. The poachers had ambushed the guard at the gate, but he had managed to call for help, and Dale had rushed out. The villains had panicked and hit him with their truck. Dale had died instantly and the attackers had escaped.

When Jo reached the Common Area, he heard the crunchy sound of tires on gravel behind him. He turned around and noticed a large tricycle used to move things around in the commune. Inside the basket were several laundry bags tied together. A young woman in her twenties was furiously pedaling the heavy tricycle. She was very pretty and a great smile compensated for the dental braces she wore. She was dressed in a short-sleeved grey coverall and her dark-blonde hair was tied in a bun behind her head, probably so that it would not interfere with her work in the laundry facility. Her name was Anna Kulik.

"Good morning, Head Councilor," she greeted him with a radiant smile. "Isn't it a beautiful day?"

"That it is, Anna. That it is. Just having my morning constitutional."

"Have a pleasant walk, Head Councilor." She gave him a quick wave, while she pedaled past, straining against the slight incline of the path. Jo watched her until she disappeared around the back of the Common Area. Then he continued his walk, feeling uplifted after seeing Anna, noticing her youthful dedication to the job. It was good to have some young people in the commune.

He thought of Erwin Johnson. His ingenious idea for the recruitment of new church members, implemented and modified by Bert Kwiss, was working better than they could ever have hoped for, and they were doing very well. That young man would go far in the Church of Oscar.

Jo had reached the end of the cultivated land, where the gardens gave way to wilderness, as yet unclaimed for the church. The area was very peaceful, and there were walking trails that were kept up by the maintenance workers. The foliage grew denser, with ferns of all kind and redwood trees. Wild lupin flowers grew in the open spaces between them. He really enjoyed his daily trips, spotting deer, birds and other creatures, like squirrels or marmots. Whenever he saw a species he didn't know, he tried to remember it and look it up later in the Nature book that a new church member had donated to the library.

He was about to turn back when he noticed something that made him halt. In the brush near a magnificent birch tree, he noticed a proliferation of small mushrooms and he recognized them at once. These were the plants depicted in Yabul's DVD. The antidote for Oscar's Breath was growing right there, on the church's property! Why had he found them now after just reading about them? Was it just a coincidence? Had these mushrooms always grown here? He stood for the longest time, not moving, his heart pounding in his chest.

Jo didn't know the first thing about mushrooms and toadstools and was secretly scared of them. After all, some types were deadly poisonous. He knew the church cultivated edible mushrooms in a special barn, but the gardens and their products were Sylvia's responsibility. Jo was more interested in flowers and small animals.

He looked at the tiny plants. There were about a dozen or so, grouped in an almost perfect circle. He wondered what he should do. Destroy them? That was against what the church preached. *Honor all life and only kill out of self defense.* Besides, they would only emerge again elsewhere. That type of mushroom had probably been around for eons and as long as people didn't know their secret, things would be fine. He would write about his discovery in the secret church annals and that would be the end of it.

When he wanted to move on, it felt as if the mushrooms' hallucinatory powers were affecting his mind even from a distance. Something inside him forced his legs to walk towards the little plants, and it seemed that the hands that picked half a dozen were acting on their own, outside his control. He brushed off the dirt and carefully stuck the mushrooms in his jacket pocket. Then he headed back to the church.

VIPERS

13

"Penny! Hurry up, or you'll be late!" Standing at the bottom of the stairs, Cramer had to shout, because his daughter's bedroom door was still closed. Cursing himself for allowing her to watch TV until the wee hours, Cramer walked to the kitchen to keep an eye on the boiling eggs.

He'd had trouble sleeping lately, but last night had been worse than ever. He'd tossed and turned, unable to keep his arms and legs still, while strange thoughts run amok in his head, as if their takeout dinner had been too spicy. Perhaps Penny felt the same; she wasn't usually this late. He heard the shower start upstairs and quickly glanced at his watch. 8:30! School started in half an hour.

When the timer buzzed, he took the eggs out of the pan and hid them under two woolen egg cozies to keep them warm. He poured himself a second cup of coffee and walked into his study, figuring he just had time to check his e-mail. When the operating system had loaded, he clicked on his mail program and waited for his inbox to open. It didn't. Damn, something wrong with the Net again! There were heavy footsteps on the stairs, and he hurried back to the kitchen. His daughter looked as if she'd dressed in a hurry. No make-up, hair untidy, a multi-colored sweater roughly pulled over a white blouse, blue jeans, and white sneakers.

"Sorry, Dad. Had a terrible night. Woke up at four and couldn't sleep at all afterwards." She sat down and hit the top of her egg with a teaspoon, as if the egg was responsible for her lack of sleep. She quickly peeled it and took a spoonful of yolk. "How about you? Did you sleep all right?"

"No. Remind me never to order takeout from that place again." They both laughed.

They quickly finished their breakfast, and Penny began to clear the table.

"No, leave that," Cramer said, "I'll do it when I come back."

Five minutes later they were on their way to school.

"Funny," Penny said.

"What?"

"Not much traffic today. And look, over there, people standing in the driveway, talking. I don't think they can get into their cars."

At the school another surprise awaited them. A large group of people, students as well as parents, stood near the doorway, but nobody was going inside. "OK, let's find out what's going on," Cramer said. He guided the car into one of the few remaining parking spaces, and they headed towards the entrance to join the crowd.

"There's Ryan and his Dad," Penny shouted, and she dashed off to see her schoolmate. Cramer followed. Ryan's father was a rotund man of about forty, dressed in an a dark business suit. Cramer vaguely remembered Penny telling him he was an accountant. His ample body betrayed a life of sedentary indulgence: rich food and drinks, and plenty of it, most likely. His moonlike face was pallid like stretched parchment, and the old-fashioned horn rimmed spectacles made him look like a dull college professor. He smiled when he noticed Penny.

"Ah, Penny, there you are. Ryan was wondering if you'd come after what happened." Turning to Cramer, he stuck out a paunchy hand. "Keith Bookhurst. You must be Tom Cramer." He pointed to a shy youth standing next to him, looking as if he desperately wanted to be somewhere else. "This is my son, Ryan."

"What did you mean 'after what happened'? " Cramer said.

"Haven't you heard?" Ryan shouted in a high-pitched voice. "The Chinese have exploded an EMF bomb in the atmosphere. Everything's dead, TV, phone, computers. We can't get into school, 'cause the night locks won't open. We're all going to die!"

"Oh, Ryan, stop being so melodramatic," his father exclaimed. "If you don't know what you're talking about, shut up."

"You've got to excuse Ryan," Keith said to Cramer. "He's got a particularly vivid imagination. From what I know, all wireless communication is dead. TV, telephones, Blackberries, computers, the lot. We don't know why, or how widespread it is, but it looks big." Keith turned to his son. "Look, Ryan, I can't wait any longer. I've got to go and see what's happening in the office." Bookhurst gave his son a hug, nodded at Tom and Penny, and walked over to his car.

There was movement behind the glass doors as they were opened from the inside. With the usual reluctance of teenagers heading for class, the students began to enter the school, and most parents began to leave. Then an official looking man in a grey suit rushed outside, waving his arms.

"Everyone, come inside, please. Parents also. There'll be an important announcement in the gym. This way please."

"That's Mr. Robinson, the Principal," Penny said, almost reverently. "Come on, Dad." They followed the noisy group of students and adults inside, through a long hallway, into the gymnasium, where rows of chairs had been set up. On the wall was a big screen TV, but it was turned off. When everyone was finally seated, Mr. Robinson, looking ill at ease, stood in front of a lectern.

"School will not be open today," he began, and a rush of excitement flew through the crowd. The Principal ignored it and continued. "There has been an event of great importance. I want you all to listen to a message from our Department of Homeland Security. We have patched it in on the audio system. Afterwards, you should all go home." He stepped back from the lectern and an uneasy silence followed. Then there was another voice, booming from the speakers on the side of the stage.

"This is Clifford Starling, Secretary of the U.S. Department of Homeland Security. Around 8:00 a.m. this morning, Eastern Time, a major solar flare of unprecedented strength caused an EMF disruption in North and Central America, Europe and parts of Africa and Asia. Wireless communication in that part of the world is disrupted. I want you all to understand three important things.

"First off, although this is an event of major importance, it is only temporary. The damage will be repaired. Our government is working on the highest level with representatives of all major electronic and electrical companies, at home and abroad, and we have their assurance that this emergency will be handled with the highest priority and in the quickest time possible.

"Secondly, this disruption only applies to wireless communications. The main electrical services as well as normal wired information networks are not affected. The Internet is partially operational, but much slower than normal. Finally, and most importantly, there is absolutely no threat to life or property and no reason to panic. Everyone should go on with their daily lives. Until normal communications are restored you can listen to our bulletins on this government emergency channel. I trust we shall soon put all this behind us. Thank you for your attention."

An exciting murmur of voices filled the room, and people began to make their way out again. Then there was a sudden commotion.

"No, wait. You have heard the official version. Let me tell you what really happened." A man in his early forties climbed on the row of benches that were stacked along a wall of the gymnasium. He was dressed in a rumpled grey suit, and his premature grey hair and a similar color beard was tousled and sticking out all over the place. Cramer's first impression was that of a rogue scientist. It was obvious by the looks on the Principal's face that the address was unexpected and not authorized by the school.

"I am Alan Harking, science teacher at Cliff High," the man said. "What you've just heard is true, but it is only part of the story." He jumped off the bench and ran to a blackboard

216

along the wall. He took a piece of chalk and quickly drew a large circle on the blackboard.

"This is our earth," he shouted, then drew another circle outside the first one. "This is the ionosphere. It is a dense natural energy field, protecting us all from any kind of incoming radiation. Now you may have wondered why this large EMF disruption has occurred. Why had this never happened before?" He drew a large freehand line on the blackboard to show the extent of the field. "Why did the ionosphere not block this monster flare? A hundred years ago, it would have. Today it didn't, and the answer lies partly in an electronic facility near a town in Alaska called Gakona.

"From here our government has been bombarding our precious ionosphere with radio waves of incredible power, stronger than the largest radio or television station in the world, millions of watts. It is called project HAARP, and our government is using it to punch holes in the ionosphere, causing it to heat up and lose its protectiveness. All this in the name of so-called research. They are affecting the weather, disrupting the patterns of rain and drought. There are more HAARP transmitters around the globe and they are threatening our very existence—"

"Dr. Harking, stop this at once," Robinson called out loudly. "You are out of line here. You heard that there is no reason to panic, so do not try to create one. Let these people go home, please."

"No, you will hear me out," Harking shouted. "Our government is not helping us with the problems we face every day, they are creating them! They disrupt Earth's natural harmony in every possible way, and we let them. This is all our own fault. Unless we start acting like responsible—"

Two burly security guards grabbed the science teacher by the shoulders and dragged him off towards the exit, accompanied by loud catcalls and boo's.

"Let him speak. It's still a free country . . ."

"He is right! What are you afraid of? . ."

"What a load of rubbish. Who does he think he is?"

217

"Come on, Penny, let's get out of here, before this turns into a three-ring circus," Cramer said, urging his daughter to the door. Several other concerned parents were also leading their kids away.

"Is it true, what Dr. Harking says, Dad? Are we the cause of the world's problems?" Penny asked, while they walked towards their car. "I like Professor Harking, he always tells good stories."

"Not much good about what he said today, Pen. It may be all our fault, but an emotional outburst like this isn't going to solve anything."

◊ ◊ ◊

"Hang on, Bob! What are you doing?" Marvin exclaimed.

They were in the Secret Springs Control room. Bob Shample was in charge of the main computer compartment. Barely twenty-five, judging from his looks, he had the sallow, pale complexion of someone who didn't see much sunlight on an average day. He'd been with the company for only two years, and what he didn't know about computers and electronics could probably be written down on a paper napkin. He was usually perky and upbeat, but this time he looked pale and worried.

"I'm shutting her down, sir. No other choice. All the WiFi circuits are fried, and I no longer know what's working and what is not. We don't know if our security system is still operational and some hackers may have gotten in already."

"No, you can't do that. Not a cold shutdown!"

"Why not?" Litto Usko had left his own station to join them. He was the company's network expert, and his job was to make sure that all the Secret Springs subscribers were registered and assigned their private bandwidth for their virtual adventures. "I agree with Bob," he said. "The only way we can find out if we are compromised is to shut it down."

"No." Marvin shook his head. "We've never done a cold system shut down like that. It's too dangerous."

"We've never been hit by an EMF wave this big, either," Litto said. "It may be more dangerous not to shut it down. We're wasting valuable time, sir."

"You're not thinking, guys!" Marvin shouted. "There are still thousands, if not millions people on line. The fiber optic cables are working fine. If you do a cold shutdown, all avatars will be suddenly reset, and we don't know what that will do to the people online. They might panic and scare themselves to death, because the Failsafe system will be off also. Look what happened to Philip Kozak! We could face massive lawsuits in the future."

Bob Shample's face turned even paler. "Didn't think of that," he said nervously. "We've got to tell everyone online to get off pronto."

"No time for that," Litto said. "It'll take hours."

"So what do I do?" Bob's hands rested on the side of his keyboard, and the others could see that his fingers were shaking.

"There is another way," Marvin said. "We can re-route all avatar circuits to a backup power supply to keep them charged. Then we can shut the system down. The virtscapes will vanish, and people may wonder what the hell is going on, but at least they have time to get out of their avatars."

"Good thinking, sir." Bob nodded. "Here, Litto, give me a hand."

Marvin stood back, while the two operators furiously began to enter commands in their consoles. His heartbeat was slowly getting back to normal. It had been close, but Philip would be safe. He looked at his watch. It was ten past eight, and a board meeting had been scheduled for eight o'clock. He'd better get going. There wasn't much more he could do here.

In the boardroom he found the others waiting for him. "Well, Marvin?" Charles asked. "Are we going to survive this latest display of Mother Nature's wrath? Have we been compromised? If this is affecting everyone else, we're safe right? Nobody can attack us."

"If only it was that easy, Charles. The solar flare that created this was cone shaped, and didn't affect the whole world. Most of South America, Africa, and Australia are OK. In a split second before everything crashed here, someone could have slipped through our security. We don't know, and that's why we've shut the system down. This is unprecedented and it's going to cost us. And not just us, but every company or organization that depends on WiFi. Six of our communication satellites are toast, so there won't be any new virtscapes until the Chinese can put new satellites in orbit. The crew on the space station is probably dead also. This is about as bad as it could be."

"Is there any positive news?" Armonde asked.

"Some," Marvin said. "Basic Internet core connections and the virtscapes are fine. There's no permanent damage and once everything is repaired and put back on line we'll be operational again. But it may take a while."

"What do you mean by 'a while'?" Sandor asked.

Marvin shrugged. "No idea. The complete recovery could take weeks, perhaps months."

"Well, I guess there's nothing we can do but wait," Armonde said. "We'll have to post a message on our website: Secret Springs, offline till further notice. Our subscribers are just going to love that. We shall have to reimburse the people who have pre-paid."

A few minutes later the meeting broke up, and the board members returned to their own departments. On the way out, Sarah Marrion grabbed Marvin by the elbow.

"Marvin, what about Philip," she whispered. "Have they reset his avatar also? Is he really dead this time?"

He smiled at her. "No. He's patiently waiting to ride it all out, just like the rest of us."

◊ ◊ ◊

It was an unusual council meeting. Ambassador Sparling had some personal business in L.A. and had taken the opportunity to visit the Church of Oscar's headquarters. It should have been a happy occasion, but instead the mood was somber. In front of each of the councilors and the distinguished guest lay a small black ribbon. When everyone was seated, Jo called the meeting to order.

"It is with great pleasure that I welcome Dr. Sparling here today," he said, nodding at Helin. "I wish it had been under more pleasant circumstances. May I ask that each of you strap the black ribbon on your arm to remember the four courageous Ambassadors who lost their lives two days ago." Jo ceremoniously picked up the small elastic ribbon, stretched it a bit, and put it around the sleeve of his council robe just above the elbow. Then he continued.

"For a while, four of our Ambassadors stationed in the African country of Zaily, had planned a mission to spread the Word of Oscar in a small neighboring country, called New Sanuga. Two days ago, that country's leader King Buassi finally gave permission for the Ambassadors to come to Oriro, the country's capital." Jo halted for a moment, to wet his lips. Then he continued.

"After they were ceremoniously admitted to the King's Palace and introduced themselves, the visitors were arrested and driven to a dilapidated farm nearby. Here they were tied up and interrogated to confess that they were followers of Satan. When none of the Ambassadors would do so, even under the most horrid tortures, the King's henchmen, armed with machetes, finished them off 'like the devil's spawn they were', according to the authorities.

"Apparently, in the language of New Sanuga, the word for devil is Occar. Afterwards, the barn was set afire to pacify the Gods. We know all this from the Ambassadors' interpreter and driver Kaxuma, a native of Zaily. Since he was a foreigner, Kaxuma was not allowed inside the palace. The Ambassadors had paid him well for a return trip, so he waited to drive his guests back to Zaily. He saw the protesting Ambassadors being driven away in an open truck, and followed at a discreet distance. When Kaxuma heard the horrid screams of the dying men and women and saw the King's mercenaries throw fuel onto the straw roof of the farm, he knew enough. He rushed back to his own country, and informed the Ambassadors' base of the dreadful news.

"I shall now read the names of our Ambassadors, and would like you all to join me in a minute of silence to remember them. Alex Zimm, Ylas Ivanno, Tammy Tilburn and Ronald Harbor." Jo let his voice trail off, then lowered his head onto his chest and closed his eyes.

"How could this happen?" Patricia Sheppard demanded, after the period of silence was over. "How come nobody made the connection between the words Oscar and Occar? Of course they would think we're devil worshippers!"

"It is very easy on hindsight, sitting here thousands of miles away, Councilor Sheppard," Father Dubois said. "It's a different matter in the field. If we want to spread the word of Oscar, sacrifices will unfortunately have to be made."

"We should have spent more time on gathering intelligence, then," Patricia said. "Common sense could have prevented this slaughter."

"I agree." Helin Sparling joined in. "Are you sure the present recruiting system is the best way to promote the Church of Oscar, Councilor Rasnell?"

Jo took a deep breath. That was all the church needed. Discord among its members. Dr. Sparling was known for her outspokenness.

"It is the only system I know that works, Ambassador. If you have a better idea I would certainly like to hear it."

"I have," Helin said firmly. "Forcing an ideology on people will not work. Wars, crusades, police actions, any form of indoctrination fails in the end. Not a single war in history ended the way it was planned. Change must come from inside people, not from the outside."

"If Councilors Rasnell and Johnson hadn't forced Oscar's Breath on you, Ambassador Sparling, we wouldn't be sitting here now," Carol remarked.

"Of course," Helin said, taking Carol's remark in stride. "We cannot tell people about the Breath beforehand, because they will not agree to have their minds cleansed. Deception is unfortunately necessary in the final stage of recruitment. But I'm not talking about that part here. What I am saying is that we must concentrate on delivering the church's message first, *before* we attempt to recruit people."

"I am confused, Ambassador," Jo said. "What exactly is your idea?"

"What I have in mind has been available for many years, and it is about time we use it. The Internet, and more especially the social networks, are great tools to spread our ideology. The biggest network, Secret Springs, would be the perfect venue for our church."

"Secret Springs? That cesspool of immorality? You can't be serious, Ambassador!" Father Dubois exploded. "How can that possibly help out cause?"

"Stripped from its virtual reality part, Secret Springs could help spread the Word of Oscar around the globe. Don't you see, Father? There isn't a country in the world that is not connected to their network. Over eight billion people would hear our message and if they are interested they will ask us to become members. They might even beg us. That is when we'll send our representatives in, when people are ready for us. Isn't that a better idea than ordering the Ambassadors into the unknown to face possible death?"

"Hold on, now," Jeremy said. "Even if people wanted to join us, their governments might not allow it. Then what?'

"The people will revolt to make it possible, Councilor Burlon. Look at how the Middle East changed in the earlier part of the century. Early social networks were the catalyst, and Secret Springs is a thousand times more powerful. The change in consciousness that is happening all over the world is unstoppable, and the Church of Oscar is the medium for it."

"Secret Springs will never allow us to use their facilities," Father Dubois said.

"The commune will need to buy it, Father," Helin Sparling said. "We have plenty of money. I have heard the virtual network is not doing well these days; they may be ready for a takeover. There was a major setback for them with that EMF cloud a while ago and a lot of people are getting tired of sin, deception and virtual games. Many subscribers have canceled their accounts. I think the church might stand a chance to buy the company, but we won't know until we try."

Helin Sparling turned around and faced Erwin. "Councilor Johnson, I believe you have a half-brother working for Secret Springs. Why don't you pay him a visit and see what you can do?"

◊ ◊ ◊

"Can we play a game, Dad?" It was about ten o'clock on a Sunday morning, and Tom and Penny had just had breakfast. Tom was sipping his coffee, while Penny slurped her V8 juice. It was a month since Heather had gone, and though it was hard, they were coping. Tom had become very conscious of all the housekeeping his wife had done behind the scenes all those years. The cooking, cleaning and washing. He had never really appreciated it until now. He lovingly eyed his daughter. It had been hardest on her, yet she was doing her best to help. She was growing up, albeit it perhaps not as fast as other kids.

They'd known for a long time that Penny was slightly slower than other kids her age. Not that there was anything wrong with her; she was as healthy as could be and had a lovely, caring character. According to Dr. Taggard, it had to do with her position on a particular bell curve.

As far as intelligence, performance, learning capabilities, sexual maturing or any other personality traits, young people were all tested and fitted on bell curves these days. According to the tests taken at school, Penny had a slighter lower IQ than average. Both Tom and Heather thought it was a lot of rubbish and would have none of it.

The fact that Penny didn't really feel like going out to parties that much, didn't have that many friends, sat at the back of the class and didn't have the solutions to some math problems right away, had nothing to do with intelligence. Her ability to say no to people who peddled drugs and booze at school made her a far better person in Tom's eyes than any of her brash, so-called smart friends. When Dr. Taggard had mentioned that there were drugs available to improve Penny's mental performance, both Heather and Tom had bristled at the idea. Their daughter was fine the way she was.

"Sure, hon. What do you want to play?"

"The Ouija Board. We played it the other day at school, in our metaphysics class. It's really cool. And it might even help us."

"Help us? With what? Finding your Mom? Come on now, Penny. That's silly. The Ouija Board has to do with the occult, you know. It's best not to tamper with that."

"What do you mean?"

"Well, from what I know about it, it's used in séances when people try to communicate with the dead and the spirit world. I personally think it's a lot of hocus pocus, and in susceptible people it can lead to all kinds of problems. And if you want to use it, you're already assuming Mom is dead. Well, she's not. I am certain of it."

"Oh, Dad, I didn't mean it that way. It's not just about the afterlife. It has to do with your subconscious and stuff. Maybe we can contact Mom, wherever she is. Don't you think it's worth a try? I mean, it has been more than a month now and we still don't know anything. What harm can it do? Even if Mom is dead, we would be better off knowing. . . *Well, wouldn't we?*"

Tom remained silent. Penny had hit a sore spot. He still had no idea why Heather had suddenly walked out on them, and they didn't have any leads.

225

"We don't have a board," he said meekly, hoping it would be the end of it. But she was prepared for that.

"Benjamin loaned me one," she said. "I'll get it." She rushed off to her room, leaving Tom in a mixed emotional state. Solving missing persons cases with a Ouija Board? The guys on the force would have a good laugh at that. Still, if it made Penny happy, he didn't mind wasting a few hours. Benjamin was one of her classmates, a nice looking, well-mannered boy. After a few minutes Penny was back, carrying a square board the size of a chess board. She folded it open and lay it flat on the kitchen table.

"We'll have to ask a question first, then close our eyes and concentrate and let our minds guide the pointer," she said, as if she was an expert on the game. "It works better with more people, because you can have an independent observer to write everything down, but there's only two of us, so we'll have to make do. I'll use both hands, and you have to put one hand on mine, and write the results down with the other. You'll need a pen and paper, Dad."

"Just a sec." Tom disappeared into his study and came back with a pen and notebook. "So what are you going to ask?" he said, sitting down again.

Penny pondered for a while. "How about: Mom, are you all right?"

"Fine."

They sat comfortably at the kitchen table. Penny placed both hands on the round, mouse-like structure with a sharp point, and Tom put his left hand on top of hers. He put the pen and the notebook next to him, on the ready. Then Penny spoke, and to Tom she sounded just like an angel.

"Mom, we miss you very much. Can you let us know if you're all right?"

They sat there, Penny with her eyes closed, waiting, hands on the mouse pointer. There was no movement.

"Mom, can you tell us where you are?" Penny whispered after a long while. Again, nothing happened, and to Tom the whole thing seemed very surreal. What on earth was he doing? This was just a waste of time. He took a deep breath, barely controlling his frustration.

"Your turn for a question, Dad," Penny said, and once more he gave in, for her sake. He thought for a moment. Then he said: "Heather, can you give us a clue as to where you are, so I can find you? We really want you back here with us."

After a few moments, Tom was surprised when his hand began to move, while the pointer slid across the board. Slowly, very slowly. It touched on the number 0, then 6, then 1. With his free hand, Tom quickly wrote down the numbers.: 0 . . 9 . . 1 . . 8. Only numbers, no letters.

After a few minutes, the mouse pointer began to move steadier, jumping from one number to another, faster and faster. He looked askance at Penny's face, and saw she was in some kind of trance, while her hands rapidly moved across the board. Tom's hand followed, but he was absolutely sure that it was Penny who controlled the pointer, not himself.

He quickly wrote the numbers down again and noticed something peculiar. There were just six numbers, and they were repeating, as if they were in some kind of endless loop. He began to feel ill at ease and took his hand off Penny's hands, but she kept moving, faster and faster.

"Slow down, Pen," he said, "you're going too fast." She didn't seem to hear him, as the pointer continued its mad movements across the board. He wrote down a few more numbers, then stared at his daughter and suddenly had enough. He grabbed her hands hard and forced them down on the board. She resisted his grip and wanted to keep moving.

"Penny, this is wrong!" he shouted. "Stop it! You're in some kind of trance. Snap out of it!"

He finally felt her hands relax, and after a few seconds Penny opened her eyes. "What happened?" she asked, as if she'd just woken up from a deep sleep.

"You scared me, girl," Tom said. The use of the word 'girl' showed how anxious he was. "I thought you'd never come out of it. I knew this was a bad thing." He removed the pointing device, closed the board with a bang and lay it on the counter top.

"What did it say?" Penny asked. "What did it tell us?"

"Nothing. Just six repeating numbers." He pushed the notebook between them, and they both looked at the numbers that filled one line, then continued on the next one and the next one, almost a quarter-sheet full.

"Six numbers," Penny said. "What does it mean, Dad? Why do they keep repeating? Look, the first four numbers: 0918. That is my birthday, September 18. Why would it spell that out?"

"I have no idea, hon," he said, glad it was over. "Just a coincidence, I guess. Come on, I've had enough of this stuff. I need another coffee. Want some more V8?"

She nodded and he could see she was sad, close to crying. She could be very emotional. He stood up and hugged her, running a hand through her hair. "It's OK, hon. You did your best to help. It just didn't work this time. Perhaps we'll give it another go later." He walked to the refrigerator and took out the V8 juice. After pouring a glass full he handed it to his daughter. "I'm just going to check my e-mail," he said. "Then we can play scrabble. OK?"

Her face lit up, and she nodded happily, the Ouija Board episode all but forgotten. Scrabble was her favorite game. Tom poured himself some more coffee, picked up his notebook and pen and disappeared in his study. Talking and thinking of Heather had upset him also. He started up his computer and while he waited for it to boot, he looked at the repeating numbers in his notebook. It was all nonsense, of course, but it was weird.

Why would a Ouija Board reveal a set of repeating numbers? Random numbers, yes, he could live with that. But the same six numbers, over and over again? What were the odds of that? And why Penny's birthday? It didn't make any sense. He took his pen and separated the numbers in groups by putting a slash after every six: 091842—slash, 091842—slash. It was spooky. Yet Tom was strangely intrigued. All his life he'd worked with facts. That's what the world ran on; things that could be seen and explained. A murder, a weapon, someone's DNA. Yet here was something he couldn't fathom at all.

His computer beeped to tell him it was ready. He clicked on his e-mail, hoping against hope that Heather had finally left a message. There was none. He left the computer on and headed back to his daughter. On the way, he picked up the Scrabble game from one of the shelves of the bookcase in the living room.

◊ ◊ ◊

Philip Kozak lay on his back in a virtual garden, his head resting on a small log. It was the exact image of the garden of their old home. It was one of his favorites virtscapes, taken quite early, before the pig farm next door had been built. He wondered what the place would be like now. Would the same squatters be there still? How dared they just steal their home and get away with it. What a bloody mess the world was in. He'd no idea how long he'd been lying there, and he didn't care. He was too depressed.

For the first time, he wondered if he'd done the right thing. He thought back about that wonderful time, when he'd just floated up and met his father. It was an experience of such magnitude, of such bliss and happiness that nothing else would ever come close. All he had wanted was to stay right there, with his Dad, forever, in the external realm of cosmic spirituality. But Yabul had told Philip he wasn't ready for that. There was something he had to do first. Much later, Philip had realized what his father had meant. His mission on earth was to save the human race by creating a place for virtual people. He'd given it all his energy, including his corporeal life. Yet nagging doubts made him miserable. Being a virtual person was a mind-boggling and exciting concept, but it had also drawbacks.

He was no longer 'in the loop', and had no control over anything outside his virtual world. He desperately wanted to get on with his idea, to talk it over with Jennifer and Marvin, but it was a one-way street: he was here, and they were out there, in the real world that he would never see again. It was so frustrating! He thought back to when he had seen his friends at the board, where Marvin had made it clear he couldn't use Secret Springs' facilities. In hindsight, Philip had to agree. The whole idea was ridiculous. Why should the company be interested in his idea? Hiding in the future was not profitable. He had to find another way.

The problem was that Secret Springs had the virtscapes, and there was no way to get them. As long as he had access to the virtscapes he was fine. He met new people every day—always in disguise, of course—and he could still see the sun going down, and feel a cool breeze at night. Virtscapes didn't run forever of course, and he had to change them frequently. When he was at rest in his avatar in between switching programs, all sense of time or space disappeared and it felt like real death. Without the virtscapes it would be like that all the time.

So he tried to be always 'on the go'. He had written a few programs—still going by that archaic name of 'batch files'—that listed all the virtscapes he wanted to see in a certain time period and in a specific order. He always had to be on guard, in case someone would recognize him and report him to Secret Springs.

The air in front of him suddenly shimmered, and there stood Jennifer. He jumped up to meet her.

"Hi. How are you, Phil?" Her smile was forced, and he knew at once she was bringing bad news.

"Hi, Jen. Frustrated would describe my state of mind, I guess."

She kissed him, but it was only a peck.

"So, what is the problem?"

"I need the virtscapes, Jen, especially if there are going to be other people like me. I just can't think of a way to get them. They're not something you can buy in a store. Secret

Springs will not last forever, and once it's gone I'll die. I'm very much up the proverbial creek without even a virtual paddle."

He could see Jennifer was hesitating, as if her mind was on something else. He felt a sudden twist in his stomach. Now what? She was looking at the property where Phil had spent his youth. Finally she turned towards him and fixed her beautiful eyes on his, and he could see she was very close to crying.

"Oh, Philip, I'm afraid I'm going to make things worse for you. I can't go on like this. I'm sorry, I won't be joining you, Phil. I won't even try. It's not for me, your price is too high."

"Price? What price? We're not going to charge people to become Virtuals."

"Now you're being stupid. Do I have to spell it out to you? I'm not talking money here. I'm talking about what you're asking me to do. I can't give up my life like that. I wasn't put on this earth to jump into some kind of suspended animation and hope for a better world in the future. I'll take my chances with the world as it is now, Philip. I've met someone else, someone I really like, and I want to raise a family with him. I am truly sorry."

"You didn't mention marriage and kids when you were with me."

"For Christ's sake, Philip, we never got down to that. All we ever talked about was you! *Your* problems, *your* mission in life. You never asked me what I wanted. We had some great times together, but this is it, Phil. I'm sure you've got plenty of choices for a virtual relationship among the women who visit Secret Springs, so go out there and meet someone else."

"I don't want anyone else. I want you."

"Well, we can't always have what we want, Phil. I'm not very good at farewells, so this is it. Have a good future, Phil." A slight shimmering in the air, and she was gone.

Philip jumped up and began to pace down the garden. No! He missed Jennifer so much every day, and now she was gone for good, just like that. He stood still, his fists balled in anger. Why couldn't he be like everyone else? Get a job, raise a family, have picnics, play with the kids. Why had he chosen this idiotic idea to become a virtual person? For the first time in his life, Philip Kozak wished he was really, truly dead. When the air started to shimmer again, he furiously vented his anger at whomever dared to interrupt his privacy.

"Go away!" he yelled. "My purple flag is up. Are you blind? I want to be alone. I don't want to talk to . . ." Then he stood, speechless, when he saw who his visitor was.

"Hello, brother," Erwin said. "They told me you were dead, and here you are, alive and well. What's going on? What's your little game here?"

14

"Ah, Anna, there you are. Come in."

Feeling very insecure, Anna Kulik entered Jo's office, wondering why she had been summoned to see the Head Councilor. Almost five hundred people depended on her for clean clothes, towels and bed linen every day. Had she messed up in her job? Sent clothes to the wrong people?

"We'll have a chat and a cup of tea, Anna." The Head Councilor gave her a big smile. He seemed nervous. She could see drops of sweat on his brow, and when he lifted his arm to direct her to her seat, she noticed a dark patch under his armpit. He closed the door and locked it. Anna wondered why.

"Thank you," she said and sat down, wondering what it was all about. Tea with the Head Councilor?

"So, how are you, Anna?" he asked, sitting down after putting two mugs of tea on the desk. The leader of the commune was known for his beautiful, deep-brown eyes and this time they seemed more piercing than ever. Anna wondered what he was thinking.

"How is the job?" There was that smile again, so much more intense than she'd ever seen before. Anna felt a sudden pang of misgiving. She took a swig of the tea and almost had to spit it out. It was very bitter. She quickly swallowed and put her cup down again.

"I am doing my best," she said. "I hope my work has been satisfactory, Head Councilor?"

"More than satisfactory, Anna. Exemplary, in fact. Quite frankly, I think your talents are wasted in the laundry facility."

"Wasted, Head Councilor? How can that be? We all have our jobs to help the church. The washing has to be done. I don't understand."

"Well maybe wasted is the wrong word," the Head Councilor said. "Perhaps I should say that you could serve the church better in another position. On the Council perhaps?"

Anna took a large swig of her tea. She was beginning to feel very ill at ease. The room seemed overly warm, and she could feel her heart thumping in her chest. What was wrong?

"A councilor? No, I can't do that, Councilor Rasnell. I'm fine where I am."

"Please call me Jo, Anna. You look so tense in that chair. I know, people often think I'm interrogating them and they tighten up. Why don't we move into the other room? It's much more comfortable." He stood up and opened a second door in his office and stepped through. Slowly Anna followed, very unsteady on her feet. She entered a small room with a bed, a computer desk and chair and, to Anna's intense relief, a bathroom.

"Please, may I use the bathroom?"

"Of course, Anna. I'll pour us some fresh tea."

Anna stepped into the bathroom and closed the door behind her. She stood in front of the sink, looking at herself in the mirror. Something was very wrong. She was sweating profusely, her heart was hammering and her ears were buzzing. Strange thoughts were trying to enter her well-ordered mind. It was a weird feeling, a dream almost. She took deep breaths to control it. In . . . out, In . . . out.

She calmed down a little. Her bladder was suddenly very active and she quickly sat down to relieve herself. Was it that tea? She flushed the toilet and washed her hands. Then, after a few more deep breaths, she opened the door and stepped back into the bedroom. There another surprise awaited her. The Head Councilor had taken off his robe and sat on the bed, wearing shorts and a casual white T-shirt. It was probably one of the shirts she had washed recently. A fresh cup of tea was waiting for her on the side table.

"Come and sit here, Anna; it's much more comfortable." He patted the bed beside him. After some hesitation, Anna sat down, as far away from Jo as politely possible. Her temporary respite had worn off and she felt worse than ever. Then something suddenly snapped in her and she turned to Jo.

"What have you done to me, Jo," she exclaimed boldly, moving closer to him. "What kind of tea is this? Why have you brought me here, in your bedroom?" It was the first time she had addressed the Head Councilor by his first name, but she didn't care. Something was stirring inside her, a feeling that had been hidden for a long time. "I want to leave," she said, readying herself to escape while she still could. To her surprise, Jo stuck out his hand and pushed her down back on the bed, gently but firmly.

"You don't want to leave yet, Anna. What's your rush? Are you afraid? Don't you like me?" He gave her one of his stares again, and she just couldn't look away.

"L . . . like you?" she gasped. "What do you mean? Of course I like you. We all like each other in the church. We're one big family."

"Oh, Anna, you're so uptight. I know why you're so tense, and I'll tell you a secret. I am also, but I'm better at hiding it. You don't have to fear me, Anna. I won't harm you, ever. Please believe me." He put his hand on her arm, and she could feel the moist heat through her dress.

The feeling inside her had fully awakened now. It was like a viper, and she was falling under its spell. She suddenly felt much younger, back in Redding, having a good time with her friends. Why did she suddenly remember how it had been, teasing the boys, kissing them? Why now? She quickly took another swig of the tea, hoping that whatever it was doing to her, it would speed things up.

Her viper was relentlessly pushing her, and there was no going back. She moved closer to Jo, threw her arms around him and raised her lips to his. To her surprise, he was just as ready as she was. They kissed for the longest time and her body remembered things from long ago. Her tightly controlled mind finally gave up and allowed the viper to take control. A powerful longing surged through her. Clothes flew through the air, and soon they were fiercely clutching each other,

235

allowing their released serpents to fight and finish what they had started.

It took the Head Councilor much longer than herself. After her viper had long spent itself and was slowly curling back into its secret hiding place, Jo was still going full pelt, moaning, shaking, pushing, pulling. Anna helped him as much as she could, and finally, with a tremendous groan, Jo grabbed her so fiercely that it almost hurt, and collapsed on top of her. She had to quickly push him to the side not to be asphyxiated. Then they lay next to each other, breathing deeply. Neither of them spoke, afraid to break the spell. Anna was soon feeling very drowsy and her eyelids began to close. The last thing she remembered was the steady rising and falling of Jo's naked chest next to her.

◊ ◊ ◊

The two men faced each other on either side of the deep, emotional chasm that time had created between them. Something blocked Philip's throat, and he couldn't speak. Was this the brother he had left when he was sixteen? Erwin would be twenty-six now, but Philip thought his half-brother looked older. A sharply defined face, smoothly shaven, and angry eyes. A devastating thought shot through Philip, as he realized there could only be one reason for his brother's unexpected visit. It felt as if a dagger penetrated his gut.

"It's Mother, isn't it? Has she died?" he asked.

"Nice to see you, too, brother! After all this time, you're still hiding from your family," Erwin snarled.

"What do you mean?"

"You're supposed to be dead, Philip! I came here to talk about a business proposal and was told you had died in a freak accident. They made me sign some papers, and gave me your ashes. Then a tall Indian guy taps me on the shoulder and takes me to some kind of sports room and asks me to put on one of those silly helmets. And there you are, hiding in an imaginary world. Couldn't you at least have the guts to meet me in the real world, Philip? Why are you playing silly games?"

"You haven't answered my question," Philip said hotly. "Has Mother died?"

"No, she is fine. That's not why I'm here."

"I would dearly like to see her again. Can you help her hook up to the Secret Springs network?"

"Don't be stupid, Philip! Why can't you come to see her in person? Why all this hocus pocus? Why pretending to be dead? Are you hiding from the authorities? Working on some kind of secret project?"

"Something like that, yes. I can't talk about it. You would never understand. We've lived apart for too long."

"And whose fault was that? Even now, after all those years, you still don't want to share things, and you know what? That's fine with me, really. I'll play your little game. I didn't want to come here in the first place, but our church has a proposal for you and I was chosen to deliver it. So instead of wasting any more time, I'll come straight to the point. We want to buy your firm."

"Buy Secret Springs? You can't be serious! What makes you think we're for sale? You're a non-profit organization. You can't just go and buy companies. And Secret Springs goes against everything your commune stands for. The whole idea is beyond ridiculous. It's outrageous!"

"I knew you'd say that, but I've done my homework, Phil. I know your firm is in financial trouble; don't deny it. You haven't paid any dividend for years, and the shareholders are not at all happy. People all over the world are canceling their accounts. We have taken quite a bite out of your precious little pie, haven't we? Your customers are beginning to wake up from the virtual dreams you serve them. The Church of Oscar, on the other hand, is based on real life and honesty. It is growing exponentially. We have five communes now, and more to come. We've even got contacts in the government. We offer people a way out in today's mad world and we're going to change everything. The earth will be ours."

Philip suddenly thought about the time he had met his mother. He'd seen a fanatic fire burning behind her eyes and he saw the same determination in Erwin.

"If things are going so well for you, why do you need Secret Springs?" Philip asked.

For a few minutes Erwin stood quietly, as if trying to compose his words. Or was he mustering courage? It was hard to tell. What on earth was his brother up to? Something began to stir in Philip's mind, as a very important thought was banging on the wall of his conscious mind to be let in.

"We wants to make a deal that can be beneficial to both of us," Erwin said.

Philip waited for the elusive thought in his mind to come to the surface, but it took its time. He stared at his half-brother. "Explain."

"We want to buy your social network and create the best, biggest, most powerful evangelical network the world has ever seen."

"I know what you're saying, Erwin, and I see your point. But I'm afraid our shareholders won't let you."

"Why not? Is our money different because we're a commune? We'll give them the best dollar value for their shares at the time of purchase. They would be stupid to refuse."

The elusive thought finally exploded into Philips consciousness, and it shook him to the core. Of course! *Careful now . . .*

"All right, Erwin. I'm not denying we've seen better times, and perhaps a takeover could be a possibility some time in the future. But we have millions of subscribers, and some have pre-paid their accounts for years. You can't just let them hang out to dry. You'll have to compensate them. And what about the rest of the company's hardware? The filming equipment? The servers? The virtscapes?"

"The what?"

"The virtscapes. You know, the virtual reality scenes that make Secret Springs possible, like the one we're in now."

"Oh, those. We'll delete the lot of them, the sooner the better, and good riddance. We don't want Secret Springs to entertain people, Heavens no. All we want is the people part: the goodwill, the subscriber accounts and the network itself. And some of your people, perhaps, to help us get things going."

"They might not want to work for your church, Erwin."

Erwin was quiet for a moment and looked Philip straight in the eye. Then he shrugged. "The consensus among the councilors was that you probably wouldn't be interested, and it seems they were right. I've done what I was asked to do, so I'll be heading back now. If you want to change your mind you know where to find us."

"No, don't go yet. This is a big move, for both of us and there'll be a lot of things to iron out, but maybe we can make a deal, brother."

"Yeah?" Erwin eyes narrowed. "Just like that, right? A minute ago you were dead against it. Now it's all smiles and talk about a deal. Why the sudden change?"

"Hey, I was just surprised to see you, all right? I was worried about Mother, and I just had a major fight with my girlfriend before you got here. I was very angry and couldn't think straight. I can see now that we can both benefit from this, and I like the idea. But the final decision is not up to me.

"May I make a suggestion? Since you don't want the virtscapes, how about we take them out of the sale? It'll bring the price down, for sure. I'll arrange for someone to remove them for you. After that, I'll do my utmost to persuade the board and the shareholders to go for it."

Erwin shrugged. "You want those virtscapes? Be my guest. Saves us the time to get rid of them." He looked at his watch. "So, can I tell our Council that, in principle, you are interested, and we can set the legal procedures in motion?"

Philip sat quietly for a while. It was a major decision, and it wasn't his to make. Marvin would have to do it, and he would bear the brunt of the shareholders' ire. They might not let Secret Springs go cheaply, if at all. But Philip knew he

239

absolutely needed the virtscapes, and here they were, almost falling in his lap. He finally nodded and stuck out his hand, but Erwin's return handshake was limp and less than spontaneous.

"Erwin, for goodness' sake!" Philip blurted. "We're half-brothers, and I don't think you would give me the time of day if I asked you. Why is there such anger and hostility between us?"

"Anger and hostility? No, Philip, you've got it wrong. It's plain indifference. You cut yourself loose from us when you left home, so don't blame me now for not being the best of pals all of a sudden. I came here strictly for a business proposal and now that it is done I'll be on my way. Whatever you're doing here doesn't interest or concern me at all. Since you want people to think you're dead, that's what I'll tell Mother."

"No, please, don't do that. Can you spare another hour or so?"

Erwin frowned in surprise. "What now? I've said all I was going to say."

"There's a good restaurant, right here in the building. Have a meal on me. Marvin can give you a voucher. I want to record a video for Mother, so that you can take it with you. Should take less than an hour. Please, Erwin, do this, not for me, but for our Mother."

Erwin considered for a moment. Then he nodded. "All right. I could do with something to eat. I'll be in that restaurant for one hour. If your man brings me that recording in that time, I'll take it with me. One minute later, he'll find me gone." There was an angry 'pop' sound, and Erwin vanished. Philip stood deep in thought for a moment, then brought his finger to the virtual menu to call Marvin.

◊ ◊ ◊

"Tom! Sit down. How's it going?" The GP sat behind his desk and pointed to the comfortable chair opposite him. On the desk stood a small pitcher with water and two glasses. Tom was here as a friend, not as a patient, the physician had insisted. They sometimes had a chat, whenever the doctor had some time in his busy schedule.

"I'm OK, Christopher," Tom said, sitting down. "Penny and I are doing fine. She's a great help these days."

"Sorry to disappoint you, Tom. You don't look fine to me and you can't be. Not after losing your wife and still not knowing what happened to her. Nobody can be fine after a trauma like that. You've got bags under your eyes from lack of sleep and you're developing a paunch from eating the wrong food and lack of exercise."

"Well, I'm not the same person I was before Heather left," Tom retorted. "Give me a break! It'll take time to get over it, but life has to go on. Physically I'm OK, and I'm doing my best."

Christopher held up a hand. "Of course. The thing is Tom, it has been almost three months now, and I can see that you still expect Heather to walk through the door again. I hope she will, but you've got to understand that will probably not happen. Somewhere you have got to draw a line and start accepting things. Let me ask you a question: Did Heather have a room of her own? A special place where she would do her own thing, like sewing, or painting, or whatever?"

"Yes. She used the spare bedroom to store her personal things. She also tried painting for a while. Why do you ask?"

"I bet you have hardly been in that room since she left you, if at all. You're still waiting for her to move back in. Am I right? Be honest, now."

Tom slouched back in his seat, breathing deeply. He looked at the other, surprised he knew.

"Yes. I just can't get myself to go in there and I've told Penny not to either. Not until I know for sure she won't be back."

Taggard reached out for the water pitcher and poured two glasses about half full. He handed one to Tom.

"Now Tom, you're sixty-two, right?"

Tom sipped some of the water. "Will be this year, yes. Why?"

"Now don't get me wrong. I'm not here to tell you how to run your life. Speaking as a professional, I can only make suggestions. If you look after yourself you have probably a good number of years left. Lots of people reach eighty, or even ninety. On the other hand, it's not as if you're twenty and still have your entire life ahead of you. The more one ages, the more precious time becomes. And it would be awful if you wasted the time you have left. I know, you can't suddenly forget about Heather, and I don't want you to. What I am suggesting is a gradual approach." Christopher took a break, sipping his water. Then he turned around, and faced Tom.

"I believe you have a crawlspace under your house, right? Is it heated and dry?"

"Yes. Never had any problems. Why?"

"OK. Get some cardboard boxes, fairly big, like moving boxes. Then go through the house and put Heather's things into those boxes. Everything. Clothes, underwear, shoes, papers, books, etc. When you're finished I want you to store the boxes in the furthest corner of your crawlspace, safe and secure, and leave Heather's door wide open all the time. Do you see what I'm trying to do here, Tom?"

"I get the picture, yes. It's like a safety net, right?"

"Exactly. By moving Heather's belongings out of your everyday life, it'll be easier to forget her and you're setting the stage for the healing process. If she somehow does come back, there is no harm done, and you can bring everything up again. Well, what do you say?"

"Thanks, Christopher. I'll give it a try."

The physician stood up and shook hands with Tom. Then he walked to the door of his consulting room. "That's about all the time I've got today, Tom. Got a patient in five minutes, so

I'd better get ready. Let me know how it works out for you. If not, I can refer you to a psychiatrist, if you like."

"No, thanks, Christopher. Not yet."

On his way home, Tom stopped at a small family-run hardware store. He walked to the counter and asked for moving boxes. The clerk, an older woman, shook her head in regret. "No, we don't sell those. How big do you need them?"

"Oh, like this," Tom made signs in the air with his hands, and the woman nodded at him. "You just wait here for a second, love," she said, and moved to the back of the store. She returned with three large flattened boxes that had contained paper towel products.

"If you can use them, they're yours," she said pleasantly. "We would just put them in the recycle bin."

"That's great, thank you very much," Tom said, giving the woman a big smile. "Do you sell tape to seal them?"

The woman waddled to one of the aisles and produced a small carton with adhesive tape. "That'll be $3.25, love." Tom happily paid and headed back to his car.

When he got home, he put the three sheets of cardboard against the wall in the living room. He walked into the kitchen and noticed it was almost twelve, almost time for lunch. But he really wasn't that hungry and decided to wait. He opened the fridge and poured himself a beer, despite the early hour. After taking a few swigs of beer, he took one of the flattened sheets of cardboard and lay it flat on the kitchen floor. He pulled up the sides and the back and front to make the cardboard into a box again, then sealed each joint with the tape. Then came the hardest part.

He went into the bedroom and stood in front of the dresser where Heather kept her clothes. He hadn't opened it since she had gone. He resolutely opened the top drawer. Heather had taken some clothes with her, but the rest was all neatly folded and stored. One by one, he picked up underwear and bras, and carefully put them into the box. Sweaters, socks, panties, everything.

243

When the dresser was empty, it was time for the closet. He took the first dress off its hanger. It was a flowery summer dress Heather had worn on their last holiday in San Diego. He could still see her, standing in her bare feet, facing the waves, with the famous Coronado hotel in the background. He folded the dress and put it with the other clothes. After her dresses came the trousers, skirts and blouses. Though Heather had good taste and ideas as far as clothes were concerned, she was also frugal. Many of her clothes had been bought at the Salvation Army and other thrift stores. With a bit of pushing and pressing he managed to get about half of Heather's wardrobe in the box.

He walked to the kitchen to make another box, then returned to Heather's room. Heather had all kinds of books and papers, stored in piles upon shelves, since cupboard space was at a premium in their little home. There were also paint brushes, tubes of acrylic paint and small canvases. Some time ago she had taken up painting, but she'd never really taken it seriously. There was also a box with jewelry, rings, brooches, ear rings. The more personal it got, the worse Tom felt. He felt he was trespassing in the worst way, despite what Taggard had said. He was acting as if Heather was already dead. Yet he knew he had to keep going.

There were photographs of the family, their wedding, the first pictures of Penny. Tom just glanced at them and placed it in the second box. Several handbags lay on the next shelf, a few wooly hats, gloves, tennis shoes and a racket. On the floor pushed against the wall stood the suitcase Heather and Penny had taken with them when they went to visit Heather's mother. Tom grabbed the case by the handle and pulled it out.

He was about to put it to the side to take to the storage area later, when he noticed it had a tag attached to the handle. He bent over to look closer. It said Haydo Arrow 42 to Minneapolis-St Paul. The Bullet train that Penny and Heather had taken. On the second line of the tag were seat numbers 12a and 12b.

42 . . . There was something about that number. What was it again? Just recently, damn, why couldn't he remember. It was on the verge of popping up in his mind. Something inside him told him it was important. He was about to give up, when it came to him. The numbers from the Ouija Board. He walked out of Heather's room to his study, and took his notebook from his desk drawer; he knew he'd written the numbers down somewhere. Yes, there it was: 091842. The last two digits of that repeating string of numbers.

He suddenly shook his head to clear his mind. What was he doing? It was just a coincidence. Hell, life was full of coincidences. He left Heather's room, sat down at the kitchen table, and grabbed the beer he had left there. He took a large swig. Facts, Tom, only facts. No more speculation. Penny and Heather had been on the Bullet train number 42, that was true. Penny, in trance, had produced a set of numbers, including her birthday and that same number, 42. Also true. So how could she have done that? Had it come from her subconscious? Or was it just random? He took another swig of his beer, and stared at the numbers again. What could they possibly mean?

Then he thought of something. Heather had had a birthday in February. She'd left him about a month later. No, wait, it was more, six weeks perhaps. He ran to the calendar that hung on the wall next to the fridge and flipped back to the pages until he found February 8th, Heather's birthday. He used his index finger to count the days after her birthday and when he reached 42, his heart thumped so forcefully that he almost fainted. His finger came to rest on March 21st, the very day Heather had left him.

◊ ◊ ◊

Jo awoke with a start. At first, he thought he had died. Everything around him was pitch-black, and he was freezing cold and very stiff. His head felt as if he had drank a full bottle of wine, though he had no memory of it. He knew he was in bed, but all the covers were gone. Very gingerly, he swung his

245

legs onto the floor and tried to stand up. His body refused to hold him upright and he fell down again. On the third try, he finally managed to stand erect and took some awkward steps in the dark, trying to find the light switch. His feet suddenly caught in something soft and flexible and he fell flat on the floor, hurting his left elbow in the process. He managed to get up again and after much probing finally found the light switch. In the sudden bright light he felt even more confused.

He stood near the door of his bedroom and he was stark naked. On the floor, in an unsightly bundle lay a white T-shirt, and it was this he had fallen over. A pair of shorts, as well as underwear, socks and shoes haphazardly festooned the rest of the floor. The only sign of neatness was his council robe, folded over the back of a chair. Shivering in his nakedness he rushed over and put on his robe, tying it together with the golden cord. What in the name of Oscar had happened here?

He looked at the alarm clock on the bedside table. 5:30 a.m. He sat down on the bed again, trying to think. His head was throbbing and he could feel the arteries in his neck pulsating in tune with his frantic heartbeat. The last time he had felt vaguely similar was the night after the massacre. He had drank a whole bottle of wine, but there had been a reason. He knew nothing that could have caused the present state of his physique.

Taking deep breaths, he tried to remember what could have happened the evening before. He ran a hand over the bed linen and it still felt slightly warm. When he brought his hand to his nose and sniffed it, he smelled a strange smell, a sweaty, musky kind of odor. He couldn't place it. After a few seconds he stood up again and picked up his T-shirt, trousers and underwear. He walked over to the cupboard, opened the door and dropped the clothes into the laundry hamper.

Laundry. The word stuck in his mind. Why did it ring a bell in his aching head? What was so important about laundry? He suddenly felt very thirsty and his mouth was dry. A drink of water. He reached for the cup of water he always had handy on the bedside table in case he got thirsty at night.

To his surprise there were two cups. Had he had a visitor? He walked to the sink, to fill one of the cups with water, than stood, transfixed.

A teapot. He never drank tea in his bedroom; it made him go to the bathroom at night. Why would there be a teapot in the sink? He picked it up, took off the lid and peeked inside. He saw no ordinary tea bag but small slivers of something. They looked like cut pieces of some kind of vegetable, or root. Mushrooms! Like the pieces of a gigantic jigsaw puzzle giving a clue to the completed picture, his mind slowly began to put things together. He had served tea, made from slivers of mushrooms, to himself and another person and ended up naked in bed. Where was the other person? When had she left?

She. It had been a woman, he suddenly knew. A larger piece of the puzzle came into focus. He felt a sudden tightening of his stomach muscles as he realized what he had done. He had had a forbidden sexual encounter. Now that the doorway to his memory had been pried ajar, it didn't take long for other memories to burst through. He'd sinned against the teachings of the very church he had founded. He had abused the secret knowledge that should have remained hidden for centuries. He'd picked the mushrooms that affected Oscar's Breath, made tea from them and called Anna Kulik, the young woman from the laundry department. They had slept together in his bed.

He suddenly knew he needed fresh air. He took off his robe and entered the bathroom. He took a long shower to clean his mind and body. While he stood there, lathering himself, as the needles of hot water massaged his hurting head, he wondered what had happened to Anna. Had she gone home as if nothing had happened? Or had she gone to the other council members to report him? The water cleansed his body, but not his mind, and he knew he could be in very serious trouble. After his shower, he put on his usual walking outfit, shorts, knitted T-shirt and a jacket. He walked over to the sink and drained the teapot, making sure he emptied all

247

the dregs into the trash. He put on his walking boots, turned off the light and very quietly opened the door.

This time of morning Excalibur was still at rest, though in the fields some workers would already have started their working day. Walking on tip toe so as not to wake the others in the building, he headed for the door and stepped out into the garden. It was only just getting light and it was still cool and everything smelled fresh. He walked feverishly, much faster than usual, to get his circulation going. Twice he greeted farm workers on their way, but he didn't stop for chit-chat.

There was something he had to do in a hurry. When he reached the edge of the wilderness he tried to remember the way from last time. When he finally found the big birch tree, he slowed down. A new crop of small mushrooms had sprouted up in the brush around it. Without hesitation, he walked over and stamped on them, over and over again, until he was certain he had destroyed every one of them.

15

The door opened a few inches and Tom could see the heavy chain hanging in front of the small, wizened face, just like last time. Irene Penstone stared at him, and if she recognized him she didn't show it.

"Mrs. Penstone, Irene, it's Tom Cramer. Remember me? I visited you a while ago and we talked about your husband. Can I come in? There is something I want to discuss with you."

A smile of recognition lit up the old lady's face. "Oh, yes, the retired detective, I remember now."

The door closed, so that Mrs. Penstone could remove the chain, then it opened again. Like last time, the old lady had a small gun in her left hand, but after she locked the door she put the weapon on the mantelpiece.

"What brings you here this time, Lieutenant? Have you found a lead to my husband's whereabouts?"

"I am not sure, Irene. First, let me explain something. What happened to you has also happened to me. My wife has left me without any reason."

"I am very sorry to hear that. It must be awful for you."

"It is, thank you. The search for missing people has become painfully personal for me, and your help would be invaluable. I have a few more questions I would like to ask you."

"Very well, but let's have some tea first. My vocal cords need lubricating if I talk a lot." She disappeared into the kitchen. Tom looked around. The room was exactly like it had been last time and it would probably stay like that until the old lady died. About five minutes later, Irene Penstone came back carrying a tray with a teapot, two cups, a little jug with milk, and a plate with biscuits.

"Help yourself," she said, sitting down. "So what have you found?"

"Something interesting," he said, while he poured the tea. "When your husband went to that school reunion in Tacoma, did he carry a suitcase with him? If so, could I have a look at it, please?"

"No. He took it with him when he disappeared."

"I see. You told me he flew down there. Do you by any chance still have his ticket or boarding pass, or anything relating to the flight he took?"

"Oh, yes. Cyril saved everything. He always said you never knew how something might come in handy later. It's all in a folder in his study. I'll get it for you."

"Thank you. What was the exact date your husband disappeared?"

"April 8th, last year."

"Do you still have a calendar for last year?"

"Sure."

While Irene went into her husband's study, Tom felt a pang of doubt. He had only a vague theory about what had happened to Heather. Was it fair to give the old lady new hope after all this time, without any solid facts to back it up? He drank some more of his tea and took a chocolate biscuit from the tray on the side table.

Irene came back, carrying a small parcel and a calendar with colorful pictures for each month. Cyril Penstone had written something in almost every little square on the various calendar pages: things to do, birthdays, doctor's appointments, stuff like that. Tom was more interested in the parcel. It had a small folder with papers inside.

"May I?"

"Of course, that's why I got them for you. Everything about Cyril's trip should be in there."

Tom flipped the various pieces of paper until he found a boarding pass. It was for Trans-Continental Airways, flight 157, from L.A. to Tacoma, WA.

"I'll leave you to it," Irene said. "I've got some washing up to do." She walked to the small kitchen, humming to herself.

Tom picked up the calendar for 2061 and opened it for the month of April. The page showed an idyllic picture of a lake with ducks flying above it. He felt highly embarrassed reading personal information, but it couldn't be helped. He noticed that the last part of the year was clear. Nothing was written in any of the squares after April 8, the day Cyril Penstone had disappeared.

OK, here goes. The flight number was 157. Tom took a pencil from his inside coat pocket and put it on the square of May 8th. Then he began to count backwards, his pencil following the squares on the calendar while he read the numbers in his mind: *157,156, 155* . . . He wondered what Irene would think if she saw him counting days. . . . *152, 150, 149* . . . Luckily the calendar also showed several months of the year before, and when Cramer reached January 1st, he flipped the pages back to December of the previous year and kept counting backwards. *45, 44, 43* . . . When he finally reached 0, Tom had great trouble to remain calm and not jump up, shouting Eureka! It was Cyril Penstone himself who had proven Tom's theory. The tip of Tom's pencil rested on November 2nd, and inside the little square was Cyril's handwriting: *My Birthday.*

"You found something?" Irene was back, and she must have seen Cramer's excitement. He almost gave in to the need to share his thoughts with her, but in the last moment he balked. No, he couldn't. Not yet.

"I did indeed, Irene. I now have an idea why your husband left you. It had nothing to do with your marriage, or anything you did. Just one more question. Cyril left early you said, while you were asleep, so I assume he used a cab. Was there a certain company he would have called?"

"Yes, Allied Cabs," Irene said. "We've used them before. Why do you ask?"

"Oh, just some loose ends," Tom said evasively. "May I keep the flight information and calendar as evidence? They'll be returned to you, when the case is solved. Thanks for your help, Irene. And for the tea." Without waiting for an answer,

Tom folded the calendar and the flight material, stuck it in his coat pocket and stood up to leave.

"Is that it?" Irene exclaimed scornfully. "You're not telling me what you have found? Thanks for nothing! I thought you were here to help me." She was obviously distressed, and Tom's heart went out to her, but he remained firm. He was still a detective, retired or not. One didn't talk about a case until things were complete, proven and sorted.

"I am sorry, I can't tell you any more for the moment, Irene," he said earnestly. "This is an investigation, albeit an unofficial one. All I can say is that you have given me invaluable evidence, and I will do my very best to find your husband. You have to trust me on that."

While Cramer walked back to his car he looked at his watch. 2:30. Allied Cabs were a well-known company in Montecito. Was it worth talking to them? Would they keep records that long? Probably not. He decided to take the chance and drive by anyway.

◊ ◊ ◊

When Ted Taylor founded the Church of Oscar, he started a diary with notes, bits of information, ideas, rules and regulations he considered important for the new church. Jo had helped him as much as he could and had taken over after Ted's untimely death. At first, it had just been a loose collection of thoughts and ideas on how to run the church, but as the commune grew and other councilors added their input, it became evident that things needed to be organized into some kind of manual, or bible. It was to be called the Word of Oscar. The task of sorting and copying the old notes and records fell to Daniel English who, after all, had extensive experience in religious dogmas.

When Jo suggested a word processor, Daniel had bristled with indignation. Wasn't the other Bible originally hand-written? Finally, considering the amount of work involved, and Jo's assertion that times had changed, English had grudgingly given in. Even with the help of modern technology,

252

it had taken him almost two years to produce a finely bound tome of over five hundred pages. Since it was the original, the book was kept in the church's vault in Jo's office, never to leave the church and only to be used in council meetings. The plan was to have some copies made for the other communes, but unfortunately, not long after completing the Word of Oscar, Daniel had died.

One early morning in June, when the eastern sky was just losing its darkness, a deeply troubled Jo sat at his desk, drinking a strong cup of coffee. He needed it to steady his nerves and shaky hands. He had taken the Word of Oscar out of the safe, and was slowly flipping the pages, not looking for anything in particular, but just relishing the touch of the paper, as if it would give him strength and inspiration before he embarked on the journey from which there was no return.

His troubles had nothing to do with the church itself. In fact, the commune was doing very well and Jo had been in the best of spirits the evening before. After a rather sumptuous meal in the councilor's dining room, he had gone back to his own quarters to read and enjoy a nice after-dinner brandy.

Just after seven o'clock there had been a demure knock on his door and Anna Kulik had entered. The young woman looked disheveled and worried. She was dressed in a loose-fitting grey gown and when she sat down in the chair opposite him, Jo noticed that her figure was a little fuller than when he had last seen her.

"Head Councilor, I need your help. I think . . . I am with child," she stammered.

Jo felt a searing pain in his stomach as if someone had made him drink molten lava. A pregnancy in the Church of Oscar! And it was his fault. He had sinned in the most abominable way, and now the Lord was punishing him for it. He knew he had to do something to put the young woman at ease and he spoke to her soothingly.

"Surely, you must be mistaken, Anna. There are no pregnant women in our church. How could there be? Our members practice celibacy."

253

"What else can it be? Could it be cancer? Is the Lord punishing me for what I have done?"

"What do you mean?"

"I had a vision a while ago," Anna said, sniffing. "I was in an unfamiliar place somewhere and there was someone with me. I think it was a spirit or angel. Strange things were happening to me, and when this entity held me we became one. It was the happiest moment of my entire life, but I also felt guilty because I knew what I did was wrong. When I woke up the next morning, I tried to remember the vision, but couldn't.

"Then I missed two of my periods, and I know something awful has happened to me, Head Councilor. I have been violated and I don't know what to do anymore." Anna began to sob, and threw herself against Jo's chest. Like an automaton, he held her, stroking her hair. His mind was in overdrive, while he tried to reassure her.

"Anna, I really can't help you," he said. "It would be better if you see doctor Fleming tomorrow. You should really get some rest now."

After Anna had left, Jo had immediately poured himself another large brandy to stop his panic. He felt like a condemned man who was to be executed the next day. How could he explain this to the other councilors and the people of Oscar? What would happen if the child was born? It might look like him and questions would be asked.

It would be best to terminate the pregnancy, but the Infirmary was not set up for that. And even if Dr. Fleming performed the operation, he would want to know why Anna was pregnant. The Church of Oscar was founded on honesty and trust, especially among the councilors. Then there was Anna herself. She had not accused him, because she couldn't remember the event. Jo himself had been confused and unsure when he woke up that morning. But it was different for him, he had known what to expect. Anna had not. The experience had been so unexpected and frightening to her, that Oscar's Breath had blocked the memory. But for how long? What if one day it came back to her, and she told the Council? How could he live with that uncertainty?

After a night of interrupted sleep, Jo had finally got up and dressed. He had hoped the new day would bring a solution, but it did not. Even the Word of Oscar could not help him. Like his good friend Ted Taylor, he had only one choice. It seemed ironic that both founders of the Church of Oscar had faced a dilemma they could not solve. He closed the Word of Oscar and returned it to the vault. One final task to perform.

He pulled a thick envelop from the back of the vault. Inside was a stack of papers, and he carefully lay them on his desk. It was one of the DVD transcripts. Quickly he looked for the paragraph that described Yabul's description of the antidote to Oscar's Breath. He picked up a pen and a sheet of clean paper and wrote: *'For Head Councilors Eyes Only'*

For a few minutes he hurriedly wrote down his thoughts, as if time itself was his enemy. He was too nervous to write in his usual flowing, calligraphic style. He just wrote the words as they came, heavily underlining some, to make certain that Sylvia, the next Head Councilor would understand their importance. After he signed his name, he took out a wax candle and lit it.

When enough drips of wax had fallen on the paper, he took his official seal of the Church of Oscar: an ebony stamp with a blue circle with three wavy grey lines inside. He pressed it into the wax to make his statement an official church declaration. When the wax had dried, he stuck the papers back in the envelope and returned it to the vault. Then he closed the vault for the last time. He stood around for a while, looking at his familiar study where he had spent so many happy years.

The weather had been unseasonably hot for the last few days, so he left his jacket in the closet and put on a light yellow sweater. When he stepped outside, the sun had just popped above the horizon. Though it was still relatively cool, he was soon sweating profusely. He set a fast pace towards the back of Excalibur's property, making sure he didn't go anywhere near the site where he had picked the mushrooms that had cost him so dearly.

There was a rock formation near a small river, several miles further in the wilderness behind Excalibur. Usually Jo didn't go that far, but this time he had to. The rocks could be very slippery with spray, and it would be very easy to slip or stumble and fall down into the river, hitting one's head, and be swept away in the current. It wasn't a foolproof scheme, but it was the best he could think of.

He walked for about an hour, then sat down for a quick break. It was just after eight and the sun was already warming the grass. While he sat there, he suddenly knew that the Lord was showing him a better way out. In the clear morning air the sharp, rattling sound was unmistakable: a rattle snake had emerged from its nightly hiding place and was probably looking for warmth and food.

Jo stood up, trying to find the direction where he had heard the sound. It wasn't far and he soon located the snake. He picked up a long stick and followed the animal when it slithered away. After he had it cornered the snake between a large rock and a tree, Jo sat down and stuck out both arms to catch it. Predictably, the rattler had other plans and went for Jo's outstretched arm.

It hurt quite badly and soon started to burn. Jo had to think quickly, before the venom would incapacitate him. He didn't want to be found here, off the beaten track; it might look suspicious. Quickly, he retraced his steps back to the place where he had rested. His vision was already giving him problems and he felt feverish. His left arm was aching tremendously. He found a spot where he could sit down, resting his back against a log.

His arm was throbbing and badly swollen. It wouldn't be long now. He looked at the sky, and the trees, while he felt the poison spreading. Resting again the log, he thought about his life in the church. He had done his best to follow the Lord's wishes, but he had failed in the end. Sylvia would be the next Head Councilor, and he wished her well. Great pains began to fill his entire body, his vision was blurring, and he was having difficulty breathing. He wondered what would happen to Anna and her child. When he could no longer support himself, he slid onto his side into the warm grass, and closed his eyes for the last time, awaiting the inevitable.

◊ ◊ ◊

Her name was Pauline, and she was the dispatcher for Allied Cabs. She sat straight upright behind her computer, like the captain of an airplane, dressed in a spotless white blouse and dark blue trousers. On top of her shoulders were epaulettes bearing the company's name. She was wearing a combination headset and microphone to answer the phone, and looked very sexy, with neatly styled dark hair. Cramer was sure she wore no make-up, simply because she didn't need it. Pauline looked about thirty, and had the prettiest smile he had ever seen on anyone. Tom wondered why she was working as a dispatcher. Her perfect face would have been quite at home on even the most demanding of fashion magazines.

"Can I help you?"

"I hope so," Tom said. "How long do you keep records of the fares your drivers pick up?"

She frowned. "Are you with the police?"

"I used to be. Retired now. I am trying to trace a person who may have used Allied Cabs a while ago."

"We don't give out information like that, unless it's to the police or a Private Investigator," Pauline said. "Are you a PI?"

"Sort of," Cramer said. "I'm working on a missing person's case."

"Can I see your license?"

Smart lady. Tom nervously shifted in his chair. "I'll be honest with you. I don't have one. That missing person is my wife. She has disappeared and I'm trying to get her back."

"That's awful!" He could see Pauline was truly shocked. "It's happening so much these days." Then her eyes narrowed and she studied Cramer.

"We've talked before," she said.

"No, I don't think so. I've never used Allied Cabs."

"I do a lot of talking here and I have a very good memory for voices," she said. "Oh, hang on." She pressed a key on her computer keyboard.

"Allied Cabs." She almost sang the words. Her fingers danced on her computer keyboard, while she spoke into the tiny microphone.

Cramer looked around the office. Apart from Pauline's station there was a row of seats along one wall, with a small coffee table in between with magazines on it. In the corner of the room stood a water cooler and two old fashioned filing cabinets. He wondered if there was a file on Cyril Penstone in there. Everything was clean and well organized.

Through a window he noticed some kind of waiting room where several men and two women were watching television, or reading, having a coffee, or smoking a cigarette. While he watched, one of the men took a pager from his pocket and looked at it. Then he stood up and headed outside to his car to pick up the fare. Cramer was impressed. Allied Cabs seemed a very streamlined and efficient operation.

"Sorry about that," Pauline said, looking at him again. "It can be quite hectic here."

"Don't apologize. You're doing your job. I shouldn't take so much of your time."

She gave him a big smile. "Don't worry about it. Seriously, though, I remember your voice," she said. "We get a lot of phone calls to order a cab, but very few queries about them afterwards. I got a call a couple of months ago inquiring if someone had ordered a cab from us. I don't remember the date exactly, but I'm pretty sure it was you."

"You have an incredible memory," Cramer said, impressed. "Yes, that was the day my wife left me, and I was trying to find out which cab company she used." He suddenly felt foolish. Why was he bothering strangers with his personal problems?

"Is that why you are here?" she asked, concerned. "To get information to find her?"

Tom nodded. "It's part of a lead," he began. Then there was the chirping of the phone again. This was crazy, perhaps he should go. He stood up, ready to leave, but Pauline waved her hand at him. "Don't go."

"All right, to heck with the rules. I'll help you," she said, after she had finished the call. "We're fully computerized here at Allied. Every call we get is logged onto the computer and we keep them for a whole year. After that, everything is archived. If anyone has used our company in the last five years, it'll be there. If you have a name and a date, it'll only be a matter of seconds."

"Cyril Penstone," he said. "I believe he ordered a cab on April 8, last year."

"Just a mo," she said, working her keyboard. "I've got to find the right archive. Yes, there it is. Cyril Penstone, of 19 Hazelwood Drive. He ordered the cab the night before. The driver took him to the Triagle Shopping Center. Does that help you at all?"

"Yes, thank you very much." Tom stood up, opened his wallet, took out a twenty dollar bill and handed it to Pauline.

"No, no! You don't have to do that!" she protested. "I'm just glad to help you get your wife back."

"I insist. You have no idea how much you have helped me. Have a drink on me."

Pauline's face lit up. She gave him another of her million dollar smiles, and put a hand on his arm. She had long fingers, like a piano player, the nails all natural, without any polish.

"Thanks very much," she said, taking the bill from him. "I will. Good luck finding her."

Just before Tom closed the door, he heard her sing-song voice again. "Allied Cabs."

While he walked back to his car Tom felt good. Pauline had restored his faith in humanity. There were still people out there, helping others just for the sake of helping. He had done all he could and he might not have any definite proof, but he now had a strong case that he could take to the authorities. In the car on his way back home, he suddenly found himself humming the notes from Rossini's *The Barber of Seville*. It was Heather's favorite piece of classical music.

◊ ◊ ◊

Sylvia Rasnell stood outside the backdoor of the Excalibur building. She had a beautiful view of the colorful gardens and the pristine wilderness behind it, culminating in the majestic rise of the Santa Ynes mountain range in the background. This time the view wasn't beautiful at all, but harsh and foreboding; the mountains looming, like the dark menacing clouds that had suddenly appeared in her life.

In the distance a group of people had just entered the gardens and were hurrying home. Four of them were carrying a stretcher between them. Sylvia could not see the figure on the stretcher, but she knew it was the Head Councilor of the Church of Oscar, her brother Jo.

When Jo hadn't shown up for breakfast, nobody had thought anything of it. He was known to go out for his long morning walks and occasionally got sidetracked or delayed, studying plants, or flowers or animals he saw. Around ten o'clock, Sylvia had sounded the alarm and a search party was organized. They would need many people, since the Excalibur estate covered more than fifty acres, not including the wilderness behind it, and no one knew the exact route the Head Councilor had taken.

There was no shortage of volunteers. The service vehicles they used in the gardens were not suitable for travel in the wilderness, so most of the search was done on foot, aided by people on horseback and others with dogs. Sylvia had not partaken in the search. She could no longer walk that far because of her arthritic knees. She had just waited, hoping that Jo was all right, that he'd got lost, or fallen asleep in the warm sun. It wasn't until noon that one of the searchers on horseback had came galloping back with the dreadful news that the Head Councilor had been bitten by a rattle snake and showed no sign of life.

When the procession arrived at the house, the four carriers stopped to let Sylvia take a look at her brother. He lay on his back, unseeing eyes staring at the sky. She had expected his face to show surprise, pain or even anger at what had happened, but it was quite neutral. He looked as if he could sit up anytime and wonder what all the fuss was about.

"My condolences for the loss of your brother, Councilor Rasnell," Dr. Fleming said. "I believe he died very quickly, within one or two hours. He was bitten in a vein in his arm and the toxin spread very rapidly. I shall deliver my full report to you later."

Sylvia thanked the doctor and the searchers. She went inside and headed for the Excalibur living room. All the councilors had gathered there, to pay Sylvia their respects and offer condolences for the loss of her brother. After a few minutes, Sylvia managed to speak to Erwin alone.

"Erwin, can we go somewhere private, please? There are things we need to discuss."

"The library would be the best place," he suggested. "You go ahead; I'll join you in a couple of minutes." The library was a part of Excalibur that the church rarely used. Rows of books, once belonging to Philip Gallagan, were stacked among bookshelves along the four walls of the room, untouched, except by the dusters of the housemaids. Ancient literary tomes, books about science, computers and technology, everything that the computer giant had been interested in. It had all been left the way it once was. It was the most tranquil place in Excalibur, and Sylvia sank down in one of the luxurious old chairs, realizing just how tired and emotionally drained she was. It was not just the death of her brother, but the fact that she was now the Head Councilor of the Church of Oscar. A few minutes later Erwin came in, carrying a bottle of brandy and two glasses.

"I think we both need some of this," he said, pouring about an inch of the amber drink in each glass. He handed one to Sylvia, then lifted his own glass. "To Jo, the leader of our Church, your brother and my mentor. May he find the peace he longed for." For a while, they both sipped their drink, then Sylvia spoke.

"It seems perhaps a bit crass, just after Jo's death, Erwin, but we must think about the future. I am to lead our Church now, and I need a second in command. I have thought about it, and I think you are the best person to fulfill that role. We need some young, fresh ideas in the church. Will you accept?"

"Of course, Sylvia. Thank you."

"Very well. Here are the keys to Jo's quarters and the vault, in case of an emergency. I shall move in when things have settled down a bit." She handed him two keys on a ring, then continued. "We shall have two days of mourning for Jo's death. I know the church does not use caskets, but in this case we must make an exception. See if you can get one of the carpenters to build one. Everyone in the commune should see their leader for the last time. I also want it recorded in video for future use. We must let the other churches know what happened. There will be a special service, of course, but I don't know where we can accommodate almost five hundred people."

"In the gardens," Erwin suggested. "I can hook up a sound system."

"An excellent idea." Sylvia nodded. "After the service, Jo's body should be cremated and his ashes be placed in the Vault of the Ancient. Could you arrange all this for me, Erwin?"

"Of course," he said. " As our new leader you are going to have quite a lot on your plate for a while. I'm sure all the councilors will help you as much as they can."

16

Marvin Tuppal walked up the three steps to his apartment, security card in hand. Below the doorknob was a small slot, and he quickly pushed the card in then pulled it out again. He opened the door and stepped inside. Most of the Secret Springs' staff lived rent-free in company apartments in the complex. It was one of the perks of working for the company. The apartments weren't luxurious, but comfortable and spacious enough. Marvin and his wife Rhana had two bedrooms, a cozy living room, a kitchen and two bathrooms, and a roomy den that Marvin had made into his VR room.

There was even a tiny garden, overlooking the Atrium, where Rhana had a few potted plants. She worked in the sleazy side of Chicago as a social worker and had a very hectic schedule that involved many late hours. Marvin didn't expect her to be in yet, and she wasn't. At first, there had been a problem. To qualify for the rent-free accommodation, both husband and wife had to be employed by Secret Springs. Then, because of Marvin's seniority with the company, the rules were relaxed a bit. They had lived at 121 Princetown Court for eight years.

Marvin took his shoes off and entered the living room. He'd been running around a lot that day, and he was tired. He walked to the food cabinet in the kitchen, took a bottle of brandy and poured himself a drink. Sitting down on the couch, he thought about Secret Springs. Philip's prognosis had been right: the firm wasn't doing well. The new subscriber's rate all over the world had gone down for the third consecutive year, and Marvin didn't quite understand why.

It almost seemed as if there was something in the air, something that made people want to give up virtual pleasures. When Secret Springs had started in 2020, as a virtual extension of sites like Facebook, Twitter, Myspace and others, it immediately became the world's most successful company ever, and for many years it had held that position. A few companies had tried to emulate them, but they had failed. Secret Springs was the paragon of virtual reality. Or so it had seemed, until the cracks began to appear.

After a few sips of the brandy, Marvin pressed one of the controls on his watch and saw he had twelve messages. Ten on his business account and two personal. He decided to check his personal messages first. He pressed one of the tiny buttons on the watch and it showed a small picture of his son, Martin.

"Hi, Dad. Guess what? We've got some time off and decided to come and see you next Sunday. Hope everything's fine with you and Mom. Let us know if it's OK, please. Love."

Marvin smiled, thinking of his son. Martin was a civil engineer, working in Atlanta. He was in charge of the upkeep and maintenance of the city's infrastructure. His wife Brenda was a computer scientist. They were just the nicest couple, absolutely made for each other. They had decided not to have children for a little while to further their careers. It had been a bit awkward when Martin was born. The name Martin was Rhana's choice, after her father. Marvin thought it was a bit confusing: Marvin and Martin? Couldn't she come up with another name? Rhana had just looked at him with those dark-brown eyes, and it had been enough. Martin it was to be.

He pressed the same button on his watch again, and there was a familiar face that would never change. Philip. Marvin sighed. He hadn't heard from Philip for quite a while. He almost loved him like a son. Philip had done what no one else had ever done and now he was imprisoned in Secret Springs. Marvin felt sorry for him. Philip could enjoy his virtual world like everyone else, but there was a big difference. He'd always have to hide his real identity and could never make any real friends or have a relationship, not even a virtual one, for fear that someone might recognize and betray him.

For some reason Marvin suddenly thought about his father, Sahitar. In his early years, he and Gurmi, his wife, had left India for Vancouver, Canada. Sahitar had also been an electrical engineer, and after living in Canada for three years, he'd found a company in the U.S. that had hired him. The family had moved to Houston, where Marvin was born. Just after he turned seventy-nine, Sahitar had two serious strokes in rapid succession. They left him paralyzed, unable to move any part of his body, except his eyes. An EEG scan proved his brain was still very active.

To Marvin it had been the most horrible time in his life, watching his father—a living mind in a dead shell. Three years later, when the doctors advised there was nothing they could do, the family had made the agonizing decision to pull the plug. Was this what was in store for Philip? A creative mind, trapped in an avatar? What would happen to him when Secret Springs would no longer be there?

Marvin took his drink and walked into the den. He had a VR suit, but recently he had purchased a new helmet. It was so much easier. He sat at his desk and started the VR computer. Then he donned the helmet and connected with Philip. Through a heuristic system of algorithms, avatars could display at least some of the emotions of the people hiding behind it. When Marvin found Philip in a virtual replica of his old office in Secret Springs, he seemed excited. Papers with drawings were spread out on his desk.

"Marvin, thank goodness you're here. I need to talk to you."

"Hi, Philip. What happened? What's so urgent?"

"I've got it, Marv! I've found the solution. I want you to build a dome for me, like before. But Chicago's not the best place, New Mexico would be better, or Arizona, any place with lots of sun. As big a dome as possible, covered with state of the art photoelectric cells, what we talked about."

"Wait. Hold it right there, Phil. I have a busy job. I'm sixty-two, ready for my retirement in three years and now you want me to go into construction? Are you insane? What are you going to do with that dome anyway?"

"It'll be a place to preserve things, Marvin. For the future. Artifacts, paintings, things made by companies . . ."

"You want me to build a frigging museum?"

"No, it'll be an exhibition. You know, the world exhibitions they had last century? Expos, they called them."

"Why, Philip, for God's sake!"

"I want to save our civilization, Marv, our culture, everything . . ."

"But . . ."

"No, let me finish. There will be two sections, a main floor under the dome ceiling and a secret basement. The main floor will hold things that people want to preserve for the future: company products, works of art, plant seeds, personal things. Everything, including people's DNA."

"First an exhibition, now some kind of ark! That will cost millions for sure, probably billions, Philip. Who the heck is going to pay for such a ludicrous scheme?"

"The exhibitors! We'll sell the space in that dome, so much per square foot. Don't you see? People are very insecure and scared about the future, and they want to make sure our human culture and heritage are preserved for eternity. I want you to build the biggest time vault ever. Once it is filled, we'll lock it up until the world is safe again."

"And that secret basement below?"

"That's where the Virtuals will live, people like me. We will be the vault's guardians. It's my mission, Marvin. This is what my father meant when I saw him. I must save people, so that in better times we can live again."

"That's rather a grandiose project, Phil, even for you, and you're forgetting something. You'll need the virtscapes for your project, remember? Your people's avatars would have nowhere to go without them. Surely you don't think Secret Springs is going to help you with this?"

"I am getting to that, Marv. You met my brother Erwin a while ago. He's Head Councilor for the Church of Oscar. I made a deal with him. That church wants to buy Secret Springs and make it into some kind of evangelical network.

266

They don't need the virtscapes and I can have them. It's all working out, Marvin."

"Now listen, Philip! That deal wasn't yours to make. You're not even with the company any more. The shareholders will decide, and they might not want to sell Secret Springs."

"They will, if you present the case for me. I really need your help, Marv. When can you start?"

"Philip, I promised to help you and I will. But not now. It's late, I'm tired, and I want to go to bed. I do have a life of my own, you know. I'll talk to you later."

Marvin disconnected. He had been a bit rude to Philip, but the thought that Secret Springs might face a takeover bid had rattled him. He walked to the easy chair in his living room, taking his drink with him. He sat down, brought up the lever of the chair and stretched out his legs. Secret Springs, being taken over by the Church Of Oscar? Ridiculous! That church had started out as a small, non-profit company. How could it possibly take over the biggest social network in history? They weren't even a proper company, and he wondered if they had enough money for a deal that size.

There was no way they could just absorb Secret Springs, they'd have to make it into some kind of subsidiary and deal with it at arm's length. What would that do to the company's stock prices? Marvin faced a dilemma. A good part of his financial portfolio was shares and stock options in the company. What should he do?

A takeover by the Church of Oscar—if it ever came to that—might cause Secret Springs' shares to plummet. If he sold his shares before that, he could perhaps save his investments. But he would have acted on insider's information and all hell could break loose. He might even go to jail for fraud.

There was also another possible scenario. The Church's evangelical network might be very successful, and stock prices could rise, instead of drop. There was absolutely no way to predict what would happen. He finished his brandy and made a decision. He was an electrician, not a banker. It was no use worrying himself sick about something that would probably never happen. He would let the dice roll and see how they fell.

◊ ◊ ◊

It had been the longest two days in Sylvia's life. It was around six o'clock on the second day after Jo had met his unfortunate end. Sylvia was parched from all the talking and greatly in need of a cup of tea. She didn't have the strength to go to the cafeteria and had asked one of the waitresses to deliver it to her room. She was exhausted. For two days the people in the commune had lined up for hours to see their leader for the last time. The line had stretched right out of the Excalibur back entrance and into the gardens. Some people waited for more than five hours, in the hot sun, but no one had complained. It had all been peaceful and subdued, marked only by one slightly unusual event. It had happened the first day, right in front of Sylvia's eyes. She had been determined to sit next to her dead brother for as long as she could, smiling at the people and thanking them.

A young woman had waited patiently in line. When she stood in front of the coffin, she looked inside at Jo's body, like everyone else. Then, instead of moving on to allow others to pay their respects, she just stood there, much longer than necessary, staring at Jo's body. Sylvia was touched by the woman's overt devotion to her dead brother, but it seemed overdone. After about a minute, the woman had moved along. Sylvia doubted if anyone else had noticed it.

The second day, after the last of the mourners had shown their respect, there was a beautiful service in the gardens that Jo had loved so much. Loudspeakers were hooked up so that everyone could hear. Father Dubois delivered the hour-long eulogy, then Sylvia, as senior council member, gave a short speech to remember Jo's life on a personal level. After the service, Erwin, Doctor Fleming, Father Dubois and Jeremy ceremoniously carried the coffin with their late leader to the crematorium behind the Infirmary. Afterwards, Joachim Rasnell's ashes joined those of the other pioneers of the Church of Oscar in the Vault of the Ancient. Sylvia had quietly returned to her room to relax.

She was just dozing off, when there was a timid knock on the door and when she answered it, a waitress rolled in a trolley with a pot of tea and a plate of small sandwiches. Sylvia thanked her, and poured herself a cup of tea and took one of the sandwiches. Then she sat back in her easy chair again. Now that the official activities were over, she put her mind to the task at hand: ruling the Church of Oscar. Was she up to it?

Lives would depend on the decisions she made. Who would they train as Ambassadors to be sent to some of the most dangerous places on earth? Many of them might not come back. How to screen the scores of new church members every day? What if one of them was a plant, like that awful man who had almost killed Father English and had been the cause of the Whitsun massacre? It had always been Jo who had the final responsibility. Now it all came down to her. Another knock on her door shocked her out of her reverie. Who could that be, so late?

"Come in," she called, and when the door opened she saw it was Dr. Fleming, carrying his black medical bag.

"Ah, Doctor, come in. Have some tea please. I want to thank you for your help, and I am grateful you didn't perform an autopsy."

"There was no need," Fleming said. "The Head Councilor's death was straightforward. Death by snake venom. I have finished the official death certificate, so we can send it to the authorities." Doctor Fleming put his bag down and poured himself some tea.

"Jo's death was slightly unusual," he said, taking a bite from a cucumber sandwich, "although not totally unexpected, of course. The average temperature in the area has been climbing for years, and with the heat come the creatures that thrive on it: mosquito's, hornets, and also rattlesnakes. They usually don't attack people unless provoked; Jo must have somehow scared it. Which reminds me, Councilor, I do not have a snake venom antidote in my Infirmary. I think we should acquire some. It may save lives in the future."

Sylvia gave him a tired smile. "Consider it done, Doctor."

For a while they both enjoyed their tea and sandwiches. Then Sylvia put her cup down and turned to the doctor. "I'm afraid I am rather tired," she said. "The last two days have been rather stressful for me. Unless you have anything else to discuss, I must ask you to excuse me."

"Actually, there is something, Councilor. I didn't want to bring it up while you were grieving for your brother, but it is a matter of concern for the church."

◊ ◊ ◊

"Where are you going, Dad?" Penny looked at Tom with inquiring eyes, as if he needed her permission for what he was planning.

"To the big City, hon," he said. "I'm going to get some help finding your Mom."

"You're going in the Bullet Train? Can I come?"

"No, the Bullet doesn't stop anywhere near Santa Barbara. It's best if you this alone. I'll drive you to school first. Come on, eat your breakfast or you'll be late."

He'd made them some warm oatmeal with a cut-up peach and some yoghurt. Penny probably would have loved cereal, but Tom had decided to go for healthier foods.

"Who are you going to see?" she asked, not wanting to be excluded from anything that could help bring her mother back. "The FBI?" She pronounced each letter slowly and articulately, almost as if it was a sacred term.

"Yes, their missing persons department. I think I can help them more than they can help me, though." He poured Penny some apple juice, then got himself another cup of coffee. The night before he had printed out all his notes and put them in his briefcase that was waiting for him on the chair near the doorway. He wondered if he should go to Pittard first. If there was a big shakeup coming, his old colleagues might wonder why he had kept them out of the loop. On second thought he decided not to. This was personal.

"OK, Pen, I'll just give Mrs. Hart a call." Florence Hart lived three doors down. A while ago, she had come to the door, wondering why she hadn't seen Heather for so long. Tom had been touched, and Mrs. Hart had offered any help she could give. He dialed his neighbor's number and asked her if she would mind picking up Penny, if he wasn't back in time. Florence said that was fine, and Tom hung up.

"OK, Pen, let's go. If I'm not at the school at 3 o'clock, you phone Florence, all right?" He ran his fingers through her hair, and they walked into the garage and got into the Volt. They didn't say much during the short drive to Cliff High and Tom suspected his daughter was disappointed he wasn't taking her with him. At the school he kissed Penny goodbye and watched her disappear into the building. Then he headed for the freeway.

He was concerned about driving in L.A.; it was a dangerous place, even in daylight. He also wasn't sure if he could find a charging station for his Volt on the way. The easier alternative was to take the bus. He could park in the bus terminal parking lot and be in downtown L.A. in about three hours. But he didn't dare. What if public transport was no longer safe? What if he suffered the same fate as Heather, Mr. Penstone and most likely countless others? Security on at least one airline and one Bullet train had been compromised, causing Heather and Cyril Penstone to leave everything they possessed and cherished. How many trains, planes or even buses would be affected? It was just too risky, after what he had discovered. Driving was the only option.

The highway wasn't so much of a problem these days. Several years ago, in an effort to stop the prevalent holdups and attacks on the freeways, the government had set up a new service, called the Road and Travel Service, which was immediately nicknamed the RATS patrol by the general public. Since there were no major wars to be fought, the service was run by army personnel. Armored vehicles cruised down the major highways, and the results had been promising. The number of hold-ups, abductions, and other crime related incidents had decreased considerably, and for once the general public had something good to say about their government. There had also been calls to bring back the computerized traffic system that had been destroyed in the EMF blast, but the repairs were expensive and slow. There was very little money in the federal and state coffers for non-emergency repairs. So people drove the freeways the way they had done for almost two hundred years: using their own eyes and hands. Luckily, the GPS system was fully functional again.

One wouldn't associate the building at 133 Wilshire Boulevard with a Federal Law Enforcement Office. Long gone were the days of pomp and splendor, and high rises with thousands of windows. The building looked more like a rundown hotel, with cheap lodgings for transients or prostitutes. Just one more sign of how the fiscal and monetary crisis wasn't showing any signs of letting up. Tom slowed down and pulled into a small car park to the side of the building. He switched his GPS off, removed it from the dash and hid it under the front seat. He checked his voltage gauge and saw there was just enough to get back.

When he entered the building he thought at first he had the wrong address. It seemed more like a doctor's waiting room. Chairs along both walls of the room, and a counter to the left. Six of the chairs were taken: three men, one child and two women. Only one of the adults, a young woman, most likely the mother of the child, looked up when he entered and gave him a fleeting smile. The kid glared at him with hostile eyes. The men had their heads buried in magazines.

"Can I help you?" The receptionist behind the counter wasn't pretty and she wasn't ugly. She was grey in every way: grey pantsuit, grey hair, and grey eyes. Even her shoes were grey. Absolutely no color on her at all. Against a grey background she would simply vanish.

"Yes, I'd like to see Agent Decker, please."

"Do you have an appointment?"

"Yes. The name is John Stirling," he lied. "My appointment is for eleven o'clock."

He could feel the stares of the woman and the kid behind him, like stinging pricks in his back, as if they knew he'd given a phony name. It was all part of the general paranoia he'd felt for the last few days.

"Agent Decker will be a few minutes," the Grey Lady said. "If you care to take a seat please." Tom sat down, keeping his briefcase on his lap. He picked up an old fashion magazine and pretended to read it. His heart was beating rapidly. He had written and rehearsed some kind of script but he wasn't sure anymore. He could still leave and go home. It seemed such an outlandish and unbelievable idea that he expected the FBI man to have a good laugh and dismiss him. But what if he was right? After a while, a door along the hallway opened and a smart looking man of about fifty or so appeared. He walked over to the Grey Lady, and she pointed at Tom. He walked over to Tom and held out his hand.

"Paul Decker," he said, shaking Tom's hand. "Could you come this way please?"

He walked ahead to his office and opened the door, letting Tom in first. It was a small office, with a large desk, a picture of a smiling President Ramsing and the ubiquitous Stars and Stripes. Tom sat down, briefcase clamped under his left arm. Agent Decker walked around and sat down in his own swivel chair. He lay both hands in front of him on his desk, and smiled at Tom.

"What can I do for you, Mr. Stirling? We are always interested in input from the general public. Please share your information with us."

Tom stared at the FBI agent and suddenly his blood seemed to turn into ice. Great shivers of apprehension ran down his spine. He clamped his briefcase tighter against his side, knowing he wasn't going to open it. He felt sick to his stomach and seemed immobilized in his seat, unable to think,

273

unable to speak. Agent Decker remained seated, waiting, eyebrows slightly raised.

"Well, Mr. Stirling? You look rather pale all of a sudden. Are you all right? Can I get you some water?"

Tom just shook his head, staring at Paul Decker as if he was an apparition from outer space. To all appearances, the FBI Agent was a normal, rather handsome middle-aged man. He looked like the prime example of an FBI agent: double breasted dark-brown suit, starched white shirt, and black tie. His hair, although graying a bit, was still full and well-cut. He had a strong looking chin, and dark-grey eyes that were beginning to look perturbed.

None of this was responsible for Tom's apoplectic behavior. It was the hands resting on the desk that had set it off. Not so much the hands themselves, but the starched white shirt sleeves, underneath the dark brown suit. Holding the cuffs together were two beautiful cufflinks. From where he sat Tom could only see one, on the agent's right wrist. The cufflink was round, about the size of a dime. It was bright blue, and in the middle of it were three wavy grey lines.

17

If only Jo were here! Sitting in the chair reserved for the Head Councilor, Sylvia thought it very unfair that at her first official council meeting, with Jo barely gone, she would face a crisis of a magnitude never seen before in the church's history. The councilors had been briefed as to what had happened, and everyone had been appalled and shaken. Today's meeting had been called to find a solution for the dilemma the church was in. It was not an ordinary council meeting. Anna Kulik had been ordered to appear, and Sylvia had no idea how it would all end.

"I call this special meeting to order," she said. "Doctor Fleming, you have the floor."

"Four days ago, Anna Kulik came to see me," the doctor began. "She was in a poor state, confused and uncertain what was wrong with her. After I gave her a thorough examination, I have come to the conclusion that she is in excellent health. She is also three months pregnant."

"Impossible!" Father Dubois called out. "Abstinence is what our church is all about. Oscar's Breath guarantees it. Your diagnosis is wrong, doctor."

"I assure you that I know my job, Father," Dr. Fleming said testily. "There is no doubt."

"In that case, conception must have occurred before Anna became a member," Dubois said. "Head Councilor, when did Anna join us?"

"I can't recall the exact date," Sylvia said. "It was about six month ago, I believe."

"Perhaps your timing is wrong then, Doctor," Dubois said suavely. "Anna's pregnancy could be more advanced."

"No." Dr. Fleming shook his head. "I could be off by a few days, or a week, but not by three months. Sexual intercourse happened here, in the commune."

275

"Councilor Evans," Sylvia said. "As interim Chief of Security, do you recall anything out the ordinary happening around three months ago? Were there any security breaches, to the best of your knowledge? Is it possible that someone sneaked into the commune and violated Anna?"

"Absolutely not." George Evans was a big, heavy set man. Though it was a council meeting, he was wearing his security uniform—without the gun, of course. He had a rather large head, with grey-blue eyes, a strong neck and biceps that would make any intruder think twice before attacking him. He was also short-tempered and bristled at the idea he had missed something.

"Since Councilor Pinehurst was killed we have been on a higher alert than before. The guard house is manned twenty-four hours a day. The fences around the perimeter are not only electric, but hooked up to the alarm system as well. Even if someone had sneaked in, Anna would have sounded the alarm. The intruder would never have made it out again. Besides, why would anyone specifically violate Anna?"

"Thank you, Councilor Evans," Sylvia said. "Does anyone have any other ideas?"

"Perhaps someone came in during recruiting hours," Patricia said. "Someone with a grudge towards Anna, from her past perhaps. He could have hidden in the building until he saw his chance."

"A possibility," Sylvia agreed. "Well, Anna? Is there anyone from your past, from before you joined the church, who could have done this to you? A disgruntled boy friend, perhaps?"

"No," Anna said. "I didn't have a boyfriend when I joined."

"It would have been very difficult for a person to hide in Excalibur and not be seen by at least someone," Erwin said. "Anyone not joining after the sermon is immediately escorted off the property. We do not allow visitors, so I can't see how someone from the outside is responsible for this."

"There is another possibility," Father Dubois said pensively. "You could be a very lucky woman indeed, Anna. Yours could be a virgin birth. After all, this has happened before; a large part of Christian religion is built on that premise."

"But why me?" Anna asked demurely. "Why would the Lord choose me?"

"That's not a question for you to ask, young lady," Dubois admonished her.

"Or there is the other side of the coin," Erwin said forcefully. "She could be carrying the Devil's brood. That's just as good a possibility. We are so concerned about changing the earth and converting people to our beliefs that we forget there is another powerful, invisible enemy out there—the Devil himself. What better place for the Force of Darkness to fight our church than from the inside, where no one expects it?"

The room fell absolutely silent, as Erwin's words sank in. Then there was a loud sobbing.

"No, no. Not the Devil. Please, don't let it be. It can't be. Oh, I want to die."

"Anna pull yourself together," Sylvia admonished the young woman. "We are here to help you. Why were you so emotional when you paid your respects to our late leader the other day?"

"Emotional?" The young woman blinked several times in succession. "I don't understand. Everyone was sad at the Head Councilor's death." Anna was very nervous. She kept running a hand through her matted black hair and crossing her legs. Her forehead was wet with perspiration.

"Yes, but not like you," Sylvia said. "I noticed that you stood at the casket much longer than anyone else. Why was that?"

Anna fidgeted even more. It seemed she was sitting on hot coals. Finally, something seemed to gave in her. She threw her head back and looked at the councilors, eyes blazing with defiance. For the first time in her life, Sylvia was petrified with fright. Something very evil was about to happen . . .

"Doctor, you may think I am fine," Anna said. "I am not. I cannot concentrate at work and I cannot sleep. I hardly eat. When I doze off at night, I have a bad dream. Every night I have the same nightmare. I am in a delivery room, giving birth to my child. I suffer great pains in my dreams. I know it is because I am punished for what has happened to me. When my child is born and they allow me to see it, it has a familiar face. Then I wake up, drenched in sweat."

"Whose face is it, Anna?" Sylvia asked.

"It is the late Head Councilor's face! I see it every night in my dreams. That's why I was angry at his funeral. It must have been he who violated me!"

There was instant pandemonium. Councilors jumped up from their seats. Confused shouts filled the air. One councilor ran towards Anna, hands high to hit her.

"No, Erwin!" Sylvia shouted. "There will be no violence in the House of the Lord. Someone stop him!"

Father Dubois and Councilor Evans who were closest, grabbed Erwin and pulled him back from Anna. The young woman had pushed her chair back and raised her hands across her face, to protect herself from the furious councilor.

"How dare you!" Erwin raged. "How dare you defile the memories of our founder, after all he did for us. You are possessed by the Devil. I'll see to it that you and your child are put to death for this."

"Councilors, please! Let us all calm down." Doctor Fleming tapped the table with his water glass. "Everyone sit down and take a deep breath."

It took quite a while for order to be restored. It was Sylvia who broke the awkward silence that followed. "Councilor Evans, could you please escort Anna to the room next door? Have one of your men guard her. Do not harm her but do not let her escape. Come back as quick as you can, because we shall need your vote."

"Well, that proves my point, doesn't it?" Erwin said. "She is carrying the Devil's child. It has not even been born and already it is causing havoc in our church."

No one said anything, while they waited for Councilor Evans to return. All the councilors were preoccupied with their own thoughts, wondering why the church was so severely tested. Sylvia was in such a conflicting state of emotions that she could hardly think straight. How could Jo have violated Anna? He had taken Oscar's Breath, just like everyone else. It was impossible. So why would Anna accuse him? It had to be the Devil's scheme.

When Evans returned, Sylvia spoke again.

"I must agree with Councilor Johnson," she said. "Horrifying as it may be, I think the Devil has taken possession of Anna, and she is carrying his child. There is no other rational explanation. Her pointing the finger at our late leader was a clever ploy to sow confusion among us. Neither Anna, nor her unborn child can be allowed to live, and we must decide on the proper method of execution."

"In the old days, possessed people like this were burned at the stake," Father Dubois stated, matter-of-factly.

"You have my vote," Erwin growled.

"Or they were ceremoniously sacrificed to the gods as a token of atonement," Dubois continued. "After all, the Lord will not be pleased that we have harbored the Devil in his Church."

"Does it have to be so barbaric?" Sylvia asked. "This is not the Middle Ages anymore. Doctor, could you not give her an injection?"

"No." Doctor Fleming shook his head. "I save lives, I do not take them. I'm afraid I cannot take part in this, Head Councilor."

It took the Council quite some time to come to a final agreement.

◊ ◊ ◊

She could no longer postpone it. Sylvia turned the key in the door lock and entered Jo's office. It smelled musty, from being closed off for four days. Sylvia knew she should have gone through Jo's things and the secret church papers immediately after Jo had died, but there just hadn't been time. Now it was a matter of extreme urgency.

The first thing she noticed was how clean and neat everything was. She had been in Jo's office many times, and although Jo was not a messy person—quite the contrary in fact—there had always been signs that he was working on something. Papers strewn on his desk, maybe a dirty cup on the table, an open book on the bookshelves. This time everything was clean. All the books on the shelves, not even a pen on his desk. Even the wastebasket was empty. Had someone been in here and cleaned up? Impossible. Jo and herself were the only ones with a key. Or had her brother cleaned everything up because he knew he would never be back?

She turned on Jo's computer. A few messages were waiting to be answered, but she didn't have Jo's password. That would be in the vault, with all the other documents that she as new leader would have to go through. Perhaps the answer lay there. From her gown pocket she produced the key that Jo had given her, long ago, after Father English had died and Sylvia had become the second in command.

She opened the vault and removed its contents: The Word of Oscar, the heavy church bible. Printouts with names of new members. Copies of letters written to the government, mostly the IRS, informing them who had joined the church and who had died. She would have to write one herself, informing them about Jo's death. Hundreds of old church papers, notes written by Jo and Ted in the early days. Bank statements. Checkbooks, although almost all monetary transaction were done online these days.

She noticed two square white sleeves with the DVDs Carol had brought into the church. Then her eye fell on a pile of loose papers, held together with an elastic band. She removed the elastic band and flipped through the pages: twenty-four pages in all. It seemed all heavy-duty scientific stuff. What could it all mean? She turned to the first page and began to read.

Official transcript of Dr. Yabul Kozak's second DVD, donated to the church by Carol Johnson.

A word of introduction by Jo Rasnell.

Part of Dr. Kozak's legacy to his wife Carol were two DVDs he had left in their safety deposit box. The first DVD is of little value to our commune, since it holds only private information for Carol Johnson. The second DVD is of great importance for our church. It contains the formula for what Dr. Kozak called VTM, which stands for Viral Thought Modification. It was this drug that became Oscar's Breath, and thanks to this formula we are now able to produce it in large amounts, allowing the expansion we have been awaiting for so many years. This DVD also contains additional information that is of no immediate value to us now, but will be of critical importance in the future, as this transcripts will show.

Sylvia sat up straight and rubbed her eyes, strained from reading the fine print. She decided she would read the rest of the transcript later. Most of it was technical, and her eyes hurt. She put the pages together and was about to put the elastic band around them, when she noticed that the last page was a different color, lighter than the others. It had obviously been written later. It contained a handwritten memo, or message of some kind. What immediately drew her attention to it, was the official seal of the Church of Oscar that was embossed on the paper. Only Jo could have written that message. Curiously she began to read.

For Head Councilor's Eyes Only.

These transcripts, and the DVD they were printed from, contain vital and essential knowledge for our future church and must be preserved and kept in the vault for future generations. This information must never leave this office, nor may it be shown to anyone, not even the church councilors. Only the current Head of Church may look at it, on assuming his or her duties. Under no circumstances may any reference whatsoever be made to it, not in the world outside, not in the church, not even at council meetings. This is an executive order, issued by Joachim Rasnell, Head Councilor of the Church of Oscar.

Dated June 21, 2062.

Sylvia stared at the writing. She was not familiar with handwriting analysis, but she did know that writing can show people's character, temperament and mood. She knew Jo's writing very well; it was precise and uniform. This short paragraph didn't seem to be written by him at all. The letters were uneven, much bigger and heavier than usual. The words *never* and *whatsoever* had been heavily underlined two times. Sylvia could see that Jo had been very emotional and uptight when he wrote it. Was he angry? Scared? Worried? Shivers of fear ran down her spine. What on earth could have upset Jo so much that he needed to write an executive order? There had to be something else, something written between the lines.

She looked at the page again, and re-read it. And again. At the third time she saw it. It was a warning! Jo was telling everyone to stay away from the transcripts and the DVDs. That's why he used such strong language: *must never be shown . . . no reference whatsoever . . .*

Sylvia herself was beginning to feel very uptight indeed. Was Jo warning her? It had to be, because she was the next Head Councilor. But what was the warning about? What could be so dangerous about a transcript? Then she looked at the date on the paper, and a thought shot through her heart, like a dagger. June 21, just four days ago, the day Jo had died and also the day Dr. Fleming had found out that Anna Kulik was pregnant. Pictures flooded her mind: Anna's lingering at the coffin in the lineup at Jo's wake, her accusatory behavior at the trial yesterday. Nervously she returned to the transcript and read it again, hoping that she had it all wrong.

About an hour later, a very tired Sylvia, shaken beyond belief, sat up straight in her chair. Her back ached from bending forward and reading so long. One more time she read Jo's handwritten letter, then put it back with the other papers. She carefully put the elastic band around the documents, collected all other bits and pieces, and put everything into the vault and locked it. She left the room and returned to her own quarters. While she prepared herself for bed, she knew for sure that she would not have a restful sleep that night.

◊ ◊ ◊

A wooden pyre was constructed in the gardens, well away from the mansion. It consisted of a pole, about six feet long, like the ones used in the wooden fences around the vegetable gardens to stop the sheep, cows and other animals from ruining and eating their precious crops. Tied all around the pole were dry bushes and twigs, anything that would sustain a fire. There were seats for the councilors, well back from the structure, to prevent the heat and flying sparks from harming them. Behind the seats, ropes partitioned an area for the crowds to stand and watch. Already scores of people were lining up for the unusual spectacle: the burning of a heretic, a person possessed by the Devil. There was a feeling of anticipation in the air, but also of fear. How could this have happened in their sacred church? The waiting was for the councilors and the heretic.

Finally, the councilors arrived with much pomp and ceremony. Though it was a warm day, the church leaders were dressed in their gala-costume, reserved for very special

283

occasions: a white woolen gown, with golden epaulets, showing the sacred symbol of Oscar: three wavy grey lines in a bright blue circle. Each councilor wore a black ribbon around the right arm for this special occasion.

When all councilors were comfortably seated there was the sudden sound of drums. A small procession appeared from the building. Four burly guards dragged the young heretic towards the waiting pyre. To the side stood a lone guard with a long stick, the top of which was drenched in tar that had been lit. It was burning with a deep yellow flame and black smoke was rising up, as a sign to the Lord that His church was about to make Him an offer of atonement. The guards tied the screaming and struggling woman to the post, then moved to the side. The drumming stopped and everyone patiently waited.

It was Sylvia, as the new Head Councilor, who had the honor of lighting the pyre. She stood up and slowly walked over to the guard with the flame. She carefully took it from him, then held it in her right hand. She headed for the pyre and stood as close as she could to the young woman, making sure her back was turned towards the crowd. Anna was still loudly protesting her innocence.

"Anna Kulik, there is very little time," Sylvia whispered urgently. "Listen to what I have to say." Something in the new leader's behavior caused Anna to stop her raving. She watched Sylvia closely, a deep frown creasing her perspiring brow.

"I am going to make the sacred sign of Oscar in front of you," Sylvia continued in a low voice. "When my hand comes close to your face, open your mouth and I shall give you a pill. Swallow it at once. It will stop the pain, so you can die in peace. But when the flames reach you, you must pretend to be in agony. The crowd will expect it."

Sylvia stood back a bit, and with her left arm she slowly made the sacred sign of the wavy lines in front of Anna. At the third pass, her hand came very close to Anna's face and the girl opened her mouth to accept the white pill Sylvia offered her. It happened very quickly and Sylvia hoped no one in the crowd has seen it. While Sylvia bent down to light the branches at the bottom of the pile, Anna spoke her last words.

"You know it was the Head Councilor." It was a whispered statement, not a question.

"Yes." Sylvia moved the torch around to light some more branches. "But I cannot allow that truth to be revealed, Anna. Sometimes one individual must be sacrificed for the greater good. May your soul rest in peace."

Sylvia had to step back from the heat, as the tinder dry brush and twigs exploded with fire. While she walked back to her seat, the first horrendous screams of agony ran through the quiet gardens. Anna Kulik shook her head from side to side, while she tore at her bonds, trying to escape the fierce flames that began to sear her body. Murmurs of satisfaction ran through the crowd. Erwin nodded to Sylvia, as she returned to her seat next to him.

"Well done, Councilor. That will teach the Devil not to infiltrate the Church of Oscar ever again." The spectacle lasted for about fifteen minutes, as the flames blackened Anna's body, engulfing her higher and higher, driven by the wind. Thick smoke filled the air and the unmistakable smell of burning flesh wafted over the spectators. Then, earlier than the crowd had expected, the voice of Satan was suddenly silent, and the only sound heard was the roaring of the flames.

18

Oh, why was he still using an old dinosaur computer, instead of investing in a new, voice-activated machine! Even after many years of writing police reports, Tom was still pecking at the keyboard with two or four fingers. He was so fired up, so full of adrenaline, that he wanted the words to appear on the screen as fast as he thought of them, and it wasn't happening. He pushed the keyboard back towards his computer and reached for his lukewarm coffee. It was about 1:00 in the afternoon, about an hour after he had returned from his visit to the FBI.

After his discovery that the Church of Oscar had infiltrated even the FBI, he'd pretended to be sick, which wasn't very difficult. He really did feel nauseated. He'd mumbled his excuses to Agent Decker and rushed out of the building. Then he'd driven straight home, made himself a cup of strong coffee and had fired up his computer.

Things had changed. Passive data gathering was getting him nowhere. It was time for action. He suddenly missed Heather tremendously. She'd always been there for him in a time of crisis, and this time he was in the biggest mess of his entire life. Thank goodness he'd used a phony name at the FBI office!

He took a swig of coffee and resumed his typing. He was methodically putting down all the information he had gathered since he had left the force. Finding the cabbie that had taken Heather. The Ouija game. His talks with Mrs. Penstone. The stakeout to find out where the trucks went. The Organic Food Emporium, and the strange symbols on the rude manager's shirt and also on the FBI agent's cufflinks.

Heather had left him because something or someone had forced her to go to the Triagle shopping center exactly 42 days after her birthday. It must been some kind of posthypnotic suggestion delivered in the Bullet train with that same number, 42. It all made such beautiful sense now. If people were forced to join that church, they couldn't just go straight down there, it would be too obvious. It had to be some kind of secretive route, and Tom realized the answer had stared him right in the face at the time of his stakeout.

There were other communes of the Church of Oscar in the country, and each one had probably an outlet similar to the Organic Food Emporium. What better way to recruit new church members, than to hide them in a busy shopping center during the day, and drive them to the commune in the middle of the night in an empty grocery truck?

When he finished typing, he read his report again and make a few corrections. Then he saved everything on a USB memory stick. He took an envelope from his desk drawer, put the little drive inside, and began to type a letter.

Christopher,

I have to ask you a big favor, my friend. I have discovered something so incredible that I can no longer keep it to myself. It is the biggest conspiracy ever. This memory stick holds everything I have discovered so far. I think I know where Heather is, and I am going to get her back. I'll drop this off on my way, and I beg of you: if you don't hear from me within twelve-four hours, please take the memory stick to the media. Do not take it to the police! I am scared, Chris, for all of us, our nation, the world. We face a great crisis and people must be made aware of it.

Tom.

He quickly read it, then typed the print command. He looked at his watch. Shit! Not much time left, he might not be back in time to pick up Penny. Thank God for Mrs. Hart. When the printer spit out the paper he quickly folded the sheet and stuck it in the envelope with the memory stick and pocketed it. He turned off the coffee maker in the kitchen and went into his office.

He opened one of his desk drawers and pocketed his Beretta. Then walked into the garage. He started the Volt and looked at the charge meter. Plenty to get there and back. He hoped the physician would be busy, so he wouldn't have to stay and talk. Luck was with him, as Linda answered the door.

"Tom! Good to see you, come in. I'm afraid Christopher is rather busy this afternoon. Want some coffee?"

"No thanks. I'm in a hurry." He handed Linda the envelope. "Do me a favor, and give this to him when he has a minute, please. It's very important. Thanks. I must go." He smiled at her and hoped she would forgive his abrupt behavior. Then he was on his way again, heading down 101 towards Montecito. His mouth was dry and his heart was doing overtime as what-ifs flooded his mind.

What if the commune would recruit him, the way they recruited others? He might never see Penny again. At one stage he almost turned the car back again, ready to forget the whole deal. Then he thought of Heather and he pushed ahead, more determined than ever. He left the freeway at Gallagan Drive and drove past the spot where he had parked early in the morning during the stakeout. He could see the Excalibur mansion in the distance. When he reached the heavy duty metal gate, he stopped the car, got out and walked to the gatehouse. An older man in a blue guard uniform looked up from a TV screen.

"Yes, sir. Can I help you?

"I would like to talk to the person in charge of Admissions, please."

"Do you have an appointment?"

"Uh . . . no."

"We don't usually accept new members this way, sir. You should perhaps go to our Sunday service first, to learn more about us."

Tom felt his heart thump like a jack hammer. How naïve could he have been to expect to walk right in. No what? He could still go back. This would never work. Then he had an outrageous idea.

"I can't wait till Sunday. I am desperate. My wife has left me, and Agent Decker of the FBI said you would help me."

"Paul Decker referred you to us?"

"Yes. I work with him. He told me your church helps people in trouble. Please, I need to talk to someone." The guard typed something on his screen. After a few minutes he looked up and smiled. "All right, sir. Relax. Someone will be with you in a few minutes. You can wait here, if you wish." He pointed to a small waiting area inside the guard hut, but Tom shook his head. "I'll stay here."

A small cart came down the long driveway. It looked like a golf cart. At the same time there was a soft humming noise as the gate slowly began to open. Tom stepped through and waited on the side of the driveway. He looked around, wondering how he would get out again, if he was in a hurry. It was a pretty high gate to scale and the wall around the property wouldn't be that easy to climb either. Not for first time did he doubt his sanity. The golf cart stopped and the young girl in the driver's seat gave him a shy smile.

"I'll take you to Father Dubois for an interview, sir."

"Thank you."

Tom sat down next to her and they headed back the way she had come. He wasn't in the mood for talking and luckily the girl didn't ask questions. After traversing the long driveway, they finally came to the Excalibur building and he could see that much construction had been going on. There was a brand-new wing built to one side. It was airy, with lots of glass, and sliding doors. The girl parked the cart and they walked into the waiting area. For a few moments Tom stood there, not quite knowing what to do. It was as if he had stepped in a modern airline departure hall. There were several rows of comfy seats and a service counter.

"Please take a seat over there. Father Dubois should be here momentarily." His driver pointed to the seats behind him, then headed to the admissions counter. Tom sat down, wondering how long he'd have to wait.

Two people, probably husband and wife, pulled a small suitcase each towards the counter. The man carried a booklet or folder in his hand. Again Tom was reminded of an airline terminal. But a terminal to what? A new life? All that was missing were the conveyer belts for luggage, the boarding gates, and the flight announcements. He could hear the couple talk to the receptionist, while she rapidly entered information into her computer, but he was too far away to hear what was said. After a few minutes, the receptionist handed the folder back and pointed the couple towards another area in the back with little cubbyholes and chairs.

Cramer looked at his watch: 2:10. How long would it take for this Father Dubois to get here? Perhaps they'd given up on him, hoping he would eventually leave. Well, he'd see about that. He started when he heard a sudden voice behind him.

"Welcome to the Church of Oscar, sir. I am Father Dubois, religious leader of our church. How can I help you?"

"You have among your flock a lady by the name of Heather Cramer," Tom said without preamble. "I would like to see her, please. I am her husband."

Father Dubois was dressed in some kind of church attire: a white cassock, with a red satin rope around the waist, and brilliant red lapels around the shoulders. He had perhaps been handsome when he was younger, but deep wrinkles around his eyes and a permanent frown in his brow showed he was at the far side of fifty. It was obvious that the priest hadn't expected a question like that.

"That is not possible," Dubois said. "Our church does not have visiting hours. If your wife has joined us, it was her decision. When people come to the Church of Oscar they make a clear break with the past."

Before Tom could reply, the young receptionist came running over.

"Father, an urgent phone call for you."

"Thank you, Lisa."

"Excuse me, please." Dubois walked to the admission counter to answer the phone.

Tom looked around. Apart from the couple he had seen before, everything was quiet. Not exactly happy hour. When Father Dubois came back, Tom noticed a distinct change in his behavior. His frown had deepened considerably, his eyes had darkened, and his lips formed a straight line. *Trouble!* When Tom looked outside, he saw something else. Two security men were approaching the admission room from the main Excalibur building.

"You are obviously a troubled person," Dubois said. "I think it is best if I show you our introductory—"

"I don't think so, Father," Tom interrupted. "I know how you recruit your new members, I have proof." From the corner of his eye Tom saw that the guards were just about to enter the admission room. "If you lay one finger on me, that information will be made public with dire consequences for your church. I suggest you call off the security guards." He had expected the priest to show at least some emotion. Anger, or fear, surprise for sure. But Father Dubois just smiled at him. *His plan wasn't working!*

"You have come to the right place," the priest said, pointing to the admission counter. "Come, let us help you."

Tom jumped forward, hit the priest hard in the solar plexus and ran towards the sliding door. He roughly pushed the admissions clerk into the path of the approaching guards. Luckily the glass door was on automatic and it swished open when he got there. Cramer dashed through and jumped into the parked golf cart. Behind him he heard Father Dubois' shrill voice. "Go after him!"

He pushed the pedal to the floor and the cart jumped ahead, like a scared horse. He tore down the driveway, while the guards reached the door. They seemed to be confused about what to do. One of them ran away, probably to get another cart, and the second man stood in the road aiming his gun. If he was any good it would be all over in a few seconds.

Tom tried to use a zigzag pattern, pushing the cart to the limit. He heard two shots, and one bullet actually hit the corner of the windscreen, shattering it into thousands of pieces. More shots were fired, but they missed. Cramer looked back, and saw that another cart had started the pursuit. If he could just get to his own car, he'd be home free. A golf cart was no match for the Volt. But there was still the gate. The old man had just gotten out, and stood in the middle of the road, his handgun aimed at Tom. Now what? He slowed down, making sure his Beretta was ready in his pocket. He stopped the cart and got out, holding up his hands.

"Don't shoot!" he cried. "I'm unarmed!" Tom himself had done quite a bit of shooting at the police firing range, and from the way the guard at the gate was holding the weapon he knew the other was not an ex-cop or army man. The man seemed confused and the hand that held the gun was not very steady. Shooting people was probably not an everyday occurrence at the church gate.

Tom glanced back and saw that the other cart was gaining. No time to lose. He yanked his Beretta from his pocket, aimed at the window of the guard hut and fired. Taken by surprise, the guard turned around, as shards of glass flew in all directions. Tom kicked the gun out of the guard's hand, and aimed the Beretta at him.

"Open the gate, or I'll shoot you in the legs," he yelled. "I mean it. Open it now!" He pushed the man inside the hut, and after a few seconds of hesitation, the guard pushed a button on a console and the gate began to open. Still aiming his Beretta at the guard, Tom ran to the gate and picked up the guards' weapon on the way.

As soon as the gate had opened wide enough, he squeezed through and ran to his Volt. He jumped in, started the engine and drove off down Galagan Drive, as fast as the electric motor would let him. In the rear view mirror he saw that the other cart had reached the gate, but his pursuers had to wait a few more valuable seconds to get through, and Tom was gaining on them. Then they came after him. Two more shots were fired, but the faster Volt was gaining and he was soon out of their range. Golf carts weren't allowed on the highway, anyway, so he'd be fine.

For the first time in half an hour, he felt relatively safe again and he took a few deep breaths, cursing himself for going into that church on his own. It had been stupid and very unprofessional for an ex-cop. If the guards had been trained marksmen, it would have ended quite differently. He had been so desperate to see Heather that he had lost it, endangered himself and, up to a point, Penny also.

He looked at his watch. Almost 3 o'clock. He was late, but with a bit of luck his daughter would still be waiting for him. When he reached the 101, he turned right and drove on quietly, letting his heartbeat slowly return to normal.

◊ ◊ ◊

Sylvia stood outside Erwin's door and knocked. From the inside came a hissing noise she couldn't identify. The door opened and there stood Erwin, dressed in summer shorts and a brown T-shirt.

"Ah, Sylvia, just in time. Come in." He showed her into the room and the first thing Sylvia saw was a large television screen, bigger than she'd ever seen. It was snowy, and Erwin was still in the process of hooking it up.

"Were did you get that?" Sylvia asked. "Is that really necessary, Erwin? Daniel English would have a fit if he could see this. Even Jo didn't have a screen that big. Why?"

"To keep in touch with our other communes," the young councilor said proudly. "Watch this." He fiddled with a remote control and suddenly the hissing sound was gone, and a lifesize picture of a woman filled the screen. It was Alison Hu, as clear as if she'd been in the room herself.

"Hello, Erwin, Sylvia. Good to see you. How are things in the church?

"Everything's fine, Alison. Thanks for the television. We'll be able to follow the cloning process here. Dr. Fleming is quite keen."

Alison smiled. "Your good doctor can ask questions. All of us speak English. We'll let you know when we're ready." The screen went blank.

When had it all began, Sylvia mused. When had they so insidiously started to bend the rules that Jo and Ted and the first council members had laid out so long ago? First a single small computer in Jo's office to keep a database of the church members. Then a video player to show potential new church members an introductory movie of what the church was all about. Next e-mail, a telephone for every councilor, and instant communication with the rest of the world via the Internet. It was all wrong.

Sylvia knew the deal with Secret Springs was set in motion, and she wasn't at all sure that was a good idea either. Could this be the real way the Devil was infiltrating the Church of Oscar? Through technology?

"Erwin, I've got something for you," she said.

Reluctantly, the young man turned away from his new toy. "What is it, Sylvia?"

She handed him a set of keys. "Here are the keys you will need."

He frowned. "You already gave me a set a few days ago, Sylvia. In the library. Have you forgotten?"

"That was when I made you my second in command. You can pass those keys on to whomever you choose as your second. This set is for you, the new Head Councilor. I am resigning my position as of today."

"You can't resign, Sylvia. Councilors are elected for life. You can't just give up your responsibilities like that. You've only been our leader for less than a week, and you've done exceedingly well, considering what we went through. Why do you want to quit?"

"The Council needs new blood, Erwin, and you're just the person to lead the church. When Jo died it was the end of a chapter, and now you can take us into the future. I'm too tired and aching to be of any use to you."

"But what will you do? Where will you go?"

"I am going to live in the gardens, Erwin. I want to be with the workers who are the true backbone of our commune. The laborers who toil the gardens, the people who pick the fruit, grow the vegetables, and look after the animals. I want to make myself useful to the community."

"You won't be able to do heavy work, Sylvia. Think about your arthritis. You're not used to working in the fields for eight hours a day."

"Oh, I know, but there are other jobs. I can peel potatoes, shell peas, bake pies. There's a job for me somewhere, I know it."

"But why so sudden?" Erwin asked. "Why not wait till the next council meeting?"

"No, Erwin, I've made up my mind. It is the privilege of the Head Councilor to select his or her successor, and I have selected you. The Church of Oscar is yours, as of now. You'll find everything in Jo's office in order. I want this to be my last day as Head Councilor. From now on I want to live in the commune. I don't want a special farewell, no speeches. Nothing. I just want to step down, so if you would be kind enough to get someone to help me move my things."

"Of course, Sylvia. If you insist. I'll arrange it and inform the Council after I have finished setting this up."

◊ ◊ ◊

"Dad! Oh, no. I phoned Mrs. Hart and she's on her way. Why are you so late?" An agitated Penny stood on the sidewalk in front of her school. "What happened? Did you find Mom?"

"I'll tell you later. Get in."

Cliff High was on Yanonali Street, near Franklin Park. Tom drove off in a hurry, turning right on Alisos. He just stared straight ahead. He hadn't reached over to kiss her when she got in and he didn't smile. At E Haley Street, where he usually turned off to go to Belmont Drive, he kept going and Penny eyed him sharply.

"What's going on, Dad? Why aren't we going home? You've got to call Mrs. Hart to apologize; she'll be furious."

"Sorry, hon, I'm just in a little bit of a panic here. We can't go home, because there are people after me. They know where we live and want my blood. We're going to Dr. Taggard till the coast is clear."

"Why are you panicking?"

He told her about his experience in the Church of Oscar.

"Are they keeping Mom there?"

"I'm pretty sure, but they wouldn't let me see her. Don't worry, I'm not finished with them yet. Now Pen, when we get to Christopher and Linda, you call Mrs. Hart, but don't say anything else. OK? Let me do the talking."

When they reached the physician's home on Alphonse Street, Tom awkwardly parallel parked in the last space on the road. Then they walked up the driveway and onto the porch, and Penny pressed the bell. It was Christopher who answered and Tom could tell the physician was not in a good mood. He glared at him.

"Tom, Penny. Come in." They stepped inside, and Linda came running from the kitchen. Out of habit, both Penny and Tom took their shoes off and put them on a mat near the front door. Then Christopher took charge.

"Linda, can you take Penny into the living room, please. Give her some juice, or something. Tom and I are going to have a little talk." He marched ahead of Tom, opened the door to his study and stood back to let Tom in. He walked straight over to the book case, opened one of the cabinet doors and took out a bottle of Scotch. He poured a liberal amount in two glasses and gave one to Tom. Then he sat down behind his desk.

"What the hell is going on, Tom? I read your note. What's all this about conspiracies and cover-ups? I think you're stressed out and it's all in your mind."

"No, it isn't. I just got back from the Church of Oscar, because I have a strong feeling that Heather is kept there and

I wanted to bring her back with me. They wouldn't even tell me if she was there or not. They're hiding something, Chris."

"Why the blazes did you go to there? That was a stupid thing to do! Are you insane? You have absolutely no proof that church is involved. You can't accept the fact that Heather has gone and now you try to blame it on everything else in the world. It's possible she joined them, yes. It's one of a million possible scenarios. Barging in there, spouting accusations like that won't help at all."

"Did you read what I wrote on that USB stick?"

"No, haven't had time yet. I have a busy practice to run, Tom, in case you've forgotten. Perhaps you can enlighten me now?"

"OK, here's what I know." Quickly, Tom explained what he had found out since he had started looking for Heather. Then he stopped to take a swig of Scotch.

"My wife was lured to that church by some kind of post-hypnotic suggestion," he continued. "Something very sinister is going on, Christopher. It's all on that memory stick."

Christopher Taggard sat quietly for a few seconds, deep in thought. Then he looked Tom straight into the eye, while he tapped his fingers on his desk.

"This is one hell of a story, Tom, and if it is true, we must do something about it at once. It's an outrageous idea, but I'll grant you this: it is possible. They could flood a train, or plane or any climate controlled place with a drug that would put people temporarily into a highly suggestive subconscious state.

"It would be a very evil, fascist and sick thing to do, but it would also be brilliant, in a way. If this is true, it'll cause the biggest scandal in U.S. history and whoever breaks it will get the Pulitzer prize for sure. I know someone at the *L.A. Times* who will help us. But you had better be right, Tom. I'm sticking my neck out here, and if this blows up into our faces you had better move as far away from me as possible. Are we clear on that? So I'm asking you again, are you absolutely sure about this?"

"Look, you now know everything I know. You decide. Do you think I'm chasing windmills here?"

When Christopher looked at Tom again, it seemed as if the physician's eyes were trying to drill right into Tom's soul, and Cramer felt guilty. He had no right to make the doctor risk his practice and everything else on just a theory. Then Christopher stood up, opened his drawer and removed the envelop with the memory stick that Tom had given to Linda before.

"Everything you've told me is on here, right?"

"Yes, except the episode at the church this afternoon. I came straight here because I didn't dare to go home."

"That's fine. Come on, we're going to L.A. right now. That church isn't going to sit back and wait till tomorrow, knowing their secret is about to be blown to pieces. They're in full damage control this very moment, and you were right not to go home. We'll take my car." The physician stomped out of the door, and headed for the kitchen, where Penny and Linda were preparing dinner.

"You and Penny are staying for supper, Tom," Linda said happily. "It's a lamb casserole. We've got plenty."

"Sorry, love. Tom won't." Christopher said. "We have to go to L.A. Would you mind looking after Penny until we come back? You'd also better prepare the spare room. They'll be sleeping here tonight. OK, Tom, let's go. I'll get the car. Don't forget your shoes. Meet me outside. Linda, we might be back late, so don't stay up." Christopher disappeared through the connecting door to the garage, while Tom walked to the front door and put his shoes back on.

"I'm sorry, Linda," he said, feeling a blockage in his throat. "I didn't expect this to happen. We'll tell you all about it later. Thanks a million. Penny, you behave now, OK?" He hugged his daughter and went out. He stood outside in the still air, feeling guilty about involving Christopher. Still, he'd done his part, and whatever the paper did with the story was up to them. For the first time in weeks he felt relief. With a little bit of luck Heather would soon be reunited with them

298

and they could get on with their lives. With a sudden whirring noise the garage door slowly opened and Christopher's Mercedes began to nose out. When it had cleared the garage Tom opened the passenger door and got inside.

"I must say, that's the first time I've heard of a Quija Board being used in a police investigation," Christopher quipped, while they drove off. "How on earth did that come about?"

"Oh, they had a demonstration in Penny's metaphysics class. Myself, I'm not really into this kind of thing, and it's certainly not something I would ever have dreamed of using, but it was just absolutely uncanny how those numbers kept repeating. And if you hadn't told me to clean out Heather's closet, I would never have found that tag on her suitcase."

Christopher laughed. "Small things, in life eh? Are you comfortable?"

"A bit warm."

"Hang on, I'll turn on the air." Christopher adjusted some of the dashboard controls and after a few seconds cool air began to flow through the car. And with the cold air came a slight burning smell, something acrid.

"There's something wrong with your air conditioner," Tom said, gasping, trying not to breathe. He reached for the windows control on his side, but it wouldn't budge.

"Can you open this window, Christopher? I'm suffocating!"

"Sorry, Tom. These are child proof windows and doors. Don't fight it. Just breathe slowly. The stinging will go in a few seconds."

Tom's body felt very heavy as all his muscles gave out. He couldn't move his arms or legs, and his body seemed glued to the seat. He desperately tried to hold his breath but couldn't, and the acrid substance began to enter his nostrils. He managed to turn his head sideways to look at Christopher who did not seem to be affected at all.

"You . . . You are one of them!" he gasped. "How could you? You're my doctor. My friend . . . I trusted you."

"Oh, Tom, I can't let you jeopardize our entire operation! You'll understand that soon enough. Just breathe deeply through your nose, and relax. Fighting it will make it more difficult."

Tom could feel the substance wasn't just heading for his lungs. Whatever it was, it had also found a shortcut to his brain. His entire body seemed paralyzed now as if all his strength and energy was needed to accommodate his expanding mind. A mind that no longer seemed to fit in his head, or even the car. Millions of sudden thoughts, exploding like mental fireworks, creating a powerful, churning vortex of emotions over which he no longer any control. Then there was a warm, soothing female voice, sounding loud and clear in the confined space of the car.

"We are the Church of Oscar. You have been selected . ."

◊ ◊ ◊

Erwin slowly turned the door handle and stepped into the room. The office that had belonged to Jo all those years was now his. He closed the door behind him and looked around. It was almost like a small apartment. The main part consisted of a living area with a table and four chairs, to entertain guests if necessary, a large book case, a couch with four flowery cushions, a coffee table and an easy chair. The second room had a bed, a computer table with a chair, and a night table. A sliding door led to an adjoining bathroom. Everything was spotlessly clean. There were freshly washed sheets on the bed, clean towels in the bathroom. A vase with flowers stood on the table.

He sat back in the easy chair and put his feet up on the coffee table, thinking about his new position. Here he was, thirty years old, and Head Councilor of the Church of Oscar. He was surprised Sylvia had stepped down so soon. Perhaps, being a woman, she didn't have what it took to be the Head Councilor. Well, he did, for sure. He deserved the position. Wasn't the use of the public transport system as a means to recruit new church members his brainchild? The church

300

needed some more fresh ideas like that. Many of the councilors were getting older and seemed to be stuck in their ways. The takeover bid for Secret Springs had been set in motion and he expected the sale to be finalized in about a month. Then there would be some real changes under his leadership.

On impulse, he decided he didn't like the title of Head Councilor. It was too ordinary, too common. He needed something more prestigious, something snazzy that would set him apart from the other councilors. He pondered for a while, until he had an idea. Provost Councilor, or just Provost. *Provost Johnson.* Yes, that had a very nice ring to it.

His eye fell on a small cupboard in the center of the book case. He had a vague idea what might be inside. He walked over and opened it. Yes, two bottles of first quality single malt whisky: Glen Cardigan and four glasses. Good old Jo. He hesitated for a moment. He wasn't really a drinker, and it was not even noon yet. Then he resolutely took out one of the bottles, opened it and poured himself a liberal amount. Why not? He had reason to celebrate. He sipped his drink for a while, thinking about the church, and what he had to do. One of the first duties would be to bring the total numbers of councilors back to twelve.

There were three vacant seats at the moment. Penny Weatherby had died recently, and Dale Pinehurst. Now Sylvia had stepped down, so they needed to find three good people. He also needed to find a deputy, in case something happened to him. In Jo's days, it had been Father English, as the supreme religious leader. Should he chose Father Dubois? He was the most senior of the councilors and his religious experience was essential. Or Jeremy Burlon? Perhaps; he was younger, and had never posed any problems. Another potential candidate was Bert Kwiss; he'd certainly made his mark in the church. Then there was Dr. Fleming. He also, was widely respected. There was another councilor whom he could chose: Patricia Sheppard, the lawyer. But she was a woman. He thought of Tammy Tilburn, and Anna Kulik who both almost had caused the church's demise. No, he definitely didn't want a woman as his second.

He decided not to worry about formalities just yet and take a look at the church documents first. Walking to the vault, he took Sylvia's key from his pocket, opened the safe with it, and took out the church papers. He carried everything to the desk, sat down, and began reading the church's official records. What immediately piqued his interest, was a small bundle of pages, held together with an elastic band.

◊ ◊ ◊

"How are you feeling?"

The sound of the voice shattered the serene peace in Tom's mind. He opened his eyes and looked around. Dusk was approaching. They had pulled over to the side of the road, and through the windows he saw some bushes and a small tree. He turned his head toward Christopher, sitting in the driver's seat.

"Very strange and different. Where are we? How long have I been out?"

"Oh, you weren't really out, just sedated. It usually takes about a quarter of an hour, sometimes less," Taggard replied. "The hardest part is the first few minutes. I just stopped here to make it easier for you to listen to our message. Did you like it?"

Tom watched, while the doctor removed a small memory stick from a slot in the dashboard. He remembered the soothing female voice, introducing him to the Church of Oscar and its purpose in the world. He felt sleepy and extremely relaxed, almost like a post-orgasmic rest.

He looked outside and saw a bush, where a tiny bird, oblivious to the car, was pecking at a small red berry. Tom wondered what it was: a bluetit? A finch? He'd never been very much of a bird watcher, but he stared at the little creature, fascinated. For a while it was as if he and the bird were in a universe all by themselves. He watched, as it took quick pecks at the berry, trying to dislodge it from the stem.

He wondered if it had a mate and baby chicks. He noticed two other birds a little further. Their yellow-and-white feathers stood out bright in the dull green thicket. Where they related? Brothers and sisters, perhaps? Did they all have families? He became aware that Christopher was waiting for an answer.

"It was a wonderful message," Tom said. "Who was that woman? She had such a beautiful voice."

"That was Sylvia Rasnell, one of the original church founders."

"That drug you gave me, Christopher? What exactly has it done to me?"

"It has cleansed your mind, Tom. Everyone who enters the Church of Oscar must have their mind cleansed of all the garbage, lies, and untruths they've collected during their lifetime. Only when that is all gone, can they understand and follow our church's teachings."

"Did you ask me if I wanted to join that church?"

"I had no choice, Tom. You discovered our secret. Would you have agreed to join, if I'd given you a choice? I don't think so. I tried to stop you before, but you just kept digging to find Heather. Why did you have to be such a bloody ferret?"

"Investigating was my job, remember? I guess that phone call to Father Dubois was you, telling him your secret was safe after all. That's why he didn't take me seriously."

"Yes. You almost pulled it off, Tom. Had you given that memory stick to anyone else, you could have brought our church down all by yourself."

"There's something I don't understand, Christopher. They won't let people out of the commune, yet others, like you and that FBI agent I met don't seem to be connected to the church at all. Isn't communal living what the Church of Oscar is all about?"

"Yes, that's exactly what we want people to think. But remember what that message said, Tom. We are at war, and to win in a war you must be smarter than your enemies and outguess their moves. You got to find out what they're planning and learn their weaknesses and strengths. You have to go behind enemy lines."

"So you're a spy."

"We use a more euphemistic term: Ambassador. I'm one of hundreds, all across the country and all over the world. It's our job to infiltrate our church's enemies: big business, multinatural conglomerates, government, other churches and organizations. We attack them from within. We collect intelligence and troubleshoot things when they go wrong."

"Like when a retired policeman finds out how you recruit new members."

"Yes. The Church of Oscar must win, Tom, and it will. The end justifies the means. Always. It's the only way to save our planet. We need good people like yourself. You've got the brains and the know-how. You could even become a councilor, given time. There will be as many opportunities in the Church of Oscar as there are in the outside world. Anyway, we had better move on. It's another twenty minutes to Excalibur and it's getting dark." Taggard started the car and they drove off.

"You know, it's very strange," Tom said after a while. "My mind is so organized and so efficient it's unbelievable. All negative thoughts and ideas have gone, and there's only room for peace and happiness. What exactly is that stuff you used?"

"It is called Oscar's Breath, Tom. That's all I can tell you."

"Why? I would have found out the truth if I'd had more time."

"You may have, so it's a good thing I stopped you. You're a member of our church, but you're not a councilor, or an Ambassador; at least not yet. There are certain things that must remain secret to the general populace."

"What about Heather?" Tom asked. "She's in Excalibur, isn't she?"

"I don't know," Christopher said. "I know she belongs to the church, but the Excalibur site is pretty well full. We've just finished building another church in Denver. She may have been transferred there. You'll find out soon enough."

"And Penny? Why didn't you bring Penny with us today?

"One of our rules. No children under sixteen allowed. She'll be sixteen in a few months, though, if I remember correctly?"

"Next September, yes."

"When her time comes, I'll drive her to the church myself. Meanwhile, Linda and I will look after her as one of our own."

"You couldn't make an exception? Three months is quite a long time for Penny to be on her own. She'll go off the wall if I'm not with her."

"The Council sets the rules, Tom, nothing I can do about it."

"Who's in charge of the Church of Oscar?"

"We've just elected a new Head Councilor. His name is Erwin Johnson."

"What? Not Patrick Johnson's son? The policeman?"

"Yes. He died some time ago. Did you know him?"

"He was my boss at work and I've known Erwin since he was a kid."

"That changes everything, Tom. Patrick was very special to our church and any friend of his is a friend of the church. I'm sure we can make an exception in your case."

Taggard looked at his watch. "Here's what we'll do. We'll put Penny up overnight, and I'll explain things to her. Tomorrow first thing, I'll call the Head Councilor. See, the number sixteen is really arbitrary. We don't want young screaming kids running around in the church, but mature kids are welcome, of course. I know Penny, so I can almost guarantee she'll be with you tomorrow."

"Thanks. What about our house?"

"The church will look after that. No need to worry. We do this all the time. Two of our church security guards will move in to make sure no squatters take over, and then the church will sell it at market price."

When they reached the entrance to Excalibur it had turned completely dark. A young woman was on guard duty, and when Tom looked closer he saw it was the same person who had driven him before. Her eyes lit up in surprise.

"Ambassador Taggard! Thank you for bringing the fugitive in so soon. We had a real problem with him earlier this afternoon. Shall I call security?"

"No need," the physician replied. "I have already processed him on the way. Tom Cramer is one of us." He handed the girl a shiny plastic card and she swiped it through a slot on her computer keyboard.

"Thank you, Ambassador." She handed Christopher his card back. With a loud click the gate opened and they headed down the driveway.

"Brownie points for bringing me in, Christopher?" Tom asked.

"No, it's not like that, Tom. She merely swiped my card to update our church records."

They didn't speak again, until they reached the same waiting area where Tom had been only hours ago. They sat down at a table and Taggard opened his briefcase. He took out three sheets of paper and lay them down on the table. "Here are the admission forms that you have to fill out and sign, Tom. There are basically just three clauses. We need your personal details, like name address, age, occupation, interests, etc. Next, it says that you are of sound mind and have decided that you want to join the Church of Oscar. The last clause gives us permission to enter your house and sell it for the Church of Oscar."

"That's a mighty long document for just three clauses," Tom said. "What's in all the fine print?"

"Oh, I don't know. It's written by lawyers, for goodness' sake. What do you expect? They want to make sure all legal angles are covered, and that the church is not liable for any of your debts or bad deals you may have made in the past. It also says that if you have a criminal record, you must tell the church about it, so that we can let the authorities know."

Tom stared at the papers. He was completely lost after reading just two paragraph. Suddenly he didn't care anymore.

All he wanted was to see Heather again and get on with their lives. He grabbed the pen and signed the forms at the bottom and handed them to Christopher, who co-signed and dated them.

"You're now a full-fledged member of the Church of Oscar, Tom. I'll ask the young lady at the desk if Heather's here, and then I'll be off."

"I'm curious, Christopher. Why didn't you recruit me before? You had plenty of opportunities."

"The Church of Oscar is not a group of sadists who enjoy tearing families and lives apart, Tom. I had the three of you on my recruitment list for later this year, after Penny had turned sixteen. Because of Heather, you got too close to the truth, and I had to protect our Church. I've got to go now." They both stood up and shook hands.

"Take care in your new life, Tom. You and Heather."

"You will look after Penny?"

"I promise. I'll do my best to bring her in tomorrow."

Taggard spoke to the young woman at the counter and handed her the admission papers. She nodded and picked up a phone. The doctor turned around, waved at Tom and was gone. With him went the last reminder of Tom's life as he knew it. Yet he felt no sorrow, no fear, no apprehension, as he sat there, waiting for Heather. It took only a few minutes. Another young woman, dressed similarly in a black skirt and white blouse with the sign of the Church of Oscar embroidered on it walked in from the outside, and next to her was Heather.

She looked exactly as she had looked five months ago. He rushed over to her and they embraced. Yet while he held his wife, happy to see her again after all that time, Tom knew that things would never be the same again. Something was missing. The spark, the intense, almost electrical longing for her had gone. He still loved her, but it was a different kind of love.

"It's so good to see you, Tom," she said. "How is Penny? Leaving her was even worse than leaving you. Is she OK?"

307

"Yes. Christopher will try to bring her in tomorrow."

"That is wonderful. That day I left you was so bad, I felt physically sick. I missed you and Penny terribly, but I had to do it, Tom. I don't know why, and there was nothing I could do about it. On hindsight, I'm glad it happened. Joining this commune has changed my life for the better."

"They manipulated your mind, Heather. Mine also."

"How did you find out?"

"Hey, I used to be a detective, remember? I just couldn't let you disappear like that. I figured it all out, but there was one thing I couldn't know. I didn't realize Christopher belonged to the church. It all started when you went to see your mother."

"What do you mean? What has that got to with it?"

"Oh, it's a long story, Heather. I'll tell you later. I've had an eventful day, and I need to unwind a bit more."

She disentangled herself from their embrace.

"A short walk, perhaps? The gardens here are very beautiful."

"But it is dark," he protested.

"There are lights, and it's quite warm still."

Soon they walked down the path, hand in hand, past the pond and the flowerbeds that were lit up by lanterns every twenty feet or so. Then Heather stopped and held him again.

"We have changed, Tom," she said. "I don't know how exactly, but it is for the better. I can think so clearly, it is amazing. The people here are all very friendly and I have this feeling of belonging, more so than I've ever felt. I have a good job in the accounts department. They'll find you something soon, I'm sure. And with Penny here also, things will be perfect. It may take some time getting used to our new outlook on life, but I know we're going to be very happy here, Tom."

"I am sure we will," he replied.

They walked on and passed an old farm shed, used to keep garden equipment. The windows were protected by steel bars and Tom's mind filled with a sudden vision. A rundown, dilapidated house. An old-fashioned room, with the door and windows barred against intruders. A handgun and delicate china cups and saucers, strangely juxtaposed on a small wooden coffee table. An old lady in a chair, sitting rigidly upright, waiting for a husband who would never come home again. Then, like the popping of a balloon, the vision vanished.

A TEAR FOR MELISSA

19

The site was about fifteen acres, forty miles east of Phoenix, Arizona; an old landfill, long abandoned. Due to toxicity in the ground, residential settlements were not allowed. For many years the land had lain fallow; a waste land with weeds, grass and brush trying to reclaim it for Nature. It was perfect, Marvin thought.

"There we are, Sandor. Buckeye, Arizona. It's not the place with the most sunshine, as Philip wanted, but it's close, and relatively near a city." Marvin and Sandor were sweating profusely in the small Iadzu compact car they had rented in town. For some reason the air conditioner had packed it in halfway on their journey. They had the windows wide open, but the outside was like an oven. There was only one dirt road leading into the area, and bulldozers were spreading and flattening the dirty earth around, to allow trucks with building materials to enter the site.

The land had been very cheap to buy, compared to the surrounding areas; it was within easy reach of Phoenix, yet remote enough for their purpose. About half of the site had already been cleared of brush and undergrowth, and small yellow stakes showed the round perimeter of what would become the exhibition dome.

"You have taken on a lot of work here, Marvin," Sandor asked. "Why? You're not exactly young anymore."

Marvin drove on for a few seconds before replying. "Oh, I know. Two reasons, really. When that deal with the Church of Oscar goes through, I'll be out of a job. I don't know about you, but even if they offer to keep me on the payroll, I'll refuse. I'm too young to retire yet, so this will give me something to do.

"Secondly, I'm doing this for Philip. He needs help. I thought his idea was idiotic, but after doing some research, I changed my mind. That young man is a genius, Sandor, way ahead of his time. Imagine if he can pull this off. A thousand years from now the human race might get another chance and start afresh. What about you? Why are you helping him?"

"I'm a scientist," Sandor replied. "We explore and solve mysteries. I just couldn't walk away from this one."

"The timing is exactly right," Marvin continued. "People are so fed up with the present, they want to preserve and keep what's left of America as it was in its better days. When I started phoning around, I found people so intrigued by the idea that I started a company called Future Holdings. In four months, I've already collected enough money to buy the land and pay for the entire photo-electric roof. It's utterly amazing. Some rich guy in Texas paid $50,000 to store the DNA of himself, his wife and kids, even of the dog and the fish in his little girl's aquarium."

"We are putting our DNA in there also," Sandor said. "Imagine if some day in the future we could be recreated. It would be similar to time travel, wouldn't it? Philip's idea is truly revolutionary, and somehow I think Secret Springs may have missed the boat for not helping him. Why did we sell out to that church, Marvin? I could not believe it when I first heard about it."

"It's all a matter of economics. We've been losing subscribers for quite some time, and that church is gaining in popularity. They have tons of money, and that's what did it in the end. It'll be sad to see the firm closing down, but hey, we've had some good years." Marvin stopped, to let a large bulldozer cross the dirt road to begin clearing the other side.

"This will be archeology in reverse, you know," he mused, driving on again. "Instead of future scientists digging their way about, scratching their heads, wondering what things were like in the past, we shove it right under their noses. A snapshot of 21st century earth, the way it was, preserved for all eternity. Meanwhile, hidden away in the dome's belly, Philip and his people can secretly roam their virtual world in peace, awaiting the day when an advanced civilization can perhaps integrate them back into the corporeal world again."

"I don't know about that part," Sandor said, shaking his head. "What if the earth becomes a wasteland and there are no more people? Philip could be stuck in there until our sun goes supernova. I can't see people becoming Virtuals. Philip may have a problem finding residents for that place. I know I could never leave my body."

"Neither could I, but you've got to look at the bigger picture. Philip explained to me how he sees it. He needs about a thousand Virtuals; more would cause an unnecessary drain on the resources. He says we can forget the rich in the cities, but should concentrate on the people on the seedy side of life. People who have problems facing the world every day. The depressed, the poor, you know. So think about it: there are more than nine billion people in the world today and Philip only needs a thousand. The odds are pretty good that it will work. As soon as we've secured the virtscapes, we can begin to look for recruits. Sarah and her husband Pedro volunteered for that part."

There was a sudden loud noise, as a pile driver began to pound the first of many foundation pylons through the top layer of waste into the undisturbed soil several feet below. Long forms for the cement foundation that was to be poured lay in piles on the earth. Several surveyors could be seen, busy with their levels and laser beams. It wouldn't be long now before the construction would begin.

"How much of the exhibition space have you sold so far?" Sandor asked.

"About a third. Mostly companies, showing off their products, but also a surprising number of ordinary people, each donating their hundred dollars or more. Artists, engineers, inventors, writers, you name it. Half of The Exhibitor's Wall is already reserved and it's not even sculptured yet."

"So how exactly are you going to get those virtscapes for Philip, Marvin? They're humungous programs."

315

"I haven't decided yet," Marvin said, heading towards the site office, a shed-like structure about a hundred yards ahead. "If that church doesn't need all the servers, they might sell us some, otherwise we'll have to buy them. We'll probably transfer all the virtscapes onto hard drives and move them down here."

"How long before you'll lock the place down?"

"Oh, not for a long time. We'll keep it open as a museum first. That'll bring in some extra money, and it'll give Sarah and Pedro more time to recruit people for Philip's cause."

When they reached the office, Marvin parked in the shade, along the side of the building. "Let's go and see how that shipment of photo-electric cells from China is doing. I sure hope the air conditioning is working in there."

◊ ◊ ◊

He looked at the young woman sitting on the bar stool next to him. He guessed she was about twenty-five, perhaps thirty. She had long brown hair, framing a round face, almost porcelain-like. Brown eyes, a delicate nose, a rather large mouth with bluish-green lipstick that looked atrocious on her. Her skin was hidden under a thick layer of makeup, and she had false eyelashes.

She was dressed in a flowery cocktail dress: yellow daisies on a blue background. It revealed plenty of cleavage. Her legs were actually the best part of her: long and shapely, ending up in two delicate high-heeled shoes with such thin straps that he very much doubted the shoes would last more than a couple of miles. Her long, slender arms rested on the bar in front of her, and she moved her right thumb and index finger up and down along the stem of her empty glass.

"Aren't you gonna buy me another drink, hon?"

"Sorry." He looked at the bartender standing a few feet away, pretending to be busy arranging glasses on shelves. There were no other customers. The bartender was the kind of guy he'd give a wide berth on the street. Short, but very broad-chested, like a bouncer. Coarse hair in a crew cut, like a

316

wire brush. A wide, almost square jaw, and a rather flat nose, as if he'd been in a few fights. Somehow he'd found enough material to put a small silver ring through it. Tattoos all over his arms and neck. One was of a naked woman, trying to crawl under the short sleeve of his T-shirt. Goodness knew what she might find there.

"Another one for the lady," he said, pointing at her glass. "I'm fine." The bartender began to busy himself making the drink, while the woman snuggled a bit closer to him. "So what's your name then, hon?"

"Harold," he said. He could smell her perfume. It was awful, but he didn't care. He couldn't be choosy, not now. He was running out of time.

"I'm Shirley." She said it as if she had trouble getting past the first syllable. Shiiiiiiirly. She probably had had a few drinks already. He was still nursing his first beer. "I can tell you ain't from here," she said, studying him with eyes like marbles. "You're not police, are you? I don't trust them."

"I'm an insurance broker." He watched, while the bartender poured her drink into a small glass. It was pinkish red.

"What do you call that?"

"It's Horny Buck." She giggled, while she reached over to pick up the glass. "Absinthe, Crème the menthe, Drambuie and cream. You want a taste?"

"No thanks. It'll spoil my beer." He hoped she wouldn't take all night to drink it.

"You haven't told me where you're from," she asked, sipping her drink. "You live in Denver?"

"No. I'm visiting from the West Coast. L.A. area."

She took a swig of her drink. "Been there once," she said. "Went to Disneyland, years ago. Didn't like it. Too crowded. Are you on holiday?"

"No. Business."

"Married?"

"No."

317

He wished she'd hurry up, and not ask so many stupid questions. He suddenly started when there was a sharp cracking sound, as if someone had dropped a bottle or something. When he looked around he saw that two young men had decided to play a game of pool. One of them had just done the break. He hoped it wasn't going to be busy, he wasn't used to crowds. He just wanted to get out of there and get it over with.

"Right." She had finally drained her glass. "I'm all yours, sweetie, I can see you're eager. Why don't you pay the man while I get my coat and powder my nose."

The bartender glanced at a little slip of paper. "That'll be $36."

He pulled his wallet out, removed two twenties and put them on the bar, waiving the change away. The bartender could smile after all, showing him two gold teeth and a whole bunch of yellowed ones.

"Have a nice evening now," he said, putting one of the twenties in the till, the other one in his trouser pocket.

Shirley was back, wearing a long imitation fur coat, and she didn't seem to be too steady on her feet. She fell against him, and he awkwardly held her. Just before they walked away, the bartender gave him a sly wink.

Outside, it was pretty cold and she grabbed his arm and snuggled up to him. "Where's your car?"

"I came by cab. We'll have to use yours."

"Here, you drive." She threw the keys at him and he almost missed them in the dark.

Her tiny little Electric Tatshu was cramped. "It's not far," she said, and he smelled a strong whiff of absinthe. "Just down the road, and left at the stop sign. Then straight ahead and right at the T. It's the fourth apartment on your left. Number 11." She suddenly leaned towards him, and plunked a heavy kiss on his lips. It reminded him of another kiss, long ago.

He kissed her back as best as he could, then quickly started the car and drove off, before she got any other ideas.

There was very little traffic and he found the place easily. He parked in the driveway, then quickly got out and walked over to open her door and help her out. She leaned into him while they walked to the door.

The apartment was small. Just one room, with a bed in the corner. An easy chair with a small side table, and a kitchen nook with a round table and two chairs. A bathroom to the side. Shirley took off her coat and hung it on a hook by the door. Then she kicked off her shoes. "Want another beer?"

"No, thanks I'm fine."

"OK," she said, standing very close to him. "First things first. I usually charge fifty, but you're such a nice guy, I'll take forty." Then she stood, waiting. He took out his wallet and offered her two twenties. She stuck them down her cleavage.

"Thanks, hon. Why don't you make yourself comfy, while I change." She winked at him and disappeared into the bathroom.

He nervously sat down, wishing it was all over. Perhaps it was all a mistake, and he should go home. He looked around. The bed was large, and looked very comfortable. Had to be, of course. On the side table stood a digital alarm clock and a light. There was a book case along the wall, with a small TV inside and an electric fireplace next to it. Very small, but cozy enough for one person.

She was back, wearing a cream-colored negligee. She rolled the bedcover back and lay down, eyeing him.

"Well? Are you going to stand there all night? If you're having second thoughts, forget it. I don't give refunds." She pulled off the negligee and threw it through the air unto a nearby chair. He quickly undressed and climbed into the bed. She pulled him close and grabbed him in a bear hug.

"Aren't you gonna take those damned glasses off?"

"No. I'm blind without them. Wouldn't be able to see your lovely face then, would I?"

She laughed out loud. "Flattering will get you everywhere with Shiiiiirley."

She kissed him feverishly and he responded, feeling his blood begin to surge through him. The Urge had awakened. He began to move with her, letting her do the work. His hands reached her breasts and he began to fondle them.

"Put your back into it, love," she whispered after a few minutes. "No need to treat me with kid gloves."

Things finally began to work as they should, and his heart began to pound as if he was running a marathon. He kissed her body wherever he could, feeling lightheaded and wonderful. Then all of a sudden he lifted his head while his whole body arched up, and the whole world vanished around him. Then everything fell back in place and he just lay there, exhausted.

"Much better," Shirley muttered, stroking his hair. "Once you got going, that is." She gave him a small push and he rolled over to his side of the bed, still sweaty and breathing fast. He looked at her naked body beside him. She was lying still, breathing slowly, a thin smile on her lips. Another satisfied client. Obviously her part of the deal was over. Not for him.

He lay back, considering the best way. He should really have thought about it before, but his mind had all been muddled. He knew he had to hurry, he was getting very tired. He'd hoped she had left something on the chair he could use, a stocking, a bra, anything, but there wasn't. He looked around and the only thing he could see was his pillow. It was a big, comfy one, and it would have to do. He grabbed the pillow as if he was adjusting it, then in one smooth movement he placed it over her face, pushing down as hard as he could. It took her a second to realize what was happening, and then she began to fight back.

Her hands flew through the air, and her nails tried to find his face. She screamed, but the pillow muffled the sound. Her beautiful legs shot up in the air, trying to kick him anywhere she could, but he easily stayed out of reach. She was so strong that he almost couldn't hold her down, and he had to put his full weight on the pillow. Finally, her movements became slower, then stopped altogether. He didn't move, pressing down on her, waiting, just in case she was faking.

When he finally removed the pillow, he almost threw up. Her doll-like face had turned a shade of purple. Her eyes, wide with terror, bulged in their sockets, and her mouth was wide open in an eternal, silent scream. He quickly reached for his clothes and dressed. He looked for the two twenties he'd given her, but there was no sign of them. She must have hidden them somewhere. It didn't matter. He had to get out of there in a hurry. He picked up the car keys, he'd put on the table before. He opened the door and looked outside. Everything was quiet. He closed the door behind him, and hurried to the car. Within seconds, he was on his way to the airport.

◊ ◊ ◊

"What is this place, Marvin?" Sandor Donavon looked at the modern building with rows of windows that looked out of place in the middle of a neglected theme park with many derelict old buildings, crumbling facades and other remnants of a once thriving entertainment industry.

"It used to be one of the biggest film studios in the area," Marvin replied, pushing a button on the side of front entrance of the building. "It closed down in 2027, I think. An old school buddy of mine bought it when the company folded. His father was involved in the creation of those special effects movies of the early century. Ernie is a mechanical and electronic wizard. His family made tons of money in special effects. I tried to get him to work for Phil's project, but he wasn't interested. Apparently he hates Secret Springs; something to do with the fact that Philip didn't hire him at one time. Best not mention that." A mechanical voice suddenly cracked the silence.

"Hi, Marv, right on time. Who's your friend?"

Marvin couldn't see any camera or microphone, but he knew they were being watched. "Sandor is a colleague of mine. I'll vouch for him."

"All right. Come on in, guys." An electric solenoid opened a hidden lock in the doorway and Marvin pushed the metal door inwards. They stood in a huge hangar. There was scaffolding everywhere, and cranes on rollers ran along I-beams, bringing metal components to an assembly area further down the hangar. It reminded Marvin of his youth, when he'd taken a tour of the Boeing factory in Washington State.

"Marvin, good to see you man!" A youngish looking man emerged from an office high up on a catwalk and rushed down the stairs to meet them. He was dressed in a green coverall, with big steel-toed boots, and a yellow hard hat. Around his waist hung an apron with electrician's tools: screwdrivers, circuit testers, wrenches, and a flashlight. He walked over to Marvin and hugged him.

"Been awhile, Marvin. You're still with that awful company?"

"No. They sold out. I'm here as a private consultant. Sandor, this is Ernie Burrows. You may think he just works here, but he actually owns the place. Ernie, this is Sandor Donavon."

"Hi." Ernie and Sandor shook hands. "That's some place you have here," Sandor said, impressed. "Did they really create those big huge steel monsters for the movies here?"

"Sure did. Anything big and mechanical that needed to move and fight. See that poster over there?" Ernie pointed to a large poster on a wall near the doorway they had just come through. It displayed a mechanical creature the size of a dinosaur.

"That was done for the fourth remake of the *War of the Worlds*. These fighting machines stood about twelve feet tall, with steel legs the size of foundation pillars for an apartment, and long hydraulic arms that could pick up a tank and throw it ten feet. Inside was a cozy little computerized control center with one guy pushing buttons. We built four of those. Of course that's all history now. The company couldn't compete with holographic software. We're doing basically consignment

322

work here, you know, small special projects. Come and see what I've got for you, Marvin."

Ernie got into an electric golf cart with room for four, and they took off, skirting around huge piles of hardware, tires, and the assembly area where several workers were welding a huge boat-like structure. "Submarine," Ernie said, pointing. "For tourism, to explore the oceans. It can go into the deepest trenches." The noise was deafening and Marvin was glad when the sliding door closed behind them. They stood in a smaller hangar, and Ernie pointed to a strange mechanical object in the corner of the otherwise empty room.

"There you are, Marv. My latest creation. I call it the Sphinx. You know, it's none of my business, but I'm really curious what kind of person would want this. It was quite a challenge to build it. It seems rather an overkill for personal security."

Marvin stared at the mechanical monster. It was the closest thing to the Devil that he could imagine. The beast was about twenty feet long and looked like a cross between a cat and a dog. It lay on its stomach—if it even had a stomach. Its two front paws were drawn back and rested along its sides. The comparison to a sphinx was an apt one. The legs were the size of elephant legs, and a thick, twelve feet long tail was curled snugly around its body. In its present position the Sphinx was about six feet tall, and Marvin guessed it would be at least ten to twelve feet high at its full height.

The creature was made of some kind of glistening dark metal alloy. It was the face that really gave Marvin the shivers. Egg-shaped, with two horns sprouting where its ears should be. The mouth was closed, but Marvin could imagine the fangs. A constant snarl curled the animal's lips, like a Cheshire cat in a very bad mood. Its eyes were still dark, but Marvin guessed that when this machine came alive, any primitive, God-fearing person would want to be a thousand miles away.

"Well?" Ernie said. "What do you think? I made it exactly to your specs, and I tell you, it gave me sleepless nights. You could defend an entire city with this thing, not just a housing complex. Why does it have too look like the Devil, Marvin? I'm curious."

"I can tell you a little bit," Marvin said. "My client is a very imaginative and neurotic person. He believes that the world will become pagan again, with billions of common serfs, ruled and oppressed by a clergy elite."

"What? You can't be serious. Going back to the Dark Ages? That's ridiculous!"

"Well, that's what my client thinks. He is holed up somewhere in the country, and he wants protection from the hordes of crusaders that he thinks are going to roam the country side soon. He wanted something to scare people off."

"Oh, that it will do for sure. Now isn't that the craziest story I've ever heard. Anyway, let's have a little demonstration of what this beast can do." Ernie took a remote control from his coverall pocket, and pressed a button. There was an electronic humming and the far wall of the hangar began to roll up like a giant garage door. Bright sunlight flooded in, and they looked out on some kind of playground, the size of two old-fashioned football fields, marked off by high wired fences all round. There were no trees, just plain grass.

"OK, here we go." Ernie pressed a few buttons on the control box he carried, and the Sphinx's eyes turned into evil, dark-red globes. Marvin felt shivers run down his spine. The beast's eyes were utterly malicious, like those of a dinosaur, getting ready for the kill. The animal slowly lifted itself on its four huge legs and gracefully walked out of the room into the open air. There it sat down on its haunches, like a giant cat, sunning itself. Its long tail was slashing about in threatening wide arcs.

"Don't ever get in the path of that tail," Ernie warned. "One swipe of it could throw you right across that field, against the back fence. Now for the entertainment." He coded another number on his remote, and a door leading to another part of the hangar opened. There was a sound like the clucking of many chicks, and in walked a group of the most incredible creatures Marvin had ever seen. They looked like stickmen; each was made up of a body like a fire extinguisher, with a head the size of a honeydew melon and arms and legs made of rigid steel wires, bent at the bottom. The creatures were all identical and had small beady eyes, triangular noses and round mouths. Each of the ten stickmen had a yellow cover around its body, with a number from 1 to 10. Like marathon runners, they ran outside and dispersed across the field.

"What he hell? Are they alive?" Sandor gasped.

"Only very rudimentary," Ernie said. "They have no mind, or consciousness or anything like that. They're just automatons, and they'll wander around like cockroaches until I stop them, or their batteries run out. They do have a certain amount of self preservation, though. I created them just for this purpose. Now, Mr. Donavon, give me three numbers under ten, please."

"Eh, 3, 5, 7."

"Ah, primes." Ernie was busy with his remote, then headed outside. Marvin and Sandor followed, not quite knowing what to expect. The ten stickmen were still running erratically across the field.

"I must warn you this may be scary," Ernie said. "I've turned the sound down, but even so."

Like his prehistoric predecessor, *Tyrannosaurus Rex*, the Sphinx suddenly stuck out his long head and growled. Marvin guessed it was close to a hundred decibels, and almost painful. Surely that sound would carry all across Los Angeles, he thought. Like a cheetah in full flight, the Sphinx sprinted off, criss-crossing the field. Then, almost as fast as it had started out, it was back again, sitting down in exactly the same spot where it had left.

"12.7 seconds," Ernie said approvingly, looking at his watch. "Not bad."

"What are these funny yellow balls out there?" Sandor asked. "I didn't notice them before."

"Let's have a look," Ernie said.

325

They walked over to the nearest of the yellow balls that had suddenly appeared in the field, like sprouting mushrooms. Even before they got close, Marvin knew the answer. He picked up the ball and held it out in front of him. It was what was left of a stickman, after the Sphinx had squashed it in his claws. It was like a soft drink can, still and quiet, rumpled and compressed by a very strong force. The yellow smudge was the cover the stickman had worn around its body.

"Had this been a real battlefield, it wouldn't have been so clean, of course," Ernie said. "There be a lot of the three B's."

Marvin cocked his eyes at the other. "Meaning?"

"Body parts, blood and bones. One machine like this in the middle ages could have decided a war instantly. An improved version could even give a present day army a run for its money, but I've kept it simple for you. This will keep any marauding group of religious crusaders at bay, believe you me."

"What about those three numbers you asked for?" Donavon asked.

"Ah! Come closer." They moved back to where the Sphinx was motionlessly waiting for its next command. Ernie pressed his remote again. The Sphinx stood up, stuck its neck out and opened its horrific mouth as if it was about to throw up a gigantic hairball. Marvin could see an array of sharp pointed teeth, the thickness of his arm. A giant tongue rolled forward, like an official red carpet, and there were the missing stickmen, marching towards freedom.

"There you are: numbers 3, 5 and 7. Saved by your command."

"Did it swallow them?" Sandor asked.

"In a way, I guess. It doesn't have a stomach, though. I think of it more as a large holding area, for things that need saving, like wounded soldiers on a battleground. Or it could take prisoners. Well what do you think, Marvin? Might this be what your client had in mind?"

326

"Absolutely," Marvin nodded, still awed by the spectacle. "How much does it cost?"

"As it sits there, without RPG's, flame throwers, lasers, and machine guns, $895,000."

"I'll take two, and they need to be shipped to Buckeye, Arizona," Marvin said.

◊ ◊ ◊

He sat on the edge of the bed, fully dressed, waiting, gloves on, video glasses ready to record. The water in the shower was making a whistling noise. She had made it easy for him—her bra hung on the chair next to the bed. He picked it up and pulled it between his fingers to test its tensile strength. Yes, it would do nicely. He listened, as the sound of the water stopped. Soon now. He adjusted his glasses and took up position next to the bathroom door. There were muffled movements inside, then the doorknob turned and she stepped out.

"If you're hungry, I have some—" He cut her off by pulling the bra around her neck, tightening it as hard as he could. She struggled, tried to kick him with her bare feet, but he stepped aside in time. Her hands clawed at his jacket, as she tried to reach for his face. She was no match for him, and it didn't take long before her hands fell loose to her side and her head rolled backwards, the eyes bulging. She made some guttural, pig-like grunts, while he pulled both ends of the bra relentlessly, hoping it wouldn't break at the critical moment.

When he was absolutely certain she had died, he let her slide onto the floor. There was no blood, just a few patches of pink froth around her mouth. He hated blood, it made things messy. He dragged her onto the bed, and straightened her out. She was in her thirties and not very attractive, but he couldn't be picky.

He draped her body with the same blanket that had covered both of them just a while ago. He was in a hurry, partially because he didn't want be in the room any longer than he had to, but also because he could feel the first twinges of tiredness. It always was that way, after the Act: the intense fatigue, resulting in a deep sleep. That's why he had reserved a hotel room this time.

He checked the room to make sure everything was the way it had been before. After he removed his gloves and glasses and stuffed them in his briefcase, he left, making sure no one in the filthy apartment block saw him leave. He wasn't too worried about leaving any clues behind. The last time police had been in the area was probably many years ago, and it was early Sunday morning, a quiet time. But he was concerned about the rental car.

While he quickly walked down the concrete steps to the outside, he felt a wave of tiredness coming over him. He had to hurry. To his relief, the car was still there and undamaged. When he got to the hotel, he parked in the lot to the side, took his briefcase and headed for the reception area. A young man with a mouth full of chewing gum sat behind a wooden counter, but didn't get up.

"Got a reservation?"

"Yes. The name is Harold Copper. Just one day." He handed Chewing Gum five twenty dollar bills, and got a rusty old key back in exchange.

"What's wrong with your eye?"

"Nothing. Mind your own business."

"It's Number 34, around the corner."

"Thanks." He put a five dollar bill on the counter. "I don't want to be disturbed, OK? Had a late night, and I need my sleep." Chewing Gum nodded and grabbed the bill.

The room was small and Spartan, but all he cared for was a comfy bed. Before he could turn in, there was one more thing he had to do. He took a diary from his briefcase and wrote down the woman's name, for his records. In the morning he might not remember. After finishing the entry in his diary, he carefully locked the door, turned off the light and fell into bed. Within minutes, he was sound asleep.

◊ ◊ ◊

It wouldn't be long now; she could feel it. Carol Johnson lay in bed in her private room in Excalibur. Her breathing was shallow and every breath could be her last. She'd been blessed with a long life at eighty-four, and done her best to love two husbands and two sons. Yet her most important decision had been to join the Church of Oscar. If she had, even in a minuscule way, helped to better the earth, it was enough. She had no fear of dying and was looking forward to join Yabul and Patrick in the hereafter.

There was movement in the hallway and Erwin entered.

"Hi, Mom." He bent over and kissed her. "How are you feeling today?"

"Not so great, son. Could you do something for me, please? I would like to see that video of Philip again. Have you still got it?"

"It's in my office. I'll get it for you."

Carol could still remember the shock, when Erwin had returned from Secret Springs with the news that, officially, Philip had died in a virtual reality accident. In reality, her first son was involved in some kind of secret experiment. He had given her a video that would explain it all. She had watched it, unable to fathom what had happened. Why would her son pretend to be dead? It was very confusing.

Erwin was back, carrying the DVD player. He put it down on her side table, then helped her sit up straight, so that she could watch it. The effort to sit up took her breath away and she almost fainted. Erwin started it for her, and then she saw her firstborn again, so young and good-looking still. She lay back, listening and watching.

"Mother, I hope this reaches you in time. I have neglected you and I am sorry. I love you in my own particular way, I am sure you know that. I'm involved in something so big, so important that it has taken all my time, even my normal life. I have a plan, Mom. I'm going to save humanity from the bad things that are about to happen. I know it is very difficult for you to understand, but I have

329

talked to Yabul. I have seen him, as real as you are seeing me now . . . "

Carol did her best to follow what her son was saying, but she felt very weak. Every breath was taking more and more effort, and she began to see Philip in a haze, as if he was getting in and out of focus. His voice was getting softer also, and further away.

" . . . . when the time comes, perhaps humanity will be reborn and people will be able to live peacefully with each other and the rest of creation. They might give me back my physical shape. I just had to do this Mother, I had to try. I couldn't just be a nobody, a conformer . . . "

It was time. She pulled the video player towards her, as if she wanted to bring Phil close to her heart. Then, while she felt death approaching fast, she marshaled all her remaining energy for just one final time.

"Just like his father," she croaked, "right up till the very end." Then she lay back, unable to take another breath.

For a while Erwin stood by her side. Then he closed his mother's eyes and stepped away from the bed. Something began to swell in his heart, a mixture of sorrow and seething anger. He was sorry that his mother was gone. Yet he was also angry that she could only think of Philip. Her no-good son who'd left home at the age of sixteen, and had only bothered to see his mother once in the last thirty years, while he, Erwin, had been at her side all the time: at home on the farm, and here in the commune. He'd looked after her after Patrick died, attending to all her wishes.

And for what? It was always *Philip this, Philip that. I miss him. I wonder how he is? Why doesn't he call?* And even here, on her deathbed, not a final word for him, who had made it to Head Councilor. All she could think of was his crazy half-brother, who was engaged in some stupid, asinine experiment. It was so bloody unfair!

330

20

As time went by, Philip adjusted to his new environment. It wasn't easy. In corporeal life, as he called his former existence, there were myriads of events that people took for granted. A sunrise, the weather, the division of day and night. With the virtscapes, Philip could get close to experiencing this, but there were important differences.

In real life, the necessity to eat, drink, make love, sleep, shower, or even just visit a bathroom, were simple routines that divided a twenty-four-hour day into manageable chunks. Not so in his virtual world. His days seemed to last forever. One could only climb so many mountains at a time, or stroll along so many beaches, before boredom set in.

Philip wasn't interested in entertainment and adventure for the moment. He missed Jennifer tremendously and wanted her back. She hadn't shown up in Secret Springs since she had left him. Furthermore, he was eager to get on with his time vault project. He wanted to be in charge, urging his team forward. It was the one thing he could not do.

Marvin was doing a great job. The construction of the time vault was moving right on schedule. Every few days, the engineer would don his VR helmet and meet Philip in a prearranged virtscape with the latest details and news about the project. The dome was being constructed from flexoglass, a new type of glass, super strong, malleable and flexible, with solar cells embedded in it.

To Philip's delight, the photo-voltaic cells provided ample power, even on cloudy days. An impressive array of high-performance batteries was constantly being charged, and Virtual City would never be short of power. To finance everything, Marvin had arranged for a bank loan that would be paid back from the fees the exhibitors paid. A friend of Sarah, a renowned sculptress, was working on the

Subscriber's Wall that would show the names of everyone who had contributed to the project. The takeover of Secret Springs had been approved, and as soon as all the details were ironed out, Marvin would move the virtscapes and Philip's avatar.

Sitting on a rock in a clearing in the forest, with Crater Lake lying below him, like a magnificent maroon sheet of ice, broken only by a few boats with people water-skiing behind them, Philip pointed his finger at the sky. From the menu that instantly appeared, he moved his finger down to a clock icon to read the time. 12:20. Marvin was very late, and Philip was getting worried. After another ten minutes, a shimmering in the cool forest air announced the arrival of the engineer. Philip quickly stood up to meet his friend.

"Marvin. Why are you so late? What's wrong? You look terrible."

"I have dreadful news, Philip. The worst possible. First of all, your mother has passed away. My condolences. I went to the Church of Oscar to start preparations for the transfer of the virtscapes and asked for Erwin, but he wasn't available. I waited for an hour, and when he finally showed up, he told me about your mother. He also said he'd changed his mind about giving you the virtscapes. I pleaded with him, Phil, but he got absolutely livid and threw me out."

"What? He has gone back on his promise? The devious jerk, I'll get him for this! If I could go out there, I'd strangle him myself. How could he do this to me, his half-brother. Virtual City is useless without the virtscapes! What am I going to do now?"

"I really don't know, Phil. I would take legal action for you if I could, but it was only a verbal agreement. Your word against your brother's, and you are not even officially alive. No hope there. You may have to give up your idea of virtual people."

"I can't accept that, Marvin. You've got to hack into Secret Springs' database yourself and copy everything onto huge hard drives, so we can put them on our own servers when they are ready."

"Oh, sure! Just like that, right? No way, Phil. I don't have the necessary security clearance to do that. I would be caught and if Armonde found out I was helping you, he would make damn sure your avatar was reset. I can't take that risk."

"Well, hire someone else, then," Philip said. "Get the best hacker you can find and have him do it. Come on, Marvin, you must do this for me! Virtual City depends on you."

◊ ◊ ◊

Lawrence Rossum knew computers. He'd been brought up with them, like everyone else. But his passion for them went much further, especially since a major car accident had left him without the use of his legs. What he lost in his legs, he made up for in his arms and hands. There were days when he only left his computer to go to the bathroom, as his fingers performed their endless symphonies on the keyboard all day long. Many people used voice recognition software and it had its uses. But not for Lawrence. Hacking wasn't like writing a novel. Most of the time he worked with cryptic words and sentences that he could not even pronounce. He was very accurate, as his fingers flew over the keyboards with very few mistakes. Among his friends he was known as the *Fingers King*.

When he first started hacking, he frequently got into trouble with the law, as he sneaked into all kinds of government computers, partly for fun, partly for money to pay for his spinal treatments. Since he had been at fault in the accident, the insurance company hadn't paid up. Unfortunately, making money through hacking attracted the Feds, and he'd been caught.

He'd spent three years in jail. It had been horrendous, especially since he was disabled. It had toughened him up. After he got out of jail at age thirty-two, he decided to stay on the right side of the law, taking up consulting and teaching people and security companies how to keep their systems safe from others like him. It was a much less stressful life, and he even managed to enter a lasting, loving relationship with a woman client of his.

He ran a website to help people who had fallen pray to treacherous and criminal cyber activities. He did not advertise, but preferred the old-fashioned way of getting business: word of mouth. His customers knew he was good, and told others about him. Sometimes he took on people who were not referred to him by others, if he was interested in their problems. Most of the time he was not.

Lawrence and his girlfriend Tina lived in an eight bedroom, hundred year old farmhouse outside a village called Deermark, about a hundred miles west of the Windy City. The property was ten acres, and the house was built in the back. An overgrown garden with several maples and a dilapidated orchard with stunted apple trees shielded the house from the road.

It was impossible for someone in a wheelchair to mow lawns, and when Tina took a look at the garden she decided it was too much for her also. Nature was left to itself. Over the years, quite a few marauding gangs, mostly on motorcycles, seeing the neglected property from the highway had considered it easy picking, and made the mistake of taking the next exit back to the farmhouse for a better look. It was not something they would do again.

When he started his business, Lawrence had faced a dilemma. He could use his earnings to pay for expensive spinal treatment, in the hope that one day he could walk again. It would leave him with very little money. The alternative was to continue life in a wheelchair, and use his funds to fortify and spruce up his property.

Much progress had been made in treating spinal injuries over the years, and for many people total rehabilitation was possible. Not so for Lawrence. The accident had almost severed his spinal cord and it was a miracle he was not a quadriplegic. When the doctors told him there was no guarantee he could ever walk again, even with the best of treatment, Lawrence made his decision. He would spend his money to protect himself and Tina, and safeguard his business in the process.

His first line of defense was an eight feet high steel fence along the entire property. A gate between two concrete posts gave access to the driveway. Embedded in one of the posts was a camera and microphone, for people who had legitimate business with him. Uninvited guests would soon find out that this particular property was protected like Area 51, minus the warning signs. Hidden emitters in the ground could spew out a variety of nerve gases. Some of it could kill in seconds, milder ones might just make its victim retch uncontrollably. Most trespassers at this stage decided they weren't really interested in the house after all, and left as fast as they could, their eyes stinging.

Since Lawrence had lived on the property, no one with bad intentions had ever made it past this stage. If someone with extraordinary determination came to within a hundred yards of the house, computer controlled high energy lasers, hidden among the fruit trees, were activated. The industrial lasers had been designed to slice through steel plates, and had absolutely no trouble drilling holes in human flesh.

Lawrence's office looked like the control room of a major traffic center. Huge screens were divided into many smaller windows, and each window showed part of his property. No one could come within two-hundred yards off the place without Lawrence seeing him. Just by flipping a switch, he could activate any one of the security systems, depending on the situation.

Though all this security might ward off marauding gangs, it would not deter a massive attack by an army with tanks, grenades and other war equipment, but Lawrence hardly expected a threat from that direction. One had to draw the line somewhere, financially. Security like this did not come cheap, and he also required his own power supply, independent of the local grid. Additionally, he used satellites for his Internet connection.

One day in October 2077, Lawrence's security system alerted him that a lone car had turned into his driveway, and stopped in front of the pillar with the communication system. He zoomed in on the car and driver and noticed it was an East Indian, well dressed. The rest of the car was empty. Seeing no immediate threat, Lawrence activated his microphone.

"State your business, please."

"Are you Lawrence Rossum?"

"I am. And you are?"

"My name is Marvin Tuppal. I saw your website online and I was wondering . . ."

"Mr. Tuppal, that website is there for a reason: to help people and businesses with security in their computer systems. That's what I do. If you need help, you e-mail my company. You don't come and bother me at home. You've wasted your time. Goodbye."

"Oh, please, Mr. Rossum, hear me out. I have good credentials. I'm the chief electrical engineer at Secret Springs. What I have to discuss is too delicate for e-mail. If I could just have two minutes of your time, please?" For a few seconds Lawrence sat in thought. Secret Springs. Not just any company. He made a decision.

"I'll open the gate. Come straight down the driveway and park your car at the end. When you get out follow the driveway and step directly onto the porch. Do not, under any circumstance, set foot in the garden."

He closed the microphone connection and toggled another switch that would open the gate. Then he wheeled his chair out of his office into an elevator and pressed the lower level button. When the door opened again, he wheeled himself into the hallway. He could hear Tina humming in the kitchen and he smelled fresh coffee. On impulse, he changed direction and joined her.

"Hi. We're going to have company."

"Who? You didn't tell me. I've got nothing in the house."

"No, not like that. It's someone who came to the gate."

"For Pete's sake, Lawrence! You have never allowed anyone in from the road. What's going on? Who is it?"

"Some guy working for Secret Springs. I'm just a little bit curious why that company would want my services. I'll see him in my study."

When Marvin rang the doorbell, Tina let him in and showed the engineer to a small room with a large desk, a single computer, and two easy chairs. Lawrence sat behind his desk. He nodded at Marvin and gestured to the chair opposite.

"Sit down, please. What brings you to the most fortified private house in the country, Mr. Tuppal?"

"I would like you to hack into Secret Springs, and—"

"Whatever it is you want, the price just doubled. Secret Springs is a tough nut to crack, even for me. Why do you want to break into your own company's computer?"

"I . . . uh . . . I want to set up business for myself, and they have something I need."

"You won't get far with me by lying," Lawrence said sharply. "You've got to be an intelligent person to become chief electrical engineer at Secret Springs, and what you're saying is rubbish. It's like hacking into Boeing and stealing their plans to start manufacturing your own airplanes. It cannot be done. Do you have a grudge against your company?"

"No, not at all. I'm sorry, I didn't want to deceive you. The truth is rather complicated. A small group of people at Secret Springs is engaged in a highly sensitive project. I can't talk about it. We need something from the company and there is no legal way to get it."

Lawrence reflected on that for a moment. Then he wheeled himself to the door.

"Tina just made fresh coffee. Would you like some?"

"Yes, please."

Lawrence wheeled himself back to the kitchen and turned on a small monitor on the counter. It showed Marvin sitting quietly in front of the desk.

"What are you doing?" Tina said. "Spying on him?" She stood next to the hacker and put her hand on his shoulder. "Look, he's just sitting there. What did you expect him to do? Raid your computer?"

"You can't be too careful in my business," Lawrence said. "Could we have two coffees please?"

He gave her a big smile and wheeled himself back towards his study.

"Now, Mr. Tuppal," he said, when he returned. "What are we talking about here? Some kind of mutiny? A takeover?"

"Heavens, no!" The engineer seemed shocked. "No, it's pure scientific research we're doing, not profitable at all, and that's why Secret Springs is not interested."

"All right, I can understand that," Lawrence nodded. "One of your guys made some kind of technological breakthrough and he wants to keep it to himself. What exactly do you want from Secret Springs?"

"We want to copy their virtscapes."

"All of them?" Lawrence sat straight up in his wheelchair. "That's impossible."

At that moment Tina carried in a tray with two cups of coffee. She smiled at Marvin and handed him one of the cups. "Is he giving you a hard time?" she quipped. "Don't worry, you're a very fortunate person indeed. Very few people get in here without an appointment." She put the tray down and left.

"How are your computer skills?" Lawrence asked after taking a sip from the hot coffee.

"OK, I suppose," Marvin replied. "I may not be familiar with all the latest and newest developments; that's not really my department. But I'm certainly not computer illiterate if that's what you mean."

338

"Right. Well let me update a few things for you. The Internet is getting bigger and bigger by the day. Bigger and also faster. At the moment, I can download at a sustained speed of a hundred Terabytes per second. One hundred thousand billion bytes, roughly. That may sound a lot, but it is really pretty slow. Terabytes are old hat these days; we've been using Petabytes for a while, a thousand times larger. The next step up is Exabytes, a thousand times bigger still.

"Those Secret Springs virtscapes are all proprietary, copy-righted programs that take up an humungous amount of bandwidth. I estimate one of them to be about twenty Petabytes, on average, but it could be more. Downloading that much information would take at least two hundred seconds, or just over three minutes. That is for one virtscape. Secret Springs has thousands of them, if not millions.

"Do you see what I'm getting at here, Mr. Tuppal? You want me to sneak into the best protected computer system on the planet, and download Exabytes of information without being found out? That's impossible, even for me. I'm afraid I can't help you."

Back into the Secret Springs building, Marvin headed for the cafeteria to have lunch, though he wasn't really hungry. It was more a way of postponing what he had to next—give Philip his death sentence. In two weeks time it would be all over. He thought of getting totally sloshed, to alleviate the pain he felt, then decided against it. He needed a clear head to face Philip. When he was finally ready, he walked to his office, sat down and donned his VR helmet. He logged on to Secret Springs and soon found Philip on the boardwalk at Venice, California.

"Hi, Phil."

"Marvin. It didn't work. I can tell from your face."

"It's no good, Phil, I'm so sorry. I just came back from visiting the best hacker I could find, and what you want cannot be done. There's too much material to copy, and Secret Springs security will find out for sure. It is the end of the road, Philip. In two weeks the church will take over, and all virtscapes and avatars will be deleted. Including yours. I'm afraid you're living on borrowed time. Virtual City will only be what it proclaims to be—a Time Vault."

Philip sat on the sand, his back resting against a log. Marvin stood next to him, staring at the ocean. He felt deflated, tired and worn-out. For a while neither of them spoke, as they watched the people stroll and roller skate down the promenade. Finally, Philip looked at his best friend.

"Thanks, Marvin, for everything you've done. I'll miss you all very much, you, Jennifer, Sarah, Sandor . . ."

Suddenly Philip jumped up, and balled his fists in the air. "No! I will not accept this. We must have those virtscapes. I can't let Erwin get away with this. We went through too much to give up now. I know we can't touch him, but maybe we can get at him through that church. They must have a weak spot. We've got to go on the attack, Marvin; hit them where it hurts. There's something very secretive going on in that church, I've known it all my life. We've got to find out what it is."

"Maybe we can send someone in who can report back to us."

"That's not how it works, Marvin. When people join that church something happens to them. I am certain of it. Even my mother told me she couldn't betray her people. They all share a secret. I don't know what goes on, but somehow people are changed when they join. Nobody ever comes back.

"Don't you find that interesting? I mean, we've had secret communes, or churches, or societies throughout history. The Catholic Church, The Masons, the Illuminati, and many others. But there have always been whistleblowers. No secret society can remain secret for ever. Except that Church of Oscar."

"What if we were to wire someone and send him in? That way we could at least get an idea."

"Nah, that church's not stupid, I'm sure they scan or check people for that . . ." Philip's voice trailed off, as he

340

stared in the distance. Then he suddenly reached over and grabbed a surprised Marvin by the arm.

"I've got it Marvin! An RFID implant. I don't think that church is checking for those yet. We've got to find one that records and transmits physical data: blood pressure, galvanic skin response, heart rate, brain activity, everything. We may never know what that church does exactly, but the results will show up in a person's vital life signs. All we have to do is sit in a car nearby and record everything. And depending on what we find, I'm sure Erwin would be very much opposed to us making those findings public. Come on, Marvin, get one of the latest implants and find us a suitable subject."

◊ ◊ ◊

SLAW. Soil, Light, Air and Water. The simple, basic equation of life. All life on earth depended on it, one way or another. Some life forms could do without one, perhaps even two of the elements, but most needed all four. It was such a simple equations, yet so powerful. If the four elements were there, unadulterated and in the right proportions, all life would flourish. Seeds would sprout, as surely as the sun would come up. Flowers would grow and people and animals would thrive. Change the equation and things would go terribly wrong. One ignored or altered it at one's peril. It was hard to understand why a society that could put men in outer space, and create realistic virtscapes, had such troubles understanding a very basic equation.

Sitting comfortably in her lounge chair on the small sunny patio behind her little cabin at the back of the Excalibur complex, Sylvia Rasnell let her mind wander, while she enjoyed her afternoon rest. In front of her, the garden plots stretched far behind the Excalibur building. It was her domain. To shield her from the afternoon breeze, workers had installed glass partitions all around her patio. To Sylvia it was the best place in the world. The soil was very fertile and the commune had used every bit of the grounds, even claiming more from the wilderness at the back where possible.

Before she had joined the Church of Oscar, Sylvia had little use for gardens, or the products they produced. Food was something that somehow appeared on the family table every day, to be consumed and then forgotten. There were other priorities in her young life: boys, jobs, marriage, seeing the world, raising a family. All that had changed one day, just after she had turned eighteen. Her brother Jo had come home with his friend Ted Taylor. Sylvia rather liked Ted; she thought he was very good-looking and smart and she was hoping he would ask her for a date. It hadn't happened, and Sylvia was far too shy to make a move herself.

Jo and Ted had acted strangely; they were all excited and secretive. Jo explained they had found this new fix, something that gave an incredible, permanent high. He had been on drugs before and he knew Sylvia wanted no part of it. She said so again, in a very firm way. Then, to her horror, Jo had suddenly grabbed her from behind and held her, while Ted had stuffed a smelly rag against her nose. The boys were very strong and she was no match for them. Whatever the stuff on the rag was, it had stung for a while, and she had been livid with Ted and Jo for doing this to her. Then her life had changed forever as her consciousness had expanded and she had joined the Church of Oscar.

At first, Sylvia had been very happy. In her new mind she firmly believed the church's main dogma—living in harmony with Nature and obeying the SLAW equation. It made such good sense, so why not start at the very beginning? The nourishment from the earth that made life possible. At eighteen, she had been old enough to see what was going on in the world: the increasing wanton destruction and depletion of farmlands, oceans, and forests, the pollution of water, soil and air, and the degradation of food. It just had never truly sunk in, as if she had been wearing blinkers.

In her enlightened consciousness she knew that the commune was a good place to start. She began to spend much of her time in the gardens. The land behind Bernard Tows' old barn had been a challenge: it was full of rocks, weeds and bad soil. The gardens behind their second home, the Magnolia Inn, had been slightly better, but the church hadn't stayed there very long. It was in their newly built church in Mission Canyon that she had found her true vocation. Only to have all her work destroyed in the Whitsun Massacre.

It was during the first year in Excalibur that Sylvia became frustrated. She wanted to spend more time in the gardens. There was so much to do: weeding, hoeing, seeding. She had lots of help, but a lot of her time was wasted on council business. Like the other original founders of the church, she had been made a councilor for life. But while the other councilors acknowledged the importance of good, organic, home grown food, they saw it only as a part of the Church of Oscar's plan. There were other important things. The Word of Oscar had to be spread. The new members needed shelter and jobs. There was also the need for security to keep people safe. The various departments of the commune had to be coordinated. Sylvia knew they were all vital parts of the church' activities, but she preferred her gardens.

When she spoke to Jo about her reservations, he waived them aside. Councilors had a very specialized, important task to perform in the church, and work in the commune was best left to the general populace. What else would people do with all their time? To pacify her, Jo made one concession. He would make her councilor in charge of the gardens. Not being a very argumentative person, Sylvia had agreed and never spoke of it again. She divided her time between the council chamber and her gardens and tried to make the best of it.

Then Jo died and Sylvia was next in line for Head Councilor. She couldn't refuse the honor and would probably have remained Head Councilor, had it not been for what she learned when she opened the church's vault. Upon finding out what Jo had done, something had snapped and she had made up her mind on the spot. Council was the wrong place for her. She had resigned her position and moved to her gardens. That had been four months ago, and it had been the happiest time in Sylvia's life. She had a little cabin in the fields with the other garden workers and, at six in the morning, after an early breakfast, she was out there, digging and weeding.

At night, she would update her diary, and on a special map on the wall in her cabin she would use colorful pins to indicate where crops were planted, which parts of the soil needed replanting and which should remain fallow. She wrote monthly reports to the Council, informing them about the status of the gardens, and giving them a prognosis about what to expect for the season. It was doubtful if anyone read her reports, but she didn't care. She also did something she didn't mention in her reports. Four farmhands had built a climate-controlled garden shed for her. Inside, they had made four racks with shelving. Sylvia procured hundreds of little boxes from the cafeteria. The shelter became her storage vault for seeds for a future time when healthy, unadulterated seeds might no longer be available. She picked the best seeds of fruits and vegetables and carefully dried them. They might not all germinate, but it was the best she could do for the future.

In the late afternoon, Sylvia allowed herself a break on her patio. She would sit there until it was time for supper. Here she indulged in her one little vice, as she jokingly called it: a glass of blackberry wine and a piece of the daily desert from the cafeteria. She could have gone there herself and joined the other farm hands in the cafeteria, but this time of day she preferred to be alone. Mary, a nice young waitress, brought her the treat around four o'clock every day. Today, Mary was late. Sylvia didn't mind. She had done her work, and now it was time for relaxing and daydreaming. There was a timid knock on her patio door. That would be Mary.

"It's open," Sylvia called out. The door slid open and a young girl squeezed through, balancing a tray. It wasn't Mary, but someone Sylvia didn't know. The young waitress put the tray on a chair and carefully placed a glass of wine and a plate with a slice of cake onto Sylvia's side table.

"That looks a delicious piece of strawberry cake, dear," Sylvia said. "I'm sorry, I don't know your name. Where is Mary?"

"I am Sonja, Miss. Mary is poorly today." The girl spoke softly. She was slightly older than Mary and not as pretty. There was a little bit too much of her, Sylvia mused, especially around the hips. Still, she seemed pleasant enough and had a nice smile. She was dressed in a white apron and her hair sat in a small bun behind her head.

"Well, Sonja, thank you very much. I'm going to enjoy this. Give my best wishes to Mary."

After Sonja had gone, Sylvia began her ritual. First she picked up the glass of wine and smelled the aroma. As always, it smelled vaguely of blackberries. Then she took a small sip. Sometimes she would sit here for almost two hours, enjoying her little treat, taking tiny sips to make it last. She noticed that the wine had a slightly different taste, a little more tangy. A new batch perhaps. It still tasted lovely. For the longest time she just sat there, looking out over her gardens, enjoying her few hours off. Then, all of a sudden, she couldn't lift her left arm and she knew she hadn't been paying attention. Somebody had altered her equation.

Mary had been late. That was the first change. Then it hadn't been Mary, but another girl she didn't know. The second change. Then the wine had a slightly different flavor. Any of these changes on their own could be considered a coincidence. Together, they meant trouble. When she looked at her gardens again, they suddenly looked blurred and she saw two rows of sticks instead of one. She felt a sudden pain in the left of her chest, as if someone had stuck a knife in her. Was it her heart? Sylvia was only fifty-three and as far as she knew in good health.

The pain was getting worse, and all of a sudden the glass she held in her right hand crashed on the edge of the table and shattered on the floor, as her fingers were unable to hold it. She needed help. She tried to cry out, but all she could manage was a soft groan that nobody in the fields below could hear. Her other fellow workers were drinking in the cafeteria and there was no one else around. She tried to get up but couldn't. Her legs refused to move and her upper body was firmly pushed against the cushion behind her, as if she was accelerating in a plane.

Sylvia was dying and she knew why. Someone had poisoned her wine. Her chest felt as if a big concrete block was resting on it. Even her head became too heavy to keep upright, and fell down, lolling on her chest. She had seen her lovely gardens for the last time. Just before she exhaled her last breath, Sylvia wondered who in the Church of Oscar would want her dead.

21

It was a recent virtscape, perhaps one of the last ones that would be taken by Secret Springs, Philip thought. The scene showed the sprawling compound of a new Church of Oscar, just outside Chicago. Philip and Marvin sat in a virtual copy of the latest model Tatshu car, parked on a little hill, giving them a good view. Like all communes, this one was surrounded by tall trees and a high wired fence, with a guarded gated entrance. From the gate, a winding driveway led through the commune's gardens to a large building further down. Several people were working in vegetable plots, neatly defined by wooden boards. Part of the front lawn was a fenced-off area were several sheep were grazing. Without the fences, the commune would have looked pastoral, Philip thought. Idyllic almost.

"Why would anyone want to live in a place like that?" Marvin asked. "It looks like a prison."

"The church members don't see it that way," Philip replied. "They feel protected from the evils of the outside world."

"What if your brother doesn't show up? We're running out of time, Philip, only ten days left."

"He will. Erwin knows there is a chance the rumor is true. He can't afford not to check it out."

Finally, half an hour late, the air outside the car shimmered, and there stood Erwin, dressed as if he'd been out running: blue tracksuit, white sneakers. He walked over to the car, pulled the door open and got into the backseat.

"I truly had hoped I'd seen the last of you, brother," he sneered. His left eye was twitching badly. "What can we possibly have to say to each other at this stage? Why are you here? Have you decided you want to have a good look at our church, now that it is about to swallow up your company?

Poor Philip, worked so hard all his life and now it's all going to pot. Less than two weeks, Phil, that is how much time you have left. So what's this ludicrous suggestion that our church is in trouble?"

"Shut up, Erwin," Philip said. "Thanks very much for not telling me about Mother. I had to hear it from Marvin. Did you show her my video?"

"All right. She died in peace, and I showed her your damned video. Happy now? As if you cared! Anyway, that's not why we are here, so get to the point."

"Take a good look," Philip said, pointing to the commune. "You're building yourself many fortresses like this, aren't you? Well protected, safe and secure communes. Well this particular one has a problem, Erwin." Philip pulled a virtual laptop computer from the side of his seat. "There's something you should see." He stuck a disk in the side of the laptop and turned it on. Soon the screen showed a series of graphs, charts, tables and columns. "This was taken a few days ago," Philip said. "It shows the vital life signs of a human being. Respiration, heartbeat, brain waves, everything."

"We're into biology now, are we, Phil?" Erwin sneered. "Well, I guess you've got to do something to fill your days. Very interesting, I'm sure, but why are we looking at this?"

"These are the readings of one of your new members, Erwin."

Erwin laughed. "We've got the best security money can buy, Philip. Do you think we're stupid? We check people out before they join. We would have found any kind of radio device. I don't know why I even bother talking to you. I'm out of here." His hand moved to the door handle.

"Do you check for RFID implants?"

"What do you mean? Implants?" The hand came back.

"You should keep up with what's going on in the world, Erwin. There are millions of RFID implants in use these days. In stores, factories and prisons. In hospitals they're used to record a patient's life sign, so that doctors know immediately when something goes wrong. Everyone in the cities will get an implant in the future. Marvin was kind enough to install such a device in one of your potential members before he entered your church.

"The implant recorded all his life signs while you recruited him. And we got some very interesting results. I'm not a medical doctor and I can't interpret the graphs, but I'm told they show elevated levels of certain neurotransmitters that play an important role in human brain chemistry. Serotonin and dopamine, for example, and there are more. This is related to a much higher than normal mental activity, Erwin. It seems you're doing something that highly excites people's brains while you recruit them. I'm sure the authorities would very much like to see this."

Like a cobra, Erwin's hand shot out and wrested the computer from Philip's hand. "I'll take that," he said, breathing rapidly.

"Oh, please," Phil chuckled. "Take it, by all means. Destroy the disk, the laptop, if it makes you feel better, Erwin. They're only virtual copies. The real disk is kept in Marvin's vault."

Erwin's left eye twitched nervously again, as if he was winking at them.

"What do you want?"

"You know what I want, Erwin. Completion of the deal we agreed on. You have no use for the virtscapes, you said. Why did you break your promise?"

"I'll tell you why. Mother had been very poorly for a while, and she knew she wouldn't last much longer. Then she wanted to see that video of yours again, even though I'd shown it to her before. And you know what? She looked at it, and then she died. Her last words were of you. Not a word for me, her other son. On her deathbed she only spoke of you, Philip. You, who ignored her all her life. So give me one good reason why I should be nice to you."

"You're a sick person, Erwin, and you're right; it is better that we never see each other again. But if I don't get those

349

virtscapes, the real disk will be made public with rather dire consequences for your church, I imagine."

"And what guarantee do I have that you haven't made a copy and will betray the church anyway?"

"If I get the virtscapes, the disk will be destroyed. There is no copy, and I shall take no action against your church. You have my word. Compared to some people, my word means something."

Erwin sat up straight and his hand grabbed the door handle again.

"The deal will be signed in ten days. After that, you have four days to take what you need. Everything that is of no use to the church after that will be destroyed." With an loud "plop" sound, Erwin vanished.

Marvin exhaled loudly, as if he'd held his breath during the entire conversation. "I know he's your brother, Philip, but he's a nasty piece of work."

"Well, at least we're getting the virtscapes," Philip said happily. "Now we can finish off Virtual City."

"That church is a bad place," Marvin said. "Brainwashing people to recruit them as new members? That's sick. We've got to tell the authorities."

Philip shook his head. "No."

"What do you mean *no*? I am serious, Phil. What they are doing there is morally wrong. How would you like to have your brain tampered with? What I don't understand is why nobody blow the whistle."

"People in the Church of Oscar don't want to come back into society, Marv. They may have been brainwashed, but they are profoundly happy with it. I know, because my mother joined them and I saw her afterwards. If they are contend with their new life, who are we to judge them? Besides, it is too big now. That church could perhaps have been stopped and investigated while it was small, but now it's too late. There are too many people involved, worldwide, and if we tell the authorities we could face a massacre a thousand times

350

worth than the one before. I don't want that on my conscience."

"In that case, Phil, let's get those virtscapes as soon as the ink of the takeover signatures has dried, and hope your brother doesn't call your bluff in the mean time."

◊ ◊ ◊

He looked so young, a choirboy almost, in his white shirt and jacket. Erwin found it hard to believe that the young man in his office was twenty years old. Sahu Deepah had been with the commune for two months. He had a very intelligent face, with large deep-brown eyes, unblemished skin, and a smile that revealed perfect white teeth. He was tall, slender like a rake, with long arms and fingers. In the world outside, he could well have been a male fashion model, or perhaps a *Wunderkind,* a classical pianist, or a famous artist. In the church he was a technician working in the communication department that Erwin himself had set up ten years earlier.

"Tell me about yourself, Sahu," Erwin said. "You were born in the United States, and your parents are Indian, with U.S. citizenship?"

"That is correct, Provost Councilor. I was born in Los Angeles, after my parents moved there from New York. They arrived from India twenty-five years ago."

"Why did you join us by yourself? What about your parents?"

A shadow clouded Sahu's handsome face. "We had a . . . disagreement."

"Was it about joining the Church of Oscar?"

"No. My parents still have old-fashioned ideas. They wanted me to marry a rich Indian girl in L.A, but I didn't want to get married so early. So I left home, and when I couldn't find any work, I joined the Church of Oscar."

"You have some schooling in electronics and communications, I have learned. I would have thought that would help you find a job in a city. Why couldn't you?"

"My father is a very influential and vengeful person. He made sure no one would hire me in L.A, and I didn't have the resources to travel anywhere else. I hoped there would be a position for me in the church."

"There very well might be, Sahu. Even a position as councilor would be a possibility, if you can help me out."

"Tell me what I have to do, Provost Councilor," Sahu said, his eyes lit up with expectation. "I'll do anything for you and the church. It is my new home."

"First of all, you will be working for me, personally. No one else needs to know, not even the other councilors. We have a rather delicate situation. There is a spy in one of our churches."

"A spy? How could that be? I thought once we received Os—"

"It was an unforeseen breach in security, something we never thought about. You will be given the chance to correct this, so that it will not happen again. Are you familiar with RFID implants?"

"Oh, yes. I have seen them on one of our trips back to India. They are used for many things."

"Someone in our church has one of those implants inside him or her, Sahu, but I do not know who it is. It happened in our Chicago commune, so you'll have to go there. I presume the implant is still active, and anyone with sensitive enough equipment could monitor this person's life signs from outside our church. It is an immediate threat to our commune, and action is needed. I want this person found." Erwin opened his desk drawer and retrieved a box the size of a briefcase. "Once you have established who it is, I want you to use this." He opened the box and showed the contents to the young man.

"Wow! That's an Colt 45. It must be a fifty years old! Why does the church use guns, Provost Councilor? I thought we were—"

"We abhor weapons of any kind, except for our own security," Erwin said shortly. "This was left here a long time ago, during an altercation. How come you know so much about guns, Sahu?"

"My father was in the army. He taught me all about weapons. This one needs cleaning and oiling."

"It is yours to use. Be careful, it is loaded. I want you to go to Chicago. While you are there, purchase a RFID scanner. You can charge it to our security department. Get a powerful one with a wide range. I do not want people to find out you're checking up on them. Once you have found our spy, use the gun to finish him off. Do this for me and I'll make sure you shall be voted in as a councilor at our next meeting."

"I'll do my best. May I make a suggestion, Provost?"

"Of course."

"Perhaps we should buy more scanners for all our churches, and use them before we recruit people. There might be more attempts to infiltrate us. We should be prepared."

"That is an excellent idea, Sahu. Yes, I have heared that the government will soon be using those RFID chips on the general population. We must check for that in our recruits. Can you look after that, please?"

"Of course, Provost Councilor. When shall I leave for Chicago?"

"Right now would be a good time," Erwin said.

◊ ◊ ◊

The old man lived in a dirty lean-to, made of two sheets of fiberglass, suspended between a tree branch and two wooden poles in the ground. The background to his 'home' was a dense hawthorn bush abloom with white flowers. Sarah could see a filthy mattress, a blanket and a collection of cardboard boxes. The man looked about seventy, haggard and ill-kempt. He had a dirty beard, and when he opened his mouth to speak, she saw he had only three teeth left. He did not seem to take kindly to unexpected visitors.

"If you're with that church, I don't want to talk to you. Piss off!"

"We're not," Sarah Marrion said. "Why are you worried about a church?"

"I'll show you why." The man began to rummage through the boxes in the back of his lean-to. It was the third attempt that Sarah and Pedro, her husband, had made to find people who would join Philip in his virtual world. After Sarah had told her husband about Philip, Pedro had asked to meet Philip in private, and they had become the best of friends. Pedro Marrion was a professor in Philosophy at the University of Chicago. He had been intrigued by Philips idea and had agreed to help him. Together Sarah and Pedro had started their search for suitable subjects. Their route this time had taken them to Delcon Park, a small patch of greenery in the seedy side of old-town Chicago.

The old man had found what he was looking for: a big, square box. As soon as he had opened it, Pedro let out a whistle of surprise. "Sarah, that's a X24G VR helmet. The latest model. Computer built in, networked, everything! Worth a fortune. Where would a tramp get that?" Sarah held up her hand to silence him.

"What is your name?" she asked the old man.

"Arnold, or Arny."

"I am Sarah Marrion, and this is my husband Pedro. We mean you no harm, and we're not affiliated with any religion. What church were you referring to?"

"That damned Church of Oscar. They've taken my life away."

"Where did you get that helmet, Arny?" Pedro asked.

"An old lady gave it to me."

"Sure. Who did you steal it from?"

"If you don't believe me, you can fuck off! Why do you always think people like me are lying? It's the truth."

Sarah glared at her husband, then looked at Arny again. "Please tell us what happened."

"Her name was Helga," Arny said. "She was from Norway. Her husband was called Einar. I saw them the first time when I was putting my garbage in the bin in the park,

354

over there." He pointed to a small garbage container at the edge of the path leading into the park. "They lived nearby, and walked their dog every day. It was a cute little poodle. Helga and Einar were very nice people, and they gave me five bucks.

"A few days later I saw them again, and I showed them where I lived. I could see they were upset at how I had come down in the world. They wanted to help me, give me money to find me a place to live, but I refused. A few dollars here and there, that's is fine, but I don't want charity. I don't want to be indebted to anyone. Anyway, we saw each other two or three times a week, and they always dropped in for a chat. Usually they brought me a bite to eat as well; you know, a sandwich, a cup of soup, something like that. Nice, friendly people. Then I didn't see them for a while, and I wondered what had happened to them.

"The next time it was just her and the dog. She was all stooped over, walking slowly, and she carried a heavy shopping bag. She told me her husband had died. Got up one morning, walked to the bathroom and dropped dead. Just like that. She was in a terrible state and she told me she was going to move and wouldn't see me again. Then she handed me the shopping bag with this helmet. It belonged to her husband, and she had no use for it anymore. She thought it might make my life more bearable."

"Not much good to you, was it?" Pedro said. "You've got no power here. Are you going to flog it?"

Sarah could see a cloud of suspicion move over the old man's face. His head was shaking left and right, in the same constant rhythm, and she guessed it was Parkinson's.

"Are you with the police?" he asked suspiciously.

"No, we're just here to help people like you," Sarah said quickly. "How did you get that helmet to work?"

Arny pointed to a lone light post about fifty feet away. It stood on the edge of the road leading into the park. "Used to be a welder in my old days," he said. "Electronics was a hobby of mine. Made my own computers and stuff, and wired my own house. I guess the fumes from the welding and soldering gave me the shakes and I had to quit work. My company was only a small one, so I didn't get a pension, and a lot of money went for my treatment. Then my wife left me, and after a few years I ended up here."

"About that light post?" Pedro asked.

"I dug a small trench from my lean-to, spliced a wire in at that post, and buried the line. I knew it was illegal, and some day they may find out about it, but so far it's been working fine. I couldn't believe my luck. Helga had even given me a full year membership to Secret Springs. I hooked up my helmet and found happiness in cyberspace. I could do anything I wanted. I was online most of the day and night. It was fantastic. Then one day . . ."

"What?" Sarah asked.

"One morning I woke up, and it was all gone. All I could get was religious mumbo-jumbo. That Church of Oscar has taken my life away, and I want it back!"

"All right, Arny," Sarah said. "What would you say if I told you that we could make that happen?"

Shaking his head, he stared at her. "What do you mean? How?"

"We're a company like Secret Springs, Arny. Very much smaller, but we do the same. See that van, over there? It's hooked up to our network. Why don't you come with us, and we'll show you. Bring that helmet with you."

They had to wait for a few moments until Arny was ready. Then he hobbled along with them to the van, and Sarah helped him inside. There was a small table and a restaurant-style bench on either side. Arny sat down heavily. "What's your company called?"

"Future Holdings," Sarah said. To her left was a large computer and she turned it on. "Now, Arny, you can plug your helmet in right here." She pointed to an outlet on the computer. "It's the same as before, but this time you just log in as guest, and you don't need a password. Why don't you have a go, and then we'll have a chat afterwards. Set your timer for ten minutes."

Very soon, Arny was on-line, and it looked very strange, the way his head was moving to and fro, but it didn't seem to hinder him. Sarah could see he was enjoying himself, his face lit up now and then, and he smiled.

"Do you want a coffee?" Sarah asked her husband, and Pedro nodded. "Yes, please. Black." Sarah walked to the small kitchen area, and plugged in the electric coffee maker. She sat down and Pedro grabbed her hand. "You know, what we're doing is crazy, right? And totally illegal, also. Assisted suicide, isn't that what they call it? You used to go to jail for that in the old days."

"Used to, yes. Not anymore, Pedro. It's happening all over the world now."

"Still, we're not even doctors. If this comes out . . ."

"We knew it was a gamble before we started, Pedro. Every new invention carries risk. This is the greatest discovery of all times, and I say to hell with the consequences."

There was a deep sigh, and the old man was back. He took off his helmet, beaming. "That was bloody marvelous! Thank you."

"Where did you go?" Sarah asked.

"White-water rafting down the Colorado river," he said. "Man, that was realistic. So how do I join this firm? What do I have to do?"

"Want a coffee? I just made some."

"OK."

Sarah stepped back to the kitchen area and poured three cups of coffee. She carried them to the table and put them down.

"Well, Arny, our company's not just involved in virtual escapism, we also do serious research. The truth is that we have found a way to create virtual people."

"What's that?" Arny asked, lifting the cup to his mouth.

"They are people who permanently live in an avatar. They have no bodies to go back to."

Arny frowned at her. "Has anyone ever done this before?"

"Yes. The man in charge of our company. He was the first to do it."

"I don't understand. If I become an uh . . . virtual person what will happen to my body?"

"You will be officially dead, Arny, but you'll live on in your avatar forever, like you did just now."

"That's a big step."

"It sure is. It's not for everyone. You have to weigh the pros and cons, Arny. Your life here, against one in cyberspace. If you want it, you must be prepared to give up everything. Your friends, relatives, and all your possessions. Without exceptions."

The old man brooded for a while. He took a long swig of his coffee, and gave them a thin smile. "I don't have much of a life here, do I? I'll give it a try." He started to put his helmet back on.

"No, Arny, that's not how it works," Sarah said. "You can't just 'give it a try'. You must go online in the absolute, unshakeable knowledge that you want it to happen. Let me tell you a story. I have a small garden with a patio at home. From our house you go through a sliding glass door into the garden. One night it was almost getting dark and we were outside, having dinner with some of our friends. I was in the kitchen and headed out to join them when I walked straight into that glass door. Someone had closed it and I didn't know. I broke the glass, cut and bruised myself badly, but it could have been worse. See what I mean, Arny? In my mind, I was absolutely, one hundred percent convinced that door was open. That's how it has to be, Arny; that's how you have to feel."

Arny's features hardened, and he took a deep breath. "I want to do this." He grabbed his helmet and connected again.

"Now we wait," Sarah said.

They both stared at Arny. They could only see the bottom of his face. His lips were tight together, not a smile on

358

his face. Then, after a few minutes, his features softened and his body began to slouch against the back of the seat.

"My God, he's doing it!" Pedro shouted. "He's actually leaving his body, Sarah."

Sarah stared at the old man, as he slowly slid off the bench onto the vinyl floor of the camper van. She reached over, grabbed his hand to feel his pulse. It was erratic, way too high, and his whole body was twitching. After a few more jerks, the twitching suddenly stopped and so did the pulse.

"This cannot be happening," she said, while a sudden blockage filled her throat. "I thought I was prepared for this, but I'm not. We've just helped someone end his life, Pedro. See if he's all right."

Pedro grabbed his own VR helmet from one of the cupboards on the side of the camper and hastily put it on. He connected to their virtual network, while Sarah rolled the motionless Arny to the side, wondering if she should try to resuscitate him. After a few seconds, Pedro roughly pulled his helmet off again, breathing deeply.

"He's there, Sarah. With Philip. I feel as if I've just witnessed the first H-bomb explosion. Or discovered the DNA helix. We're making history here today, you and I. Nobody is going to believe this."

"Help me drag him back into his lean-to," Sarah said matter-of-factly. "If anyone finds us here, we'll be in trouble." Together they dragged Arnolds body back to his home and put him on the mattress. The body was emaciated and not heavy at all. Then they walked back to the camper, still awed by what had happened.

"Now what?" Pedro asked.

Sarah grabbed her cell phone and punched in a number.

"What are you doing?"

"I'm calling the authorities. We can't just leave his body here."

"I want to report a death," she said, when she was connected. "We were just walking in Delcon Park, and noticed a dead homeless person here. He must have died recently."

She listened for a second, then said: "OK, fine," and disconnected.

"Well?" Pedro cocked an inquiring eye at her.

"They'll deal with it," she said. "Let's move the van a bit further away and wait. I want to see what happens."

It took about half an hour. There was a low rumbling noise and a vehicle came down the path. It was a big truck, loud music blaring, with two men standing on little steps at the back. The men were wearing coveralls with yellow hazard stripes down the front and back. The two of them jumped off the truck, and walked towards the lean-to. For a few minutes nothing happened, while all Sarah and Pedro could hear was the loud music and the engine idling. Then the men were back.

One had Arny's body slung over his shoulder, like a roll of carpet. He walked to the back of the dump truck and threw the body inside. The other man carried Arny's mattress and a pile of clothes, and threw that in also. Then they went back for the rest of Arny's stuff. In about ten minutes they were done. The men jumped back on the truck, and one of them hit the side with his fist. The truck began to move again, and soon disappeared down the lane ahead, the loud music following it. The lean-to had been demolished and removed. Even the hawthorn bush been pulled out. It was as if an old man by the name of Arnold had never lived there.

22

"Good afternoon, Provost Councilor! How was the convention?"

"Splendid, Bertha, splendid. We covered a lot of stuff. How are things here?"

The housemaid, dressed in her white uniform had just come out of one of the councilor rooms, carrying a stack of clean towels. She was a buxom, middle-aged matron with a pretty face and a ready smile. She made a face at Erwin and didn't seem to notice the nervous twitch in his left eye. It was getting worse these days.

"The same, always the same," Bertha said. "Nothing new and exciting. It's only you who gets all the perks here." She said it with a twinkle in her eye, and Erwin smiled at her.

"That's because I am the Provost. I have to work for it, believe me. Anyway, I'm rather tired, so I had best be on my way."

"Of course, Provost Councilor. Good to have you home." The housemaid moved on towards the next room, while Erwin headed straight for his own living quarters a little further down the hall. Once inside, he locked the door behind him, took off his tie and shoes and lay down on his couch. He was pooped, and not just from the convention in Chicago with other chapters of the Church of Oscar. After a few minutes he got up and walked to the liquor cabinet below a set of bookshelves. He poured himself a small glass of Scotch and carried it to his computer desk.

While the computer booted up, he took a swig of the Scotch and felt it go down like fire. He first checked his e-mails. Twelve messages but none of them urgent. He fell down on the couch again, enjoying his drink and the fact that he was home. Traveling was great now and then, but it was

361

also tiring. After a few minutes he stood up again. Down to business.

He turned the combination lock of the safe to the required numbers and pulled the crank handle. He took out all the church's valuables: official notes, bills and receipts, the DVDs and the Word of Oscar. The last item in the safe was the original flask of Oscar's Breath that had started the commune. The church kept it for sentimental reasons. After Erwin took the flask out, the safe seemed empty. It was not.

He stuck his left hand inside the opening and pressed his thumb on a particular spot on the bottom plate of the safe. After a few seconds there was a clicking sound as the plate hinged open, revealing a false compartment underneath, about two inches deep. It contained two computer memory cards, one current, the other a backup. Erwin removed them both, put the backup one on his desk and the current one into his laptop. He took another swig of his Scotch and walked back to the couch where he had left his jacket.

He pulled a pair of glasses from his inside jacket pocket and lay them down on the desk. They were the spyglasses that originally had belonged to Clive Wadding before he became one of the first Ambassadors in Washington. Erwin had noticed them among Jo's old belongings some time ago, and he had found a perfect use for them. Next he pulled a notebook and a small vial with some dark-brown dust from his pocket and placed them on the desk also.

He took a small cable from his desk drawer and fitted one end in a free computer port, the other end to the spyglasses. Next, his fingers danced over the keyboard while he called up a copying program. A small blue bar showed up along the bottom of the screen with a thin yellow dot on the left side. The yellow dot became a line and it slowly began to fill the entire bar. The screen already showed three icons for three video files. While he waited for the video to be copied he thought about his 'experiments'.

He'd had quite a shock that day, quite some time ago, when he first read the transcript of the DVDs and Jo's warning at the end of it. It didn't take much imagination to realize that Jo, his mentor, the man he had looked up to, had weakly given in to temptation and desecrated the church and its policy of celibacy. He had taken the mushrooms and been intimate with that young woman. That the same young woman had later been put to death in a rather horrid way left Erwin cold. He had returned everything to the vault, and decided not to make the same mistake. The information was best left for future Head Councilors, when the time had come to repopulate the earth.

After a while, his curiosity got the better of him and he changed his mind. Shouldn't he, as Provost Councilor, know everything about the Church of Oscar? Should he not know about all church policies, past, present and future? He wondered where Jo had found the mushrooms. It had to be on the church's property, because Jo hardly left the commune. Intrigued, Erwin decided to investigate. He donned his walked clothes and headed out into the wilderness behind Excalibur. After walking around for quite a while, he finally found some of the mushrooms, picked a few, and headed back.

Then there was a problem. What to do with them? Eat them raw? Cook them? He had no idea. They might not be the right mushrooms and kill him. There was no one in the church he could ask, so he tried to find the information on the Internet. Here he had a stroke of luck. There was a company that actually sold the same mushrooms in a freeze-dried powder form that could be dissolved in a glass of water. He immediately ordered a small vial and decided on a plan of action. Jo had made a terrible blunder when he had selected a young woman in the church for his plans. Erwin wouldn't make the same mistake.

A few weeks later, when the parcel arrived, Erwin told the councilors he was going to Denver, to help the new commune sort out some 'teething problems'. On arrival in his hotel in the city, he drank some of the mushroom extract and went to town. He had met Shirley in a bar near the airport. He still remembered how scared and worried he'd been, but it had to be done. He needed to know the truth, for the church's sake.

The mushroom extract worked well, and gave him the necessary Urge to make love to Shirley. Then there was the second act to silence her. There could be no witnesses. After he smothered the woman, Erwin decided he'd learned enough. It was a messy business, and dangerous to boot. The mushroom extract did indeed give people back their sexual powers, and he would make a note of that in the Word of Oscar for future generations. He had returned home next day, happy that it was all over.

Only it wasn't. A few weeks later, sitting at his desk, reading the latest updates on the cloning of Oscar, he felt the Urge again. It was there, hiding inside him, like a viper, stirring in its nest. He tried to ignore it, concentrating on his work, and for a while it went away. Then, a few days later, it was back again, and he became ill tempered and depressed. Action was needed. On his next trip, he met Gertrude in L.A., and about two months later it was Melissa, in Washington. On his latest visit to Chicago he had been with Pamela. Each of the women had earned a star on the files in his computer disk.

There was a short ping sound, letting him know that the Pamela file had been transferred to his laptop. He finished the last of his Scotch and looked at his watch. Almost six o'clock. He suddenly felt famished. Time for dinner in the councilor's dining room. He hooked up the backup memory stick to the computer and copied the latest file onto the backup disk. Then he picked up the disks, his glasses, the diary, and the freeze-dried mushroom extract and put everything into the false compartment. He put all the other stuff back on top and closed the vault door. His secret would be safe forever, even after his death. Then he was off to a well deserved dinner.

◊ ◊ ◊

It was eerily quiet in the dome, almost spooky. Marvin stood in front of the Exhibitor's Wall, the sculpture that held the names of all the companies and people who had donated money to have their names remembered for the future. It was a huge, curved structure, like a monolith that had doubled up along its vertical axis in a ferocious windstorm. It didn't touch the roof of the dome, but it was the highest of all the exhibits. All in all, it had more than twenty thousand names inscribed in it.

Thirty-six hours earlier, the place had been filled with a huge crowd, as everyone who hadn't seen the time vault had rushed over for the last day of the exhibition. At six o'clock, the closing buzzer had gone off for the last time. The Mayor of nearby Phoenix, the Honorable John Balmor, had given a short speech at a free banquet, and then the people had shuffled out, leaving a mess of drink cans, bottles, paper plates, napkins and other signs of a hungry crowd feeding itself.

Early that morning an army of janitors had marched in, to prepare the vault for its long rest. All day long, they had cleaned and polished the floors, emptied the scores of trash cans, wiped the exhibits, cleaned the lavatories, and even pressure-washed the Exhibitor's Wall. Around five o'clock, they had taken their gear and left the building never to return.

The hosts and hostesses of the exhibits had also collected their belongings, and one by one had signed out with Marvin, to make sure that no one would be left behind. Still, even after everyone on the time sheet was accounted for, Marvin had walked around the gigantic exhibition himself, to double check. When the doors closed that evening, they might not open again for thousands of years. He had checked the toilets, the food and beverage stands, the cloak room and the bandstand where the Mayor had given his speech. Everyone had gone. The only part of the building he had not entered this time was the basement, the home of Philip Kozak and his Virtual people. He had already said goodbye to Philip the day before.

To Marvin, Virtual City was truly a miracle. As per Philip's wishes, he had constructed the basement first. When that was done, and the electrical system put in place, they'd brought in the hard drives with the virtscapes from Secret Springs, and installed the programs. It had taken three whole days. Marvin had carefully removed the avatar that contained Philip's consciousness and brought it to Buckeye himself.

The setup of the exhibits had run flawlessly. Day after day, trucks had driven up the specially constructed access road and delivered their goods from all over the country, and even from abroad. When everything was in place the Time Vault was officially opened to the public. The plan was to keep it open for as long as it would take to find people who would become Philip's followers inside the dome. Sarah and Pedro Marrion, and two friends of theirs, had started to search the seedy areas around the big cities to recruit new inhabitants for Virtual City. To everyone's surprise it had taken them less than a year to recruit a thousand people. Despite Philip's plea, Marvin had never considered becoming a Virtual. It wasn't for him; he still considered it suicide. He was astonished that so many people had been able to leave their bodies so that their spirits could live forever.

After he had made his final round, there was one more task to perform. Marvin had liked being the director of the Time Vault project and he greatly looked up to Philip, whom he considered a real genius. He walked back towards the main entrance and entered a restricted area to the left, beside the sliding door. For the last time he swiped his security pass through the slot and entered the dome control center. The room looked like the small version of a power plant, with scores of gauges, screens and controls.

He began by checking the electrical charging system. The millions of solar cells on the roof were working fine, the batteries fully charged. The Sphinx watchdogs were on standby, ready to be deployed if Philip perceived a serious threat to his habitat. The cameras on the dome surface were working, and at any time Philip could see what was going on outside.

Marvin set the master thermostat for the building at 56 degrees and turned off all unnecessary electrical circuits in the Time Vault. Immediately everything went dark, and he realized it was later than he had expected. In a different area, he shut off the water supply. That only left one switch, operating on a timer. He took one last minute to double-check everything, shining the beam of his flashlight around, like a burglar. Then he set the timer for ten minutes. It would give him ample time to get out. Soon, an air mixture, consisting mainly of nitrogen and a few other inert gasses would flood the entire dome. This would stop the exhibitions from rusting, corroding or disintegrating for as long as the dome was closed.

He walked out of the control room and closed the door. The two big doors that would allow the two Sphinxes out, if need be, were already locked and sealed. He aimed the remote at the main exit door and it swished open. While he walked out, he felt a sudden strong pressure in his ears, as some of the pressurized inside air rushed out with him. Outside the dome he halted for a moment. This was it. When he pressed the remote next, the door would close, and there would be no way for anyone outside to open it again. The moment seemed to warrant some kind of speech.

"Well, Philip," he said. "You were truly one of a kind, and I was privileged to work with you. May you find the peace and happiness you could not find in your real life. God Bless." He firmly pressed the remote and with a big *woosh* sound the door closed and sealed. He couldn't even see a line or joint afterwards. The Time Vault was activated. He looked at the giant dome, with the moon light reflecting off the solar collectors, like a gigantic insect eye.

What would the Virtuals find when Philip opened that door again? It was hard to imagine. Marvin walked to the grassy area that had served as a parking lot. His car was the only one left. Just before he got in, he took one last turn at the dome and felt rather sad that it was all over, at least for him. It had turned almost completely dark and the steel blue dome looked somehow foreboding, gleaming in the moonlight. He started his car and turned around, heading for the rough road that would take him to the main road further down. His high beam flooded the darkened scenery around him.

When he came to the main road he quickly turned left and accelerated. He didn't notice the large, old fashioned gasoline powered SUV that was hidden by a large tree at the corner of the two roads. It wasn't until he heard the siren and saw the sudden flashing light behind him that Marvin realized he was followed by a police cruiser.

Oh, hell, not tonight of all nights! Why the blazes would a police car hide there, in the middle of nowhere, at this time of night? He thought of speeding off, but his little electric car would be no match for a police cruiser. Funny though, the police no longer used old cars like that. What was going on? While he pulled over, he had bad forebodings.

The siren and flashing light died, and in the little light that was left he saw the car door swing open and a big man get out. He was carrying a flashlight and slowly ambled towards Marvin's car. Marvin knew at once he was in big trouble. This was no ordinary police officer.

In the light of the flashlight, Marvin noticed that the other's boots were old and dirty, and the uniform trousers creased and filthy. His coat was about two sizes too small, two buttons were left undone, and it also was stained and dirty. It looked as if the man had been in a war zone for the last six months. No policeman would dare to appear in public like that.

When Marvin finally saw the other's face, his apprehension turned to outright fear. The bogus police man was a man of about forty, with a stubble of at least two days. He was very heavyset, with a thick strong neck, a pallid round face, with dark-brown eyes, a nose like a boxer's and a mouthful of bad teeth. He was a very unrealistic policeman, but there was nothing unrealistic about the gun that dangled from his belt.

"Bit in a hurry, were we, sir? That was a stop sign you ignored. Step out of the car, please."

Reluctantly, Marvin took off his seatbelt and opened the car door. *OK, take him by surprise.* He slowly got out, then immediately made a dive for the other's gun, but the heavy bogus policeman was surprisingly agile and got hold of Marvin first. He had him in a grip of steel, forcing Marvin down, body against his own car.

"Let go of me, you moron," Marvin yelled, "You're no more a cop than Santa Claus, so why don't you just piss off and leave me alone. I've got no time for games."

"Games?" The man laughed noisily, but kept Marvin in his vise-like grip. "You think this is a game?" He stood back and drew his gun. "I could shoot you right now, but I might as well take your money first. Come on, give me your wallet."

Looking into the barrel of the gun, Marvin knew he had very little choice. He handed the bogus cop his wallet, and the other quickly rifled through the bills.

"Two hundred and fifty. Not a bad catch, I guess. So, gimme the rest: your phone, car keys, everything. Come on!"

"Look, take the money, I don't care," Marvin said. "But I need my car. I want to go home to my family, I've had a long day. Be reasonable, sir. Do you have a family?"

"Sure do," the cop said, nodding. "Three of them. See my patrol car? They're all in there, including the wife. That's not just my car, it is my home. That's where we live. I used to be a cop once, you know, a sergeant with the Arizona State Police. Then I made just one small mistake and they kicked me out without even a pension. Now we live in a 2024 Jeep Jabuck, because there ain't any cheap housing available, while people like you build stupid domes that nobody has any use for. Oh, yeah, I've seen the inside of that place, millions wasted on nothing, while others like us suffer. And you want me to be reasonable? Have you ever lived in a car for months in a row?"

"Can't say I have," Marvin tried to humor the man. "But it's not my fault that the world is in such a mess. I'd help you if I could." Oh, if only Philip could see what was happening. One of the Sphinxes would make a piecemeal of this idiot. But Philip was probably busy doing other things on his first night alone in his virtual world.

"Oh, you will help us all right. You're going to be our meal tickets for a while. Now empty your pockets and give me your keys, or I'll put a bullet in your kneecap."

Furiously, Marvin took out his cell phone, his flashlight and keys and threw them on the ground.

"Your jacket also, and your shoes. Then turn around and sit down there, knees up and hands around the back of your head. Come on, I mean it!"

Something snapped in Marvin, and he blew up, livid with rage. "You bloody asshole! I know you're going to kill me, and you don't even have the nerve to look me into the eye, you coward! I won't be shot like a mad dog, you hear!" He swung his fist at the cop, but the latter easily sidestepped the blow.

"All right, if that's how you want it." The bogus cop raised his gun, then he relaxed a bit. "Actually, you're a brave man, and I like that in people. You'll be dead in about twenty seconds, but you're entitled to know the truth, I guess. This ain't really a chance event. Couple of days ago, I was approached by a stranger. He was a nervous wreck, shifty eyes, one of them twitching like hell. I didn't like him much, but he paid me handsomely to do this."

Marvin's eyes followed the gun, as it was slowly raised level with his eyes, and the last thing he saw was a hairy finger that pulled the trigger.

◊ ◊ ◊

"The last time I saw a car like that it was full of U.S. government people," Erwin said, staring at the big black sedan that had turned into Excalibur's driveway. "I wonder what this lot wants."

"Probably nothing good," Councilor Sahu Deepah said. "Shall I call the others?"

"Yes, I think so," Erwin said. "The boardroom, please, Sahu, thank you."

That promising new star on the church firmament would certainly make a very good Provost one day, Erwin thought. Sahu needed a bit more training perhaps, some coaching and polishing. He was reliable, clever, obedient and brimming with youthful energy, and knew when to speak and when to be quiet. As an added bonus, he did exactly as he was told. Sahu had proven himself on his recent trip to Chicago, where he had liquidated Philip's spy. As a result of Sahu's idea, all chapters of the Church of Oscar now used RFID scanners in their recruitment of new members.

The black car had reached the end of the driveway and parked near the front entrance. Two men in dark suits came out, and Erwin knew his instinct had been correct. Another government visit. He waited till they had reached the front door and then quickly opened it.

"Can I help you?"

"We are with the FBI," the oldest one of the two said, presenting a badge. "I am Special Agent Fulcram and this is Agent Starr. There is something we need to discuss. May we come in?" It sounded more like a demand than a request, and Erwin knew trouble lay ahead. Fulcram was the quintessence of an FBI agent: dark-blue, expensive looking suit, black shoes polished to a shine. White shirt, and dark grey tie. Well groomed, but perhaps not as physically healthy-looking as the other, younger agent.

"Certainly. I am Provost Johnson, leader of this commune. I have informed the other councilors of your arrival. This way please." In the boardroom, Erwin quickly introduced everyone, then they sat down behind the long table. Agent Fulcram placed his briefcase on the seat next to him, cleared his throat, and looked at Erwin.

"Provost Councilor, are you aware that our President signed Bill C 150 into law on February 15th a years ago?"

"No," Erwin said. "The Church of Oscar does not concern itself with politics."

"You should. It is called the Federal Privacy Initiative bill. Some feel it was years overdue. Bill C 150 entails the insertion of a small, harmless RFID chip in a person's arm. This implant will guarantee people's privacy forever. Read under a proper scanner the chip will instantly reveal a person's genealogical, medical, and social history, as well as any law enforcement records. Everything is tied to the person's DNA, so identify theft will be a thing of the past. As an added bonus, emergency workers at the scene of an accident will immediately know the complete medical history of the patient. Millions of lives will be saved."

"Providing of course, one doesn't lose the arm in an accident," Erwin interrupted.

"Well, if so desired, the implant can be put elsewhere," Fulcram retorted. "Just to be on the safe side, secondary identification is always required also. However, in most cases, the chip will give instant access to everything emergency personnel will need. The RFID program will slowly be phased in for the cities first, and in the future it will be mandatory for everyone."

"Why are you telling us this, Agent Fulcram?"

"I am getting to that, Provost. We have reason to believe that in the last three months you have allowed thirty-two people with a RFID implant to join your communes across the country. We would like you to stop doing that."

Something began to stir in Erwin's insides and he had difficulty keeping his temper. "I see. And just when were the United States Constitution and Bill of Rights revoked, Agent Fulcram?"

"What?"

"You know what I mean: those pieces of paper that gave people the right to religious freedom, among other things?"

"This is not funny, Provost Councilor."

"I'm not laughing," Erwin said. "Anyone who wants to join our church can do so. We made an agreement with your people years ago, that only criminals actively wanted by the government would be handed over to you. So far we have never refused anyone admittance to our church and we're not going to start now. You have absolutely no right to come in here and dictate how we should run our church."

"Actually, we have. If your church continues to accept people with a RFID implant we shall unfortunately be forced to shut you down. You and the other councilors will be sentenced and face jail time."

"On what charge?"

"Stealing U.S. government property."

Erwin's mouth dropped, and he was unable to speak. He felt like throwing the two FBI agents out of the building. What the hell did they mean? Stealing government property? What property? A soft voice broke the silence.

"Provost Councilor? May I?" Sahu Deepah cocked his eye to Erwin inquiringly. Erwin sat back and nodded.

"Go ahead, Sahu, before I do something I may regret."

"Agent Fulcram, would you mind telling us how many people with implants have joined this particular commune, here in Santa Barbara?" Sahu said, in his lilting accented voice.

Fulcram opened his briefcase and took out a sheet of paper. "We have broken the figures down for your various communes. Over the period of March, April and May this year, twelve people with implants have joined this commune. Five others joined your church in Denver, five more in the New York commune, four in Washington, D.C, and six in Chicago. A total of thirty-two. We like you to release those individuals from your communes."

"How do you know that twelve people with implants have joined our commune here?" Sahu asked.

Fulcram shrugged. "Your monthly reports, of course. We knew the names of the people, so we just checked them out."

"Ah, yes, indeed. You are correct. In March, three people with implants joined us, in April three, and in May six, for a total of twelve. I have, however, a slight problem with that, Agent Fulcram. Today is May 25th, and our report for May has not yet been forwarded to the government. How do you know that six people with such an implant have joined us this month?"

The two agents were getting restless. They looked at each other, and there was concern on Agent Fulcram's face. It was Starr who answered. "We can't answer that question, Councilor Deepah. It is classified information."

"Well, let me declassify it for you, sir. I think those RFID implants in question are rather more than just a database of information about people's health, social status and ID. I believe they also contain a micro-GPS unit that allows the government to monitor people's activities. The only way you could know that six people have joined us in May, was when their GPS signals led you straight to our church. Am I correct in that?"

"Absolutely not," Fulcram burst out. "This is just an example of the hundreds of conspiracy theories that are alive on the Internet these days. It was done by ordinary sur-veillance. The situation is very simple. We know you have bought electronic scanners for all your churches in the country. What other use could they have then the detecting of our implants? We suspected all along that you would try to remove the implants and we cannot allow that. Our government has invested a lot of time and money in this project. The implants are ours."

"I see. Excuse me." Sahu put a hand in his robe pocket and produced a small box the size of a pack of cigarettes. He put it down in front of the flabbergasted agents.

"What is this?" Fulcram asked, his face reddening. "Some kind of joke?"

"Perhaps you should open it," Sahu said suavely.

When Starr picked up the box it made a rattling noise, as if it contained peas or other small items. He awkwardly pulled the lid back, then put the box back on the table. Inside were round glassy beads just a shade larger than a grain of rice.

"Provost Councilor Rasnell, what is the meaning of this?" Fulcram shouted, his face now crimson. "Why are you wasting our time here? We came to speak to the person in charge, not to play games with someone barely out of diapers!"

"Councilor Deepah is a fully authorized member of this Council, Agent Fulcram, and I would ask you to treat him as such. He has our full support and I think you owe him an apology."

Fulcram shifted nervously in his chair. He glanced at agent Starr for support, but the other agent just raised his eyebrows. *It's your mess, you clean it up.*

"OK, All right. I'm sorry, Councilor Deepah. I shouldn't have lost my temper. Where did you get those?"

"Well, isn't that obvious? These are the twelve implants in question. For a while now, we have been scanning our new members for implants like this. When we find one, we remove it, because they do not belong in our church. As you said, they are government property, and I am herewith returning them to you. I have instructed our other churches to do the same. From now on, any implants we find will be removed and returned to you with the monthly reports."

"You are interfering with a National Security policy here," Fulcram shouted. "You had no right to take these implants out!"

"And you had no right to put them in," Father Dubois thundered. "You may own those confounded bugs, but you don't own the people!"

Fulcram picked up the little box, closed it and carefully put it in his brief case. Then he pushed his chair back, and stood up. "This is pathetic," he growled. "Your church is no match for our government. You'll be sorry you did this. This isn't over by a long shot."

375

"Oh, but I think it is, agent Fulcram," Erwin said. He had finally composed himself, his anger under control. "You say you used ordinary surveillance to follow up on the movements of people with implants? Don't insult our intelligence! I find Councilor Deepah's GPS theory much more acceptable. There are still millions of Americans out there, fed up and angry with the way this country has been run for the last hundred years. If you as much as lay a finger on us, we shall post a message on the Internet to the effect that the U.S. government is using GPS implants to track each and every move its citizens make. In that case you can be assured that in next election the very few people who still vote these days, will be doing so with their fist and boots, rather than with their fingers."

◊ ◊ ◊

As the scene for the opening ceremony of Virtual City, Philip had chosen a virtscape of the famous Coliseum in Rome. It was as breathtaking as the real thing, or what was left of it, of course. Time and weather had not been nice to it. The group of a thousand Virtuals seemed lost in the humongous space, and Philip had to shout while he gave his welcome speech.

"I do not know the personal reasons why each of you made the decision to join our group," he began. "I do know mine. I have always known that human evolution is an ongoing process and I wanted to show the world the next stage of our development: the separation from our conscious-ness and the corporeal world that our senses show us. It had to happen. We are more than our bodies. For many of you, leaving the corporeal world may not have been easy. Others failed altogether. But I do know the effort was worth it.

"I want you all to understand that Virtual City is not the end of human evolution, it is a mere stepping stone. As long as our sun supplies us with the necessary energy, we are here to ride out the dark tides that will come. It may take centuries, perhaps even millennia, but eventually a new earth will emerge, where compassion, intelligence and respect will have replaced dogmas, ignorance and greed. When that happens, we shall be ready.

"In the meantime, feel free to explore the many virtscapes in our library. Remember that we also have a wealth of information inside each of us that we can share with each other. We need no longer feel bound, or held back, by the old ties of insecurity and fear from our past. Status, envy, and money are no longer our concern, nor will disease and time's ravages impact us." Philip felt the excitement of the moment grow inside him, and he raised his fist in the air, for a final shout of victory.

"We are free! We are the Virtuals. We are forever!" Immediately many voices echoed between the old walls of the Coliseum, as his slogan was repeated, over and over.

For a while Philip stayed were he was, high up on a broken part of the Coliseum's façade. He looked at the crowd below. A few of the avatars vanished, then more and more, as if some giant invisible hand scooped them away. The Virtuals had begun the exploration of their new world. Philip felt as if his heart was emptying, just like the Coliseum grounds. He'd given up everything for this moment: his old life, his friends, his job, and also love. Yet instead of being exhilarated that he had pulled it off, he felt melancholic and utterly alone.

Someone was missing, and it was gnawing at his insides. While working on his project, he'd managed to push thoughts of Jennifer to the back of his mind, but now they returned in full force. Why did she have to leave? She could at least have tried to join him. He raised his right hand and pointed at the menu that floated in the clouds. Searching through the various virtscapes, he selected one of a beach on the Caribbean island of St. Maarten. They'd been there before, lovely wide sands and a quiet surf. He wanted to walk and put his mind at ease.

Before he could make the connection, the air in front of him shimmered and two people popped up. He hadn't set his privacy flag this time. Some of the Virtuals might have questions or problems. After all, he was their leader. Shutting himself off on the very first day could be considered rude. The two visitors were very tall and had obviously not wasted time to get to know each other. Philip felt the emptiness in his own heart intensify. It was obvious that they wanted to have a chat. The man was tanned, handsome and about forty or so. The woman clinging on his arm looked slightly younger and she had lovely dark eyes, a flawless complexion and chestnut brown hair, blowing in strands around her face.

"So you managed to get it all organized then, did you?" the man asked. "The virtscapes and stuff?"

"Eh . . . well, yes. It all worked out well."

"I'm surprised," the man said. "I didn't think it could be done." He suddenly held out a thin, manicured hand. "Lawrence Rossum. This is my partner, Tina. We know who you are of course, Philip Kozak, who made all this possible. Great speech, Philip."

"Thanks," Phil said. "I'm sorry, am I supposed to know you?"

"Well, yes." The man seemed surprised. "Didn't your chap tell you about me? That Indian fellow?"

Something clicked in Philip. "Of course, you must be that hacker," he said. "No, Marvin didn't mention you were planning to become Virtuals."

"Information analyst, if you don't mind," Lawrence retorted. "I was quite intrigued with your problem. How did you solve it in the end? I bet my virtual boots you didn't hack into the Secret Springs site to get those virtscapes. If I couldn't do it, nobody could."

"Let's just say I found an alternate solution," Philip said. "Can I ask you a question?"

"Fire ahead."

"What made you both become Virtuals? How did you find out about us?"

"Ah. It's kind of complicated, but what the hell, we've got lots of time now, don't we." He laughed, then suddenly turned serious. "When I was eighteen I had a nasty car crash and injured my spine. Lost the use of my legs, and even now, twenty years later, they still couldn't make me walk again. So I was confined to a wheel chair. I was lucky in a way, mind. I still had the use of my upper body and arms, so I could keep doing my job. I have . . . had this big house in the country, guarded like a bloody fortress. Had to, because I had tons of expensive stuff in there.

"Anyway, thanks to Secret Springs, Tina and I could walk together and enjoy life, like other couples. But there was always the homecoming. The reality, hitting me every time we got back: the wheelchair . . . Still, I guess I could have lived like that, but then two bad things happened. One just bad, the other really, really bad. That church took over and closed down the virtual reality part of Secret Springs. All the virtscapes were gone!

"So there went part of my life, cut off just like that. But even without that I could perhaps have continued. Then came the real bad part. Tina, here, my light and love, got sick. Ovarian cancer, prognosis not good, major surgery for sure. So the two of us did some soul searching. What kind of life did we want? Then I thought about your man, Marvin Tuppal, and wondered why he had wanted those virtscapes. I supposed he wanted start something like Secret Springs, so I got kind of curious. I gave him a call and he told me all about your idea. Is he with us here, by the way?"

Philip shook his head. "No. Becoming a Virtual wasn't Marvin's style," he said. "He was the one who closed Virtual City. I miss him very much."

"Yeah, he was an all right guy. Anyway, he sent us to that nice woman, Sarah. She explained the procedure and well . . . Here we are. It was a close call, though. I almost couldn't do it."

"Not everyone can," Philip said.

"No, I don't mean it that way. We both wanted to, really. No way was I gonna live in that big old place, with nowhere to go and the love of my life dying next to me. We were both ready to leave everything behind. Except for one thing . . . I couldn't part with my dog. I just loved that mutt, and I cried and cried. In the end I found a good home for her and then we joined."

"It is really wonderful here," Tina said. "Thank you for giving us a new life." Her smile went straight to the pit of Philip's stomach. It reminded him so much of Jennifer's smile.

"Well, we'd best be going," Lawrence said. "Lots of things to explore, places to go for walks." The three of them shook hands, and Philip watched the happy couple walk away. He felt tears in his eyes. They were obviously much in love, even in virtual life.

He changed the virtscape and stood on the beach in St. Maarten, thinking about Jennifer. If only . . . He'd walked for about ten minutes, when a shimmering of air ahead of him caught his attention. Not again! He wasn't going to get much privacy today. But when he saw who it was he felt his virtual heart almost burst with excitement. Jennifer!

For short moment, his confused mind sought for an explanation. Virtual City was shut off from the rest of the world. Marvin hadn't said anything about Jennifer. Yet here she was, waiting for him. How was that possible?

He suddenly sprinted to her while she ran towards him. It all seemed like one of those old-fashioned romantic soap operas. Without a word they held each other almost fiercely and he kissed her repeatedly, as if he expected her to vanish again.

"Jenny, how come . . . I thought . . . You said . . ."

"I missed you, Phil," she simply said, still hugging him. "I didn't think I could do it, but well, here I am, a Virtual, like yourself."

He had pulled himself together.

"So what happened to the husband, the new job, and the family with kids?" he asked.

She made a face. "I tried, Phil, I really did. I applied for three jobs, without success. But I didn't care, because I had found the man I loved. Eric was his name. Then it went all wrong."

"I know. He couldn't match my wit and charm."

She punched him playfully in his virtual stomach. "Don't be silly." Then, more seriously: "Actually, in a way, you're right. I couldn't stop thinking of you. Eric was all nice and romantic for a while, but then he changed. He became very materialistic, always talking about a better job and more money. It lasted about a year, Philip. I had some other dates, but none worked out. One guy wanted me to do unspeakable things in bed, another wanted me to meet his mother first, to see if she approved.

"So, two days before Marvin was about to lock the vault, I went to see him and he was kind enough to lend me a VR suit. Well, it worked first time, Phil. I just kept thinking of you here in your virtual world, and how I wanted to be with you. Poor Marvin. I hope he doesn't get into trouble. He had to get rid of my body."

"Don't worry, Jen. You're here now. I'm sure Marvin will be all right."

"What about the others? Have they joined us?" Jennifer asked.

"Marvin and Sandor are scientists. They want to prove everything in corporeal terms. Consciousness doesn't fit that paradigm. Becoming a Virtual is an act of surrender, a leap of faith into the unknown. They couldn't do it. But Sarah and Pedro are here. He's a delightful old chap."

"So how did it go? The virtscapes and everything? Marvin told me about the deal you made with that church."

"Oh, it went very well. Marvin downloaded the virt-scapes on huge hard drives and shipped them here from Chicago. We loaded everything on our own servers and it's working fine."

"One day, just after I broke up with Eric, I went to the Church of Oscar, Philip. I was so depressed. I was seriously thinking of joining."

"You went to one of their Sunday services?"

"Yes. There were about forty people, I guess. I've never been much of a church person, but the service was actually quite good. Afterwards, we were given a choice: continue with the admission, or go home. There were two doors, one for the people who wanted to stay and one for the people who didn't. While I stood there, enjoying coffee and refreshment, trying to make up my mind, someone who was going to join held the door open for another person, and I caught a glimpse inside that room. It looked just like a big airport terminal, Phil, honestly.

"But where were they going? People were lining up, emptying their pockets, and they were all scanned and patted down. Then they disappeared into another area. It was surrealistic almost, as if they were planning to leave the planet in some kind of Rapture event. It felt spooky. I mean, isn't that weird, all that security to join a church? It gave me the shivers, and I went home. Anyway, enough of that. This is like the old Secret Springs, right?"

"Well, not quite. For a start, there will never be any new virtscapes. Nor are we connected to the rest of the world. It is a private network now, just for us Virtuals. A lot of personal stuff from previous members has been removed."

"How do you mean?"

"Well, many subscribers added their own input to the virtscapes throughout the years. After all, Secret Springs was a social network. There were 3D videos of peoples' homes, their families, work places, holidays, bedroom scenes even. Most of it was terribly boring, some parts quite crude and obscene. When I got the virtscapes, I asked Marvin to delete all that. It made the virtscapes a lot leaner and easier to load. So we save energy as well. We kept all the nature scenes, towns, cities, 3D movies and the archives with historical stuff."

"Everything is still the same quality as before?"

"Absolutely, yes. Nothing changed there."

"And we can still . . . you know . . ." She winked, and he gave her an understanding smile.

"Of course. No change there, Jennifer."

"Good." She lay down in the sand, giving her one of her gorgeous smiles. Instead of joining her, he aimed his finger at a menu in the sky.

"What are you doing?"

"Just a formality." Philip made a selection, closed the menu, and lay down next to her.

"We've got our new world all to ourselves," he said, stroking her hair and kissing her. "None of the other Virtuals can find us now."

23

It was a celebration unlike any other the commune had ever seen. The Church of Oscar was fifty years old. Everyone but essential personnel had the day off. The church had even formed a small orchestra that gave a performance in the gardens at a special luncheon banquet. Several years year ago, Provost Councilor Erwin had set aside a fund to purchase musical instruments for the people who could play. Time had been allowed for rehearsals and practicing. Even the weather cooperated, providing a balmy, sunny day. More old-fashioned leaders, like the late Daniel English, might perhaps have objected at this display of worldly behavior, but the Provost Councilor had gained massive support and admiration for allowing it.

To the other councilors, Erwin had proven to be an innovative leader. He had deployed several ideas that former church officials had frowned upon. One of his first suggestions had been a reduction of the council from twelve to seven members. None of the present councilors would be asked to leave, but some would not be replaced in the future. When some councilors queried the rather unusual number, Erwin had explained it was necessary to speed up the council meetings, and to prevent 'hung votes'. As Provost, Erwin reserved the right to the final, deciding vote.

Another new idea had been an investment in electronic equipment, with the assistance of Ambassador Hu, in China. During Jo's times, the church had only one computer, used mostly for research by Jo himself. As an enlightened Provost, Erwin had made computers available to all councilors.

After the banquet, Erwin addressed the world via the church's new Evangelical Network. The event was broadcast from the Excalibur's library, where Erwin sat in an old-fashioned chair, dating back to the Philip Gallagan era, while a young woman quickly applied some makeup to his face. When she had finished, the man behind the teleprompter held up a hand with the fingers splayed: five, four, three, two, one. *Go!*

"People of Oscar, this is Erwin Johnson, your Provost Councilor," Erwin read from the prompter. "I want to say a few words on this very historic occasion. Fifty years ago, to this very day, two young men walked into the Santa Barbara municipal office in California, here in the Unites States of America, to register a commune they called the Church of Oscar. They did so because one of them, Ted Taylor, was chosen by our Lord to lead mankind on a quest to save our planet from the ravages and destruction that has been going on for centuries.

"By opening this commune to the homeless, and those who lost everything, we have given many people shelter and a new purpose in life. We now have many other communes, at home and abroad, where people like yourselves are dedicating their lives to nurture the Earth back to health. We grow wholesome, organic foods, breed livestock in a proper, humane way, and teach young people to become skilled tradesmen for the small businesses this country so desperately needs.

"There is still a long way to go, and many places have not yet heard our message. Spreading the Word of Oscar is not an easy task, and sometimes sacrifices need to be made. But I am confident that given time, we shall succeed in bringing salvation to everyone, and reclaim our true place as a guardian of Nature. I thank you all for your courage and dedication. May the Lord of all consciousness bless you and our church."

The teleprompter technician gave a thumbs-up sign and began to wind down the transmission. Erwin felt angry and sick to his stomach and he was glad the ordeal was over. He stood up and headed straight to the Excalibur boardroom where the councilors had followed the speech on a large TV screen.

"Great speech, Provost Councilor," Patricia Sheppard said, when Erwin stomped in. Though she was eighty-three, Patricia was still active in the Council. Like the other councilors, she was dressed in formal dress code uniform for the occasion: a white robe with golden epaulettes, and the red satin cord. Great waves of white hair seemed to meld with her councilor's attire. The woman was getting on Erwin's nerves. How dare she censure his speech! Perhaps he should change the rules some more, and force councilors to step down at sixty-five, instead of letting them drag on until they died. They were all well past retirement. Look at that Bert Kwiss, a walking skeleton almost. Erwin desperately wanted to dissolve the entire Council, except for Sahu.

"Very well presented, Provost Councilor," Father Dubois said. Erwin dislike the man intensely. He was no comparison to his predecessor, Daniel English. Bert Kwiss, Jeremy Burlon and Dr. Fleming also nodded their approval, like the parrots they all were. Only young Sahu Deepah, the fresh blood on the Council, sat quietly, looking straight ahead.

"It was sentimental trash!" Erwin raged. "Thanks to you, Patricia. I should never have agreed to let you write my speech. It has given me a bad headache."

"Look, Erwin, we've all been through that," Patricia said. "If you are going public there are certain things you cannot say."

"Oh, really? Why is that? I thought you people told me we had a secure connection. What's the use of that if you can't speak your mind?"

"Erwin, you're being unreasonable. Even with a secure line we can not be absolutely certain that unauthorized people won't listen in. This is the Internet, in case you have forgotten. You can't go out there spouting the church's secrets. I know you would like to give our people a pep talk about fighting the enemy, like generals did before major battles, but that's not how our church works and you know it. You can't mention Oscar's Breath. Or the fact that we must destroy all big companies, organized churches, greedy multinationals and corrupt officials. We still have some kind of government, and if you had said anything like that, they would have come down on us hard. You don't own this country, much less the world, Provost Councilor."

"Not yet," Erwin growled. He sat down at the head of the table, still fuming. "That speech was a soppy childhood's fairytale. There are much more important things I wanted to tell our people. They should get ready for the next stage of our plan to save the world, but they don't even know about it."

"Of course they don't," Father Dubois exclaimed. "Why should we tell them more than they need to know? We need to discuss these things first. That's why we have a church council. We must finish stage one first."

"I didn't know we voted you in as Provost, Father," Erwin said sharply. "Perhaps you should simmer down a bit. I know we haven't finished the spreading of the Word of Oscar, but the longer we wait the more damage is done to the earth. Stage two is vital, the cleanup of the air, the water, and the land. We need to remove derelict houses, offices and factories. Trees must be planted, we need to create good soil, and save more seeds and plants before they are all altered and modified by big companies. Spreading Oscar's Word is a cakewalk compared to cleaning up the earth."

"That is true, of course," Dubois relented. "Just be careful what you shout from the roof tops."

"Well, I think we're done here," Erwin said curtly. "We're all supposed to have the day off, so I'm out of here. Unless anyone else has something of importance to share?"

None of the other councilor had, and without another word Erwin stood up and stormed out of the boardroom. He headed straight to his living quarters, and once inside, grabbed his bottle of Scotch and poured an inch. From his desk drawer he took a little tube of pain killers, peeled off two tablets and swallowed them with a swig of the amber liquid.

He could not go on like this much longer, something had to give. He should not antagonize the other councilors like

387

that. They could make life difficult for him; they could even force him to resign. He was surprised nobody had said anything yet. He'd been irritable and short tempered for quite a while, and he knew exactly why. He hadn't had a good night sleep in months. He took a swig of Scotch and tried to breathe deeply to relax. Most of his life he'd felt upbeat and optimistic about the church's future. The Church of Oscar was unstoppable. It would just get bigger and better and in the end it would rule the world. It was inevitable.

Lately, that dream had fallen apart. The church would never get anywhere at the rate it was going. Couldn't the others see what was happening? Sure, they might recruit some poor people and others who were fed up with their lives. But there were still the rich and the super-rich, millions of them, ensconced in their secure cities. They would never join the Church of Oscar. Why should they? Everything was going exactly the way they wanted. They would have to be forced out. To conquer the entire world they would have to fight, just like old Bernard Tows had said. Blood would have to flow. There was no other way.

Of course, his short temper, the sleepless nights, the depression, and the headaches were not the cause of his problems, but the result. He had lost his faith in the Church of Oscar. It was completely gone, destroyed by the mushroom extract he'd taken. His mind was cluttered with emotional garbage again, the way it was before he joined, only much worse.

He dreaded going to bed at night, knowing he would just lie there, unable to relax or sleep, with thoughts racing through his mind, like cattle chasing each other during a stampede. Erwin knew enough of the human psyche to know that chronic sleep deprivation could drive him mad, or even kill him. The nervous tick on his left eye was almost constant now, and sooner or later Dr. Fleming would feel it his duty to examine him. He felt tired and drained, unfocused, without any hope for the future. He was no longer capable of ruling the church. On top of all that, he also had his private little dilemma.

The files on his memory sticks in the vault contained four icons. Four missions, daring and dangerous, and he had gotten away with them all. But eventually he would be caught; no one is lucky all the time. He was getting older, less alert, more prone to make mistakes. The idea of capture was unthinkable; he would rather die than face the disgrace. Yet whenever he got the Urge, it needed satisfying. What to do? He took another swig of Scotch and suddenly threw the glass against the wall of his study. It shattered in several pieces, the liquid running down the wallboard like amber blood. He just stood there, swaying, breathing heavily.

"Damn you, Yabul Kozak, I hate you!" he shouted. "First you create a drug that takes away what makes us human, and then you give us an antidote that will surely kill us. You are truly the Son of Satan!"

So what were his options? Stay in the church, like Jo had done, but use protection when his Urges needed attending to? No, it was still too dangerous. He could ask Dr. Fleming to remove the offending . . . No, that wasn't an option at all. He still had Claude Sparling's gun. One quick move, and it would be over. No, that wouldn't do either. Deep inside, Erwin knew he was a coward; he would never have the courage to pull that trigger. There was also the fear of a backlash, of what people in the church would say afterwards. A Provost Councilor who had killed himself? What would that to the church's image?

Perhaps he should leave the church. Find someone and live on an old farm. Yet where would he ever find a respectable woman? They were all the same; he'd seen them on his trips, provocatively dressed, almost waiting to be raped. He hated them all. It had all started with that Tammy. She'd been bad, real bad. Not just because of what happened in her apartment, but of what she did afterwards. Blackmailing the church! The Lord had punished her for that,

389

though, when she had been chosen for that mission to New Sanuga. She and that greedy boy friend of hers.

He hated his mother, for preferring Philip to him, even on her deathbed. Then there was Helin Sparling, pompously lecturing him on how to deal with Secret Springs. Nor did he think much of Patricia Sheppard, the interfering bitch. Even Sylvia, the most likeable of them, had to be dealt with. She might have read the transcript and realize what he had done.

No, life outside would be too complicated and dangerous. He much preferred the safety of the commune, and his position of power. How could he possibly give that all up, just to satisfy the Urges? The more Erwin thought about his situation, the more he realized there was only one possible solution—he would have to return into the church's fold. He'd have to take the Breath again. He didn't know if it would work a second time around, but he had to try.

He made up his mind, left the room, and walked down the stairs to ground level. Everything was quiet, as most people were outside, enjoying the festivities. There would be fireworks shortly. He entered the recruitment room and used his Provost ID card to enter a restricted storage area. He carefully selected a mask, then hooked it up to a flask of Oscar's Breath, and filled the little container in the mask. When it was about half-full, he closed the valve on the flask and put it back into the box. Then he returned to his living quarters.

He carefully closed and locked the door behind him. He walked over to his window that looked out over the gardens and the wilderness in the back of Excalibur. There were large crowds in the open area around the pond, eagerly awaiting the fireworks that would soon start. He knew people would wonder why he wasn't there, but he didn't care. He could always blames it on his headache. He closed the blinds and sat down again. He raised his hand with the mask, ready to take Oscar's Breath for the second time in his life. Then he hesitated. No. *Not quite yet . . .*

He put the mask down on the side table beside him and walked over to the vault. He took the ordinary church items out and put them on the table also. He pressed his left thumb down in the corner of the vault to access the hidden compartment. He retrieved one of two memory cards and walked over to his desk, his heart pounding with expectation. He quickly pushed the card in the appropriate slot in his computer and started it. It was already hooked up to his big screen.

Soon the four stars showed prominently on the big TV. He took a deep breath, and scrolled through them with the mouse. Shirley, Gertrude, Melissa, and Pamela. The choice was easy. He quickly poured himself some more Scotch and double-clicked on the star named Melissa. When her image filled the screen it took Erwin's breath away.

Melissa—he didn't even know her last name—was a buxom young black woman. Her skin was flawless, her teeth white like pearls, her lips the most sensuous lips of any woman Erwin had ever seen. Not for the first time he wondered why she had ended up in her profession. Just the sight of her made him feel hot, and he felt the Urge awakening inside him.

When she took off her sweater, then her blouse and finally her bra, it made him feel so excited that he, also, threw of his shirt and trousers and soon sat there, in his easy chair, stark naked, his eyes fixed as Melissa walked towards him on the screen, giving him that wonderful smile with those beautiful lips. His manhood was on fire now, and he knew he had no choice but to help himself, since Melissa wasn't there with him.

It took a while. The Urge wasn't ready to release him yet. He saw his own hands on the screen, tightening the scarf around Melissa's beautiful neck. That part had not been easy at the time, but it had to be done. Her beautiful face became distorted with anger and pain, and she was fighting back, her fingers clawing at him, splayed like talons, ready to scratch out his eyes. He had been stronger and easily held her back.

Then, just as Melissa breathed her final, lingering breath on the screen, Erwin's Urge was finally satisfied and he jumped up, crying out in ecstasy. Precisely at that moment, the first fireworks went off outside, masking his screams. When he saw Melissa's limp body, her lifeless head lolling forwards, Erwin felt a single tear running down his cheek. Then the screen went dead, and he fell back onto the couch like a rag doll. He was totally spent and his heart was pounding as if he had just jumped from an airplane on his first parachute jump.

After a little while his heartbeat slowed a bit and he felt cold. He walked to the bathroom and turned the shower as hot as he could bear and stood under it for the longest time, washing himself with soap again, although he had already had a shower that morning. For a few moments he thought about Melissa. *If only* . . . When he got out of the shower, he dressed in clean underwear, a nice clean white dress shirt with black tie, and dark blue pants. He put on a smart black and red striped sweater and clean socks. He reached for his drink and sat down to relax for a while. Outside, the festivities had begun. After a few minutes, he sat up straight at his desk, and picked up the mask. He almost ceremoniously placed it over his mouth and nose, and took a deep breath.

For the second time in his life, Erwin Johnson felt Oscar's Breath surge up his nostrils. He welcomed the tingling feeling, and noticed it was not as sharp as the first time. Very soon, his mind was in a controlled uproar, as hundreds of thoughts ran amok, chasing each other, while they were being sorted, like sheep rounded up by a guard dog. He closed his eyes, as vivid pictures flew through his mind. He saw his mother, and while he lay back, her image changed. She remained in his memory, but the hatred, the feeling of frustration and hurt towards her were suddenly gone.

One by one, his thoughts were cleansed of their emotional impact, allowing others to break through again. He suddenly knew the Church of Oscar wasn't finished at all, not by a long shot. Its mission had only just started. He could see it clearly now, all it needed was time. He was focused again. He stood up and kneeled on the floor, head down in prayer.

"Thank you, Lord," he murmured softly. "Thank you for taking me back. I shall not let You down again for as long as I live."

He stood up and opened his fridge. On one of the racks stood a big brown paper bag. It was filled with apples. A young woman had given them to him this morning, as a gift to the Provost Councilor for the celebration. He carefully took the apples out and put them loose on the rack. It was the bag he wanted. He walked back to the vault and took out his backup disk, the spyglasses, the glass vial with mushroom extract and his diary, and put everything in the brown bag. He took the disk out of his computer and bagged that as well. On impulse, he also added the mask. Then he pushed the false bottom of the vault down for the last time. It had served its purpose. Feeling completely revived, he put on his official council robe and stuffed the brown bag inside one of its spacious pockets. He stood for a second, looking around, to see if he had forgotten something. Then he left his room and headed for the stairwell.

The incinerator supplied hot water and heat to Excalibur. It was four floors down in the basement. Erwin walked down the stairs and through a short tunnel with heavy-duty piping and cables suspended along the ceiling. In the furnace room, he picked up two mittens that hung from pegs on the wall. He put them on and carefully opened the furnace door. It had a small porthole in it, so that the maintenance men could see when it was necessary to add wood. A waft of searing air hit him and he stood back.

He took the brown bag out of his gown pocket and threw it into the flaming logs. The bag went up in flames at once, then there were two sharp hisses, announcing the end of his two memory disks. Two small explosions heralded the end of the mask and the vial. When he was sure all the evidence was gone, Erwin closed the door of the incinerator and turned around, just as he heard steps outside in the corridor. An older man, dressed in a blue coverall entered the room.

"Can I . . ." he began, then he recognized Erwin.

"Oh, hello Provost Councilor, I didn't expect to find you here."

Erwin smiled. "Just some sensitive church stuff I had to burn."

The man nodded. His name tag said John Morking. "Of course. That was a great speech you gave, Provost Councilor. I watched it in the office."

"Yes, I'd rather liked it myself," Erwin said. "Did you manage to take part in any of the festivities?"

"In between my rounds, I took a quick peek outside," the man said, smiling. "Fifty years! Hard to believe, isn't it? What do you think will happen in the next fifty years, Provost Councilor?"

"Well, it's never easy to predict the future, of course," Erwin said, turning back towards the door. "However, I am very much convinced that whatever happens, our church will play a very dominant role in it."

"Amen to that," John Morking said, nodding.

"Well, have a good evening, John."

"You too, Provost Councilor."

Erwin walked back through the short corridor and up a flight of stairs back to the Excalibur main floor. It was empty and quiet, as the celebrations had ended. He crossed the open space towards the stairway that led to the councilors' living quarters. He was happy for the church and also for himself; his future was finally sorted out and secure again. After all this time, he could finally devote his life exclusively to the Lord again, but first he needed a good night's sleep.

When he inserted the key into the door lock of his living quarters, he noticed the door was unlocked. He frowned. He always locked his room. How could he have been so careless? When he opened the door and walked inside, he knew at once that sleep would not be forthcoming. Seated behind

Erwin's desk, as if he owned the place, was young Councilor Deepah.

"Sahu! What on earth . . . What are you doing here?"

"I have a key, Provost Councilor." The young man did not smile and kept his expression and voice neutral. Erwin felt the first misgivings that something was wrong.

"Yes, of course. When I made you my second-in-command, I gave you a set of spare keys, in case I died, or for some other reason became incapable of fulfilling my job. That doesn't mean you can just barge in here without asking me. This is outrageous! Your chances of becoming the next Provost Councilor have suddenly dropped rather dramatically, I can tell you that."

"Oh, I don't think so, Erwin."

"What? Are we on first name terms now? What's going on here, Councilor Deepah?"

"I know why you went to the incinerator, Provost Councilor." Though Sahu's face betrayed no emotion, there was anger and defiance in his eyes.

"I had to get rid of some confidential stuff. Are you keeping tabs on me now? Is this some kind of silly game? Explain yourself."

Sahu shook his head. "No game. The Council has been very worried about you for quite a while, Erwin. Your behavior lately has been rather erratic and provocative. Not suitable for a member of the Church of Oscar, and most certainly not acceptable for a Provost Councilor. So I made it my business to find out why you've been acting the way you did."

"I get bad headaches, I've told you."

"Yes, but we both know these headaches are only symptoms of an underlying cause that is of great concern to our church. You have sinned and betrayed the very cores of our belief. I know what you did, Provost Councilor."

The shivers down Erwin's spine were turning into tremors. *Sahu couldn't possibly know. He was bluffing.*

"I have no idea what you're talking about, and this subordination has gone far enough, Sahu. The Church of Oscar may not actually incarcerate people but we do have security. As of now you are no longer a councilor, and I am placing you under house arrest until the Council decides on a way to deal with you permanently." Erwin walked over to the phone on his desk and began to punch in a number.

"It'll make no difference, Erwin," Sahu said. "Once I make my findings public you will be finished, and I shall be the new Provost Councilor."

"What findings?" Erwin put the phone down again.

Erwin pointed at a smoke alarm attached to the ceiling, dating back from the Gallagan days. "Some time ago I installed a small surveillance camera in there. It gave me quite a good view of what happened in this room. I did have some problems with the secret compartment in your safe at first, but I solved that eventually. I know what you threw into the incinerator, Erwin. I've seen the mushroom extract, the glasses, and the videos for your private entertainment. I sent John Morking to save the evidence, but he was too late. I've also seen the disgraceful and disgusting show you put on here tonight."

"You have no proof of any of this, Sahu. Why would the Council take the word of a young, inexperienced member against that of the Provost? They won't believe it, and it will be you who is finished, not me."

Sahu shook his head. "I have all the proof I need, Provost Councilor. I saved the surveillance videos. You also forgot one important thing. Among your papers, I found a receipt for a vial with mushroom powder. Why did you order that, Provost? You should have destroyed that also."

Erwin sat down, knowing it was over. The Council would meet out some kind of harsh punishment and that would be it. Inwardly he felt calm, as if it didn't really matter. Oscar's Breath was shielding him from the devastating news. He had gambled and lost. If this conversation had taken place a few hours ago, before he had renewed his faith in the church, he would probably have strangled Sahu on the spot. Perhaps he could still diffuse the situation.

"OK. Yes, I have sinned, Sahu. I was weak, and gave in to temptation. I harmed Oscar's Breath in me and from there on things went out of control. But I've taken the Breath again, and things are as they used to be. I still believe in our church."

"No, Erwin. That's not how the Church of Oscar works. Surely you, as Provost Councilor, should know that. We don't absolve people. You are guilty of a crime against our Lord Oscar and you must be punished."

"But Sahu, many of our members may have sinned before they joined us, and we recruit them anyway. Can't you forget about the past? I'll never touch that mushroom stuff again, that's why I burned it, honestly. Nobody else needs to know. You can't ignore all the good things I've done here. Come on, forget it. I'll step down and you can be the new Provost Councilor."

Sahu stood up and walked over to the kitchen area. He took a glass from the cupboard above the sink, half-filled it with water and carried it to the desk. "I don't think so, Erwin. Believe me, it won't give me any pleasure to expose you to the Council. You were my mentor and I admired you. I owe you a lot. But I can't just forget about this." He took a small plastic pouch from his trouser pocket and opened it. Holding the pouch at an angle, he let a darkish green power slide into the water.

"What is that?" Erwin asked suspiciously.

"Concentrated root extract of *Altrope Belladonna*, commonly known as Deadly Night shade."

"You want me to commit suicide?"

"Yes. I'm giving you an honorable way out, Erwin. If you drink this, you will be remembered as an enlightened Provost Councilor, and your ashes will be kept in the Vault of the Ancient. I'm sure that doctor Fleming will agree with me that your headaches were a sign of a potential aneurysm in the brain that finally ruptured."

"And if I don't drink it?"

"Then I shall tell the Council the truth, Provost Councilor, and they will decide on a way to punish you." Sahu stood quietly for a few seconds. "Perhaps you are thinking about leaving us to find a new home in another chapter of our church. I would advise against it, Erwin. If I find out you have disappeared, I shall warn the rest of the church and they will not let you in.

"In that case I shall also inform the authorities about the four heinous murders you have committed, and you will be hunted down and face the death penalty, or a life-long term in jail, among vicious criminals. I'm sure you'll agree that my solution is far more elegant. The choice is yours." Sahu folded the pouch, returned it to his pocket, and left without another word.

For the longest time Erwin sat motionless, staring at the glass. The water had turned slightly green. He wondered what it was like to be poisoned. Would it be painful? Or would he just doze off and fall asleep, never to wake up? It was a strange feeling to know one would be dead in a few hours. Yet somehow Oscar's Breath kept his panic at bay. It was no use thinking of options to save himself; there were none. He had better get it over with.

Pulling the glass closer, he thought of the happiness he had felt when he had joined the Church of Oscar. He had done more than most, and made it to the top. Without his input the commune would never have grown the way it had. His thoughts went back to his early life on the farm, with his father and mother, and his half-brother Philip. The hand that held the glass suddenly tightened. His half-brother . . .

Officially, Philip was dead. Yet he was alive; they had talked together. After their mother had died, Erwin had unceremoniously dumped his brother's ashes in the gardens behind Excalibur. He had never paid even the slightest attention to Philip's work, but suddenly it seemed vitally important. Had there been a cover up? Philip had said he was involved in some secret program. Perhaps the ashes Erwin had brought home from Chicago had belonged to someone else . . .

Erwin pushed the glass back and sat very still, breathing rapidly, thoughts about poison and sleep pushed from his mind. Were was Philip? He tried to remember his last meeting with his half-brother. Something important had happened there, what was it? Oh, yes, those virtscapes! Philip has insisted on having part of Secret Springs' software and computer equipment because he needed them for his plans. So where had it all gone?

Erwin pulled his laptop computer close and turned it on. He connected to the church's website and began to hunt. The details of the acquisition of Secret Springs would all be there. He searched through scores of legal documents, but nowhere could he find any mention of virtscapes. He was hardly surprised. It had been a verbal agreement between himself and Philip. What he was looking for were official bills of loading, documents relating to the move. Virtscapes were humongous files, and Philip had opted to put them all on large hard drives and had everything shipped somewhere. If he could find the software it would lead to his brother. Philip would help him; he owed him for those virtscapes. He was family, and he would hide him from the authorities.

He finally found a document relating to the virtscapes. All the files, as well as three servers and some projecting equipment, had been moved by a company called Future Holdings. Everything had been taken to a place called Buckeye in Arizona. He stood up and began to pace the room. He'd seen that name in the news before, not too long ago. Something had happened there. He quickly typed the words in his search engine, and after a few seconds he stared at a large silver dome. *The Arizona Time Vault.* An ark in time. Erwin had heard about it on the Internet. Was that where Philip was hiding, inside that glittering dome?

He picked up the telephone and pressed the number for the main gate, impatiently waiting to be connected. "This is your Provost Councilor," he said to the guard who answered his call. "Please call a cab for me in about half an hour. Tell the driver to come to the back entrance." Without waiting for a reply he replaced the receiver, and checked his watch. It was 1.15 a.m. He picked up the glass with poison, carried it to the sink and emptied it down the drain. *Too bad, Sahu, I have found my own way out.*

For the next twenty minutes, Erwin was busy packing a suitcase with as much clothes, shoes, toiletries and money as he could cram inside. When he was finally done, he stood still, and looked around the familiar room. He would miss his sanctuary and the safety of the Church of Oscar, but he had no choice. He resolutely picked up his case and left, not bothering to close the door behind him.

In the dark, he carefully walked down the hallway, wheeling his suitcase behind him. Excalibur was quiet, everyone sound asleep after the exhausting celebrations. He opened the back door and stepped onto the patio. The air was cool and fresh, and there was still the slightest hue of orange behind the mountains in the distance.

In the quiet of the night, he heard the faint sound of a car coming down the driveway, and a little while later, two cones of bright light appeared at the side of the building. Then a cab turned the corner and stopped in front of him. Erwin rushed over, opened the passenger door and stowed his case on the back seat. Then he climbed in and sat down next to it.

The driver was a young chap in a dark suit, looking smart and alert for the time of night, as if he had just started his shift. He wore a black cap with *Downtown Cabs* printed on it.

"Where to, sir?" the young man queried, leaning back to look at him.

Erwin took a rather large bundle of money from his pocket and held it in front of the driver's surprised face. "Yours," he said, "if you take me to Buckeye, Arizona."

www.ingramcontent.com/pod-product-compliance
Lightning Source LLC
Chambersburg PA
CBHW060341260626
47160CB00006B/2166